Publisher:
Wildside Press

Editor:
John Gregory Betancourt

Associate Editors:
Darrell Schweitzer
Sean Wallace

Distribution Manager:
Warren Lapine

Assistant Editors:
P.D. Cacek
Diane Weinstein

Adventure Tales is published twice per year by Wildside Press LLC, P.O. Box 301, Holicong PA 18928–0301. Postmaster & others: send change of address and other subscription matters to DNA Publications, attn: *Adventure Tales*, P. O. Box 2988, Radford VA 24143. Single copies: $7.95 (magazine edition) or $18.95 (book paper edition), postage paid in the U.S.A. Add $2.00 per copy for shipping elsewhere. Subscriptions: four issues for $19.95 in the U.S.A. and its possessions, $29.95 in Canada, and $39.95 elsewhere. All payments must be in U.S. funds and drawn on a U.S. financial institution. If you wish to use PayPal to pay for your subscription, email your payment to: wildside@sff.net.

Tell us what you think!
Visit the official *Adventure Tales* message board at:

www.wildsidepress.com

Wildside Press
P.O. Box 301
Holicong PA 18928–0301
www.wildsidepress.com

We invite letters of comment (via email or regular mail), and we assume all letters received are intended for publication (unless marked "Do Not Publish") and become the property of Wildside Press. Please note that we cannot reply personally to every letter received. If you have specific questions, please check the message boards at our website.

CONTENTS

WINTER 2004-2005   **Vol. 1, No. 1**

CLASSIC FANTASY

LORD DUNSANY

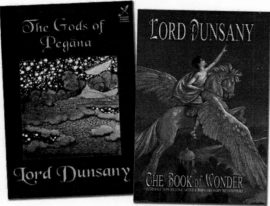

"Dunsany was the second writer (William Morris in the 1880s being the first) fully to exploit the possibilities of . . . adventurous fantasy laid in imaginary lands, with gods, witches, spirits, and magic, like children's fairy tales but on a sophisticated adult level." —L. Sprague de Camp

"[Dunsany's] rich language, his cosmic point of view, his remote dream-worlds, and his exquisite sense of the fantastic, all appeal to me more than anything else in modern literature." —H. P. Lovecraft

THE BOOK OF WONDER	$12.99
DON RODRIGUEZ	$17.50
A DREAMER'S TALES	$15.00
FIFTY-ONE TALES	$13.95
PLAYS OF GOD AND MEN	$17.50
TIMES AND THE GODS	$15.00
THE BLESSING OF PAN	$17.50
THE GODS OF PAGEANA	$12.95
TALES OF WAR	$12.95
UNHAPPY FAR-OFF THINGS	$13.95

JAMES BRANCH CABELL

FIGURES OF EARTH	$17.50
CREAM OF THE JEST	$17.50
THE LINE OF LOVE	$17.50
DOMNEI	$17.50
CHIVALRY	$17.50
GALLANTRY	$17.50
THE CERTAIN HOUR	$17.50
JURGEN	$17.50
LADIES AND GENTLEMEN	$19.95
THERE WERE TWO PIRATES	$15.00

 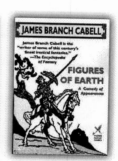

JAMES BRANCH CABELL (1879-1956) is best known for his tales of the imaginary land of Poictesme, where chivalry and galantry live on. All of Cabell's works from before 1930 were assembled into the grand "Biography of the Life of Manuel," the supposed redeemer of the land of Poictesme, and they form a series which follows Manuel and his descendants through the centuries.

Cabell has been a favorite author of many famous writers, ranging from Lin Carter to Robert A. Heinlein.

The Blotter

WELCOME to the first issue of *Adventure Tales*. The general idea of *AT* is to reprint some of the greatest adventure-oriented fiction ever written for pulp magazines (and sometimes the "slick" magazines). We're not talking about moldering old work by authors nobody has ever heard of, but rare and classic fiction that retains its original excitement and meets current high literary standards. Here you will find everything from fantasy and science fiction to mystery, suspense, and (as the magazine's name implies) high adventure.

For the premiere issue, we have drawn from *Argosy* — perhaps the most famous pulp magazine of all time — for two stories by Hugh B. Cave, our Featured Author: "Island Feud" and "The Man Who Couldn't Die." Don't miss the interview with Hugh, too, as he talks about his writing career and pulp magazines.

There are also stories by H. de Vere Stacpoole (best known as the author of *The Blue Lagoon*, filmed no less than five times, most famously starring Brooke Shields). "Under the Flame Trees" originally appeared in *Short Stories* magazine.

James C. Young, a well-respected pulp author who is unfairly forgotten these days, contributes "Rats Ashore," a nautical tale with horrific overtones.

H. Bedford Jones was in many ways the king of the pulp magazine writers, contributing hundreds of stories (under his own byline and more than a dozen pseudonyms) to all of the top adventure and fiction pulp magazines. Here he contributes "Skulls," a gruesome little revenge story, also from *Short Stories*.

Noted mystery author Vincent Starrett (1886-1974) contributes "The Evil Eye," the first entry in his Lavender series, about a Chicago detective. (We will have more Lavender stories in future issues.)

"Watson!" by Captain A. E. Dingle, is an early Sherlock Holmes pastiche. The good Captain was a frequent fixture in pulps in the early 20th century, contributing a long string of nautically-themed stories. Not surprisingly, Holmes and Watson find themselves at sea in this one, too. There is a sly sense of humor to it — and a twist ending that will leave Sherlockians gasping in surprise! It originally appeared in the October 10, 1921 issue of *Short Stories*.

H. P. Lovecraft, Robert E. Howard, and Clark Ashton Smith, with whom I assume most readers will already be familiar, contribute verse this time around, along with a few lesser-known poets. And the wonderful logos for the contents page, the Blotter, and the Morgue are by the incredibly talented Thomas Floyd.

YOUR editor (me) is John Betancourt. I run Wildside Press, the small publishing company which produces this magazine, and I also write novels now & again in my spare time.

This is actually the fifth magazine I have worked on. My love of magazine editing began when I got a job in college in 1983 working as an assistant editor at *Amazing Stories*, the classic science fiction magazine. (It used to be a pulp, of course, but had long been a digest when I worked on it.) From there, I went on to help launch the revival of *Weird Tales*. After I left *WT* for a book-editing career, I launched a non-fiction news magazine called *Horror*, which

covered (perhaps not surprisingly) the horror field. *Horror* took too much time, so I turned it over to another small press (which ultimately folded *Horror* a half dozen or so issues later). Then I wandered back to *Weird Tales*, becoming the co-publisher (with Warren Lapine of DNA Publications). After that, I started *H.P. Lovecraft's Magazine of Horror*, selecting much of the first issue's content before passing the editorial reins on to Marvin Kaye. I'm still the publisher of *HPL's*.

Which brings us to *Adventure Tales*. I love and collect pulp magazines, and over the years Wildside Press has done quite a few pulp-related projects — from *The Best of Weird Tales: 1923* to a line of facsimile reprints of pulp magazines (including issues of *Spicy Detective Stories*, *Spicy Mystery Stories*, *Ghost Stories*, *Golden Fleece*, *Phantom Detective*, and more.) *Adventure Tales* fits squarely in the middle of all the company's pulp roots (and pulp-revival aspirations).

Assisting me on *AT* are Wildside Press staffers P. D. Cacek, Sean Wallace, Diane Weinstein, and Darrell Schweitzer, plus Warren Lapine of DNA Publications. Darrell edits *Weird Tales* magazine with George Scithers and has an encyclopedic knowledge of pulp writers and fiction. Sean Wallace is a book editor with a love for classic pulp fiction. Warren Lapine, who runs DNA Publications, is assisting with circulation management. (All the stuff I don't want to do, like keeping track of subscribers and mailing out subscription copies.) Diane Weinstein is a terrific proofreader and is always happy to lend her considerable art direction skills. Together, I think we make a great team, and I hope that *Adventure Tales* becomes your new favorite

fiction magazine. If not, it won't be for lack of trying!

One note for collectors: we are producing two distinct editions of *Adventure Tales*, one on newsprint for casual readers (it's much cheaper — only $5.99 per issue) and one on book paper for collectors who want to save it ($15.95 per issue). Because we need a minimum of 108 pages (our printer's requirement) for the book paper edition, we are going to add a little extra material in to fill it out. With the first book-paper edition, we will feature *The Spider Strain*, a short novel by Johnston McCulley (best known as the creator of Zorro). With the second issue, we will begin the serialization of a 60,000-word novel, *The Golden Dolphin*, by J. Allan Dunn. *The Golden Dolphin* will also be available as a book from Wildside Press if you can't wait to finish it!

You can subscribe to either version (or both). The newsprint edition is $19.95 for 4 issues; the book paper edition is $29.95 for 2 issues, postage paid in the United States.

Till next time . . .
— John Betancourt

IN MEMORIAM: As this issue was about to go to press, we received news of the passing of Hugh B. Cave. He was a great writer and a wonderful person. He will be missed by all who new him. We are all grateful to have been able to work with him to create this special issue of *Adventure Tales* honoring him and his work.

BRITANNIA VICTURA

When Justice from the vaulted skies
    Beheld the fall of Roman might,
She bade a nobler realm arise
    To rule the world and guard the right:
She spake — and all the murm'ring main,
    Rejoicing, hail'd Britannia's reign!

The mind of Greece, the law of Rome,
    The strength of Northern climes remote,
On one fair Island made their home,
    And in one race their virtues wrote:
The blended glories of the past
    In England evermore shall last!

Untrodden wilds beyond the sea,
    And savage hordes in lands unknown,
At Albion's touch rose great and free,
    And bless'd the sway of England's throne:
Discordant tribes, with strife o'errun,
    Grew Britons, and join'd hands as one!

When Greed and Envy stand array'd,
    And Madness threats a peaceful earth,
Britannia's sons with sacred blade
    Defend the soil that gave them birth:
Nor is their cause to that confin'd —
    They fight for Justice and Mankind.

Tho' Fortune frown and trials press;
    Tho' pain and hardship weigh the heart,
the dawn of vict're soon will bless
    Each Briton who sustains his part:
For Heavn'n's own pow'r is close allay'd
    To Virtue's and Britannia's side!

— H.P. Lovecraft

EDGAR RICE BURROUGHS

"It was Burroughs who turned me on, and I think he is a much underrated writer. The man who can create Tarzan, the best-known character in the whole fiction, should not be taken too lightly!"

ARTHUR C. CLARKE

available now

THE LOST CONTINENT

The year is 2137. Two hundred years ago—in our time, more or less—Eurasia fought a war to end all wars, a war that meant, for all intents and purposes, the end of the Old World. The Americans managed to retain their civilization—but only by engaging by the most extreme form or isolationism imaginable for two centuries, now, no American has ventured east of the thirtieth parallel. "East for the East . . ." the slogan went, "The West for the West!" Until a terrible storm at sea forced American lieutenant Jefferson Turck to disobey the law, seeking safe harbor in England—where he found that two centuries of isolation have desolated the land. The damaged ship found a Europe that is no longer an enemy—a ruined land that is utterly unable to be an enemy—or a friend.

THE MAD KING

Edgar Rice Burroughs wrote this tale of confused identity and royal intrigue in 1914 and 1915: it means to be an homage to Anthony Hope's *Prisoner of Zenda*. Of course it isn't Hope writing, but Burroughs: the events that led to the war inform the book, and it speaks to the real events happening as Burroughs wrote. That makes it a very different story from Hope's almost-whimsical novel. Part of the reason Burroughs left such a lasting mark on the world is because he was engaged in the events that surrounded him; the news troubled him deeply and personally. As well it might! He was writing, as he always did, on fantastical topics; but it is the fantastic nature of the twentieth century that is the real text of the man's career. The events that shape our own times now inform the work at hand: Edgar Rice Burroughs is generally described as a "Pulp Writer"—that's code for a successful hack—but the truth is that he was much, much more.

THE GIRL FROM FARRIS'S

Few authors, not even with the exception of Rudyard Kipling, have covered so wide a field in their fiction as has Mr. Burroughs. His maiden effort, which was published in the old ALL-STORY in 1912, dealt with the adventures of an American who made a trip to Mars. . . .

EDGAR RICE BURROUGHS:

The Man Who Held the Hero's Horse

by Mike Resnick

There have been a lot of theories advanced as to why Edgar Rice Burroughs remains a popular author more than 90 years after he first broke into print, when dozens of Pulitzer and Nobel winners (and a few Hugo winners as well) can't be found this side of Bookfinder.com.

A lot of people credit his imagination, and yes, it certainly worked overtime, coming up with Tarzan, Barsoom, Amtor, Pellucidar, Caspak, Poloda, and the rest.

Others point to his break-neck pacing. You follow Tarzan until he's unarmed and facing a ferocious man-eater at chapter's end, then cut to Jane until she's one grope away from a Fate Worse Than Death at the end of the next chapter, then back to Tarzan, and so forth. Works pretty well.

A few point to his remarkable facility at creating languages. And truly, what *would* you call an elephant except Tantor? What could a snake possibly be other than Hista? What better name for an ape-king that half-barks and half-growls his language than Kerchak? Yes, he was damned good at languages.

But there's another aspect to Burroughs that lends enormous verisimilitude, especially to his younger readers, and it's an aspect that has been addressed only once before, by the late Burroughs scholar (and Royal Canadian Mountie) John F. Roy — and that is the interesting fact that ERB wrote himself into almost all his greatest adventures.

When I first discovered *A Princess of Mars* at age 8, I *knew* the story was true. I mean, hell, Burroughs was writing about his own uncle, the man who had entrusted him with the manuscript of his adventures on that distant and wondrous planet. Wasn't that proof enough that Barsoom existed?

Well, if you were young and impressionable, it was proof enough — but even if you weren't, it was a very effective and informal way of getting you into the story.

And while ERB was not a trained writer, at a gut level he knew it worked. He might not have known what "distancing mechanism" or "stream of consciousness" meant, but he sure as hell knew how to lasso a reader and pull him along, and his favorite and most effective gimmick was to tell you how he himself had been thrust into the company of this book's hero.

So here he was, the nephew of John Carter, gentleman of Virginia and Warlord of Mars, explaining how he can come upon this remarkable manuscript, how he had watched his uncle standing outside at night reaching out his arms to Mars, how he had followed instructions and buried him in a well-ventilated coffin that could only be opened from the inside, and only now understood the meaning of it all.

And it didn't stop with the one book. He meets John Carter again and is given the manuscripts to *The Gods of Mars* and *The Warlord of Mars*. Some years later he meets Ulysses Paxton (a/k/a Vad Varo) by proxy when John Carter delivers Paxton's long letter (i.e., *The Master Mind of Mars*) to him, and he is visited by John Carter at least twice more. It is made clear that ERB is now an old man (as indeed he was), while the Warlord remains the thirtyish fighting man he has always been.

But ERB's interaction with his characters wasn't limited to Barsoom.

For example, he knows the man who knows the man who knows Tarzan — or some permutation of that. The very first line in his most famous book, *Tarzan of the Apes*, is: "I had this story from one who had no business to tell it to me, or to any other." A Burroughs scholar would probably conclude that the "one" was Paul d'Arnot, but it makes no difference. The point is that here is ERB, inserting himself in the beginning of the story again to lend some degree of authenticity.

Did he ever meet Tarzan? He never says so explicitly, but he did meet Barney Custer, hero of *The Eternal Lover*, and his sister, and based on the interal evidence of the book, the only place ERB could possibly have met them was on Lord Greystoke's vast African estate.

It was while vacationing in Greenland that ERB came across the manuscript that became *The Land That Time Forgot*. (Yes, he was pretty sharp at finding saleable manuscripts.)

Burroughs gets around. *At the Earth's Core* finds him in the Sahara, where he stumbles upon David Innes, who in turn had stumbled upon the hidden world of Pellucidar and felt compelled to spend the night telling ERB his story. A reader in Algiers summons him back a few years later, where he is reintroduced to David Innes, who once again pours out his story, which was published as *Pellucidar*.

After moving to California, who should ERB's next-door neighbor turn out to be but the brilliant young scientist Jason Gridley, creator of the remarkable Gridley Wave, by means of which Burroughs received still more tales of that mysterious world at the center of the hollow Earth. (And Gridley himself later went to Pellucidar, which means the ERB rubbed shoulders with still another hero.)

Burroughs even wrote his company's secretary, Ralph Rothmond (who was later fired, more than a decade after ERB's death, for carelessly allowing a number of copyrights to expire) into one of the books. Rothmond introduces ERB to young, handsome, blond, heroic Carson Napier, the Wrong-Way Corrigan of space, who takes off for Mars and someone winds up on Venus. Napier remains in telepathic contact with Burroughs long enough to dicate *Pirates of Venus* and three-plus sequels.

There was just something about ERB that made heroes seek him out and tell him their strange stories, always on the condition that he not publish the tale until they were dead, or if he couldn't wait that long, to at least change their names. The last to find him and unload on him was Julian V, who narrated the tale of *The Moon Maid*.

ERB never met the author of *Beyond the Farthest Star* — after all, that would have been quite a voyage — but of all the people in the universe, the author was, perhaps unsurprisingly by this time, drawn to Burroughs, and mystically compelled ERB's typewriter to produce the story one night in Hawaii while ERB watched in awe.

The interesting thing is that though he associated with Tarzan and John Carter and David Innes and Carson Napier and many others, ERB never once performed an exciting or heroic deed in any of the books, and that lends a little verisimilitude too. These are extraordinary men, these heroes, and neither ERB nor you nor I can begin to match their skills or heroism, so it makes much more sense for him to tell us about it and for us to read and appreciate it. Fighting lions or green men or allosaurs is for heroes; reading about it is for the rest of us mortals.

And maybe that's why we loved and identified with Edgar Rice Burroughs. He didn't lop of heads with his longsword, or bellow the victory cry of the bull ape over the corpse of an enemy, or make his way to the center of

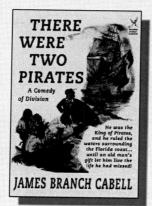
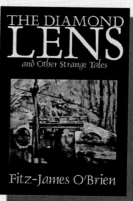
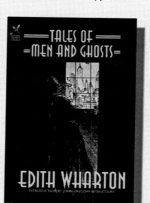

the Earth. But he seemed to know the re-markable men who *did* do those things, and, by golly, he got to hold the hero's horse. Most of us would have traded places with him in a New York — or Barsoomian — minute.

THE SKULL IN THE CLOUDS

The Black Prince scowled above his lance, and wrath in his hot eyes lay,
"I would that you rode with the spears of France and not at my side today.
"A man may parry an open blow, but I know not where to fend;
"I would that you were an open foe, instead of a sworn friend.

"You came to me in an hour of need, and your heart I thought I saw;
"But you are one of a rebel breed that knows not king or law.
"You—with your ever smiling face and a black heart under your mail —
"With the haughty strain of the Norman race and the wild, black blood of the Gael.

"Thrice in a night fight's close-locked gloom my shield by merest chance
"Has turned a sword that thrust like doom — I wot 'twas not of France!
"And in a dust-cloud, blind and red, as we charged the Provence line
"An unseen axe struck Fitzjames dead, who gave his life for mine.

"Had I proofs, your head should fall this day or ever I rode to strife.
"Are you but a wolf to rend and slay, with naught to guide your life?
"No gleam of love in a lady's eyes, no honor or faith or fame?"
I raised my face to the brooding skies and laughed like a roaring flame.

"I followed the sign of the Geraldine from Meath to the western sea
"Till a careless word that I scarcely heard bred hate in the heart of me.
"Then I lent my sword to the Irish chiefs, for half of my blood is Gael,
"And we cut like a sickle through the sheafs as we harried the lines of the Pale.

"But Dermod O'Connor, wild with wine, called me a dog at heel,
"And I cleft his bosom to the spine and fled to the black O'Neill.
"We harried the chieftains of the south; we shattered the Norman bows.
"We wasted the land from Cork to Louth; we trampled our fallen foes.

"But Conn O'Neill put on me a slight before the Gaelic lords,
"And I betrayed him in the night to the red O'Donnell swords.
"I am no thrall to any man, no vassal to any king.
"I owe no vow to any clan, nor faith to any thing.

"Traitor — but not for fear or gold, but the fire in my own dark brain;
"For the coins I loot from the broken hold I throw to the winds again.
"And I am true to myself alone, through pride and the traitor's part.
"I would give my life to shield your throne, or rip from your breast the heart

"For a look or a word, scarce thought or heard. I follow a fading fire,
"Past bead and bell and the hangman's cell, like a harp-call of desire.
"I may not see the road I ride for the witch-fire lamp that gleam;
"But phantoms glide at my bridle-side, and I follow a nameless Dream."

The Black Prince shuddered and shook his head, then crossed himself amain:
"Go, in God's name, and never," he said, "ride in my sight again."

The starlight silvered my bridle-rein; the moonlight burned my lance
As I rode back from the wars again through the pleasant hills of France,
As I rode to tell Lord Amory of the dark Fitzgerald line
If the Black Prince died, it needs must be by another hand than mine.

— Robert E. Howard

Michael Chomko, Books

2217 W. Fairview Street
Allentown, PA 18104-6542

Purveyor of Pulp-Related
Books & Periodicals

**BLOOD 'N THUNDER   GIRASOL REPLICAS
G-8   HIGH ADVENTURE   ILLUSTRATION
LOST TREASURES OF THE PULPS   THE SPIDER
ZORRO   ADVENTURE HOUSE   ARKHAM HOUSE
BATTERED SILICON DISPATCH BOX
BOLD VENTURE PRESS   CRIPPEN & LANDRU
DARKSIDE PRESS   HAFFNER PRESS
MIDNIGHT HOUSE   NIGHT SHADE BOOKS
WILDSIDE PRESS   *and more!***

THE PULP REPRINTS OF HUGH B. CAVE

by Michael Chomko

Hugh Barnett Cave was born in 1910 and seemingly began writing as soon as he could lift pencil to paper. While still in high school he was a published author, having sold a few stories to Sunday School papers and poetry to newspapers. Not long after obtaining his first and only job with a Boston vanity publisher, Cave made his first sale to the pulps. "Island Ordeal" was published in the July 1929 issue of *Brief Stories*. It was quickly followed by others sold to a variety of magazines. *Action Stories, Short Stories, Astounding Stories, Wide World Adventures, Outlaws of the West,* and *High Spot Magazine* all published stories by Cave during the next year. He was soon able to give up his day job and survive as a full-time author. By 1933, he had established markets with many of the leading publishers of the pulp industry, including Popular Publications and Street & Smith. According to his records, Cave published about eight hundred stories in the pulps, the bulk of them appearing prior to 1942. By then he was writing predominantly for the book trade and "slick" magazines, selling stories to such mainstream publications as *Colliers, Country Gentleman, Good Housekeeping, Liberty, Redbook,* and *The Saturday Evening Post*.

Although other prolific pulpsters such as Edgar Rice Burroughs, Lester Dent, Frederick Faust, Walter B. Gibson, and Robert E. Howard had found their way back into print by the late sixties, it was not until 1977 that the pulp work of Hugh Cave would begin to reappear. It was then that the late author and editor, Karl Edward Wagner, hoping to preserve the work of writers he felt had been unjustly neglected, released *Murgunstrumm and Others*. This long out-of-print collection, published by Wagner's Carcosa House and illustrated by the great Lee Brown Coye, went on to win a 1978 World Fantasy Award. It's best described using the language found on the inside flap of its dust jacket:

> *Murgunstrumm and Others* abounds with haunted houses, ravenous vampires, slobbering monsters, fiends human and inhuman, nights dark and stormy, corpses fresh and rotting. These stories exemplify the gothic horror thrillers of the 1930s — no-holds-barred lurid chillers of violent action and scream-in-the-night terror . . . savored best on a stormy, lonely, night.

Largely drawn from the pages of *Strange Tales, Spicy Mystery Stories* (where Cave's tales originally appeared under the pseudonym Justin Case), and *Weird Tales, Murgunstrumm and Others* will soon be reissued by Wildside Press in both hardcover and trade paperback.

Although Wagner's collection helped to reëstablish Hugh Cave as an author of dark fantasy — his short novel, *The Mountains of Madness*, was released earlier this year in a limited, signed edition by Cemetery Dance Publications — it would be another ten years before the next collection of Cave's pulp work would see the light of day. *Spicy Detective Encores No. 2*, one of a series of six tiny volumes, each about the size of a "Big-Little Book," reprinted three of Cave's "Eel" stories. Cave had introduced this character in the June 1936 issue of Culture Publications' *Spicy Adventure Stories*. Urged by his editors at Culture to supply them with more tales of the "Eel," Cave went on to produce about twenty stories featuring the character, all of them credited to Justin Case.

Published by Winds of the World Press in card-stock covers, *Spicy Detective Encores No. 2* is a collectible rarely seen on today's used book market. However, the three stories it reprinted are available in a more recent and extensive collection of "Eel" yarns. *Escapades of the Eel*, published in 1997 by Tattered Pages Press of Chicago, assembled fifteen of the best stories featuring the "gentleman correspondent" of *Spicy Adventure Stories* and private dick of *Spicy Detective* and *Spicy Mystery Stories*. Told in the first person using the tongue-in-cheek style of the spicy pulps, the "Eel" stories range from the wilds of Borneo to the urban jungles of Depression-age and World War II-era America.

In 1988, the next Cave collection saw the light of day — *The Corpse Maker*. Assembled by Sheldon Jaffery for the now-defunct Starmont House, it was a short, paperbound collection of seven stories drawn largely from the pages of such weird-menace pulps as *Dime Mystery Magazine* and *Terror Tales*. Jaffery's collection reproduces its stories directly from the pages of the pulps and features personable, yet informative introductions to each story. The title yarn was originally published in the second of the "weird-menace" issues of *Dime Mystery*, the magazine that introduced the genre to pulp readers. Like *Spicy Detective Encores No. 2*, *The Corpse Maker* is now a difficult book to find.

Nearly another decade passed before the Hugh Cave floodgates opened. It began with a collection that Carcosa House had intended to be the sequel to *Murgunstrumm and Others*. Fortunately, in 1995, following their success with collections of pulp fiction by Robert Bloch, Carl Jacobi, and Donald Wandrei, Minnesota-based Fedogan & Bremer rode to the rescue and released the long-delayed collection of Cave's best tales of weird menace, *Death Stalks the Night*. Featuring seventeen tales from shudder pulps like *Dime Mystery, Horror Stories,* and *New Mystery Adventures, Death Stalks the Night* like its predecessor, *Murgunstrumm*, was also nominated for a World Fantasy Award.

According to editor Karl Edward Wagner, weird-menace stories "were calculatedly gothic and grisly . . . (with) no pretensions of art — just go for the throat . . . (and) the wildest and weirdest menacer of them all was Hugh B. Cave. . . . Cave's weird-menace stories still have the power to chill and thrill. . . . This really is a curl-up on a dark and stormy night book." And you know, he was right!

In 1997, Fedogan & Bremer dipped again into the shudder pulps to harvest ten more stories by "the wildest and weirdest menacer of them all." Compiled by the author himself, *The Door Below* featured stories selected from throughout the author's career. Alongside such pulp stories as "Servant of Satan" and "The Thing from the Swamp," were tales written during the last three decades of the twentieth century, fiction "written most often for magazines published by people who fondly remembered the pulps and sought to keep those memories alive by recreating them." Thus, although "From the Lower Deep" and "Damsels for the Damned" could very well have

been titles for stories featured in *Strange Tales* and *Spicy Mystery Stories,* both yarns missed those magazines by half a century.

Two paperbound collections from Tattered Pages Press — the previously discussed *Escapades of the Eel* and a companion volume entitled *The Dagger of Tsiang and Other Tales of Adventure* — joined *The Door Below* to make 1997 a banner year for Cave reprints. Assembled by Doug Ellis from the pages of *Short Stories, Top-Notch Magazine,* and other periodicals of the early thirties, *The Dagger of Tsiang* collects eleven "colorful tales of Tsiang House, a British outpost deep in the jungles of Borneo . . . adventure at its finest, written by a master of the craft." Both of the Tattered Pages books are entertaining packages, assembled and published by a small press devoted to reproducing some of the best stories of the pulp era.

Another small press was next to reprint the work of the man sometimes known as Justin Case. In 1998, Black Dog Books, headed by artist, designer, and pulp fan Tom Roberts, published the first of its five Cave collections — *The Death-Head's March and Others.* Subtitled *The Geoffrey Vace Collection,* three of the four stories included were written by Cave's older brother, Geoffrey. Along the lines of Talbot Mundy's tales of India, the Vace stories were originally published in *Oriental Stories* and *Magic Carpet Magazine,* the adventure-oriented companions to *Weird Tales.* The fourth story of the collection, "Step Softly, Sahib!" was written by Hugh Cave, using his brother's pseudonym. "I did my best to keep that Nom-de-plume alive for him with stories in many different pulps . . . always hoping he would one day return to his typewriter."

Other Cave collections from Black Dog Books include *White Star of Egypt,* which re-

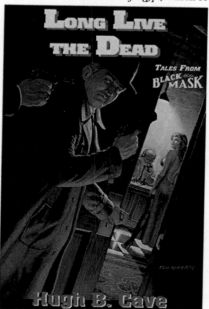

prints a pair of tales from *Spicy Adventure Stories; The Desert Host,* the sole "sword-and-sorcery" story that Cave contributed to the pulps, written for *Magic Carpet; Dark Doors of Doom,* a trio of weird-menace yarns from the pages of the spicy pulps, all originally credited to Justin Case; and *The Stinging 'Nting and Other Stories,* four adventure yarns first published in 1931 in two pulps rarely seen today — *Far East Adventure Stories* and *Man Stories.* Black Dog's Cave collections are digest-sized books with card-stock covers, available from the publisher for between five and nine dollars.

Although Hugh B. Cave is predominantly regarded today as a writer of dark fantasy, a large portion of his pulp era work was created for the mystery genre. At least one quarter of his pulp production was aimed at the rough-paper detective market. Beginning in 2000, modern readers were reintroduced to this versatile author's crime fiction through three reprint collections issued by the small presses.

Fedogan & Bremer celebrated the author's ninetieth birthday with the republication of Cave's nine "Peter Kane" stories, originally written for Popular Publication's *Dime Detective.* According to Don Hutchison's introduction to the volume, "Kane . . . was introduced as (the) 'ace shamus of the Beacon Agency, chronic drunk, two-fisted, hard-headed private dick with nothing to live for except the next drink' . . . a man who can down three liquid meals a day, get hit on the head more often than is really healthy, and still land on his feet right side up."

While the first half-dozen Kane stories, originally published in 1934 and 1935, owe a large debt to the weird-menace field for which Cave had then been laboring for several years, the final three tales set a more comic tone and feature rather puzzling plots.

Dime Detective was also home to another Cave hero, truant officer Nick Coffey. The protagonist of three stories contributed to the Popular magazine in 1940, Officer Coffey was a favorite of *Dime Detective*'s editor Ken White as well as Cave's agent, Lurton "Count" Blassingame. The stories concern good kids, driven into trouble via circumstances beyond their control. In 2000, Subterranean Press reissued two of the three Coffey stories in a chapbook limited to 250 numbered and 26 lettered copies, all signed by the author. The Sidecar Preservation Society issued the third Coffey story separately in 2001 as a fund-raising effort.

Black Mask was the premier detective magazine of the pulp era, the periodical where the hard-boiled detective story took root and evolved. Home to such greats of the mystery genre as Dashiell Hammett, Raymond Chandler, and Erle Stanley Gardner, *Black Mask* would also publish ten of Cave's tales of detection, contributed to the maga-

zine from 1934 through 1941. Ranging from the tough-guy cop of "Too Many Women," to the greeting card executive who investigates crimes as a hobby in "Smoke Gets in Your Eyes," to his last story for the magazine, the Hitchcockian "Stranger in Town," Crippen & Landru's *Long Live the Dead* amply demonstrates Cave's versatility as an author.

Although *Black Mask* and *Dime Detective Magazine* were probably the best of the many detective pulps that were published during the pulp era, it was for *Detective Fiction Weekly* that Cave wrote most of his crime fiction. From 1936 through 1941, he contributed sixty-three tales of mystery and detection to the Munsey magazine. Crippen & Landru's *Come Into My Parlor* collects nearly a dozen of these stories, which, according to the author, were "among the best of the pulp stories I wrote."

"What I had, in many of my tales for *Detective Fiction Weekly,* were folks like you and you and you, who never wore a policeman's uniform or were licensed to be crime fighters. These characters were just everyday people who became involved in crime-fighting more or less by 'accident.' And when I began writing that kind of story, with a hero who was not a professional crime-fighter, but just an ordinary Joe like most of us, the editor of *Detective Fiction Weekly* liked them and so did the readers."

Both Crippen & Landru volumes were published in two states — a trade paperbound edition and a limited clothbound edition, signed and numbered by the author. Included with the latter was a separate pamphlet, reprinting an additional Cave pulp story not found in the paperbound edition of that particular book.

With over eight-hundred stories moldering away in the crumbling pages of seventy-year-old magazines never meant for permanence, these seventeen collections reprinting over 130 stories have only scratched the surface of Cave's prodigious output. Hopefully, the appearance of *Cave of a Thousand Tales,* a biography of the author written by Milt Thomas and released by Arkham House in June of this year, will provide the impetus for further collections of this wonderful craftsman of the pulp era.[1] After all, the Arizona Kid, Wildcat and Range Wolf, and Senor Bravo are all still having "Trouble Tamin' Tumbleweed" in the pages of *Western Story Magazine* and *Wild West Weekly.*

[1] Starmont House published a short biography of Hugh Cave, *Pulp Man's Odyssey,* written by Audrey Parente, in 1988. It was followed in 1994 by Cave's autobiographical *Magazines I Remember,* based on his long correspondence with fellow author Carl Jacobi and published by Tattered Pages Press.

ADVENTURE TALES INTERVIEWS HUGH B. CAVE

Hugh B. Cave surely needs little in the way of introduction to any fan of pulp fiction. Under his own name and pseudonyms such as "Justin Case" he wrote more than a thousand stories for magazines, before turning his attention to books. We were pleased when he accepted our invitation to be the Featured Author in the first issue of *Adventure Tales*, and he consented to this interview.

Adventure Tales: How and when did you enter the pulp field as a writer?

Hugh B. Cave: While still a student at Brookline, Massachusetts High School, I sold poetry and crossword puzzles to Boston newspapers and other publications, stories to Sunday School magazines, and did cartoons for the Boston YMCA News. One such poem, called "Men," originally published in *Sunset Magazine* on the West Coast, was set to music by Carlyle Davis, sung by him in Carnegie Hall, and published by the Oliver Ditson Company.

After high school I worked for a Boston publishing company for a year or so. One book of poetry that I had a hand in designing was by W. Adolph Roberts, editor of a pulp magazine called *Brief Stories*. He suggested I try a short story for *Brief Stories*, and the suggestion resulted in "Island Ordeal," my first pulp sale, which was published in July, 1929, when I had just turned 19.

There were more than a hundred pulp magazines being published at that time — so-called because they were printed on rough wood-pulp paper. I eventually sold a total of some 800 to 95 of them, then moved on into the higher-paying slick-paper magazines such as *The Saturday Evening Post* (to which I sold 46 stories), *Good Housekeeping* (41), *American*, *Redbook*, *Ladies Home Journal*, *Collier's*, *Liberty*, *Esquire*, etc. etc. Three hundred fifty stories in all. And my next two books, due out this year, will be Number 49 and Number 50 on my list of books published. Five of these are World War II books written as a correspondent. Two are books on Haiti and Jamaica. Twenty are novels. The others are hardcover collections of my pulp and slick-paper magazine stories.

Some of these books and many of my shorter works have been reprinted in foreign countries. About a dozen of my books have been reprinted by John Betancourt's Wildside Press.

And along the way, two books have been written about me. These are *Pulp Man's Odyssey: The Hugh B. Cave Story* by Audrey Parente, published by Starmont House in 1988, and a brand new one, *Cave of a Thousand Tales* by Milt Thomas, due out this year, 2004, from Arkham House.

AT: Of all those stories, do you have any favorites?

Hugh B. Cave: Two favorites come to mind quickly. The first is a very short story called *Two Were Left*, which was originally published in *American Magazine* in June, 1942. It's about an Eskimo boy and his beloved sled dog who are marooned on a drifting ice floe and, when hungry enough, one of them will have to eat the other to survive. The story has been reprinted more than one hundred times in school books and anthologies.

The other is one of many tales I have written about Haiti after having lived there for five winters. I note there is a question about Haiti coming up in this interview, so I won't go into my adventures there now, but this story, called *The Mission*, first appeared in the old *Saturday Evening Post* of March 14, 1959 and was reprinted in *The Best Post Stories* of that year, in the first issue of the new *Saturday Evening Post*, and in seven foreign magazines. Just recently, when Haiti was in turmoil over its president, a group that wanted the world to have a better opinion of that country requeted permission to feature the story on a web-site. It's about a six-year-old country girl who, after the tragic death of her mother in a landslide, walks miles to Port-au-Prince, the capital, to find her "famous artist" father who actually existed only in her mother's imagination. After the *Post* printed it, Doubleday did it as a handsome gift book, calling it "a little classic of the spirit."

The Post, by the way, reported that this story had received more reader mail than any story ever published in the magazine. Part of the story's success was due, I'm sure, to the portrait of little Yolande by artist Peter Stevens, which was featured in the Doubleday book also.

AT: For the collector, would you care to talk about some of your pseudonyms and their histories?

Hugh B. Cave: My brother Geoffrey Cave, four years older than I, was editor of his school paper when he attended a high school in Boston, Mass. But he didn't plan to make writing his career. Instead, he went on to business school and became an accountant.

Still, Geoff tried his hand at writing some pulp stories, using the name Geoffrey Vace, and sold some to Farnsworth Wright, famous editor of *Weird Tales*, for such magazines as *Oriental Stories* and *Magic Carpet*. So for a while, whenever I had two stories in any issue of any pulp, I would use his writing name, Geoffrey Vace, on one of them to win him more exposure.

In 1998 Tom Roberts, publisher of Black Dog Books, put out a neat booklet that he called *The Death-Head's March and Others: The Geoffrey Vace Collection*, by Geoffrey Cave and Hugh B. Cave." But Geoff didn't continue as a writer, the way I did. He gave it up to be an accountant.

Another pseudonym I used — and used much more often — was Justin Case. This was a name I developed for the Spicy pulps — *Spicy Mystery*, *Spicy Detective* and

Spicy Adventure — because they paid me as high as six cents a word but I was aiming at the slicks and didn't want to use my real name. (I wonder if any real people named Case ever named a son Justin!) Black Dog reprinted some Justin Case tales as well, calling the booklets *Dark Door of Doom* and *White Star of Egypt* after two of the stories in them. And in 1997 Tattered Pages Press of Chicago published a handsome paperback collection of my Justin Case tales featuring a character I called "The Eel," calling it *Escapades of The Eel.*

And, finally, even in the slicks I occasionally needed to use a pen-name, in which case I called myself H.C. Barnett, Barnett being my mother's maiden name and my actual middle name. I can't think off-hand of any others I used, but there probably were one or two more.

AT: How has your interest in Haiti and voodoo influenced your work?

Hugh B. Cave: Let's begin with why I went to Haiti in the first place. At age 25 I married Margaret Long, a physical education teacher in the Providence, R.I. school system. We had two sons, Kenneth and Donald. When Ken was 10 and Don 5, the older boy began having some strange nightmares, and their doctor recommended we get him out of cold New England for the winter. As it happened, I knew a man who was teaching English in Haiti and asked him if he could find a house for us to rent. He found one in Petionville, and our Haitian adventure began. The boys attended an English-speaking school run by the U.S. Embassy. I began exploring the country and writing about it.

And then voodoo. We were told about a voodoo *maman* named Lorgina in Port-au-Prince, the capital, who was highly regarded. We obtained permission to attend one of her services, but, when we got there, found her ill with a badly swollen, painful leg. My wife, remember, was a phys. ed. teacher. "Go find me some olive oil and I'll try to massage the pain away," she told me.

Well, I drove all over Port-au-Prince in the middle of the night and finally found some in a little all-night eatery. Meg massaged the mambo's pain away. And Lorgina was so grateful she said, "Anything you want from me, just ask. Anything!"

What we wanted — what I wanted, anyway — was to learn about the real voodoo so I could write about it. We spent five winters there in Haiti, and I am happy to say that the same cook, same housekeeper, and same yard boy worked for us the whole time, and our boys did well in school. I came up with some short stories for various magazines and then wrote a book called *Haiti: Highroad to Adventure* about which noted author Kenneth Roberts wrote to the publisher: "If there was anything printed about Haiti that I didn't read (when I was writing *Lydia Bailey*) either in French or English or in diaries, I couldn't find out about it; and Cave's *Haiti* seems to me to stand head and shoulders above all of them in its vivid depiction of the land and the people. If you want a quote, I suggest 'The most perfect depiction of present-day Haiti, the land and the people, ever drawn.'"

Then I wrote a novel, *The Cross on the Drum*, about the conflict between a voodoo houngan and a protestant minister (which ended with the two of them calling each other "my brother") and it was a Doubleday Dollar Book Club selection and a Literary Guild bonus book. And I wrote many magazine short stories about Haiti which have been reprinted in a collection of my West Indies tales called *The Witching Lands.*

AT: Despite your success in the slick magazines, you kept coming back to fantasy and horror themes in your work. I note that many of your later novels are, in fact, horror. What's the appeal of dark fantasy for you?

Hugh B. Cave: Well now, I have a hunch it all began when I was a kid singing in the men's-&-boys' choir at a church in Boston. We choir kids attended a camp for two weeks every summer near Cape Cod, as I may have mentioned before, and every night around a campfire our choir-master read us creepy stories by Poe and other such

writers. I got to be very fond of them and still am. Most horror stories, it seems to me, have a touch of fantasy, and fantasy gives a writer space to expand in. I've done many other kinds of stories and books, but feel so "at ease" in the fantasy-horror field that I keep coming back to it.

AT: You mentioned that the "Spicy" magazines paid 6 cents a word for fiction. Wasn't that a lot of money for a pulp magazine? How did the other pulps compare?

Hugh B. Cave: My record-books show that most pulp magazines paid from 1 to 3 cents a word. I don't know what the "Spicies" paid other writers, but my Justin Case stories got a lot of covers and apparently were popular with the readers. Some have been reprinted in book form, as I mentioned before. I don't know what the "Spicies" paid other writers. My old records give only the title of each story sold and when it was published. Other pulps, such as *Short Stories, Adventure, Dime Mystery,* and *Dime Detective,* paid me more than a cent a word, I seem to remember, but I can't think of any that paid me what the "Spicies" did.

AT: When you were writing your pulp stories, what were your working hours? What was a typical day like for a writer in, say, 1935?

Hugh B. Cave: Before I married (which I did in 1935), I worked long hours at those old-style typewriters. (I remember having one whose carriage I had to lift up to see what it had typed from underneath!). Then along came electric machines and computers. When a story I'm working on grabs my interest really hard, I'm likely to work all day at it and sometimes even half the night. It has always been that way for me, even in my pulp-writing days. Now I have slowed down a bit. After all, I'm 93 as I write this. But if a great story idea comes my way, I'm still likely to work long and hard at it, and I still enjoy doing so.

AT: Is there a question you haven't been asked in interviews before, that you would like to answer?

Hugh B. Cave: Well now, no interviewer has ever asked, "Do you ever wish you had been something other than a writer?" If anyone ever does ask that, my answer will be a resounding "No!" because it has been a fulfilling and fascinating life.

After all, I started at age 16 or thereabouts and am still writing at 93. Amen.

AT: Thank you very much for your time!

SKULLS

by H. BEDFORD-JONES

I

THE entire affair occupied an incredibly short space of time, considering what was involved. It happened in a corner of the smoking room of the *Empress of China*, the evening before we were to dock in San Francisco.

Looking back on it now, I suppose it is impossible to convey the full shock which accompanied the ghastly denouncement of Larsen's story, Larsen was sharing my stateroom; we were friends. He was returning after spending a year away out in western China, gathering specimens for some museum. A thin, dark, sallow man, he possessed that rare charm which comes of deep, strong character. He was full of surprises; and, I have since thought, full of an inexorable, grim puritanical sort of righteousness, as well.

Mainwaring, who occupied the odd chair in our corner of the smoking room, had taken a liking to Larsen from the start, and stuck with us the whole voyage. We liked him, also. He was lonely and homesick, poor devil, anxious to be back home. He had spent several years in the Orient, in the silk business; a big chap he was, bearded, with gently imaginative blue eyes and a great reticence of manner.

We had the place pretty much to ourselves that evening, since everyone was packing, Mainwaring showed us a couple of very fine old netsukes, abominably indecent, which he meant to bring past the customs in his pocket. At this, Larsen flushed slightly and rose.

"I'll show you chaps something interesting," he said, and left us.

He returned presently, bringing a small Chinese box. This he opened, and took from wads of cotton two shallow, oval bowls, handing once to each of us. I examined mine. At first I took it for rhinoceros horn; it had the same rich brown coloring and feel. Then I perceived the lines upon it, and knew the thing for what it was — the top of a skull.

"Hello!" exclaimed Mainwaring with interest. "You must have been up in Tibet to get hold of these, eh? I've heard the lamas use human skulls for bowls."

"Yes and no." Larsen lighted a cigar and leaned back in his chair, smiling oddly. "I got these at a lamasery, right enough, but it was across from the Tibetan border — up in the Lolo country in northern Yunnan."

Mainwaring glanced up from the skull in his hands. His brows lifted in quick interest.

"Oh! By the way, did you ever hear of an expedition that got lost up in that country a couple of years ago? Three Americans — I can't recall their names. I heard something about it at the time, but never learned whether they got out."

Larsen nodded. His eyes held an air of singular intensity, yet his words were calm.

"Yes. Oh, yes! The Bonner party, eh? I knew old Bonner very well indeed, years ago. And his nephew Stickley; a fine chap, and an excellent botanist, Creighton was the third of that party. Yes, I got the whole story from the lamas up there. Rather interesting, in connection with these skull-bowls."

"They got out, then?" questioned Mainwaring.

"No," said Larsen, inspecting his cigar ash. "No. They're still there — in parts." An indescribable gleam flashed in his eye as he said this.

"Yes, of course," I put in carelessly. "It was quite a famous case at the time — they were murdered by the Lolos or by bandits. If you've learned the truth of it, Larsen, I suppose you'll take it up with the government? Washington should do something about it."

Larsen looked at me, and his dark eyes held a devil.

"What do you really suppose, now," he drawled, "that Washington would do about it? Saint Paul mentioned two kinds of faith, I believe. You've just been up in Assam? Well, if some native had stuck a spear into you, what would have been done about it? No, no; I believe in faith through works, not in faith through notes. I shan't trouble poor Washington."

Mainwaring leaned forward. "Tell us about it, will you?" he asked quickly. His blue eyes were alight with eagerness, "What happened to them?"

"They died," said Larsen. "I got their papers, some of them, from the lamas, and then got the whole story. Well, I don't mind, if you fellows want to listen to a yarn; it has an intimate connection with those skull-bowls, as I mentioned."

We assured him that we did want to listen.

II

BONNER was an elderly man, fussy and crotchety — said Larsen — but a fine old chap in his way. Young Stickley, his nephew, was headed for the top notch in botanical fame; both of them were keen on exploring the Lolo country. Creighton, who joined their party, was after big game. He was a handsome brute, with plenty of money, and I understand he partly backed the expedition. Most people liked Creighton at sight.

At all events, they reached the Clouds of Heaven lamasery, an isolated place up in the hills. They reached there alone, for the mafus had abandoned them for fear of the Lolo men, who were raiding the hill people about that time. The lamas were hospitable, put them up in a small outlying temple, and the three of them went to work at their own lines of endeavor.

Third parties and accidents cause most of the trouble in this world. The third party in this instance was a Lolo woman, the daughter of a chief. She stepped out of the brush just as Creighton, who had seen her tiger-skin garment, thought he was being attacked by Stripes and let go with both barrels of his shotgun. You can imagine what the two loads did to the girl.

I imagine this smashed Crieghton's nerve completely. It would, you know, to bowl over a girl that way. Old Bonner took the matter in hand at once and paid over good indemnity to the Lolos; but indemnity would not satisfy the fellow who had been about to marry the girl. He swore death to the white men, and took to the brush with his arrows. The Lolo, like the Chung Miao, use a virulent poison on their barbs, you know.

After that, Creighton probably fancied that he discerned this warrior lurking behind every bush and tree. He ceased his hunting trips, and only went out in company with Bonner and Stickley. The picture of the dead girl must have haunted him frightfully.

Well, the end came very suddenly. The three of them went out to visit some traps Bonner had set for small animals. A mile or so from the lamasery, they were going up a narrow, steep hill-trail with one pack-mule. Creighton was ahead and beyond sight of the other two, trying to get a sambur they had seen when, abruptly, out of the brush stepped the warrior who had sworn to get them, the fiancé of the dead girl.

Creighton might have warned his friends. He might have shot the man. He did neither. Instead, he gave one gasping, incoherent cry, threw down his rifle and fled. Broke for it — ran straight ahead like a madman.

The Lolo calmly waited there until Bonner and Stickley came along, all unsuspecting.

Then he gave them two arrows. They died there. The Lolo went on and caught Creighton by himself. From the story the priests told, he must have thrown Creighton over the cliffs, and at the last

moment Creighton used his pistol. At all events, the lamas did not find Creighton's body, while they did bring in the dead Lolo, Bonner, and Stickley.

And that's the whole story — the tragedy of Creighton's broken nerve.

III

WHEN Larsen had finished, he lighted a fresh cigar and leaned back in his chair.

Mainwaring sat fingering the skull-bowl in his lap, pursing up his bearded lips and shaking his head as he listened. Presently he looked up, and his gentle blue eyes were wide, as though the tale of that tragedy had filled him with horror.

"But you said," his voice was husky, and he cleared his throat, "you said that there was some connection between the story and these skulls?"

Larsen nodded. A flash darted in his eyes and was gone again.

"Yes. Exactly. The bowl in your lap was made from Bonner's skull. The other was made from Stickley's."

Lord! How to describe the loathly horror that I felt at these words! It is one thing to play with the cranium of some forgotten, unknown savage; quite another thing to play with the brain-pan of a scientist, honored and revered, a man almost a friend.

Mainwaring turned absolutely livid. His beard moved. You know how a cat's fur erects? That way; his beard curled and writhed with the frightful feeling that was upon him. Sweat started on his brow. He reached out and laid the skull on the smoking stand, his fingers shaking. Then he came to his feet.

"I think," he said, taking a deep breath and shaking his head, "I think — it's too much for me to stomach. I — I don't like these ghastly stories."

He left us abruptly, striding out of the smoking room. Larsen looked after him, then turned his dark eyes upon me. I had set the other skull with the first.

"Gave him quite a turn, didn't it?" said Larsen. His voice was cold, brittle.

"Confound you!" I answered, nettled. "It gave me a turn. It'd give anybody a turn!"

"Take a cigar," said Larsen, extending one. "There's a bit more to the story."

I took the weed, but made a gesture of protest.

"Never mind the rest of the story," I said. "You're too cursed fantastic as a storyteller, Larsen. I don't fancy this Grand Guignol stuff myself in the least!"

Larsen smiled. "I must confess, my dear fellow, that I told a beastly lie. If you'd examine those bowls, you'd see they are about a hundred years old — the patina shows it. I bought 'em at the lamasery. Bonner and Stickley were decently buried."

At this, you may judge how I stared at him!

"Well," I said, angered at the way he had played on my nerves, "all I have to say is that you told a lie in rotten bad taste! Those two men were friends of yours, weren't they? Then —"

"That," he interposed cryptically, "was why I told the lie."

I did not understand in the least. There was a restrained tension in his manner that puzzled me. His fingers were nervous on his cigar.

At this instant we heard a sharp sound punctuating the steady throb of the ship's engines — a sharp, bursting sound about which could be no mistake. It was a shot.

"Ah!" Larsen came to his feet and took the two brown skull-bowls in his hand. "Ah! There is the rest of the story, old man, as I promised."

"What the devil d'you mean?" I exclaimed.

"That was our friend Mainwaring — shot himself. I thought he'd do it. That's why I told the lie in question. You see, Mainwaring was not his real name. His real name was — Creighton."

And Larsen departed, leaving me to enjoy my cigar as best I could.

THE SINGER IN THE MIST

At birth a witch laid on me monstrous spells,
And I have trod strange highroads all my days,
Turning my feet to gray, unholy ways.
I grope for stems of broken asphodels;
High on the rims of bare, fiend-haunted fells,
I follow cloven tracks that lie ablaze;
And ghosts have led me through the moonlight's haze
To talk with demons in the granite hells.

Seas crash upon dragon-guarded shores,
Bursting in crimson moons of burning spray,
And iron castles open to me their doors,
And serpent-women lure with harp and lay.
The misty waves shake now to phantom oars —
Seek not for me; I sail to meet the day.

— Robert E. Howard

EXOTIQUE

Thy mouth is like a crimson orchid-flow'r,
Whence perfume and whence poison rise unseen
To moons aswim in iris or in green,
Or mix with morning in an Eastern bow'r.
Thou shouldst have known, in amaranthine isles,
The sunsets hued like fire of frankincense,
Or the long noons enfraught with redolence,
The mingled spicery of purple miles.

Thy breasts, where blood and molten marble flow,
Thy warm white limbs, thy loins of tropic snow —
These, these, by which desire is grown divine,
Were made for dreams in mystic palaces,
For love, and sleep, and slow voluptuousness,
And summer seas afoam like foaming wine.

— Clark Ashton Smith

UNDER THE FLAME TREES
by H. de Vere Stacpoole

I was sitting in front of Thibaud's Café one evening when I saw Lewishon, whom I had not met for years.

Thibaud's Café, I must tell you first, is situated on Coconut Square, Noumea. Noumea has a bad name, but it is not at all a bad place if you are not a convict. Neither is New Caledonia, take it all together, and that evening, sitting and smoking and listening to the band and watching the crowd, and the dusk taking the flame trees, it seemed to me for a moment that Tragedy had withdrawn, that there was no such place as the Isle Nou out there in the harbor and that the musicians making the echoes ring to the *Sambre-et-Meuse* were primarily musicians, not convicts.

Then I saw Lewishon crossing the square by the Liberty Statue and attracted his attention. He came and sat by me, and we smoked and talked while I tried to realize that it was fifteen years since I had seen him last and that he hadn't altered in the least — in the dusk.

"I've been living here for years," said he. "When I saw you last in Frisco I was about to take up a proposition in Oregon. I didn't, owing to a telegram going wrong. That little fact changed my whole life. I came to the islands instead and started trading, then I came to live in New Caledonia. I'm married."

"Oh," I said, "is that so?"

Something in the tone of those two words "I'm married" struck me as strange.

We talked on indifferent subjects, and before we parted I promised to come over and see him next day at his place a few miles from the town. I did and I was astonished at what I saw.

New Caledonia, pleasant as the climate may be, is not the place one would live in by choice. In those days, the convicts were still coming there from France. The gangs of prisoners shepherded by wardens armed to the teeth, the great barges filled with prisoners that ply every evening when work is over between the harbor quay and the Isle Nou, the military air of the place and the fretting regulations, all these things and more robbed it of its appeal as a residential neighborhood. Yet the Lewishons lived there and what astonished me was the evidence of their wealth and the fact that they had no apparent interests at all to bind them to the place.

Mrs. Lewishon was a woman of forty-five or so, yet her beauty had scarce begun to fade. I was introduced to her by Lewishon on the broad veranda of their house, which stood in the midst of gardens more wonderful than the gardens of La Mortola.

A week or so later, after dining with me in the town he told me the story of his marriage, one of the strangest stories I ever heard and this is it, just as he told it.

"The Pacific is the finest place in the world to drop money in. You see it's so big and full of holes that look like safe investments. I started, after I parted with you, growing coconut trees in the Fijis. It takes five years for a coconut palm to grow, but when it's grown it will bring you in an income of eighteen pence or so a year according as the copra prices range. I planted forty thousand young trees and at the end of the fourth year a hurricane took the lot. That's the Pacific. I was down and out, and then I struck luck. That's the Pacific again. I got to be agent for a big English firm here in Noumea and in a short time I was friends with everyone from Chardin, the governor, right down.

"Chardin was a good sort but very severe. The former governor had been lax, so the people said, letting rules fall into abeyance like the rule about cropping the convicts' hair and beards to the same pattern. However that may have been, Chardin had just come as governor and I had not been here more than a few months when one day a big, white yacht from France came and dropped anchor in the harbor. A day or two after, a lady appeared at my office and asked for an interview.

"She had heard of me through a friend, she said, and she sought my assistance in a most difficult matter. In plain English, she wanted me to help in the escape of a convict.

"I was aghast. I was about to order her out of the office, when something — something — something, I don't know what, held my tongue while, with the cunning of a desperate woman in love, she managed to still my anger. 'I understand,' she said, 'and I should have been surprised if you had taken the matter calmly, but will you listen to me and when you have heard me out, tell me if you would not have done what I have done today?'

"I could not stop her, and this is what she told me.

"Her name was Madame Armand Duplessis. Her maiden name had been Alexandre. She was the only child of Alexandre the big sugar refiner, and at his death she found herself a handsome young girl with a fortune of about twenty million francs — and nothing between her and the rogues of the world but an old maiden aunt given to piety and guileless as a rabbit. However, she managed to escape the sharks and married an excellent man, a captain in the cavalry and attached to St. Cyr. He died shortly after the marriage and the young widow, left desolate and without a child to console her, took up living again with her aunt, or rather the aunt came to live with her in the big house she occupied on the Avenue de la Grande Armée.

"About six months after, she met Duplessis. I don't know how she met him, she didn't say, but anyhow he wasn't quite in the same circle as herself. He was a clerk in La Fontaine's Bank and only drawing a few thousand francs a year, but he was handsome and attractive and young, and the upshot of it was they got married.

"She did not know anything of his past history and he had no family in evidence, nothing to stand on at all but his position at the bank, but she did not mind — she was in love and she took him on trust and they got married. A few months after marriage a change came over Duplessis. He had always been given rather to melancholy, but now an acute depression of spirits came on him for no reason apparently. He could not sleep, his appetite failed, and the doctors, fearing consumption, ordered him away on a sea voyage. When he heard this prescription he laughed in such a strange way that Madame Duplessis, who had been full of anxiety as to his bodily condition, became for a moment apprehensive as to his mental state. However she said nothing, keeping her fears hidden and busying herself in preparations for the voyage.

"It chanced that just at that moment a friend had a yacht to dispose of, an eight-hundred-ton auxiliary-engined schooner, *La Gaudriole*. It was going cheap and Madame Duplessis, who was a good business woman, bought it, reckoning to sell it again when the voyage was over.

"A month later they left Marseilles.

"They visited Greece and the islands, then, having touched at Alexandria, they passed through the canal, came down the Red Sea and crossed the Indian Ocean. They touched at Ceylon and while there Madame Duplessis suggested that, instead of going to Madras as they had intended, they should go into the Pacific by way of the Straits of Malacca. Duplessis opposed this suggestion at first, then fell in with it. More than that, he became enthusiastic about it. A weight seemed suddenly to have been lifted from his mind, his eyes grew bright, and the melancholy that all the breezes of the Indian Ocean had not blown away suddenly vanished.

"Two days later they left Ceylon, came through the Straits of Malacca and, by way of the Arofura Sea and Torras Straits, into the Pacific. The captain of the yacht had suggested the Santa Cruz islands as their first stopping place, but one night Duplessis took his wife aside and asked her would she mind their making for New Caledonia instead. Then he gave his reason.

"He said to her, 'When you married me I told you I had no family. That was not quite the truth. I have a brother. He is a convict serving sentence in Noumea. I did not tell you because the thing was painful to me as death.'

"You can fancy her feelings, struck by a bombshell like that, but she says nothing and he goes on telling her the yarn he ought to have told her before they were married.

"This brother, Charles Duplessis, had been rather a wild young scamp. He lived in the Rue du Mont Thabor, a little street behind the Rue St. Honoré in Paris, and he made his money on the Stock Exchange. Then he got into terrible trouble. He was accused of a forgery committed by another man but could not prove his innocence. Armand was certain of his innocence but could do nothing, and Charles was convicted and sent to New Caledonia.

"Well, Madame Duplessis sat swallowing that fact, and when he'd done speaking she sat swallowing some more as if her throat was dry. Then she says to Armand:

"'Your brother is innocent, then,' she says.

"'As innocent as yourself,' he answers her, 'and it is the knowledge of all this that has caused my illness and depression. Before I was married, I managed to forget it all, but married to the woman I love, rich and happy, with enviable surroundings, thoughts of Charles came and knocked at my door, saying, 'Remember me in your happiness.''"

"'But can we do nothing for him?' asked Madame Duplessis.

"'Nothing' replied Armand, 'unless we can help him to escape.'

"Then he went on to tell her how he had not wanted to come on this long voyage at first, feeling that there was some fate in the business, and that it would surely bring him somehow or another to Noumea; then how the idea had come to him at Ceylon that he might be able to help Charles to escape.

"She asked him if had he any plan, and he replied that he had not — that it was impossible to make any plan till he reached Noumea and studied the place and its possibilities.

"Well, there was the position the woman found herself in, and a nice position it was. Think of it, married only a short time and now condemned to help a prisoner to escape from New Caledonia, for, though she could easily have refused, she felt compelled to the business both for the sake of her husband and the sake of his brother, an innocent man wrongfully convicted.

"She agreed to help in the attempt, like the high-spirited woman she was, and a few days later they raised the New Caledonia reef and the Noumea lighthouse that marks the entrance to the harbor.

"Madame Duplessis had a big acquaintance in Paris, especially among the political and military people, and, no sooner had the yacht berthed than the governor and chief people who knew her name began to show their attentions, tumbling over themselves with invitations to dinners and parties.

"That, again, was a nice position for her, having to accept the hospitality of the people she had come to betray, so to speak. But she had to do it. It was the only way to help her husband along in his scheme and, leaving the yacht, she took up her residence in a house she rented on the sea road; you may have seen it, a big white place with green verandas, and there she and her husband spent their time while the yacht was being overhauled.

"They gave dinners and parties and went on picnics; they regularly laid themselves out to please. Then one night Armand came to his wife and said he had been studying all means of escape from Noumea and had found only one. He would not say what it was, and she was content not to poke into the business, leaving him to do the plotting and planning till the time came when she could help.

"Armand said that before he could do anything in the affair he must first have an interview with Charles. They were hand in glove with the governor and it was easy enough to ask to see a prisoner, but the bother was the name of Duplessis, for Charles had been convicted and deported under that name. The governor had never noticed Charles and the name of Duplessis was in the prison books and forgotten. It would mean raking the whole business up and claiming connection with a convict. Still, it had to be done.

"'Next day Armand called at the governor house and had an interview. He told the governor that a relation named Charles Duplessis was among the convicts and that he very much wanted to have an interview with him.

"Now the laws at that time were very strict and the governor, though pretty lax in some things, as I've said, found himself up against a very stiff proposition and that proposition was how to tell Armand there was nothing doing.

"'I am sorry,' said the governor, 'but what you ask is impossible, Monsieur Duplessis. A year ago it would have been easy enough, but since the escape of Benonini and that Englishman Travels, the orders from Paris have forbidden visitors. Any message you would like me to send to your relation shall be sent, but an interview — no.'

"Then Armand played his ace of trumps. He confessed, swearing the governor to secrecy, that Charles was his brother. He said that Charles had in his possession a family secret that it was vital to obtain. He talked and talked and the upshot was that the governor gave in.

"Charles would be brought by two wardens to the house on the Sea Road after dark on the following day. The interview was to take place in a room with a single door and single window. One warden was to guard the door on the outside, the other would stand below the window. The whole interview was not to last longer than half an hour.

"Next evening after dark, steps sounded on the path to the house with the green veranda, Madame Duplessis had retired to her room, she had dismissed the servants for the evening and Armand himself had opened the door. One of those little ten-cent, whale-oil lamps was the only light in the passage but it was enough for Amand to see the forms of the wardens and another form, that of his brother.

"The wardens, unlike the governor, weren't particular about trifles. They didn't bother about guarding doors and windows. Sure of being able to pot anyone who made an attempt to leave the house, they sat on the fence in the moonlight counting the money Armand had given them, ten napoleons apiece.

"Half an hour passed during which Madame Duplessis heard voices in argument from the room below, and then she heard the hall door open as Charles went out. Charles shaded his eyes against the moon, saw the wardens approaching him from the fence, and walked off with them back to the prison he had come from.

"Then Madame Duplessis came from her room and found her husband in the passage. He seemed overcome by the interview with his brother.

"She asked him had he made plans for Charles' escape, and he answered: 'No.' Then he went on to say that escape was impossible. They had talked the whole thing over and had come to that decision. She stood there in the hall likening to him, wondering dimly what had happened, for only a few hours before he had been full of plans and energy and now this interview seemed to have crushed all the life out of him.

"Then she said: 'If that is so there is no use in our remaining any longer at Noumea.' He agreed with her and went off to his room, leaving her there wondering more than ever what could have happened to throw everything out of gear in that way.

"She was a high-spirited woman and she had thought little of the danger of the business; pitying Charles, she did not mind risking her liberty to set him free, and the thought that her husband had funked the business came to her suddenly as she stood there, like a stab in the heart.

"She went off to her room and went to bed, but she could not sleep for thinking, and the more she thought the clearer it seemed to her that her husband, brought up to scratch, had got cold feet, as the Yankees say, and had backed out of the show, leaving Charles to his fate.

"She was more sure next morning for he kept away from her, had breakfast early and went off into the town shopping. But the shock of her life came at dinner time, for when he turned up for the meal it was plain to be seen he had been drinking more than was good for him — trying to drown the recollections of his own weakness, it seemed to her.

"She had never seen him under the influence before and she was shocked at the change it made in him. She left the table.

"Afterward she was sorry that she did that for it was like the blow of an ax between them. Next morning he would scarcely speak to her and the day after they were due to leave for France.

"They were due out at midday, and at eleven Duplessis — who had lingered in the town to make some purchases — had not come on board. He did not turn up till half an hour after the time they were due to sail, and when he did it was plain to be seen that all his purchases had been made in cafés.

"'He was flushed and laughing and joking with the boatman who brought him off, and his wife, seeing his condition, went below and left the deck to him — a nice position for a woman on board a yacht like that with all the sailors looking on, to say nothing of the captain and officers. However there was nothing to be done and she had to make the best of it, which she did by avoiding her husband as much as she could from that point on. The chap had gone clean off the handle. It was as if his failure to be man enough to rescue his brother had broken him, and the drink which he flew to for consolation finished the business.

They stopped at Colombo and he went ashore. They were three days getting him back and when he came he looked like a sack of meal in the stern sheet of the pinnace. They stopped at Port Said and he got ashore again without any money, but that was nothing, for a chap coming off a yacht like that gets all the tick he wants for anything in Port Said. He was a week there and was only got away by the captain of the yacht knocking seven bells out of him with his fists and then handing the carcass to two quartermasters to take on board ship.

"They stopped nowhere else till they reached Marseilles, and there they found Madame Duplessis' lawyer waiting for them, having been notified by cable from Port Said.

"A doctor was had in and he straightened Armand up with strychnine and bromide, and they brushed his hair and shaved him and stuck him in a chair for a family conference, consisting of Madame Duplessis, the old maiden aunt, Armand, and the lawyer.

"Armand had no fight in him. He looked mighty sorry for himself but offered no explanations or excuses, beyond saying that the drink had got into his head. Madame Duplessis, on the other hand, was out for scalps — do you wonder! Fancy that voyage all the way back with a husband worse than drunk! When I say worse than drunk I mean that this chap wasn't content to take his booze and carry on as a decent man would have done. No, sir. He embroidered on the business without the slightest thought of his wife. An ordinary man full up with liquor and with a wife touring round would have tried to have hidden his condition as far as he could, but this blighter carried on regardless, and, when the whisky was in, wasn't to hold or bind.

"Of course she recognized that something in his brain had given way and she took into account that he was plainly trying to drown the recollection of his cowardice in not helping Charles to escape. All the same she was out for scalps and said so.

"She said she would live with him no more, that she had been a fool to marry a man whom she had only known for a few months and of whose family she knew nothing. She said she would give him an allowance of a thousand francs a month if he would sheer off and get out of her sight and never let her see him again.

"He sat listening to all this without a sign of shame and when she'd finished he flattened her out by calmly asking for fifteen hundred a month instead of a thousand. Never said he was sorry, just asked for a bigger allowance as if he was talking to a business man he was doing a deal with instead of a wife he had injured and outraged. Even the old lawyer was sick, and it takes a lot to sicken a French lawyer, I can tell you that.

"What does she do? She says: 'I'll allow you two thousand a month on the condition I never see your face or hear from you again. If you show yourself before me,' she says, 'or write to me, I'll stop the allowance. If you try to move the law to make us live together, I'll turn all my money into gold coin and throw it in the sea and myself after it, you beast,' she says.

"And he says, 'All right, all right, don't fly away with things,' he says. 'Give me my allowance and you'll never see me again.'

"One day an old woman turned up at her house asking her to come at once to where he was living as he was mortally ill and couldn't hold out more than a few hours.

"She didn't think twice, but came, taking a cab and being landed in a little old back street at the door of a house that stood between a thieves' café and a rag shop.

"Up the stairs she went, following the old woman, and into a room where his royal highness was lying with a jug of whisky on the floor beside him and a hectic blush on his cheeks.

"'I'm dying,' he says, 'and I want to tell you something you ought to know. I was sent to New Caledonia,' he says, 'for a robbery committed by another man.'

"She thought he was raving, but she says, 'Go on.'

"'Armand and I were twins,' he says, 'as like as two peas. Armand could do nothing. He stayed in Paris while poor Charles — that's me — went making roads on Noumea. Then you married him.'

"'But you are Armand,' she cries, 'you are my husband or am I mad?'

"'Not a bit,' says he. 'I'm Charles, his twin brother.

"'A year ago you and him came in a big yacht to Noumea and the governor sent me one night to have a talk with him. When we were alone he told me how his heart had been burning a hole in him for years, how he had married a rich woman — that's you — and how when he was happy and rich his heart had burned him worse so that the doctors not knowing what was wrong with him had ordered him a sea voyage.' Then Charles goes on to tell how Armand had come to the conclusion that even if he helped Charles to escape this likeness between them would lead surely to the giving away of the whole show, make trouble among the crew of the yacht and so on — besides the fact that it was next to impossible for a man to escape from Noumea in the ordinary way. But said Armand, 'We can change places and no one will know. Strip and change here and now,' he says, 'the guards are outside, I'll take your place and go to prison and you'll be free. I've got a scissors here and two snips will make our hair the same, and by good luck we are both clean shaven. You've done half your sentence of ten years and I'll do the other half,' he says. 'The only bargain I'll make is that you'll respect my wife and live apart from her and, after a while, you'll break the news to her and, maybe, when I'm free in five years she'll forgive me.'

"Charles finishes up by excusing himself for the drink, saying if she'd served five years without the chance of a decent wet all that time she'd maybe have done as he'd done.

"He died an hour after and there was that woman left with lots to thank about — first of all her husband wasn't the drunkard that had disgraced her, but he was a convict serving his time and serving it wrongfully.

"The thundering great fact stood up like a shot tower before her that Armand wasn't the drunkard that had disgraced her in two ports and before a ship's company, wasn't the swine that took her allowance and asked for more. That he was a saint, if ever a man was a saint.

"She rushed home, telegraphed to Marseilles and recommissioned the *Gaudriole* that was still lying at the wharves. A week later she sailed again for Noumea.

"On the voyage she plotted and planned. She had determined to save him from the four years or so of the remains of his sentence at all costs and hazards, and when the yacht put in here she had a plan fixed on, but it was kiboshed by the fact that the governor, as I have said, was changed. However she took up residence for a while in the town. People she had known before called on her and she gave out that her husband was dead.

"You can fancy how a rich widow was run after by all and sundry, myself included — not that I had any idea about her money. I only cared for herself. She knew this as women know such things, by instinct. She had asked for my help. I'm a strange chap in some ways. I had liked her enough to ruin myself for her by risking everything to give her husband back to her, and between us we had worked out a plan that was a pippin.

"It would have freed Armand only that we found on inquiring about him that he had already escaped — he was dead. Died of fever two months before she came.

"I heard once of a Japanese child that said her doll was alive because she loved it so much, adding that if you loved anything enough it lived. Well, in my experience, if you love anything enough you can make it love you.

"That woman stayed on in Noumea and I made her love me. At last I married her. You know her — she is my wife. She loves Armand still, as a memory, and for the sake of his memory we live here. It's as good a place to live as anywhere else, especially now that they have settled to send no more convicts from France."

AN OPEN WINDOW

Behind the Veil what gulfs of Time and Space?
What blinking mowing Shapes to blast the sight?
I shrink before a vague colossal Face
Born in the mad immensities of Night.

— Robert E. Howard

BY ANOTHER SEA

The Western gull is whiter than a dove
Or the ungathered foam.
I close the eyelids, and again I roam
The meadowlands of forty years ago.
I see the osprey circling far above,
Come back to the old nest from Mexico,
And we are young once more, O boyhood love!

The spray of that last wave is on my face.
Time breaks. We hide again
Beneath the cedar from the April rain.
O Youth's forgotten music, lost to me!
Ocean and sea wind echo now your grace;
But what one wave can tell us of the sea
Is more than all I learn of time and place.

Dear days, a little while our very own!
Dear mouth I never kissed!
The years between us gather like the mist.
It is enough to know you are no more.
It is enough to know I walk alone.
Still cries the ocean on that distant shore,
But farther than the osprey have you flown.

— George Sterling

RATS ASHORE
by James C. Young

WE WERE twenty days out of Rio when Captain Andy remarked to me that he never had seen so few rats on the old *George Crabtree*. After that I kept a sharp eye, and it seemed as though only a few dozen rats were aboard us. This worried me, because we had rats aplenty at Panama and all the way to Rio. When I began to think about the thing I remembered that the rats had started to disappear before we reached Rio. That was a bad sign. The only place we had stopped in between was a little mudhole port called New Madrid. And suddenly I recalled that the rats were scarce after we pulled up anchor there.

"Have the boys noticed it, Mr. Spriggins — about the rats?" asked Captain Andy, speaking properly to me as first officer.

"Why, not so far as I know, sir," I said, "but there's no telling when they will. I can't understand it."

"Must have gone ashore at Rio," he observed.

"But I missed them after we left New Madrid, although there seemed to be plenty left. In Rio there were not so many, and now I can find only a few."

"They couldn't have ducked overboard," said Captain Andy, asking the question rather than telling me any news.

"No rats ever left a ship at sear which wasn't sinking," I said.

"Sinking?" repeated the old man. "But we are not sinking."

"Then where the devil — beg pardon, sir — are the rats?"

"Blessed if I know," was all he could say, walking away and shaking his gray head.

It might be thought strange for a man to worry about the rats missing from his ship. But I knew just how the men felt. There was likely to be trouble if they missed them. Maybe some of the crew knew it already. We were swinging up with the trade wind and would soon drop anchor at a port of call. If the men ever started to talk of the rats leaving us we would not get out of port again with the same crew. And crews were scarce.

In this pinch I advised Captain Andy to skip the port of call, but he said that he would make port, rats or no rats. In fact, he damned all the rats afloat and me, too, his first officer, which was not a proper way of speaking.

I found myself anxiously watching for some of those ugly rodents. Two or three times I went below to look for them, and called myself worse names than had Captain Andy. I felt like I was going into a decline or something, the rats bothered me so much.

On one trip I saw a big fellow sitting in a passageway on the third deck below, and I could have shaken hands with him, I was so pleased. Then a strange thing happened. I was not more than twenty feet away when the rat disappeared and I heard something slap against a case with a vicious swing. That looked peculiar to me. I went forward, to see what was the trouble, but found nothing. One minute the rat had been there and the next he was gone — then silence. I decided that he must have jumped, and being an extra big fellow had slammed himself against the case. Anyway it was a small matter, though I almost hoped that rat had not hurt himself. I wanted a few to show the men in case of trouble.

Trouble came soon enough. We had a large crew for a freighter, but the prospect of losing a half dozen men was not a pleasant one for a first officer to have ahead of him. They called on me, properly enough, as being next in command to the old man, and wanted to know if they could leave ship at the first port we touched. That was a white man's way of doing things, and I tried to treat them civilly, asking about the trouble. They wouldn't say, but I could see, and they knew that I understood. It would have been mighty bad form for any man to tell his mate that he wanted to leave ship because the rats had gone. But I almost felt that way myself.

There was something wrong with the old *George Crabtree*. From the day that the men asked about their discharge every hand aboard was uneasy. We fouled a propeller on a floating spar and began to limp. Then one of our turbines started to show its temper and we almost stood still. Captain Andy swore longer and louder every day, which was not a proper way of speaking, to my mind.

Things were just about at this pass when I started to watch "Foolish" Thompson. He had been wearing a grin for a week, and was the only one of us who appeared to be pleased about anything. Some men's idea of fun is hard to explain. Thompson was that sort of man, the dare-devil kind, without any particular sense. He went through life grinning at everybody, always playing some trick. But he and I had reached the point where that grin had to end.

I got him in a corner, with a hand on his throat.

"What the devil are you grinning about?" I asked, eyeing him hard.

He wouldn't say anything, and I was ready to let him go when a remark of mine brought him to time.

"There's something funny going on below," I said, thinking to bluff the men through him, "and I mean to find out what it is mighty quick."

Thompson's face went a little white, and he said quickly:

"Be careful, sir, or you'll get hurt."

"Hurt?" I demanded. "What do you mean — mutiny?"

Then I saw his eyes change and guessed that it was something else, for he looked relieved, and answered: "Oh, no; not mutiny, sir. I didn't mean anything."

When I got through shaking and persuading him, he opened up with his yarn.

IT WAS this way, Mr. Spriggins," he said. "Me and Bill Toots and Sam Sparks, and a couple of other fellows from the engine room, went ashore at New Madrid. You know where that mountain is back of the town? We decided to go up on top and have a look at the country. It was a stiff climb, but we got there about noon and sat around in the shade to rest. 'Fore long Sam Sparks yells and starts to run. We looked about. Not far away and coming toward us was a big boa constrictor. He wasn't coming fast, just sneaking along the ground, and maybe wanted to see what we was like. But, believe me, Mr. Spriggins, he was coming plenty fast for us. We all ran and soon got out of his way. Then we turned and saw that snake moseying around where we had been sitting, eating our grub, which we had brought from New Madrid. That I couldn't take. I told the fellows we must go back and lay out that snake. They wanted to bolt at first, but decided to stick after we talked it over. Bill Toots, who used to work in a circus, got to thinking about how much more that snake would be worth alive than dead. He told us we should catch and sell him. Right there we almost lost our crew, but some of them wanted to know who would buy such a thing. Bill said there were plenty of fellows in New York or New Orleans who would give us a thousand for the snake. He looked about forty feet long, and big as a barrel. Bill said he was a beauty, better than anything he had seen in the circus. I didn't express my sentiments on his beauty, but said I would help do the trick.

"That boa was stuffing himself on our grub in a way to make you mad. One or two of the boys wanted to back out when they saw what an appetite he had, but we kidded them along, me and Bill Toots, who knew all about these boas. He said the fellows who buy them might give us a couple of hundred extra on account of the boa's size.

"Well, we cut a lot of limbs, with forks big enough to put over your body, and started to do our job. I began to feel sort of sick as we got near the boa. He was the biggest thing in the snake line I'd ever seen outside of a dream. But that grub of ours must have made him sleepy. He wrapped part of himself around a log and stretched out a few yards, laying still as a dead one. We could almost hear him snore, Mr. Spriggins. He didn't pay no more attention to us than if we hadn't been around, just went right on with his nap.

"We watched that boa a long time before we starting anything. Then Bill Toots told us he would slip up and hit the boa a wallop to put him out. At the same time I was to slap down a notched stick on the back of his head and hold on for dear life. The other fellows were told to grab his tail. Then we would tie him onto a log.

"Everything worked fine. The boa was sound asleep. Bill got a club as big as my leg and let the old boy have it on the head. He never hit him to kill, only intending to knock the big fellow out. I was a little too quick and came down with my notch over his neck about one second before Bill landed. The boa almost tore my arm

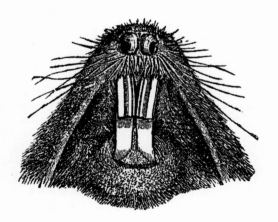

off with the jump he made, but Bill hit him so quick that it didn't do the boa any good to jump. I held the fork over his neck and some of the other fellows nailed him down along the body. Sam Sparks got the worst of it. He was on the tail end, and the boa hit Sam a crack which laid him in the shade. One of them big engine room huskies caught that tail and held on, see-sawing like a man holding a loose sail in a gale. Gee, it was awful."

"What happened then?"

"Mr. Spriggins, we got that snake on a log 'fore he really came to and tied him down some way. Then we started to carry the log, which wasn't very large. But the whole crowd of us had a tussle with it, that snake being so heavy. After a long time we crawled down the mountain, skirted around New Madrid and came to our dock after dark. From there we slipped the boa aboard when no one was looking —"

"And where is he now?"

"Down below, sir. He got off that log and is running loose."

Now I knew where the rats had gone!

C APTAIN ANDY was just coming up from the engine room when I went in search of him. He and the engineer had been having a session with the turbine, and he was in a sweet humor — ready to bite a spike in two. I had to tell him, but it was a case of gaining time. So I asked about the engine, and began petting Maggie, the mastiff which dogged his heels. She had been part of the crew for so long that we almost regarded her as one of us. And Maggie was the old man's special pride.

The fuss I made over Maggie soothed his temper a bit, and I judged this to be the proper time and place. So I said:

"Captain, there's a boa constrictor down below and running loose. He's cleaned out the rats and may start on some of us next."

"Boa constrictor?" questioned the old man. "Have you been drinking, Mr. Spriggins?"

That was no proper way of speaking to me, a man who never was anything but sober. I saluted, in a stiff kind of way, and said nothing. Then Captain Andy broke loose and dealt me a choice line of conversation. Thompson had slipped away. I had to tell the whole tale.

"Where is Thompson?" demanded the old man, "Put him in irons."

That would have been a bad thing to do, with the men already upset, and at least a half dozen of them knowing there was a giant boa below decks. I tried to turn the old man's wrath and finally got him to heed a little reason. He came around with the wind, and took charge of things like a captain should, and as he knew well how to do.

"Where is this varmint?" he asked.

"Third deck below, up forward, when last seen, Captain."

"Take Thompson and the rest of the men who put him on this ship and make them get him."

And that was about the largest order of my long time at sea.

"How are we going to do it?" I asked.

"Don't ask me," said the old man. "Let Thompson and those other fools find out."

We sent for the half dozen rascals, and I said a few words straight to the point. Then I gave them the bad news.

They fell back and looked sullen. So I singled out Bill Toots and inquired, "Bill, how did they work these things in that second-rate circus you used to follow around? What did you do when one of these big boas got on a rampage?"

According to Bill, he had no experiece in this line. I called for suggestions, but failed to get any.

"Very well," I said, "if you fellows could catch this boa, you at least can kill him. We will issue rifles to every man. Get your knives, too, and search the third deck. The first thing which you see that moves — shoot."

I was going to add, "or which you feel," but that did not seem to be a happy ending just then. As it was, the men went about their job mighty reluctant. A roar from the old man set them in motion. We issued rifles, some of the lot which had been put aboard during the war, and the men started on the boa hunt. We gave them pocket flashlights to light up dark corners.

I had to go along, of course, and brought up the rear, not so much from fear of the boa as to see that none of the lads dodged their task.

When we got down to the third deck everybody was jumpy. I could hear the men breathing hard. Then I remembered that this was the deck where I had seen the big rat disappear, and heard something slap against a case. The hair began to rise on my head. I had been within twenty feet of the boa — and didn't know it!

Now I understood what Foolish Thompson had meant about feeling sick when he got near the boa. I was pretty sick right at that moment. It seemed as though I could feel something cold slip about me, then tighten, and my senses begin to go. But I steadied a bit and started to talk. That was the next best thing next to whistling, and my courage certainly needed some whistling to help it along.

"Look here, men," I said. "We've got to get that reptile. Scatter out and work down the passageways. Shoot — and shoot quick — anything which you see."

Did you ever hunt for something in the dark which you didn't want to find? That was the way with us. Of course we had the flashlights, and the incandescents were burning here and there, so it wasn't wholly dark. The flashlights sent little beams of light ahead as we moved along between the big packing cases.

That was a devilish bad job. Unless the boa was in a passageway, we had small chance of finding him. He might be hiding behind a pile of freight, or stretched out on top of the cases. I got to thinking of this and was ready any minute for something clammy to fall about my neck. But we moved along the deck and found nothing. As the men came nearer to the bow bulkheads, they got mighty nervous. Still nothing happened, and after a half day's hunt we gave it up.

There was no boa on the third deck. At least — none we could find.

We had coffee on the other decks, with a thousand hiding places among the sacks. It took three days to finish the hunt among those sacks, and still no boa. Where he had gone was a question that everybody tried not to think about.

The captain's dog took part in the hunt, and we hoped for big things from her, figuring that she would be able to smell the reptile. But in all our search Maggie never once let out a yelp. Captain Andy suggested that the boa might have gone overboard. I doubted it, for there was a book in the cabin telling about wild animals and such things. I found the chapter on boas and the fellow who wrote it said that no boa ever took to the water. Besides,

though I didn't tell anybody, I had come upon a rat, pretty well lashed up — and recently. The boa was still around.

I didn't lose any time clearing out from the neighborhood of the dead rat. But I got sort of ashamed afterward and led a searching party. No mate of the *George Crabtree* could lose his nerve and hold the job. I didn't mean to part with my berth just then, even though boas were out of my line.

It was Maggie who found the reptile. She had a crony down in the stoke hole and went to see him. While the man was playing with her she suddenly threw her head in the air and started to bark, with ears standing straight out.

Maggie was no coward. She had been fighting everything that came aboard the *George Crabtree*, man or beast, for many years. Before the stoker could stop her she had jumped on the coal and into the darkness of the bunkers. The next instant the men heard a terrible threshing, with Maggie barking and snarling. Then they knew where the boa had hidden.

I don't like to call those fellows names, seeing as they were a good crew, but I believe that every man ran. One or two reached the main deck, although most of them recovered their nerve and went back before we drove the other fellows down.

By the time I reached the stoke hole poor Maggie was dead. We could not hear a sound. Again our pocket flashlights and the rifles came into play. We crawled up on the coal, badly scared as men could be. But we meant to get that boa and end it once for all.

I have been a game man in my time because I had to be. But never was I so ready to run as the hour I crawled about in the coal. We could not find the boa. He was gone, nobody knew where. Nothing could be done but give up the hunt.

We found poor Maggie, with her sides crushed. The boa had done for her at one stroke. When she was taken on deck and the old man saw her I thought he was going to weep. Two big tears came into his eyes, and he motioned the men away, saying nothing. We buried Maggie with honors, a weight at her feet just like any of us might have had.

As all things come to an end, like the poet fellow said, so our troubles with the engine got straightened out. We started to move again. The hunt for the boa went on, in a half-hearted way. I believe the crew felt better, even with the boa aboard, than when the rats were disappearing and nobody knew why except the fellows who brought that snake on to the ship. Most men will face things they can see, even such a thing as a boa constrictor. Of course none of us had seen him except the fools who kidnapped the devil, but we all knew he was there.

It had been an ugly day at sea and I was in command when a call from Captain Andy's cabin startled me. Many times he had proved himself a brave man, and that cry sent a chill through my heart. I left the deck in a run and scrambled down to the cabin. Something seized me about the legs as I ran, and I fell with a crash. The old man cried again, a kind of wavering cry that turned me cold all over, even as I hit the deck. But I had no time to consider anything. For I knew what had taken me around the legs.

I didn't understand it all then, but the devil had thrown me with his tail. I felt the coil tighten and the blood fly upward as the flow stopped below my knees. I reached for my knife — and couldn't find it. The boa was threshing about this way and then another, and every instant I heard the cry of the old man. Now I was crying out myself, calling for help loudly as I could. There is a recollection in my mind of flying footsteps, then my head struck the wall and everything went black.

I DIDN'T see what happened. Some of the men told me. Foolish Thompson had been in my watch on deck. He came down after me with the others. When they saw that boa all but Thompson ran for the rifles. Thompson was a dare-devil man.

He said when it was over that he had got us into the scrape and that it was up to him to get us out again. But he risked his life and did it like a man.

The boa had Captain Andy pinned to his bunk. It never wrapped around him, probably because the captain was laying on the bunk, one edge of which was flush to the wall. But that devil of a reptile just stayed there, half coiled on the old man's chest. Captain Andy couldn't move, the weight being so great. And every minute he expected the writhing death to get him. Still he had the courage to call out.

When Thompson went into the cabin the boa got busy. He left the old man with a spring straight at Thompson. But Thompson ducked and swung his sheath knife. He must have landed, for the fight began in dead earnest. Thompson may have been foolish most of the time, but he had sense enough to get behind a table and to hold a chair in front of him. That bothered the reptile. Every time it lunged Thompson struck back with his knife.

I was in a bad way, for the devil was threshing around with his tail. And every time the tail moved I hit something. But my mind had gone to Davy Jones and the rest of me was in a fair way to follow.

Some of the men returned and started to help Thompson. They were afraid to shoot, fearing to hit one of us. We were all mixed up with the big boa in the little cabin. The furniture was going to pieces, and the old man had been laid out by a lick from the boa.

Thompson said that I was nearing the end of my rope. Another crack or two and I'd have gone under. Anyway he pushed over the table and drove the knife home with a blow which severed the boa's neck. That didn't end matters, for the villain's body kept writhing about the cabin. The men went into action and slashed the devil so many times that finally he quieted down and they pried me loose. I didn't see the cabin for several days, but they said it wasn't a pretty sight about the time they freed me. Besides a couple of cracked ribs and a body covered with bruises I was all right. The old man hadn't been hurt.

We went into port with a new third officer, Mr. Thompson by name, and Captain Andy bought a silver plate for the cabin wall, in honor of Maggie. But he has a bad temper, the old man, and whenever things go wrong nowadays he warns Mr. Thompson that any foolishness will land him in irons, which isn't a proper way of speaking to your third officer, I allows.

SOUTHWARD-BOUND

Lightning and rain and the roar of the thunder,
Splash of the prow through the curling sea,
Hiss of the wind 'round the mast and the rigging,
And a shaggy old ship sailing brave and free.

Pitching and tossing and twisting and turning,
Breasting the storm with a bone in her mouth,
Bravely she bears to the land of all dreaming,
And sweet through the storm is the smell of the south.

— Edmund Leamy

THE EVIL EYE
by **Vincent Starrett**

"**T**HE peoples of earth," said my friend Lavender, "are divided into four classes: criminals, victims of criminals, detectives, and readers of detective literature. Each division, of course, has its subdivisions; these are obvious. The fourth class comprises the majority of mankind, and is responsible for the other three; but the detective class is growing. Only the fact that for every detective there must be a criminal, and for every criminal a victim, prevents the detective class from increasing so hugely as to threaten the supremacy of the reading division."

I laughed. The speech was characteristic; typical of Lavender's whimsically ironic philosophy. He regarded me reproachfully.

"Even so," he continued, "how the detectives of London must jostle in the streets! From Holmes to the latest amateur is a far cry. And New York is as bad or worse. Here in Chicago," he added, "I am less handicapped by competition."

Outside, the snow was piling up in the streets, and the elevated railroad station across from the windows had lost much of its ugliness in its white and glistening insulation; it rose on gleaming pillars, a fantastic dream structure, above the whiter isolation of the street. Lavender's hearth fire snapped cheerfully as he stretched out his hand for the afternoon paper. Dusk was stealing over the city, but the incarcerated, leaping flames gave him sufficient light to read.

"There is nothing here," continued the fathomer, scanning the first page, "that cannot be duplicated in the newspapers of any large city. Indeed, they might as well be composed with a rubber stamp, they are so much alike, these stories, whatever their locale. It is only the occasional masterpiece of crime that makes the game of detection entertaining, and even in masterpieces there is a family resemblance, as you may observe at any first-class art gallery."

"You are bored at present, then?" I suggested.

"To the contrary," he returned, "I have the beginning, at least, of a very pretty puzzle. I have been retained in the Hurst case, which promises well. Hurst will be buried tomorrow, and my first important work will be done at the funeral. Are you partial to funerals?"

"No," I said with a grimace, "but I have a presentiment that I shall attend this one. Just what is the Hurst case? The newspaper accounts were delightfully vague. He was a bank teller; he was found dead in a deserted house, and he had not been murdered.

Intriguing, but hardly sensational."

"The papers know a little more, but not much," said my friend. "They have been waiting for the bank to check on its losses, which now are definitely placed at more thousands of dollars than you or I ever are likely to possess. Otherwise, the known facts are very much as you state them.

"Hurst was paying teller for the Columbian National, a small but sound bank in the suburbs. Two days ago, there was an unusually large balance left after settling with the clearing house. Hurst, a thoroughly trusted man, took care of clearing house settlements for the bank, and afterward, it was his custom to lock up his own funds, merely telling the cashier that he had done so. On this occasion, he did not lock up the balance. What he did with it remains to be discovered. The money is missing. Hurst was found dead in a small, empty house at Henrietta and Division Streets."

"And was *not* murdered!" I again suggested.

"That is to be proved," said Lavender. "If you mean that there were no indications of murder, you are right; nor, as a matter of fact, has the autopsy divulged a hint of foul play. Yet I believe Hurst was murdered!"

"By a partner?" I asked quickly. "Hurst must have been party to the removal of the funds, Lavender!"

"Ye-es." He hesitated. "The obvious theories occur readily enough. He may have taken the money himself, have hidden in the empty house, and have been robbed and murdered by a second criminal who did not even know him. He may have been lured to the house, in some manner; or, as you suggest, he may have had a partner who is now responsible for his death. In any case, it is difficult to avoid the thought that Hurst took the money."

"The real problem, then, is the manner of his death?"

"Oh, I know how he died," Lavender shrugged. "He froze to death! You can't leave a man in a barn with the thermometer below zero, and expect him to pick up his bed and walk, in the morning. But what I should like to know, Gilruth, is what prevented him from leaving that house! He was not stunned. Apparently he had fallen asleep while in hiding. But what sane man would — or could — go to sleep in such a place, in such weather?"

I pondered this for a moment, and then asked, "What shall you do at the funeral?"

"Curiously enough," he answered. "I am looking for friends of Hurst rather than enemies. What the newspapers don't know,

Gilly, is this — Hurst was not found by accident. The president of the bank himself received an anonymous message telling him where to find his missing teller. The police were notified, and Hurst was found — dead. Now, what does that mean?"

"That somebody, perhaps perfectly innocent, discovered the body and was afraid of being mixed up with a crime," I answered, after a moment.

"Not bad," smiled my friend. "The police would laugh at you, but it is not at all an impossible case. It is often fatal to overlook the obvious solution simply because it is obvious. Just the same, I think you are wrong. I figure it like this: If Hurst was found in the house, and robbed; or if he was lured to the place to be robbed, by someone unknown to him, there is little reason to believe this unknown criminal so tender-hearted that he would endeavor to save Hurst's life, or that he would be eager to start the police on the trail. It is a rather nice point, but it seems to me that the anonymous message was the work of a friend of the victim — willing perhaps to rob him, but unwilling to take his life. And so, in the hope that Hurst will be rescued alive, he takes the risk and sends off a note to the bank."

"And you think he will attend the funeral?" I jeered. "I don't!"

"Oh, he might," protested Lavender. "Why not, if he is not suspected? Wouldn't the absence of a particular friend call greater attention to that friend than his presence? And, anyway, there will be many friends present. I may pick up a word that will be invaluable."

He paused to light a cigarette.

"Look here, Gilly," he continued, "unless you are a real funeral fan, and wouldn't miss one for worlds, you can serve me better by staying away from this one. I'd like you to get into that empty house, early tomorrow, and stay there all morning. It's unlikely that the man we want will come back, but your objection has weight, and I admit that if he does come back it will be while all the rest of us are at the funeral. I want to cover both ends. Savvy?"

"Yes," I said, a bit downcast. "All right, Jimmie! Where do we meet?"

"Say here, at noon."

"Noon," I agreed. "Shall I look for footprints at the empty house?" I added, with a chuckle.

He smiled shrewdly.

"You think that's funny, no doubt, but the fact is it's exceedingly strange. Somebody must have been there with Hurst, but there's not a footprint or a mark to show it! And in a sheltered part of the porch we did find footprints of Hurst! Chew on that, Gilly! Snow all around, too. It's as if he went there alone, and lay down and froze to death as calmly as if he were going to sleep in bed. Furthermore, there was a rather awkward print in the snow on the doorstep that could only suggest that Hurst had set down a satchel. And there was no satchel with him when he was found! And on top of that, there is the anonymous message. Who could see him — without approaching the house? Somebody must have been there who walked on wires or flew with wings."

"Fine!" I said. "A ghost story!"

"I've heard of stranger things," smiled my friend. "Don't you believe in ghosts?"

"No!" I replied. And then I added, "But I am afraid of them."

II

AS it happened, I attended the funeral of Samuel Hurst, after all, arriving not long after Lavender himself had put in an appearance. For I had found the police in charge of the empty house in Henrietta Street, and felt that in the circumstances my assignment was useless.

It was an unsavory neighborhood, and I speculated vainly on the strange conduct of Hurst that had brought him there to his death. Certainly it was not the sort of place he would frequent for amusement; or so I argued. But bearing in mind my friend's ceaseless instruction to "keep my eyes open," I had a look around the neighborhood before I left, although I was sure there was nothing that Lavender himself had not seen on the occasion of his own visit.

It was a polyglot district. A dozen nations were represented in the lines of shops in nearby Division Street, and children of half a dozen played in the surrounding arteries and vacant lands. The house in which Hurst's body had been found was practically on the corner; the actual intersection was marked by a vacant lot. It was a tumbledown shanty, two stories in height, and in a sad state of disrepair. It leaned perilously to one side, like an ancient ruin, and when a high wind struck it broadside it must have creaked alarmingly. The fantastic decorations of packed snow now added to its sepulchral appearance. In my youth I should have instantly set it down as a haunted house, and, avoided it with scrupulous care. On the other side of it there was a second vacant lot, and then a line of brick flat-buildings of the vintage of 1895.

I approached the decrepit door, and tried the handle. To my horror, it was instantly snatched backward, and the door opened inward disclosing a man in the opening, who looked upon me with a sardonic gaze. But a return of my reportorial instinct saved me from funk; my shocked mental processes began to function normally, and I recognized him, by sundry signs, as a plain-clothes policeman.

"Good morning, Sergeant," I said, politely. "I'm representing Mr. Lavender of Portland Street. I had no idea the house was occupied."

"Come in," he said, standing aside. "Jimmie's a friend of mine. I suppose you're Gilruth. Glad to know you." As I entered the bare room, he added, "My partner, Crawley!"

A heavy, elderly man nodded his head in curt acknowledgment.

But there was no reason for my presence, and I determined to get out. I apologetically explained that Lavender had thought the place needed watching.

"An' it's being watched!" observed the Irish Crawley sagely.

"Wherefore," I said, "I shall make myself scarce, and leave the job in better hands."

Gordon accompanied me to the door.

"What does Lavender make of this, Gilruth?" he asked confidentially.

"I don't know," I said honestly. "If you know Jimmie, you know he doesn't talk much till he's sure."

"He's right," nodded Gordon. "Well, look here, lad! There's a bit of gossip about the neighborhood here that I don't take much stock in, and it would do me no good to repeat it at headquarters. It's right in the line of young Lavender, though, and I'll give it to you. Just remember that you don't know where you got it, see? It's this: the folks hereabouts are afraid of this house! They cross to the other side at night, and that sort of thing. And why? Because somehow the rumor has been spread that it was marked by the 'evil eye,' and is death to them that cross its threshold. Moonshine? Sure! But there you are!"

He winked cheerfully, and I left him broadly smiling on the threshold whose sinister properties he had just described.

The nearest place in Division Street was a converted saloon, now a Greek ice-cream parlor. A pool room, a bakery, an undertaker's establishment, a restaurant, a pawn shop, and three or four groceries and markets filled the rest of the block, with old houses, like punctuation marks, here and there between.

The evil eye!

Well, it was an admirable locality for its exercise; I could not deny that. The most attractive window displays were those of the bakery and pawn shop, and into these I gazed for a passing moment. Noticing my seeming interest, the proprietor of the pawn shop hastened to his door and endeavored to engage my enthusiasm in his wares. He offered revolvers, binoculars, hourglasses, pottery and retired musical instruments at a staggering sacrifice. But I refused to be tempted.

My mental map of the vicinity completed, I hurried to catch a car to join Lavender at the final ceremonies in the home of the late paying teller.

Lavender approved my course, when I had finished my recital.

"The police are getting wiser every minute," he remarked. "One of these days they'll beat me out in something big, and you'll transfer your allegiance. That's an interesting yarn about the evil eye, Gilly, and it stirs something in the back of my brain. Can't put a name to it, yet!"

We were on the veranda of the house wherein Samuel Hurst once had lived; his mother's home. Inside, the solemn services were going on, but Lavender preferred the colder atmosphere of the porch.

"Who were the fellows at the house?" he asked.

"The man who talked was named Gordon," I said. "His partner was called Crawley, I think."

"Pat Gordon," said my friend. "I know him. I don't know Crawley, but Gordon's a good man. Well, he may be nearer the truth than I am!"

At that moment the front door opened and a man stepped out. He shook Lavender's hand heartily.

"Beastly warm inside," he said, opening his coat to the keen air. "Poor old Hurst!" he added.

"May I present my friend, Mr. Gilruth?" Lavender asked. "This is Mr. Cousins, president of the Columbian Bank, Gilly."

I responded suitably.

"Look here, Mr. Cousins," continued my friend. "I came here to look over the crowd. I want a line on Hurst's friends. Are they all here? That is, can you say whether anyone is conspicuously absent?"

The bank president started and looked shrewdly at the investigator. His brow clouded. Then he turned to the door.

"I have only a vague idea what you are driving at," he said, "and it frightens me. But wait, I'll get Burns out here. He was Hurst's most intimate friend at the bank. He's sure to know."

In a moment we were talking to a clean-cut young Irish-American of more than the average intelligence. He appreciated Lavender's question at once, and rapidly considered. He looked speculatively at Lavender.

"Only two missing," he said, at length. "Of course, there are lots of chaps who knew Hurst who are not here; but of those that knew him best only two are missing. One is Henderson, who used to be in the same cage; but Henderson's been off sick for more than a week and probably doesn't even know Hurst is dead. The other is Amick, the third assistant cashier. He and Hurst used to be pretty thick, and it is a bit strange that he isn't around today."

"Used to be?" repeated Lavender.

"I didn't mean to insinuate anything," answered Burns, less readily. "I believe they were excellent friends to the last. It just happens that I hadn't seen them together so much lately."

"Both Henderson and Amick are well trusted men, Mr. Cousins?"

"Very much so! I should as soon think of suspecting myself — or Burns here! — as either of them. The fact is, Mr. Lavender, my whole staff has been with me for years, and it hurts to think that any of the boys might be — you know! We've got to find out, but I'm afraid of what you may have to tell me!"

"I understand," said Lavender. "Well, we must make no mistakes. I suppose I can see Amick at the bank, tomorrow?"

"Certainly! I can't imagine why he isn't here today."

"Then, as the services seem to be drawing to a close, I think Gilruth and I will leave you. Good-bye until tomorrow!"

The two men turned hurriedly within, while Lavender and I went down the steps and walked slowly to the nearest corner. A little group of those strangely curious individuals who seem to enjoy the sorrow of others had gathered in the snow at the corner. This group we joined, and ourselves waited.

In a short time there was a bustle on the veranda we had left, and immediately thereafter Samuel Hurst came down the front steps for the last time, borne on the shoulders of six of his friends.

When it was all over, Lavender continued to loiter in the neighborhood. Apparently he saw nothing out of the usual, for after a few moments he turned away, and together we proceeded on our journey.

We walked briskly, for it was a cold day. The heavy snowfall of the day before had been cleared from the sidewalks, and our heels rang sharply on the icy pavements. Lavender's slight stoop and steady rhythmic tramping suggested that we were in for a long walk.

"Where to?" I asked, at length.

He halted.

"By George, I don't know, Gilly! I was thinking about empty houses and evil eyes!"

"The evil eye is sorcery, of course?"

"Yes," he smiled. "And the belief in witchcraft, in this day, is surprising, although it is largely confined to the so-called lower classes. A man possessed of a devil may have an evil eye, and by its malevolence may cause an arm to wither, a house to fall, or an infant to die. So runneth the tale. Our Henrietta Street mystery is in the very heart of that sort of nonsense, as it happens, and I am not surprised by the reputation of the place. A clever crook might use the superstition to advantage — if he wished to keep people away from the house, for instance. It is no longer an original thought, Gilly, but it is still a fact that if walls had ears and lips, they would hear much and could tell as much as they heard. At least, we shall find out who owns the place, eh?"

"We can easily find that out at the City Hall," I said.

"All right," responded Lavender. "I suppose the police already know, and I can't afford to be behind them."

We hastened to the corner and boarded the first car. As the bell was pulled for the coach to go ahead we were treated to one of those humorous spectacles that sometimes beguile the tired citizen who journeys to and from his labor on the surface lines. A man ran across the road and tried to catch the car before it had started.

He was too late, but with admirable determination he pushed his hat down upon his brows and gave chase, to the huge delight of the observers on the rear platform. He was a swift runner, however, and managed to overhaul us, swinging onto the platform with a grunt of satisfaction.

Everybody who witnessed the incident chuckled and felt better for it; but the moment I saw the man's face my smile died away. The face was perfectly known to me, almost intimately. Yet its identification bothered me. The situation is always provoking, and I thought desperately.

"What now?" languidly murmured Lavender.

"I know that fellow," I said, "and I can't place him."

"Then you know an interesting individual," he said, with a keen glance at the man on the platform, "for that fellow's an East Indian."

"What!" I cried, but as the exclamation left my lips I remembered. "Got it, by Jove!" I added. "Lavender, I saw that fellow less than two hours ago, in Division Street. He runs a pawn shop! He came to his door while I was looking in his window, and I actually exchanged words with him. What's he doing here?"

"I don't know," said my friend, "but the coincidence is interesting, if it is a coincidence. He may be following you. You didn't steal anything from his shop?"

I turned from him, disgusted.

"Forgive me, Gilly!" pleaded Lavender. "It really is an interesting coincidence, and we won't forget it. Just now, though, it doesn't fit in. You don't want me to arrest him for the murder of Hurst, do you? What is the charge? He is a pawn broker; he lives in Division Street. It isn't enough."

But I was hurt, and accompanied him in moody silence to the City Hall, where he gave over his railing and commanded immediate attention. Assistants rushed around pulling down huge canvas-bound volumes, which Lavender rejected. Then the right one was found, and with a triumphant twist of his single white lock, Lavender was bending over the book.

He had not searched long when a little exclamation of satisfaction caught my half attentive ear. It aroused my curiosity. I stopped sulking and eagerly swung about.

Lavender's finger was upon a line of writing in the book. I did not understand the lines of figures and what they stood for, but I could and did understand the significance of a name.

Here was the owner of the shabby property in Henrietta Street, where Samuel Hurst had come to his death.

A woman. Mrs. Frederick Amick!

III

LAVENDER lighted a cigarette, and leaned back against the desk. He described an elaborate pattern in the air with the smoke.

"At the very least," he said, "young Mr. Amick will have some explaining to do. This Mrs. Frederick Amick is more likely to be his mother than his wife, however, and her ownership of the empty house proves nothing after all. But it is interesting and instructive. It seems to point to something not yet clear, but on the point of clearing. I shall enjoy talking with Amick."

"You suspect him?"

"I suspect nobody definitely, but it seems plain that Amick has some connection with the case, possibly a quite remote one. And, of course, he may be perfectly innocent."

Whatever Lavender thought, however, there was one close at hand who had no doubts. Looking up, I caught this person's eye.

"Great Scott, Lavender!" I whispered. "Here's that East Indian again!"

My friend did not turn his head.

"What's he doing?" he whispered back.

"Looking at us casually," I said, "and trying to let on he isn't. By George, he's going to speak to us!"

I was right. The dark-skinned man now came rapidly forward.

"I ask your pardon," he said, in perfect — almost too perfect — English, "but am I addressing Mr. James Lavender?"

He looked at me, but Lavender answered.

"I am James Lavender," said the fathomer, and now he looked up and met the man's gaze.

"You will forgive me," continued the stranger, "but I have been following you for some time. I was not sure that you were the men I wished to see, although I recognize your friend as having been in my neighborhood this morning."

"You tried to sell me an accordion," I said, dryly.

"Yes," he smiled. "Selling is my business. And it was a good accordion, my friend. But I watched you, and saw your interest in the house where the young bank officer — Hurst — was found dead. Then I thought that you were the celebrated Mr. Lavender, for I knew you were not a policeman."

He turned to Lavender.

"I salute you, sir!" he said, with a bow. "If I may, I shall be glad to assist you. I have information."

"I shall be glad to listen to your information," said my friend, without eagerness.

"Thank you. It is this: It is known to me, through friends, that this Mr. Hurst who is so unfortunately dead, frequented the receptions of the celebrated Hara Singh, a countryman of mine, of whom no doubt you have heard."

He ended on an upward note, and Lavender nodded.

"A well-known charlatan," said my friend. "I do not know him personally, but by reputation. He is a mystic, I believe — an adept, a sorcerer, or something of the sort."

"At least, something like a wise man," said the East Indian. "We must not quarrel about the nature of his profession. He is honest, also, and he will have nothing to do with a crime. As he is my countryman, I know him; but he is far above me, and his movements I know chiefly through some of his servants.

"Through these friends of mine, Mr. Lavender, I am told that a young man named Amick also frequented the receptions of Hara Singh. Sir, it is my belief that Mr. Amick is responsible for the theft of the bank's money and the death of Mr. Hurst!"

He leaned swiftly forward, and tensely whispered, "Have you heard of the evil eye?"

I all but jumped, and looked hastily at Lavender. His eyes did not leave the face of the questioner. He seemed unexcited. His answer was a brief nod.

"This Amick is known to be possessed of the evil eye," continued the Oriental, his face working almost savagely. "His spell was upon the unfortunate young bank officer, who did what his evil friend commanded. How Mr. Hurst was slain I cannot tell you, but Mr. Amick can be made to tell. It is perhaps no secret to you that the house in which Mr. Hurst was found is owned by this Mr. Amick?" His glance sought the big book on the desk beside us. Lavender smiled.

"That is known to us, as you correctly infer," said my friend. "May I ask how it is known to you?"

"I have lived for years in the neighborhood," said the other with a shrug. "I know the history of every house. I know the man from whom Mr. Amick bought it. I have even seen Mr. Amick there, several times."

"You think, then, that Mr. Hurst was murdered, do you? And by Mr. Amick? How?"

Lavender's blunt questions shook the East Indian.

"My dear sir," he protested, "I have not said that! I do not know. I have told you that this Mr. Amick has the evil eye. That is well known to my friends. It would be easy for him to command Mr. Hurst to steal money, and then to command his friend to remain in the house until he had perished. It is a dreadful gift!"

He shuddered effectively.

"Is not your friend, Hara Singh, also possessed of the evil eye?" asked Lavender, shrewdly. "Does he, perhaps, teach its use?"

"There is nothing that Hara Singh does not know," replied the dark man earnestly. "But he has no friendliness for those who are thieves or murderers."

Lavender nodded absently. I knew he was doing some rapid thinking.

"What is your idea?" he asked at length.

"Sir," said the stranger, "Mr. Amick is going to the house of Hara Singh tonight. If you allow it, I, as your agent, shall also be there, and report to you what passes."

"And you are — ?"

"My name is Daniel Alexander, in the English. I am an American citizen."

"All right, Daniel Alexander," said Lavender, suddenly making up his mind. "For this evening you are my agent. I shall depend upon you for a complete report of the meeting between Hara Singh and Mr. Amick. You must be careful. Come to my rooms tomorrow."

"Thank you, sir," said Daniel Alexander. "Tomorrow I shall be at your rooms."

He was out of the door in a few steps, and his tread was as silent as if he wore sandals. Lavender laughed softly.

"What do you make of your friend?" he asked.

"What do you make of him?" I retorted. "He's your agent. Whatever possessed you to listen to his scheme? I wouldn't trust him as far as I could throw him by the nose. I seem to have convinced you, at last, of his importance."

My friend's laughter increased.

"Rest easy, Gilly," he said soothingly. "When Daniel Alexander calls upon his friend, Hara Singh, this evening, you and I will be on hand to greet him."

"You know this Hara Singh?"

"I know enough about him to gain entrance to his home. Well, we have some rapid work ahead of us. We have two visits to make before evening, and the episode of the helpful East Indian has delayed us a bit. We shall have to hurry. First, we'll run out and see Henderson, the first of the two who failed to turn up at the funeral. He may be ill, as claimed, but we can't take anyone's word for anything. Later we shall visit Mr. Charles Amick, and still later the splendors of India."

WE gained little at the rooms of the clerk Henderson, and were enabled to cut the visit short. The old woman from whom the young fellow rented the rooms was able to confirm the report of Henderson's illness. He had not been out for more than a week, and for several nights he had been dangerously ill. He was now convalescent.

"Out of his head, he was, poor fellow, for several nights," said the garrulous old body. "Knew he was bad, he did, poor chap, and kept telling himself he must wake up. I thought he was gone, sir, that time, but —"

She would have gone on indefinitely and given us the whole history of the case, including the story of her own life, had not Lavender checked her.

"Thank you, thank you!" he hurriedly interposed. "Well, we won't bother him. I'm sure he's in good hands. When he wakes, just tell him a friend from the bank was asking about him. He's had a doctor, of course?"

"Oh, yes, sir, every day, and I expect he'll be along again soon, if you care to wait, sir."

We got away at last, and to save time took a taxi to the bank.

"So much for Henderson," said Lavender. "Now we'll have that talk with Amick."

The president of the bank introduced us, and we found Amick to be a dark young man of the type characterized as "sporty." He was not pleased to see us, or so I thought, but Lavender paid no attention to his evident discomfort.

"Of course, Mr. Amick," echoed my friend, "I remember you quite well. I think I saw you at the funeral, did I not?"

"I think you did not," replied Amick, with deep suspicion. "I was not at the funeral, Mr. Lavender."

President Cousins at this juncture unwittingly asked the right question.

"No, Mr. Amick was not there," he broke in, apparently surprised that Lavender had forgotten. "I looked for you, Amick. I thought you and Hurst were pretty warm friends."

"We were, Mr. Cousins," said Amick desperately, "but the fact is, I simply couldn't go. I hate funerals, and to think of Sam — well, I couldn't do it. I wanted to remember him as I saw him last."

"When was that, by the way?" asked Lavender.

"The day before," answered Amick, with increasing suspicion. "He was here at the bank."

"I should like to know where Mr. Hurst spent the night before that," said Lavender. "That is, the night before the night of his death. You couldn't tell me, I suppose?"

"No, I'm afraid I can't," replied Amick, with better grace.

"Well, I'm obliged to you, Mr. Amick," said Lavender. "I don't like to bother people with questions, but we must do what we can with this unhappy business."

"I agree with you," said the assistant cashier, "and of course if I can be of service, I want to be."

"We are all entirely at your disposal, Mr. Lavender," said President Cousins.

The taxi was waiting, and we took it through the snowy streets to Lavender's rooms. Throughout the cold drive my friend sat in silence, for the most part, drumming on the window sill with the fingers of one hand. The monotonous refrain got on my nerves.

"Well," I interrupted brusquely, "who is it? Amick or Daniel Alexander?"

"Or both?" he added, looking up. "There's more than one man in on this."

"Oh!" I said blankly.

WE dined at Lavender's rooms, and later climbed into evening raiment. "Tony old boy, this Hara Singh," quoth Lavender, "and we must be dressed for the part."

"Just who is Hara Singh?" I demanded.

"Crystal gazer, palmist, phrenologist, faker!" he responded, laconically. "Probably a millionaire, incidentally. The social set flocks there in droves. Nothing succeeds like successful humbug, Gilly!"

And so, shortly before eight o'clock, that evening, we departed for the Astor Street mansion of Hara Singh, the Master of Mysteries. We drove up in style, sent our driver on his way, then mounted the steps in leisurely fashion. With Lavender's thumb on the bell, a long muffled peal came faintly to our ears.

In the doorway, as the door swung open, stood a magnificently attired Oriental, in an imposing headdress. All the colors of the rainbow seemed to have been hung upon his lithe frame, and his small mustache curled upward like that of the ex-Kaiser.

He bowed deeply and stood to one side as we passed him. In the hallway beyond, a second and similar pageant of color bowed at our approach, and indicated a lighted room to the left. Everything was done in silence. A heavy incense hung in the air.

We passed through red hangings into a wide chamber decked in a fantastic fashion with Eastern designs and colors. Fine rugs were upon the floor, and fantastic footstools. Around the walls were gorgeous divans of inviting aspect, and Oriental weapons hung upon the walls.

At the head of the room, looking inward, beneath curtains of red velvet, a great crystal ball reposed on a pillar of marble.

A gigantic dark-skinned man entered the room as we looked around us, and in a high-pitched voice that curiously belied his formidable appearance, said respectfully, "Please to have seats, gentlemen. The master will be down in a moment. You have an appointment?"

"Oh, yes," lied Lavender, easily.

In several moments we heard soft steps on the stairs, and an instant later the hangings parted and the negro appeared.

"Hara Singh, Master of Mysteries!" he intoned shrilly; then rapidly disappeared.

A man in flowing white robes entered the chamber with quick, soft tread, and stopped short inside the threshold. I uttered an exclamation of astonishment.

Lavender seemed highly amused, as if something he had quite expected now stood before us.

The robed and whiskered Hara Singh was Daniel Alexander, dealer in revolvers and accordions in Division Street.

IV

A MOMENT of vocal silence followed; then the Master of Mysteries shrugged his shoulders with elaborate unconcern.

"Yes," he said, as if replying to a question, "it is I! Are you surprised?"

"Not at all," said my friend. "I have known since our recent conversation that you were Hara Singh, Master of Mysteries. Surely no one but a master so readily could have solved the mystery of the death of young Mr. Hurst."

There was a trace of mockery in Daniel Alexander's bow.

"You are jesting," he said reproachfully. "But you shall see! I am right, my friends, and tonight I shall prove it to you. Yes, I am Hara Singh, The Master of Mysteries, and also I am Daniel Alexander, the dealer in antiquities. There is nothing disgraceful in either profession, but it is not strange that I keep them apart. Foolish persons suspect a man who is known by two names; yet both my ventures have been profitable, and I do not care to sacrifice either. Some day, perhaps, Hara Singh will retire, and the world will know him no more. On that day Daniel Alexander will begin to be seen more often at his shop, and both he and his neighbors will be glad. The present life, my friends, is often fatiguing."

"I should imagine so," said Lavender dryly. "But your business is your own, Mr. Alexander. You offered to help us, and we are prepared to accept your assistance. And so we are here."

"I am sorry," he said, "but there is no help for it, now. I could have done better alone. You will only frighten the young man who is coming. Yet I cannot ask you to go away. Will you mind, my friends, if I conceal you during the interview?"

"A good idea!" exclaimed Lavender. "By all means, let us be concealed."

"Come then, for the young man is almost due."

With extravagant courtesy, he led us through the red curtains that fell on either side of the great crystal globe. We passed into a smaller chamber beyond, dimly lighted by an Oriental lamp in a far corner. Comfortable chairs were indicated by our host, and cigarettes were placed at our elbows.

"I shall order that drinks be served you," said Hara Singh, as he left us, and shortly thereafter the giant negro appeared with a tray of liquors and a small basin of ice.

"I fancy it is perfectly safe," smiled Lavender, noting my hesitation. The giant had vanished. "Here, I shall start the ball!"

He mixed himself a mild highball and tossed it off.

"No," he continued; "there is nothing to fear except the potency of the liquor. It is uncommonly good, and we must restrain our natural inclinations, my dear Gilly! I do not want to have to take you home in a condition suggesting collapse."

We sat in the semi-darkness, puffing at our cigarettes and waiting the advent of Charles Amick.

Inside of ten minutes the long muffed peal of the doorbell again thrilled through the house, and in a few moments we knew that our acquaintance of the bank was in the reception chamber a few feet beyond.

The soothing voice of Daniel Alexander, or in this case Hara Singh, came to our ears, as he greeted his visitor.

"It is some days since I have seen you in my poor home, my friend!"

The concentrated fury of Amick's utterance took me aback.

"It will be a good many days before you see me again, Singh!" he rasped harshly. "I'm through with you and your tricks!"

"My friend!"

The gentle voice of Hara Singh was filled with reproach.

"Don't play the innocent babe," snarled Amick. "I'm sick of it! I want to know only one thing from you — what happened to Sam Hurst?"

"My friend!" The voice of Hara Singh rose almost to a scream.

I glanced at Lavender. In the half-darkness, I could see that he was smiling wickedly.

"I'm not your friend!" screamed Amick. "If I were, no doubt I'd follow Hurst. Come quick, now! You'll tell me, Singh, or you'll tell the police. Sam Hurst was my friend, and if the police haven't sense enough to know where to look for his murderer, I have. Dead, and without a mark on him! I'm not a fool, Singh, and your Indian blarney doesn't go down."

There was a painful silence. Lavender rose to his feet and crossed the floor in two swift, noiseless strides. He peered through the curtains, and beckoned me to his side. An extraordinary sight met my gaze.

The men stood facing each other, their eyes fixed, their faces pouring perspiration. It was as if each, by sheer will, was endeavoring to force a break on the part of the other. The face of each was ghastly; but the face of Hara Singh was more — it was diabolic.

"My God!" I whispered. "The evil eye!"

Then spoke the voice of Hara Singh, soothing now, and tender as a woman's. "You force me to speak, Mr. Amick," it said gently. "Your violence does not frighten me. You are yourself the slayer of your friend! He was found dead in your house. You sent him there with the money. You are his slayer."

"Liar — liar — liar —" mumbled the changed voice of Amick. He seemed to be struggling with himself for articulate utterance, but the baleful eyes of Hara Singh continued to bore into his vision. "I did not kill him," muttered Amick. "How could I kill him? I was not near him. It was not my house — my mother's house — you sent him —"

His voice trailed away. "With your evil eyes you sent him there," continued the steady voice of Hara Singh.

"This won't do, Gilly!" said Lavender, in a quick whisper.

Swiftly he pushed aside the curtains and entered the chamber, thrusting his form between the eyes of Hara Singh and the shriveling Amick. He seized the bank officer by the shoulders and shook him vigorously. A nasty scowl disfigured the brow of Hara Singh, but he said no word.

"Come out of it!" roared Lavender, in Amick's ear. "Do you hear, Amick?"

The man addressed stared solemnly, then a light of intelligence flashed again from his eye. He squared his shoulders truculently.

"I know!" he cried. "Nearly gone, that time! Obliged to you —"

His vision cleared.

"Lavender!" he cried. Then quickly, "Where's that devil, Singh? He nearly had me."

He caught sight of the East Indian and lunged forward for the dark throat. Lavender held tightly to his arm.

"Wait, Amick!" said my friend, sharply.

He turned sternly on Hara Singh.

"There must be no coercion in this," he said. "If you have anything further to say to Mr. Amick, you must say it in my presence."

The East Indian shrugged.

"I am sorry," he said. "I have my own way, and you have yours. In a moment you would have known all. Now —" He shrugged again.

"What's the truth of this, Amick?" demanded Lavender. "I have heard this man accuse you of the murder of Samuel Hurst."

"He lies!" said Amick, laughing bitterly. "He knows he lies. He's trying to pull the wool over your eyes, Mr. Lavender. I know where Sam Hurst was the night before he was killed. He was here. Whose evil eye was on him then? Who sent him to the bank next day, with instructions to steal the money? Who lives around the corner from my empty house, and was there next night to receive the money? Don't waste time on me, Mr. Lavender. There's your man."

Hara Singh's voice was conciliatory.

"My friend," he said, "can it be possible that we have wronged each other? That we are both wrong? What you say is partly true. Mr. Hurst was here that night before, but he was here only for a moment. He had an engagement and went away. I hardly spoke to him, for he was in a hurry. He was going to the bedside of a friend who is ill —"

"Again you are a liar," said Amick. "The only sick friend Hurst had is Henderson, and Henderson is —"

The doorbell rang.

"I think Henderson is at the door," said Lavender, with a pleasant smile. "Keep your gun on Alexander, Gilly!"

Followed by the giant, Henderson entered the room.

"Amick!" he cried.

"Mr. Henderson," said Lavender, "it gives me great happiness to arrest you for the murder of Samuel Hurst, and the theft of the money from the Columbian Bank!"

The face of Henderson went a dirty yellow. Hara Singh stood motionless, but the face of Charles Amick lighted with a slow smile.

"By God, Lavender," he said, "you're all right! If you need any help, I'm right here!"

A sudden, low cry broke from Henderson's lips.

"Sam!" he whispered. Then his voice rose in high crescendo as he sought the eyes of Daniel Alexander.

"It is you who have done this," he cried. "It is you, Hara Singh, who have ruined us all. Until we knew you, we were friends. You turned us against each other; you played with us — your tools — your fools!"

He aimed a dramatic finger at the East Indian's stolid face.

"There is the real murderer!" he cried shrilly. "I — yes, it was I who sent Sam Hurst to his death. It is I whom the world will know as the slayer of my friend. But there is the assassin brain that schemed it all. And tonight he would have been a murderer in fact; he would have killed Amick if he had failed to master him by will.

It was for this I came, at the request of this murderer and thief, to aid in slaying another friend!

"And now it is I who am to suffer, while he is only an accessory, a receiver of stolen goods! It is unfair!"

There followed a movement so rapid that even the quick-witted Lavender was taken by surprise, and suddenly instead of the rigid, pointing finger, the sinister eye — the evil eye — of a revolver looked into the eyes of Hara Singh.

Lavender's spring was an instant too late. The crack of the revolver and Alexander's squeal of terror seemed simultaneous. Then the smoking weapon was wrenched from Henderson's hand before it could be turned upon himself.

I bent over the fallen body of Hara Singh, with Amick, and knew that life was extinct. But a strange pity was in Lavender's gaze as his eyes rested upon the face of Henderson, and I knew that one good word for that unhappy youth would be spoken at the subsequent trial.

V

IT was a case of the 'evil eye,' all right," said my friend Lavender, as we sat together in his rooms, "but we call it nowadays by another name — hypnotism. All three of them were dabblers — Henderson, Amick, and Hurst. The affable Hara Singh was their instructor, and they became his victims. Henderson, poor fellow, used his knowledge evilly. He needed money, I suppose; they always do. The idea occurred to him, undoubtedly through Alexander, to get Hurst to commit the actual theft. Hurst, of course, was perfectly innocent. Henderson hypnotized him. No wonder the poor fellow slept in that house until he froze to death! He was in a hypnotic trance."

"You mean that Hurst robbed the bank without knowing what he was doing?" I demanded.

"Just that! Undoubtedly Henderson had experimented with him in many ways, and Hurst was an excellent subject. He had been hypnotized so often, I fancy, that Henderson could send him to sleep, as it were, by a mere snap of the fingers. In that condition, he could be made to do remarkable things, especially in the way of post-hypnotic suggestions. That is, Henderson could command his victim to perform a certain act at some future time; and, waking, Hurst would have forgotten the suggestion. But at the time set he would perform the act unconsciously, as though by his own volition. If the original command ordered him to fall asleep after performing the act, he would fall asleep.

"This sort of thing is all understood. It is easy to follow the case. Hurst visited his sick friend — who was shamming — and was hypnotized by Henderson. Henderson ordered him to take the money next day; then take it to this empty house, which Henderson and Alexander knew belonged to Amick's mother, and there fall asleep after delivering the satchel. Hurst did fall asleep, and slept into death.

"Alexander — who was Henderson's fake doctor — got the satchel, of course. Hurst, following instructions, dropped it from a window after carrying it to the house. It was picked up in the lot, outside the house, by Alexander, who also sent the anonymous message to President Cousins — too late to save Hurst. Henderson probably ordered the message sent."

"When did you first suspect Henderson?" I curiously asked. "Both Amick and I suspected Alexander, or Hara Singh, but never thought of Henderson."

"I suspected him vaguely from the first," said Lavender. "That is, from the day of the funeral. But there was nothing to base even a suspicion upon, really. Then when we called at the rooms he occupied and listened to that poor old dupe of a woman, I clinched it, although I had to check on it throughout, afterward. You remember what the old woman said? That Henderson had been calling on himself to 'wake up!'

"Of course, Henderson was doing nothing of the sort. He was doing his best however, possibly conscious-stricken, to wake Hurst — miles away in that empty house!"

"What science would have called it, had he succeeded, heaven knows!"

OLD SONGS MODERNIZED

Take, oh take those lips away —
Osculation's quite forsworn!
Bacilli, the doctors say,
Make it but a creed outworn.

So thy glance for favor suing, favor suing,
Pleads in vain, there's nothing doing, nothing doing!

— Corine Rockwell Swain

"WATSON!"
by Captain A.E. Dingle

"WATSON, my dear fellow, this inaction is maddening. I am *ennuied*," drawled a lanky, cadaverous individual reclining lumpishly in a long deck chair, a black cigar in his teeth, his brows drawn down, and his fingertips touching in approved Sherlockian fashion. A ripple of mirth passes around the small circle of which he formed the centre, and his expression darkened in outward resentment.

The man addressed as Watson glanced at the amused ones with a faint smile on his own face and replied indifferently, "Better take a dose of dope, my dear Holmes. The steward uncorks a rippin' brand of Scotch. Shall I call him?"

Holmes unfolded himself out of the chair without a reply and stalked away in the direction of the smoking room.

"He's on the scent!" chuckled a fiery-haired youngster.

"That's a scent you all can follow!" replied a merry-eyed girl, seizing the red one and dragging him off to play shuffleboard. Watson remained in his chair, and behind lowered lids his eyes glittered shrewdly.

Percy Anstruther's big steam yacht *Vagrant* never went to sea without a happy, careless party of youth aboard.

Percy himself was of the type dubbed porcine. Finding himself tremendously wealthy quite early in life, mainly by dint of ignoring the Golden Rule and playing up the Rule of Three — which he interpreted to mean, one for the firm — of which he was head — and two for Percy Anstruther — holding no scruples which might prevent profits accruing through some such idiocy as consideration for others, he soon decided, on retiring, that a steam yacht was the thing to gain him entry into the society of the exclusive set he desired to adorn. Percy knew enough to refrain from attempting the impossible; he paid high salaries, not wages, to the best of secretaries, the cunningest of chefs, the very paragon of stewards, and he possessed that native shrewdness which prevented him offending by any vulgarity of speech in select company, no matter how free he might be among his own kind. No amount of

shrewdness could warn him of the bad taste, or inadvisability, of loading himself with costly, bizarre jewelry. He saw ladies and gentlemen of the class he envied, each wearing such gems as they possessed when occasion demanded. In his small mind there was only one reason for their not wearing more — the lack of possession; only one reason for limiting the times of wearing what they had — fear of losing them. And since neither fear of losing them nor limited possession applied to himself, Percy Anstruther's fat fingers were ever loaded with flawless diamonds, his fat neck glowed from the fires within a great single ruby in his scarf, his fat watch fob scintillated like a cluster of stars against his fat little paunch.

"I've got 'em, why shouldn't I sport 'em?" he had demanded many times in answer to suggestions from his friends. "I can afford to wear 'em, and the crook isn't born who'll take 'em away from your Uncle Percy. No, sir!"

Which all brings us back to Holmes and Watson; for it was the long, lean, cadaverous Holmes who first expressed entire agreement with Percy's ideas on the subject of fashion in gems. They had met, and become acquainted, at the great Casino of Ocean View, off which the *Vagrant* lay anchored while her owner and his guests disported in a dance or two, a turn or so at the wheel, or a little chopping, according to individual taste. Percy, furthermore, strongly desired to become acquainted with somebody who would accept his hospitality without making him see and feel that he became a debtor by receiving the honor of the present company. He was gratified by the celerity with which he attained his object. There could be no doubt regarding the desirability of Mr. Holmes or his friend Watson. Those names appeared on the register of their hotel, and by them they were known and introduced to Percy by the croupier of the roulette table. There could be no cavilling at friends secured through such a sponsor. And, best of all, they quite certainly did not seek his acquaintance merely to have a finger in his pocket-book, for they politely insisted upon buying wine themselves; and their taste was proven when they ordered a brand which Percy always hesitated about, though he knew it was quite the thing, simply because he wasn't sure how to pronounce the name.

"I say, you chaps must come for a cruise with me," he had said eagerly at the third bottle.

"The ocean's rather a bore, old man, but perhaps we could endure it for a few days, ah, Watson?" Holmes had replied in a drawl which seemed incongruous with the sharpness of his big, steady eyes.

"Oh, just for a week, perhaps," Watson had conceded, with similar lack of eagerness, and the thing was done. They vacated their hotel that same day; the *Vagrant* steamed just beyond the blue skyline in the cool evening.

WITH a young party on board, it was inevitable that Holmes should speedily acquire the name of "Sherlock." For Dr. Watson to be dubbed "Doctor" followed as naturally as night follows day. At first they mildly resented it, although, queerly enough, Holmes rather deserved it than otherwise, for he was forever reading the detective books in the yacht's well-stocked library, and he could easily be led on to expound the methods of the famous sleuth of fiction. But soon they accepted the titles bestowed on them, and gradually Percy, seeing the fun the others got out of the little pleasantry, and seeing that his new guests suffered nothing actually by it, fell into the mood himself, and often cast out bait in the hope of getting Holmes into a tangle of explanations over some really trivial circumstance. Such as the time, for instance, when the crew's cook, who looked after the fowls carried to supply the owner's table with fresh eggs, reported the best layer missing, and the boatswain, at the same time, pointed out to the chief officer chicken tracks up the side of the freshly painted smokestack.

"You let the bloomin' chicken loose yourself while washing down decks," was the mate's emphatic decision. "You scared her trying to chase her back, and the bally thing flew up against the funnel before she volplaned overboard. You want to be more careful, bo'sun."

But Percy, urged on by his young friends, suggested to Holmes that there might be another solution to the missing chicken mystery. Holmes placed the tips of his long, white fingers together, drew down his brows, and nodded sagaciously. From the stokehold grating came the merry whistle of a happy fireman whose spirits were proof against the discomfort of his work. A windlass clanked, and two firemen just off duty drew up a can of ashes and dumped them down the lower-deck shute; from the galley door a sculleryman emerged, staggering under the kitchen garbage pail. Both containers discharged their waste into the blue sea at once, and tigerishly Holmes darted to the rail and keenly scanned the floating refuse. Then he resumed his chair, lighted a huge briar pipe filled with strong plug, and placed his finger-tips together again, while Percy Anstruther and the merry band of youngsters waited for his next utterance.

"You are right, Mr. Anstruther," he said crisply. "There is another, very different answer to that seemingly simple riddle of the chicken."

"Oh, surely you have not solved the mystery so soon?" protested Percy. His young friends giggled.

"My chain is almost complete, sir," Holmes replied. "You hear

that peculiar whistle emanating from the fire-room? I dare say it is the first time you have noticed it. But I, who note the meanest trifles, can assure you that there has been, is, method in that whistle. Where are the poultry pens? Right beside the stokehold ventilators, are they not? Very well. The messmate of the whistling fireman slyly opens the cage, the whistler pipes up a cunning note, the chicken creeps out, the cage is once more fastened, and the miscreant who opened and closed it darts below to join his fellow criminal. The whistling goes on, the poor deluded chicken follows it, and now it takes on the quality of ventriloquism. It seems to emanate from the funnel. The silly fowl walks up the smokestack, the fumes overcome it when it gets to the rim, and it falls down into the hands of the hungry pair waiting for its advent, singed and cooked ready to devour. That, gentlemen, is the solution of an apparent mystery. Quite simple."

A roar of merriment pealed out across the sea, and Holmes appeared annoyed.

"Fine!" laughed Percy, with the conscious superiority of having discovered a palpable flaw. "But tell us, old chap, how these awful criminals got the chicken out of the furnace? It would be burned up long before it reached the bottom of that chimney."

"You may amuse yourselves unravelling that point, gentlemen. I will give you a tip, though. I stepped to the rail just now. You imagined I did so idly, or simply to knock out my pipe. It was not so. I examined the refuse thrown over at that instant. Feathers, some burnt, some whole, floated away on a mass of ashes. It is the trifles which count in detecting crime. Now, Watson, I think we will investigate a rumor that the steward was seen breaking out a new case of Scotch this morning."

There was a medley of voices in the group he left. Some actually wondered if he really believed in his own deep cunning, since he was never seen to smile even while expounding his most outlandish notions. Others were only disgusted. There were two who warned Percy without reserve that before the cruise was up he would be touched for money by the Sherlockian Holmes and his friend Watson.

"Oh, I don't think that," objected Percy. "He's rather idiotic, of course, but I think the chap's only fooling himself. They're both gentlemen, anyway, and we're having some fun with them."

"Why not let us make up a real mystery, Percy?"

"Oh, goody!" cried a merry-eyed girl, dancing joyously. "Oh, let's! You can have a tremendous robbery, or something, and have all the clues point to all of us, and all of us have an alibi, and you can scatter my hair-pins and combs about, and —"

"That's the identical scheme!" chuckled Percy, shaking like a jelly in his mirth. "Let's dope out a plot."

"Presently!" interjected the red-headed youth, intensely. "Here's the Watson chap. Not a word!"

Watson strolled along the deck, having left Holmes in the smoking room, and he wore a grimace of mingled boredom and contempt. He glanced around the little group inquisitively, then addressed Percy.

"Holmes begins to irritate one, doesn't he, Anstruther? A little of his nonsense is amusing; too much is sickening. I wonder what he'd do if faced with a real case. Sometimes I think he's really keen on scientific investigation of problems, at others I feel disgusted at his childishness. The chicken twaddle, for instance."

Percy hesitated for a minute, then, smiling fatly in justification of his resolve, he said.

"I say, Watson, you must be a thought-reader. When you came along we were discussing playing a little joke on your friend to see how far he would dig into a real puzzle. You won't mind if we keep you out of it, will you? Might drop him a hint, you know, and spoil —"

"Not at all," replied Watson quickly. "Make your plans and start him going. I'll have my fun looking on, I assure you. I hope you concoct a real mystery, though, with something far deeper than vanishing poultry as a motive. Good luck."

THE first outcome of a long and close secret confabulation was the sudden increase of Percy's jewelled embellishments. That evening at dinner he simply blazed with light from gorgeous gems, and in place of his customary offering of big, sleek Cuban cigars in a handsome snake-skin case after dinner, he preferred still choicer weeds in an amazing gold case on both sides of which his monogram leaped out at one in diamonds. Then, under pretence of showing the men some intimate curiosities, he took them into his great stateroom where, obviously through oversight, a stout cash box stood open on his table, crammed to the top with bank notes of high denomination.

"Confound that man of mine!" he exclaimed, closing the box, but leaving it on the table. "He's always leaving valuables about as if they were pebbles."

While exhibiting the trivial curiosities he had brought the men in to see, he shot keen side-glances at Holmes, and chuckled shakily as he led the way out to the after deck, omitting to reprimand his valet, however, for his carelessness.

"It's a gorgeous night," he remarked, when the space under the awnings resounded with tuneful music from an excellent machine.

"Let's have a bit of dancing, hey, folks?"

IN THE quietest hour of the most silent watch, about two o'clock in the morning, the yacht rang with sounds of dire mis-happening. A pistol shot shattered the stillness on deck, a heavy splash was heard over the side, and in a minute the decks were alive with alarmed seaman and excited officers; a huddle of sleepy guests milled about each other in well feigned panic. Watson was there, as panicky as the rest; and Holmes, true to his assumed character, took up the burden of discovering the meaning of that midnight alarm.

"Where is Mr. Anstruther?" he demanded, peering around like a scrawny hawk. "Find him, steward. Fancy him sleeping through such a racket! He's getting far too fat."

While Watson looked on in silence from the companionway door, and a little giggling group nudged each other delightedly, Holmes flashed a pocket torch about the decks and rails. On hands and knees at times, he nosed along waterways and peering overside into the silken blackness of the smooth sea. Presently he brought forth a huge magnifying glass, and the red-headed youth laughed outright. The sound seemed creepy in the darkness and quiet, broken before only by swish of water and that flickering circle of light from Holmes' torch. But the steward's sudden appearance and agitated announcement diverted attention again.

"Mr. Anstruther's — Oh, his room, it's horrid!"

Prepared as they were for such an announcement, it required all their self-control to prevent the conspirators uttering little gasps of sheer suspense, so vivid was the steward's terror. Watson glanced keenly toward the absorbed figure of Holmes, who was scrutinizing the steward pitilessly, every inch of the man's outward aspect coming under the inspection.

"That will do, my man," snapped Holmes at length. "You may show us the way to Mr. Anstruther's stateroom. Come, Watson, I may need you." The steward led the way trembling, and the muffled giggling burst forth again as the youthful jesters saw the Sherlockian one tumbling into the trap they had set for him. All the details of the plot had been left to Anstruther, and they were sure he had done a good piece of work, for he had outlined most of what he intended to do, but none had anticipated the perfection of theatrical setting which seemed to leap out at them through the door of Percy's room.

"Ooh!" cried the merry-eyed girl, and shrank back with fright which was more than half real. Her companions too, playing out their hands, peeped inside, drew back, gasped and stared in simulated terror. Watson looked in, then stepped inside, his ruddy face wearing an enigmatical expression. Holmes alone maintained an utterly expressionless air as he waved everyone back from the threshold and took from his pocket a tape measure.

Well indeed had Percy done his part. The bed was upset, and the coverings strewed the carpet. One curtain flew loose through the wide porthole, the other hung by one hook, torn in halves. The table and writing desk in a corner were bare; the drawers, both hanging open almost out of the slides, lay empty. The stout cash box was on the floor, empty but one forlorn note of small denomination lay pinched under one corner of it. Across the room, near the bed, which was a four-poster and not a bunk, was a woman's hair comb, broken; a yard away lay a pyjama button, still a yard further a red and green grass bath slipper, obviously far too small for Percy to have ever worn. And, stabbing the dim light like a spear, a great red smear ran from a dark stain on the bed-head clear up to and through the open port.

Watson stepped over and touched the red smear with a finger, smelling it and peering at it under a light globe. A queer curl wreathed his lips, and he glanced curiously at Holmes who was on his knees with tape and lens. Afterward, when talking over the events of that night, some of the young men recalled that queer glance of Watson's, and remembered, too, that he contrived to get into the foreground quite as much as Holmes, yet without in the slightest degree seeming to want to. Anyhow, in all the after pictures of that night which rose up before any of the guests, the short, heavy figure of Watson loomed as large as the long, thin, stooping figure of Holmes.

"What's happened, d'you think?" whispered somebody. The merry-eyed girl giggled hysterically, and rejoined, "Give Mr. Holmes time. Don't you all see there's been a horrid crime committed, and that poor Percy has vanished? Don't breathe. You may disturb something, mayn't they, Mr. Holmes?"

For answer Holmes suddenly appeared before the little group in the door, his eyes ablaze.

He seemed to arrive from the other side of the room without, motion, like a shadow; and without warning he plunged his hand into the tumbled mass of shining hair over the girl's startled eyes. In the other hand he held the broken parts of the hair comb he had picked up from the floor.

"Same color," he muttered, matching comb with hair. "Where

is your comb, miss?"

Confronted with the very thing she had suggested herself, the girl looked less happy than she had expected. Confusion seized upon her, and her saucy tongue failed her. She stammered, sheepishly enough, "That is it. I er — I lent it to Percy to, er — to —"

"That is all, thank you," Holmes interrupted her sharply. "I will ask for you when I require your statement. You may retire." A tiny murmur of protest rippled around at sight of the girl's crestfallen air as she turned away toward her own room; but then the hugeness of the joke struck all concerned, and they crowded close to hear what was coming next.

Holmes closely examined the carpet, the bed, the curtains; he even measured the length and breadth of the red smear on the side panel. He sniffed at some dust he scraped up, he struck his head through the porthole and peered up and down, fore and aft, like a raw-necked vulture seeking prey. Then, stepping to the centre again, he looked for a moment at the faces before him and at the red and green bath slipper. Suddenly he went to his knees before the red-headed youth and forcibly lifted his right foot knee-high. He flung aside the leather Romeo the young man wore and clamped the grass slipper to the foot.

"H'm! You, too, I shall know where to find when I need you," he remarked. "You may retire, sir; and I warn you that this very serious occurrence may lead into unpleasant places. If you wish to tell me anything, you may do so in the morning. That is all, thank you."

Now he held out the pyjama button, scanning the sleeping suits before him. One jacket lacked a button, and one only. Like a tiger Holmes sprang before the wearer, clapped the button to the vacant place, and glared terribly into the young fellow's face. "B-but, Holmes, it isn't the same pattern!" giggled another bystander, scarcely able to talk for repressed mirth.

"Married?" Holmes jerked out abruptly to the man who lacked a button.

"Surely," laughed the youngster, recovering his nerve.

"Pattern doesn't matter then," was the unexpectedly sophisticated reply. "You will be called in the morning, sir. That will do."

"Say, Holmes," put in the last onlooker, who, except for Watson, alone remained unspotted by suspicion. "I don't lack a shoe, nor a button, nor even a comb. Can't you discover some clue which indicates me as the brutal murderer?" There was a keen note of sarcasm in the man's suggestion. Holmes looked at him gravely.

"I shall permit nothing to escape my notice which bears on this monstrous mystery," he said. "Place your left hand here, please."

With excessive care he pressed the man's hand down into the nap of the thick carpet, and scrutinized the edges through his powerful lens; then released the man and told him to go, but, like the rest, to hold himself ready to be questioned.

"Meanwhile," remarked Holmes, "we shall turn in toward some port. This is a matter for the regular police, to whom I hope to be able to deliver the criminal."

"Sure you can't find something which incriminates Watson?" gurgled the young fellow just released. "This is such a scream it would be a shame to keep him out of it."

"You will kindly keep your witticisms for a more suitable moment, sir," was the dry retort, and the guest departed, leaving Watson gazing thoughtfully at the stooping back of Holmes.

"My dear Watson," the sleuth said presently, "pray ring for the steward." The steward answered the bell, and Holmes told him, without turning around, to go and order the captain to change the course for the nearest port, and to notify him immediately which port it would be. In answer, the captain appeared in person, and a very angry, irritable person he was. He opened fire at once on the sleuth.

"What's the meaning of this?" he demanded warmly. "Why am I not called in to be consulted about this? And who are you, to order me into port, I'd like to know. Where's the owner?"

"Mr. Anstruther has disappeared, captain. There has been some foul play. That is why I suggest running into port —"

"And this is the first I hear of it!" bellowed the captain. "Shooting goes on aboard my ship, somebody tells me my owner has gone, and I'm not asked for an opinion but told to run —"

"Just a moment, captain," Watson put in quietly; "I will explain a lot to you if you'll give me a moment outside. There has been mischief, certainly, but not so serious as might be. Come, let Holmes continue his investigation. I'll tell you about it."

He led the mollified skipper out to his own roomy cabin, and Holmes flashed a look of appreciation after them as he shut the door.

AN EXPECTANT party gathered about the table at breakfast in the morning, for daylight brought back all the brightness of the farce which night and its gloom had almost made to seem like tragedy. They awaited Holmes, who presently appeared looking haggard and pale after an obviously sleepless night. He crushed up a white pellet and stirred it into his coffee, which he drank before eating anything; then coldly, and with an incisiveness worthy of a graver situation, he plunged into a bald recital of his discoveries and decision. On deck, listening through the skylight, a gleeful yacht captain chuckled hugely, slapping his leg, utterly reconciled to the temporary loss of his employer.

"We shall be in port in a few hours now," Holmes began. "The culprit in this brazen piece of villainy will be taken ashore then, I promise you. You all heard the shot in the night, and —"

"How about the shoes and buttons and other haberdashery?" grinned the red-headed youth maliciously.

"I shall come to that, my young friend," replied Holmes, glaring fiercely. "You heard the shot, I believe. You all saw the scene of the crime —"

"That shot was on deck!"

"The scene of the crime," the sleuth proceeded as if no interruption had been offered, "and even my friend Watson could discern the obvious signs of violence there. You saw the odd slipper, the pyjama button, the broken comb, and the gory smear on the wall. Now there is one chance remaining for the guilty one to make reparation, and thereby perhaps gain leniency. I shall run over the facts, and on our arrival in port I shall summon the police to take the criminal, unless meanwhile he confesses.

"Now that slipper would fit only a child or a woman. That button might have come from a lounge pillow. The comb could easily have been picked up broken somewhere else and dropped in the cabin by the owner himself. I have some little skill in reading signs, and I say that pistol shot was fired out through a porthole, sounding thus as if it were on deck; the slipper is one of a heap of about fifty pairs of all sizes, kept by Mr. Anstruther for the use of guests who may have forgotten to bring bath shoes. The button assuredly came from the cushion in Anstruther's own arm chair, and the comb was probably dropped by him when he returned from the deck."

"Why, Holmes, you might be accusing Percy himself!" roared the party in mirth. Then, realizing suddenly that they ought to wear more of an air of gravity, since Percy was apparently murdered in his own yacht, and they were all more or less under suspicion, their faces fell, and they leaned closer to Holmes in deep attention.

"Making due allowance for youth and frivolity," Holmes proceeded coldly, "I will bear with you. Here is a tip, which you may find useful. Pray try to assist the course of justice, rather than hinder it because you do not see things as I see them. You would find the assassin and thief? Very well then. Look for a person of this description: A tall, lean man, rather stout, and about five feet eight inches high; he is florid and pale of complexion, and wears a number seven or number ten shoe. On one hand he has a crooked finger, which he can straighten whenever he wants to."

As one man the party got up from the table, and on every face was a sneer. They had expected something far better than this, else Percy would surely never have submitted to many hours of discomfort in order to play out the jest. The merry-eyed girl lingered behind to state, forcefully, her opinion.

"Mr. Holmes, I think you are a beast! If you are such an idiot as your silly words seem to indicate, you should at least have decency enough to refrain from uttering such nonsense at a time like this!"

She flirted out, and a slow, deep smile overspread Holmes' lean face as she disappeared. The captain, on deck, turned away to face a stammering, pop-eyed steward at his elbow.

"Mr. Anstruther, sir! He's down —"

"S-sh!" the skipper warned the man sharply. "Keep your mouth shut, steward. This is all right. Don't say a word."

"B-but, sir, he looks —"

"I tell you it's all right. It's a game he's playing. Keep quiet, I tell you."

Watson was having a similarly difficult time persuading his fellow guests to let the joke go on a little longer. They were, to a man and girl, for seeking out Percy and telling him it was useless to remain in hiding any longer.

"Why, Watson, it's too darned silly to be funny," cried the redheaded one. "It's simply idiotic to let old Percy sweat himself sick down in some dark hold just to draw this faker Holmes. I never heard such rubbish, even from half-witted kids."

"Don't spoil it," Watson advised quietly. "I know Holmes rather better than you, and I tell you he's only trying to scare you off while he makes out a case. If you leave him alone, say until we get to port, he'll have something amusing to tell you, even if it is all wrong. At any rate it will be a logical sequence of points comparing perfectly with all the clues."

"But how about poor old Percy?"

"I'll see him myself. He'll be agreeable, I know, since he arranged the joke himself. I'll take him down some wine and see what else he wants."

"Oh, then you know where he's hiding? He didn't tell us."

"I know, yes. Just keep quiet and watch awhile. You'll have something truly interesting to talk about soon, I promise you."

The yacht ran into harbor before noon, and as she steamed up the sail-dotted bay Holmes came on deck in town clothes. Every eye fastened on him, and smiles were carefully concealed.

"I am going on shore to bring the police, gentlemen," he stated sharply. "There is little time, but still time enough, for the culprit to reveal himself."

He turned away and stood at the rail. Behind him muffled giggles and chuckles broke out, and the merry-eyed girl chirped recklessly, "Oh yes, let him go! It'll be bully sport seeing the real police tear his silly old theories to rags."

Holmes seemed to notice nothing that was said, but presently the steward appeared absolutely dripping with the perspiration of fear, and in a moment all was changed from farce to earnest.

"Captain!" the man yelled to the bridge, "I've found Mr. Anstruther, and he's hurt! He ain't fooling, no, sir! He's been tied —"

Watson stepped forward, laid a hand on Holmes' arm coolly, and jabbed a pistol muzzle into his ribs. He faced the group with a smile.

"The steward is right, gentlemen. You thought to play a joke, but Long Holmes here turned it into a real game. That is, he almost succeeded. But I have been keeping tabs on him for a long time, and I've got him now with the goods. Yes, I'm a detective. You might see after Mr. Anstruther. I shall come back and report to him as soon as I've placed my prisoner in safety."

Holmes twisted his neck and glared down at Watson with murderous eyes; but the smaller man kept his pistol pressed to the other's side until the yacht docked, then put it into his pocket, warned his prisoner, and marched him ashore and into a taxicab.

Percy was brought up from the darksome depths of the storerooms, blinking and furious, but more than a little frightened. He shook a fat, abrased fist after the disappearing taxicab when the captain told him who was in it, and launched into a feverish recital of his adventures.

"By the Great Horn Spoon!" he gabbled, reddening up like a turkey's wattles. "That chap's smart, but he ain't a patch on the quiet Watson. There's a sleuth for you! Followed his man, he has, for months, I'll go bail; why, I'll bet he made his acquaintance at Ocean View just to keep right after him until he pulled something.

"And nobody suspected him all the while Sherlock was turning our little game into a damn nasty reality. I knew something was wrong—kind o' felt it, y'know—but it was too late to do anything when the suspicion grew to certainty. I was hobbled then.

"Oh, I give it to Holmes, fellows, he fooled me nicely! I came into my stateroom as we arranged, scattered those fool clues about, and was just ready to gather up the loot and blow off the gun out of the porthole, when in comes Sherlock like a ghost, slams me up against the wall and busts my nose, wraps me up in my own bathrobe and ties it with the cord, and carries me down below. Then he passed up again, and I heard the pistol go off, and there I've lain ever since until just now."

"By George! It was a clever bit of trickery," exclaimed a wide-eared listener. "Lucky it failed, eh?"

"Yes, thanks to Watson. I knew that chap was the real thing," vowed Percy, dabbing tenderly at his swollen nose. "You got to hand it to him, though he didn't deceive me for a minute. He had just the look of a real, clever crime-hound. I'll do something handsome for him when he comes on board."

None of the party wanted to go ashore until Watson had returned. They lounged under the awnings, sipping long cool drinks and chatting over the affair. About half an hour after Watson had taken his captive ashore, a wide-winged flying boat flew overhead close down, circled once or twice as if inspecting the fine yacht, then flew swiftly seaward in the general direction of a long line of islands belonging to many different nations, lying far down over the horizon. Flying boats have ceased to be objects of intense curiosity, and nobody took more than a fleeting interest in the low-flying machine, until it had almost speeded out of sight in the sea haze and the radio man suddenly appeared in obvious excitement and handed Percy a message. Percy read it idly, re-read it with staring eyes, dropped it on deck and sprang to the rail, gaping into the blue sky for that vanished speck which was the flying machine. The merry-eyed girl picked up the message, smoothed it out, and with a hesitating glance at the stupefied Percy read it aloud to the shocked company.

"Thank you, Percy," it said. "We've had a lovely time, and bear you no malice for your friends' ridicule of our methods. We'll write you from Mars, or Venus, or some place. Ta-ta, old boy. Sherlock and the Doctor."

Faces gaped into faces in utter amazement, then all turned to Percy. But Percy was already taking the companionway stairs six steps at a time, bound for his ravaged stateroom from which a treasure in gems and cash had all too surely vanished.

TO ONE WHO GOES ABROAD

Guarded through enormous space
*   By the unseen Captain's eye,*
Where gigantic shoals of suns
*   Fill the night with majesty,*

Stars on every side awash,
*   Earth's our ship that travels far,*
Plunging to the ports of God
*   Swifter than a falling star.*

Go, then, if you will, and find
*   Other countries, other friends;*
We've a common voyage still
*   Down a way that never ends!*

— Barry Kemp

THE MAKE-WEIGHT
by HAROLD LAMB

ARTHUR KENT breathed a sigh of relief as the last trick of the last hand was turned. He had been lucky. Indeed lucky, if neither of the other two players at the green-covered table in the billiard room of the officers' club had seen him cheat that last hand.

Checking up the score, Kent held it out for the others to see. His dark eyes were half closed, his full, handsome face impassive. The moisture around his eyes came only from the early evening heat that enveloped Rawal Pindi, in Upper India.

"'Fraid I'm winner, gentlemen. Sorry Captain Gerald has had enough."

The third man, a nervous subaltern, tried to smile as he wrote out an I.O.U. for seventy pounds. With a nod Kent folded the sheet of paper on the table and fell to shuffling the cards together until the subaltern had left the room.

Into the pack of cards he deftly slipped the three discards that he had secreted. He smiled, for now there would be no proving that he had cheated. Luck usually ran his way. His was a clever mind and quick to seize advantage — consequently he had made a name as political agent. True, two years ago when native under-officials had complained of extortion, Kent had been transferred from a Bengal province to the small frontier post of Dalgai, near Rawal Pindi. But here he had married a first-rate American girl with a little money.

"Well?" he observed.

Captain Fred Gerald, surgeon, attached to the cavalry regiment at Dalgai — called Daktar Sahib by the natives to whom he sometimes administered aid — took a five-pound bank-note from the breast pocket of his tunic and thrust it across the table. "I'm riding up into the gorges to attend a patient." His gray eyes hardened swiftly. "Wouldn't you better return that — paper to the young cub, and explain that a mistake was made in the score?"

"Eh?" Kent flushed as he grasped the other's meaning. "Kindly explain what the devil you're getting at?"

The Daktar Sahib counted off on his fingers "Three cards. You palmed them, you know."

A curious smile played under Kent's mustache. So he had been seen! And by the one man in the world who did not want to denounce him publicly as a card cheat. His luck was still good. He called to the one house boy who lingered near the window lattice by the table and sent him to fetch Gerald's stick and pith helmet.

When the two were alone Kent pocketed the promissory note.

"What do you propose to do about it, my dear fellow," he asked, a strained note in his full voice, "make a fuss or keep quiet?"

Gerald took his hat and stick from the boy who had returned, dismissed the native and rose. His alert, tanned face was emotionless. No one in the border station or Rawal Pindi guessed, for instance, that the surgeon worshiped the girl who had married Kent a year ago.

He paid her no marked attention, avoided meeting her in fact.

The only one who suspected his feeling for Ethel Kent was the man who sat by the table before him — the man, in fact, whom he had just seen cheating.

No one better than the Daktar Sahib knew the rigid code of ethics that bound the men of the army stations of India. To denounce Kent would inevitably make misery for Ethel Kent.

The luck of the political agent still held good, you see. When Gerald started to speak, shrugged and turned away, Kent sprang up, his smile hardening. To the shifting mind of Kent it was whispered that the man who would avoid open quarrel with the husband must have an understanding with the wife.

For a long moment gray eyes clashed with black; the cold anger of the surgeon and the gnawing fury of the political agent were on the verge of being unleashed. The heat that day had been wearing. "I shall say nothing about the cards — now — Kent," the surgeon observed evenly, "for your wife's sake. I warn you, though. The hill natives have an apt proverb. They say that one who digs a pit for others will find that he has made his own grave."

Glad that the tension was broken, Kent pocketed the cards, veiling the suspicion that flamed in his eyes at mention of his wife. "You forget, my Daktar Sahib," he pointed out ironically, "the little thing called proof. Whatever your chums the hill beggars say, proof is required by the white man's law when you accuse a man. I have not forgotten that."

Gerald's deep eyes studied curiously the man who could make his way conqueringly in the world without thought of the rights of others. It did not occur to the straightforward mind of the surgeon that Kent's words were aimed at him. Because it was impossible for Gerald to conceive that any man could think evil of Ethel Kent.

"True," he nodded. "There is, however, one court that requires no proof of evil before administering justice. And that is Providence, or the judgment of God."

This chimed with Kent's inner thoughts. "Yes, may Providence or God or the devil judge between us, Captain Gerald. And may the officer of justice be whatever tool is handiest!"

Now, by one of those minute coincidences that link together the chain of life, both men started and stepped back, although they had heard no sound — were, in fact, alone in the billiard room.

Intent on each other they noticed only vaguely what seemed to be the dart of a snake out from the lattice of the open window upon the bare green table between them.

But it was not a snake. It flashed back through the lattice, leaving behind it, however, a folded square of torn, yellow paper.

On the upper side of the paper, traced in a curious, curving hand, was the name: "Kent Sahib."

THE blooming, thievin' beggar had the chit in the cleft of a stick. Pushed it in through the lattice-work, pulled back his stick and slipped down the veranda post, out into the bush before I had a fair look at him."

So said Kent, irritably, as he returned from his sally out on the upper veranda of the club. Twilight, aided by a mist of rain, had enabled the fugitive messenger to penetrate the Rawal Pindi compound unnoticed.

As the political agent deciphered the flowing Turki script on the paper, an oath came from his bearded lips.

"A dinner invitation, and a pressing one, for tonight. Also, from the worst murderer in the Hindu Kush." He jerked his thumb up over his shoulder at the lattice, behind which the curtain of rain concealed the outline of the giant foothills of the Himalayas.

Sparing of speech or motion — a trick of all old service men — Gerald took the missive up from the table where Kent had tossed it contemptuously and painstakingly read it through.

"The Kadi, Kent-Sahib, will come to the home of his unworthy servant, Jehan Khan. He will come tonight. He will be afoot, without his police. Inshallah."

"Sheer insolence," growled Kent. "*Inshallah* — by the will of God. I'll stay in Pindi, thank you. The Pathan, Jehan Khan, calls himself the descendant of kings, and has a nest somewhere up in the gorges that my men can't find. I might have marked it down once, but a hill native ran full into my horse at a bend of the *kud* — the precipice path."

The political agent was not lacking in courage. When the native had accosted him, Kent had struck the fellow with his riding crop. The blow, falling on the man's head, had knocked him down. "End over end, about a thousand feet or so," Kent was fond of saying.

He remembered it clearly, because there had been something peculiar about the eyes of the hill native. Kent did not know what it was, but from time to time he found himself thinking about those eyes —

"I am going there tonight," observed Gerald. "Fact is, I got the mate to this *chit* two hours ago. Only it said a woman needed my care."

"Then it's a trick! No Moslem would let you look at the face of one of his wives, let alone touch her. You don't really mean to go? You'll have a knife in your back if you do."

"Better to chance that than have a musket ball, long range, in my head if I don't. Jehan Khan invariably pays off a grudge. You see, I treated a wound of his once and said I'd do as much again." Gerald spoke lightly, while he puzzled over the duplicate messages received by himself and Kent. It seemed to be nothing more than a bit of effrontery; but long experience had taught the surgeon that nothing the Pathans did was without a distinct purpose. "Has Jehan Khan any score against you, Kent?"

The other shrugged and shook his head. Gerald's lips tightened at a sudden thought. "Has the Pathan ever threatened your wife?"

Again the hard smile came to the lips of Kent. "Ethel pretends to like the rascals that you dote on. She rides alone in the upper gorges, in spite of my warning —"

The smouldering light of suspicion was in his eyes as he watched Gerald stride away and heard him call quickly for his horse. When the Daktar Sahib rode out the compound toward Dalgai, Kent overtook him.

"Think I'll go with you," the political agent grunted, "as far as Dalgai."

"That would be best."

THEY pelted through the mud, heedless of the rain, and at the Kent bungalow in the cantonment, Gerald's sudden fear was realized. His few visits to the bungalow veranda were treasured up in memory, but this one was to endure in his thoughts so long as he lived. Ethel Kent had disappeared.

She had gone for her usual evening ride, the frightened native butler said. The *mem-sahib* had refused to take her groom. A half hour ago the police riders, sent out to seek her, had returned with the *mem-sahib*'s horse, found lame by the ravine of the Panjkora River.

The Panjkora, Gerald knew, was one of Ethel's favorite haunts. He had met her there once and warned her it opened into the brigand's preserves.

The river? He knew Ethel was unhappy in her marriage with Kent. But she would not —

"Jehan Khan has carried her off," he said to Kent, who was staring at him blankly.

"The thieving dog! By God, he'll know a thing or two when I've finished with him. I'll take a company of my men, surround his eyrie —"

"Won't do, you know, Kent. You couldn't find it without guides; the Pathans would snipe off your fellows, and, don't you see, man, Jehan Khan holds your wife hostage?" Gerald unbuckled his belt, wrapped it around his revolver and holster and handed it to the trembling butler. "I fancy I'll have to accept Jehan Khan's invitation, on his own terms."

Kent started. He had forgotten the note.

"He said," Gerald summed up, "to come alone and on foot. We'll ride our horses as far as the Panjkora trail and send 'em back by one of your men. That is, if you are coming." He looked at the other squarely. "If you and Jehan Khan have any score to settle between you it would be better for me to go alone —"

A low laugh in the darkness answered him. Nor did Kent see fit to discard his revolver as he spurred forward.

At the cantonment entrance a shadow rose from the roadside and began to trot beside the two horses. The shadow was that of a tall Pathan in dripping finery, a long *jezail* over his shoulder. This did not surprise Gerald.

The Daktar Sahib was meditating on the strange turn of events. An hour since, secure among the police troopers of Rawal Pindi, an influential political officer had laughed at a Pathan's *chit*.

Now this same officer was hastening — in a gnawing rage and armed, but nevertheless hastening — to obey the summons of the Pathan.

JEHAN KHAN'S name signified the Lord of the World. A pretentious title, considering that Jehan Khan's domain consisted of as much hillside as he had been able to wrest from neighboring tribes who were his foes — and the Tower.

That was the secret of Jehan Khan's power. Jehan Khan had won it in a hand-to-hand scrimmage with another chief who had been tumbled headlong to his death in the Panjkora. The Tower was ideally situated for an execution, and was inaccessible except to his own men, impregnable, and invisible.

You see, Jehan Khan was a philosopher. In the small Koran that hung from his bull neck he had written two prayers — that he would never miss his aim, and that he would never allow a wrong to go unpunished.

Gerald, who had met the Pathan chief, considered that the Lord of the World had two redeeming traits. He reverenced his aged father; he kept his word. He was of course a most gifted liar, but when he made a promise he kept it. Witness, the coming of Arthur Kent to the Tower.

WHEN the shadow of the Panjkora gorge closed in on them their Pathan guides made known that the two sahibs must dismount and send back their two horses.

Kent demurred, but Gerald dismounted and set the example of cutting his mount with a blow of the riding-crop. When the horses had disappeared, galloping homeward, the Pathans produced from somewhere two shaggy, miniature ponies and the white men mounted and carried on.

"You would better," suggested Gerald, who had been pondering the episode of the ponies versus their own mounts — nothing that a Pathan did would be without good reason — "rid yourself of that revolver. It might make more trouble for us."

"Not much," growled the burly political agent. "I may use it, and if I do it would be trouble for Jehan Khan, not for us."

Gerald said no more. He wished mildly to point out that the Pathan held Ethel Kent, beyond a doubt, and that the safety of Ethel Kent must be gained by mutual terms, not by weapon-play. And the safety of the woman was the one thing that mattered.

For this reason Gerald had discarded his own revolver. But Kent had a perfect right to keep his side-arms.

The political agent had the knack of shooting from the hip. He could, in this fashion, perhaps shoot more quickly than could Jehan Khan. But not more accurately.

Their ponies were threading up along a cliff path as broad as the extended arms of a man at the widest point. Afoot, or on plains-bred horse-flesh, they might slip on the damp stones and fall a thousand feet or so into the Panjkora in flood.

It was useless, Gerald found, to try to piece out the turns and twists of the way. The rain had ceased, but the cloud banks shrouded the moon, and the brisk wind that whipped at them seemed to come from every quarter of the compass.

They ascended, in time, beyond the timber line. The clouds enveloped them as their horses edged over a crescent-shaped rock bridge that gave the illusion of swaying above a limitless abyss. A stone was detached from the bridge and Gerald listened for its impact below in vain.

Gerald remembered that he had seen Ethel Kent once in the lower valley — a trim figure, hatless, her gray eyes intent on the hills that rose over the ravine like the buttresses of heaven itself. A flush under her eyes had told Gerald that she had been crying. He would have given an arm to have spared her that.

This love he had guarded rigorously from Ethel's eyes and the eyes of the world. She was another man's wife.

He wondered why she had come back to the spot. They had exchanged only a few words. She had smiled, wistfully as a child.

Here Gerald struck viciously at his boot and his horse shivered.

"Sahib," growled a voice, "for the love of God, take care. Not a

year ago a man fell to his death from here, a holy man."

As the voice of the Pathan reached him there was a glimmer of veiled lightning and Gerald caught a glimpse of a *mazar*, a native shrine, close to the path on the near side. It was nothing but a heap of rocks ornamented with rags stuck on sticks planted in the rocks. On an outcropping of rock it overlooked the path, where, on the off-side, was a sheer drop.

Gerald saw, at the same time, the dark face of Kent peering at him. Then they passed around a bend in the cliff and halted. Gerald wondered whether his horse had been startled by the blow of the whip or whether there was an aspect of the supernatural about the spot.

He wondered, because he himself had had a distinct prescience of death at that moment, and Gerald's imagination was not usually sensitive to such impressions.

On foot again, they were led up a stony incline, passed by a sentry who challenged them in the darkness, and lifted to the shoulders of their guides. Ascending through what seemed to be a dense tamarisk thicket, they were hoisted into the aperture of a black structure that loomed abruptly out of the clouds.

"Long life to my guests!" said the Lord of the World, and he laughed as he said it. "Hast thou no fear?"

A torch revealed him to Gerald, a man broad of girth, his shoulders too big for his soiled coat. Yet the face under the gray turban was lean and hawk-like, and the fine, dark eyes were eloquent and unreadable as an animal's eyes.

What Kent noticed especially was the bandolier of cartridges over the bandit's shoulder, the heavy revolver in his belt.

"Where is thy father?" he responded in fluent Turki, scanning the array of bearded faces that clustered in the shadows of the castle hall behind the Lord of the World, "And where is the *memsahib*, my wife?"

Although the Pathan still smiled, his thin nostrils quivered.

"My venerable father," he explained, "is dead of the bite of a mad dog. The woman is here!" He motioned the two toward a room opening into the stone-flagged hall. "The *meiman khanwn*, my guest room."

It was a place that Jehan Khan had, or fancied he had, fitted up in the manner of Europeans. Three-legged chairs stood about in the most inconvenient places imaginable; a photograph of Colonel Younghusband, a bullet hole marking one eye, hung against the cheap print paper.

From the sofa under the portrait Ethel Kent rose, and her beauty was like a flower in the hideousness of the room.

"Captain Gerald!" she cried. She was tucking a strand of the bronze hair into place, and she smiled at the two men. Ethel must have expected her husband's coming, and the arrival of the Daktar Sahib surprised her.

He had noticed that she limped, and he kneeled to touch the stockinged ankle from which the riding boot had been removed.

"Not a bad sprain," she answered his unspoken question. "I merely wrenched my ankle when my horse threw me; I was riding near the mouth of the Panjkora ravine. But I could not walk and Jimmy, my horse, was lame too, poor fellow. The Pathans rode up then and made me come up here on one of their ponies."

"Didn't you offer them money to bring you back to our lines?" Kent demanded.

"They wouldn't. I can only speak a few words of Hindustani,

and when I said that you would be angry and the policemen would punish them they only laughed."

Gerald, who had assured himself that the woman's hurt was no more serious than she had stated, turned in time to check the outburst that Kent was ready to launch upon their host. The taciturn Daktar Sahib had been thinking.

The messages from Jehan Khan had reached the club at Rawal Pindi in less than two hours after the seizure of Mrs. Kent. It was not accident that had brought the Pathan and his men on the scene. They must have been watching from one of the lookouts on the mountain slopes. Jehan Khan had prepared the messages before he had shown himself to Ethel Kent.

"Is this thy hospitality?" he rated the Pathan soundly. "A cold room for thy guests and no food offered?"

Jehan Khan seemed abashed. Under his directions a supper of cold mutton and *chuppaties* was brought, and a smoking blaze ignited in the brazier by the sofa. This done, Gerald asked him to order his followers from the room.

"Wilt thou share with us, Jehan Khan," he inquired, "the *chota hazri*?" (the little breakfast).

With a glance at Kent, the Pathan shook his head, his fingers playing with the thick mesh of his beard the while.

"Nay, my Daktar Sahib, the honor is too great."

At this Kent scowled and burst into long pent-up speech. "Dog and thief, dare ye hold the *memsahib* captive? Release us at once, and provide horses. Then come to the *Sirkar* to beg forgiveness for thy crimes, or thou wilt be thrown from the Tower to the vultures."

The Pathan's face darkened at the insult. It is not well to call a Moslem of rank a dog. His smile vanished in a trice and his eyes became hot coals. "I dare, *Sahib*!" Then he made a gesture as if putting aside an unpleasant thought. "Are any crimes written under my name in the book of the *Sirkar*? Nay. As for the *memsahib*, I knew not her speech and did but carry her to shelter for the night. Is that a crime?"

"Thou liest. The message written by thee proves it." Kent's anger beat impotently against the iron restraint of the native. "Thou hast a price; name it."

Jehan Khan smiled again. "A price for what?"

"My — our release."

"Has anyone said that thou and the other sahib and thy wife are not free to go?"

Kent was nonplussed. He had believed that the Pathan was holding Ethel for a heavy ransom, and had sent to Gerald and himself to arrange terms. He had come, with Gerald, because of the suspicions taking shape in his mind against the other.

"Thy message — " he repeated.

"It was to summon thee, Kent Sahib. Is the woman not thy wife? For whom should I have sent?" Jehan Khan enjoyed to the full the bewilderment of the massive white man. "Yet, since thou hast said it, I will take a small price for my pains as a make-weight." On the last word he hesitated briefly.

"Ah."

"A very small price: two thousand rupees."

"How much?" The exclamation broke from Gerald, who was frankly astonished. Two thousand rupees was barely the price of three reasonably good polo ponies.

"As I have said, rupees, two thousand. It will be a make-weight."

Jehan Khan repeated his words, and assented to Kent's swiftly framed conditions. The three visitors — as he insisted on calling them — were to be allowed to depart from the castle the next day; horses were to be provided; they were not to be followed.

"Good!" Kent closed the bargain, and felt in his pockets. He and Gerald had both come without such a sum on their persons. "I will give thee a signed note for the money." His bluster returned, under assurance that Jehan Khan would not dare molest them. "Well for thee, Pathan, that thou dost obey me. Otherwise, this." He tapped the butt of his revolver.

Long and curiously the Lord of the World looked at the white man and his weapon, as if trying to read the thoughts of a child. His black eyes under heavy brows were wolfish. Clapping his hands loudly he summoned a native and ordered writing materials brought.

When the brief promissory note was written he checked Kent when the latter was about to sign.

"The Daktar Sahib," he explained softly, "will write his name alone. Thus and not otherwise will I know the *chit* will be honored."

This was his way of returning Kent's compliment of a moment ago. A Pathan never lets an insult pass unanswered. Tucking the paper into his girdle he bowed and retired.

"His price was cheap enough," grunted Kent, who had flushed. There were certain gambling debts for which he had signed notes at the club — notes still unhonored. "Why did you ask that scoundrel to breakfast with us?"

Receiving no answer Kent sat down and attacked the mutton cutlets vigorously. He flattered himself he had handled the situation well. To tell the truth he was rather relieved. There had been something spooky about their trip to the tower hidden among the clouds, and Jehan Khan's eyes . . . Had he seen those eyes before? Well, the beggar knew his place now.

"Is there danger?" Ethel broke the silence in which she had been studying Gerald's grave face.

"We're quite all right," snapped her husband. "You'll keep your infernal rides within our lines, I expect, after this." It was her fault, he considered, that he would have to pay Gerald the hundred and thirty pounds when they reached Dalgai. And Ethel had had no money for some time. "What's the matter, Gerald? You look like the skeleton at the feast I mentioned at the club. Haven't you an appetite?"

"No, thanks." Gerald nodded reassuringly to Ethel. "Now, you must sleep. I'll chat a while with the Pathan."

He was thinking that, according to the Pathan code, if Jehan Khan had shared bread and salt with them, they would have been safe in his hands. But Jehan Khan had refused. Gerald knew that danger threatened one of them.

SOMEWHERE a wind sprang up in the precipices of the Hindu Kush. The snow peaks changed from black to gray to blood color.

The wind added its whisper to the mutter of the Panjkora. A great bird, hovering against the blue of the morning sky, seemed to be trying to peer down into the blackness of the Panjkora ravine.

A slender girl in a tattered shawl rode an ox from the huts of the village to the spring. Dogs barked.

Heedless of the cold of dawn, the Lord of the World sat cross-legged on the summit of his tower, caressing the stem of a hubble-bubble pipe. Gerald, also, paid no attention to the chill wind, save to thrust his hands instinctively into the pocket of his drill coat. He was noticing how, over the rocky eminence on which a native stood sentry, the shrine beside the trail was taking shape. It had not occurred to him before that the shrine could be seen from the tower-top, which was all but invisible from the trail.

Patiently he had been working to make the Pathan talk. His last speech had accomplished his purpose, which was to plumb the depths of hatred in the other's soul. "Thou dost not make war upon a woman, Jehan Khan," he had said. "Yet thou didst watch for her coming to the gorge."

A direct question, he knew, would have been answered only by silence or an elusive lie. The Lord of the World puffed at the bubbling water-pipe and did not look up. "True," he acknowledged finally. "For a year have I watched the comings of the *memsahib*, the time when I could bear her here. As thou hast said, she will suffer no hurt."

So, Ethel was not the one. Gerald stifled a sigh of relief and waited. Silence, the patience of the white man, wrought upon Jehan Khan to give voice to the thoughts that had preyed upon him for a year.

"Hear, then, this tale, my sahib. Thou knowest I had a father who was the morsel of my life and a piece of my liver. Until misfortune came upon him and he was afflicted — aye, he was the drop of water that came to me from the river of God's mercy." Jehan Khan's handsome face was reflective, even gentle. And Gerald knew that he was telling the truth.

"When he was afflicted, my father prayed often at the shrine below," pointing to the heap of stones and the rags that lifted in the wind. "One day, for he knew well the way, he walked there alone with his staff. A rider, sahib, was coming up the trail and when my father did not run back the man struck him. An evil blow. It was only with the whip — a heavy whip — yet it caused him who was the life of my eyes to fall, and my father fell — outward."

The Pathan waved his hand over the ravine. "My father was blind. For two years he had not been able to see the way before his feet."

Gerald bit his lip, and waited. "Sahib, my father could not see to get out of the way of the horse. And the rider of the horse was Kent Sahib."

No longer did Jehan Khan blow on the ashes of the hubble-bubble. His eyes were like embers blown into life by a passing gust of wind. Gerald walked to the rampart of the tower. He was thinking of the Moslem law, a life for a life.

When Kent had knocked the native over the cliff, he had taken care to wheel his horse and ride back quickly to the cantonment. He had not noticed that the tower overlooked the site of the shrine. So he had not seen that he was observed, and he could not have known that the native was Jehan Khan's father. In fact Kent had painted the episode, in his version at the club, in colors that made it seem a brave piece of work on his part.

No matter. The death of the old hillman lay at Kent's door. Jehan Khan had taken up the pursuit of blood. Not all the gold in India would pay for the wrong. Probably Kent had not known that the old Pathan was blind. No matter.

The debt must be paid, and not with money. Jehan Khan would exact a life as payment. Gerald had no longer any doubt on whom the vengeance would fall.

"So," he said swiftly, "thou wouldst slay the sahib, when you have taken his money for his release?"

The shadow of a smile passed over the bearded lips of the Pathan.

"Did I say that? Nay, Kent Sahib is free to ride hence."

Gerald glanced over the plateau behind the tower, where a cluster of huts, fronting the pasture that nestled against a sheer wall of rock rising overhead a thousand feet or so. There was no way out of the domain of Jehan Khan except by the shrine and the trail up which they had come. This was guarded.

Even if they could overcome or steal by the guards they could not hope to escape, with Ethel lame. And they had no horses. Gerald perceived at once that flight was useless.

He reflected that Jehan Khan had not promised that Kent would reach the border alive. The Pathan's acceptance of the money might mean anything — dulling Kent's suspicions, for one. And his tale of a moment ago merely signified that he was so sure of his vengeance that he could afford to make known to the two white men the cause of it.

The vengeance would be all the sweeter, Gerald knew, if Kent was aware of its coming. No bribe could alter the Pathan's purpose. The political agent was doomed as surely as if a Christian court had sentenced him to be hanged.

And Ethel? Gerald went hot, then cold. Alone, the two men might have made a fight of it. Now that was impossible. If she and her husband were to be saved it must be done another way.

"Let the woman and Kent Sahib go unharmed," offered Gerald, "and let thy vengeance be upon me. I will remain. I am the friend of the man. Thou art a bazaar-born thief and a murderer."

Jehan Khan laughed deep in his throat. "A brave man thou, but a fool. The beauty of the woman holds thee — not I. I have seen it."

"Then," cried the Daktar Sahib, "why didst thou summon me here?"

A direct question, that, and useless.

"Perhaps, Sahib, to witness what is to come to pass this day."

"And that?"

From below the tower came the low voices of men at prayer. Gerald heard the *Allah-Akbar* chant that is the dawn prayer of the Moslems.

"God is great," echoed Jehan Khan sententiously and that was all he would say. Gerald went to the door of the guest room.

Ethel came to the door and closed it behind her. She had heard his step.

"My husband is asleep," she said. "But I could not sleep. What did Jehan Khan say?"

Instinct told her that Gerald was not assured of their safety. He put aside her question by leading her to an embrasure in the tower wall overlooking the gorge. Sunlight flooded in on her, and the rarefied air brought a flush to her cheeks. The never-ceasing wind whipped strands of brown hair about her forehead.

"Oh!" she cried, her eyes resting on the splendor of crimson and blue. Their hands touched and Gerald's fingers closed on hers. She looked up at him swiftly.

Gerald's boyish face was alight, its mask of gravity gone. His eyes clung to hers, saw her cheeks whiten, and read the love that Ethel had hidden from him.

He could feel the pulse in her fingers that answered his own. He checked the whispered words that sprang to his lips and looked away. She must have known that he loved her. She did not withdraw her fingers.

Gerald had only to keep silence, do nothing, say nothing to Kent and the man would be slain, without a breath of blame to him. But that could not be.

Kent, unable to save himself, must be saved by Gerald. The Daktar Sahib had already decided that, and how it was to be done. He would have to risk his life in the other's stead. A life for a life, was the Moslems' toll.

But the knowledge that Ethel cared for him quickened every fibre in him, and the Tower became a paradise, soon to be lost, but a paradise of the gods.

"YOU see, the beggar could pot you on the return journey from a dozen places. He might even wait until we're out of the gorge, where he has an outlook over the spot where Ethel's horse fell lame, you know. Evidently he counts on me as a kind of witness on his behalf that no harm came to you at the Tower. And the business of the money payment as a make-weight was to provide evidence that he didn't intend to murder you. You see the crafty old chap even had me sign the *chit*, so that he could collect payment afterward."

They were seated on a tangle of rocks and thorn bushes, overlooking the pasture where Jehan Khan's followers were selecting horses for their departure. Gerald was finishing a cigarette with relish, but Kent's cigar was cold in his fingers.

The bluster had gone from the political agent. Although it was fairly cold in the garden of the Tower, his face and hands were damp with sweat. Gerald's account of what the Pathan had told had shattered Kent's optimism.

He knew what it meant when a Pathan took up the pursuit of blood. Jehan Khan was squatted a score of paces away, apparently oblivious of them but actually intent on the fear that had transfigured Kent's face.

The hand of the political agent stole toward his revolver and then dropped to his side. From the corner of his eye he had seen a rifle muzzle raised from behind a boulder.

There would never be a chance to draw his weapon. Gerald had noticed his action.

"It won't do," he pointed out, "on Ethel's account. You'll take care of her — eh — after you and she get free?"

It was as much of an appeal as he could bring himself to make to Kent. The man at his side nodded. Ethel was then looking at the ponies. He could hear her singing, under her breath, actually singing. Of course Gerald had said nothing to her about the danger, but it annoyed Kent that she seemed so light-hearted.

Why, even then, the confounded Pathan was plotting his death. He did not see why Gerald had deliberately delayed their departure until late afternoon, almost evening. True, the other had explained that darkness would cover their flight. But — the delay was torment. Neither of them could guess what form Jehan Khan's vengeance was to take.

The natives, too, had gathered on rising ground overlooking the trail down which they must ride. They were sitting in the rear of the Tower, where a steep grassy slope led down from the pasture to the Panjkora path at the edge of the cliff, the path that disappeared around the bend behind which was the shrine.

"They're coming to look at me. What is the devil thinking of?" he cried.

"We can't tell." Gerald shook his head. "We'll act first."

The cigar dropped from Kent's quivering fingers. He had seen for the first time the eyes of Jehan Khan, stripped of the mask of good-humor, and they were like the blind eyes of the old Pathan he had killed.

And with that glance Kent's nerve forsook him. There was no outward sign of this, except an involuntary quivering of the lips, and the silence that held him.

But Jehan Khan, who missed nothing, saw Kent's eyes wander uncontrollably over the hillside and the precipice seeking vainly some way of escape from the hidden menace that would threaten him before nightfall. It was already the hour of sunset.

"Time," observed Gerald, tossing away the cigarette. Edith was safely mounted on a pony. "Remember, Kent, when I make a move, ride for it. Take Ethel's rein and be sure that she goes around the turn ahead of you, because there will be no passing each other on the trail and you have the revolver. The sentries on the rocks have come down into the crowd."

He rose, drawing the other man with him, and moved toward Jehan Khan.

"Once around the bend," his whisper continued, "you'll be safe."

But Kent's stare was glassy. In his mind he could see the face of the old man who had fallen from the cliff.

He moved mechanically to the horses, and with a sudden, jerky motion, took the rein of a docile pony that Jehan Khan himself brought forward. The Pathan's followers stood aloof on the hillside, well back from the slope that led down to the trail at the cliff's edge.

"Looks like a cricket match, eh?" Gerald observed to Ethel who was watching him with strained interest, a frown on her smooth brow. "Or rather, I should say, the crowd at a Derby —"

He had drawn near to Jehan Khan, when Kent, without warning, made his spring into the saddle of the waiting pony. The political agent clapped heels to the flanks of the startled animal. Jerking its head around, the man urged it into an uneven trot down the slope away from them.

Kent had given way to panic.

But Gerald, at the instant the other acted, proceeded to carry out his part of the plan they had agreed upon. A quick thrust of his foot sent the rifle upon which Jehan Khan had been leaning out of reach. Gerald's left arm passed between the Pathan's elbow and body.

Jehan Khan was held firmly, his back to Gerald. And the right hand of the Daktar Sahib plucked the revolver from the other's girdle, thrusting its muzzle under the Pathan's shoulder-blade over the heart.

"Stand where you are," Gerald cried in Turki, at the staring natives, "and do not lift a weapon, or Jehan Khan dies." Over his shoulder he added in English, "Ride for it, Kent. Let Ethel — For God's sake, Ethel, *ride!*"

For the first time he perceived that the other had fled without thought of the woman. And that Ethel had not moved. He could hear the hoof-beat of Kent's horse receding down the slope.

"Do not move," he said grimly to Jehan Khan, and to Ethel,

"The way is clear, now. I'll hold the Pathan hostage for a while, you know. Follow your husband."

Ethel, however, did not stir. It was not that she was bewildered or afraid. She was an expert horsewoman, and the way, as Gerald said, was open for a space. The Pathans, taken by surprise and temporarily leaderless, would be some time in cutting off the retreat down the cliff trail.

They could not shoot Gerald; he was too close to their chief. If they came nearer, Jehan Khan would be shot. The Pathan, in fact, was strangely quiet as if listening for something he had not as yet heard.

"I'm going to stay right here," said Ethel suddenly, a little break in her voice.

Gerald groaned under his breath. He had taken pains not to have her know the danger that threatened Kent. It had never entered his thoughts that Kent would leave her, or that she would not obey orders to seek safety with her husband; that she would choose, instead, to share Gerald's fate.

He had not taken into account the heart of the woman.

And then they both were voiceless. A scream had cut into the silence of the ravine, a scream that came from the bend of the trail around which Kent had vanished alone.

Ethel put her hand to her throat to stifle a cry. They could no longer hear the hoofs of Kent's pony.

Twisting around, and drawing Jehan Kahn with him, Gerald strained his eyes on a patch of the path that was visible beyond the shrine. The shrine itself and the turn of the trail were hidden from view. Minutes passed, and Kent did not appear on the patch of the cliff path.

The twilight of the hills was deepening rapidly into night. Silence held the watchers by the Tower. Gerald knew at last that Kent would not appear again to them. The man had cried out when he was abreast of the shrine.

Had his horse been startled by something at the shrine? Had Kent's fear overmastered him? Had the spirit of the dead Pathan confronted horse and rider? Gerald's thoughts were wildly futile.

"Sahib," the voice of Jehan Khan came to him, "thou art a brave man, but a fool. The thing that I foretold has come to pass and now there is no danger for thee or the *mem-sahib*."

It was not his speech or the gathering darkness that made Gerald release him. Ethel Kent had swayed in the saddle in a faint. Gerald caught her as she was falling, and faced the Pathans with the drawn, revolver. But Jehan Khan continued passive as before.

DURING the hours of early night Gerald rode down to the cantonments, a mute, frightened woman clinging to the comfort of his arms. The Pathans guided him as far as the end of the gorge. He saw no trace of Kent.

When Ethel had been left at her bungalow in the care of the women of the station, Gerald changed to a fresh horse and collected a party of white men to return to the Panjkora. Kent, he learned, had not been seen in Dalgai.

Kent's body lay, as nearly as Gerald could determine, directly under the Tower and the shrine of Jehan Khan. Beside the body was the pony, crushed by the fall to the rocks.

The night was far spent, and Gerald was swaying on his horse from weariness when they found what they sought on the rocks at the bottom of the gorge by the edge of the mountain torrent.

"How did it happen?" Gerald was asked.

He shook his head, inspecting by the light of a lantern the two forms that bore no sign of a bullet or any injury other than the fall. Kent's face was set, ghastly. Gerald covered it with a blanket and gazed long at the pony's head. He bent close to search the curiously pallid eyes of the beast that Jehan Khan had brought for Kent to ride.

He had seen such eyes in horses before. But this one was dead, and there was no proof of the thought that had come to him.

"The Pathan gave Kent this pony to ride," he said wearily, "this blind pony. It must have trotted over the cliff at the first turn."

Gerald knew that it had been murder, but when he pointed this out to the authorities at Rawal Pindi, they knew and he knew that there was no way of proving in the white man's court that it had not been an accident.

In fact, the Pathan tendered his note at Dalgai, and it was paid. The only thing that the white men could do, they did. When the note had been honored they informed Jehan Khan that his Tower would be taken from him.

The Lord of the World laughed, and a year later when, divested of his stronghold, he was wandering through the hills he was ambushed and shot down by his tribal foes.

But by then Gerald was on leave in America, to seek out the home of Ethel Kent who had returned to her own country, and who was waiting for his coming.

THE STREAM

I must follow the stream that leads
Through the marshes and through the meads.

It, like mine, has a rover soul
In the depths and over the shoal;

Dimpling, and then darting far
Under the sun and under the star.

Now 'mid peace and now 'mid strife
I must follow the stream of life!

—Clinton Scollard

ISLAND FEUD

by Hugh B. Cave

MATT Martinsen's *Witch* was long overdue at Teala Town. When she came at last, with her sails shining white in the South Pacific sunlight, the whole town held its breath.

Tom Trefflan, the shopkeeper, saw me standing on my hotel veranda and came across the road from his establishment, blowing as he climbed the steps. "This is it, John," he said. "The day of reckoning."

Phil Pawley, the Burns Philip agent, hurried up from his office on the pier. "We're about to see history made," he declared. "I can feel it under my ribs."

The three of us turned, as one, to look along the shore toward the house of Doc Harty.

You've never heard the story of Doc Harty's downfall, I expect. It's too big a world. With wars and such hogging the headlines, the little human tragedies go unnoticed. Doc was too young, anyway, to be important.

Full of ambition and the milk of kindness, he came out to the

islands to study beriberi for some medical foundation, and stayed on to work with the natives. For headquarters he chose Fanuwin, a handsome island whose people were a dreary lot, haunted by sickness. They eked out a living, the Fanuwin natives, by growing copra and selling it to Matt Martinsen for a third of its worth.

Doc Harty got rid of the parasites crawling about inside Fanuwin's people and taught them how to stay healthy. A labor of love. During the two years it took him, Martinsen called every three months in the *Witch*. They came to know each other well.

Martinsen's daughter, Ruth, came to know Doc well, too.

She was nineteen, and you had a hard time believing she was the daughter of a hard-bitten trader such as Matt. He was a glum, grim man with quick fists and a ready oath; she a slim, pretty girl with a look of far places in her eye.

An odd business, but no odder than many in the islands. The girl's mother had died when Ruth was young, and the child was brought up by an aunt in Sydney until old enough to know her mind. Back she went to Matt then, to keep his books and help with the work.

But at Fanuwin she seldom stayed aboard ship while Matt did his trading. Up the hill she would go to Doc Harty's little hospital, to help Doc with his patients. She should have been a nurse, Doc told her.

There were some on Fanuwin who predicted a wedding. Martinsen, when asked about it, only grunted.

Then . . .

One day Martinsen took his ship into Fanuwin and found no copra sacks on the wharf. To all his questions, the natives simply wagged their heads and pointed to Doc's house on the hill. The trader, his face a thundercloud, stormed up there.

"What's going on?" he demanded.

Doc Harty poured whiskey into two glasses — a ritual when Martinsen called — raised his and grinned. "Matt, you'll have to mend your ways."

"What?"

"You've given these people a rotten deal for years. Now they know the facts of Life. Either you pay the going price for their copra, or I arrange to have someone come here who will."

Martinsen heard but didn't believe. "Say that again," he challenged.

Doc repeated it.

The trader curled his lip and looked Doc up and down. Then, "You meddling young whelp!" he said in a voice he usually saved for his native crew. "I'll have you on your knees!"

"Now, Matt, you know well enough —"

The whiskey glass was in Martinsen's hand. He smashed it on the floor at Doc's feet, wheeled and stormed out of the house. But just beyond the foot of the veranda steps he paused. The inspiration for what happened later must have exploded in his raging soul at that very moment, even before his thinking had properly begun.

There on the hillside path, strolling up from town with a market basket on one shapely hip, was Doc's housekeeper, Loliti. Martinsen halted before her with a leer.

"Well, now, this *is* a pleasure!"

Loliti laughed, tossing her hair.

"To look at you," Martinsen said, "no one would dream you'd buried a husband. Widowhood's becoming to you, lass. Come along to the ship with me for a drink and a bit of talk."

Loliti went. And when the *Witch* departed next day at dawn, she was aboard it.

DOC Harty hadn't a ghost of a chance because, you see, it was Loliti, not Martinsen, who filed the complaint. Martinsen's name never officially entered into it at all. He was too shrewd.

The doctor was a wicked man, Loliti complained. Oh, very. She said this in Suva, in the office of a quite high official to whom the welfare of the natives on such islands as Fanuwin was a matter of gravest concern. She said it with such innocent-seeming grief that the gentleman paid profound attention.

"He made eyes at me from the time he came there," said Loliti, her own eyes brimming with tears. "Of course, I paid no attention. I was faithful to my husband, as anyone on Fanuwin will tell you. But then my husband sickened. He went to the doctor for medicine. And instead of getting better, he died."

"The doctor was kind to me after my husband died," Loliti went on. "He allowed me to be his housekeeper and paid me good wages. In my innocence, I did not know why. And then — ah, then —"

Martinsen must have coached her well in the two weeks she spent with him on the *Witch* between Fanuwin and Suva. Blessed with the lusty imagination common to girls of her sort, she could easily have embellished that portion of her tale beyond all belief and thereby lost her audience. She didn't. Her account was subtly touched with allusions to Doc Harty's "secret drinking." And how was a government desk man in Suva to hear the voice of Martinsen back of her sobs?

"But," said that gentleman, "how do you *know* the doctor caused your husband's death?"

"He told me."

"Told you!"

"When he was drunk one night and angry," said Loliti. "He called me names and said he wished he had never gone to the trouble of getting rid of my husband. I wasn't worth it."

She was questioned, naturally. From the first official she was passed along to a second, third and fourth. Each did his best to find a discordant note in the song she sang. A man of Doctor Harty's standing? Unthinkable! Still, the islands did strange things to some men, and Fanuwin was such a lonely place, so out of touch. In the end they sent for him.

He denied. He explained. Pale of face, seething, he called them fools. But even he, when faced with the girl, could not shake her story in the smallest detail.

It was unfortunate. No formal charge could be placed against him, of course. The girl had no proof. On the other hand, his own angry accusations . . . there, too, the proof was lacking, wasn't it? A mess, the whole affair. Nasty mess.

Big thing was, a man shouldn't get himself involved in these things. They gave the government a bad name. Such a tale traveled — like a tidal wave, actually. And the usefulness of a man with a cloud over his head was limited — ah, yes, limited. Better not go back to Fanuwin. Not just yet. No shortage of men to carry on there. Some other place, perhaps. . . .

Doc Harty didn't wait for them to find some obscure niche for him. He found a place for himself outside their jurisdiction: an island in our group where, he told us later, he thought he might begin again. But he didn't stay long. Knowing where he was, we got off an urgent plea when an outbreak of measles began to wipe out the native population of Teala. So the Doc arrived one day in an outrigger sailing canoe, with his medicines in a wooden chest and became the fourth white resident of our little island community.

He was worth all the rest of us put together. Day and night he labored, dragging us along as his assistants and making us labor, too. The measles were stopped. Doc, like us, stayed on.

Only once was the affair at Fanuwin mentioned. We were building Doc a house by the beach and Trefflan, glancing seaward, saw a fishing boat in the reef passage. "Doc," he said, "one day you'll look out there and see the *Witch* coming in. Martinsen calls every few months for coconuts. What will you do?"

Doc gazed at the fishing boat in silence for a moment. "We'll have rain if this wind doesn't shift," he said.

But among ourselves we speculated. "I know what I'd do,"

Pawley said. "I'd beat the dog to a pulp!" Amusing, this, from Pawley. He stood a shade over five feet and never stepped out of doors in a high wind.

"I think I'd put a gun to his head and make him sign a confession," vowed Trefflan. "And if he refused, I'd blow his brains out."

None of our business, you say? Agreed. But we knew what Martinsen was up to. A letter would come for Pawley from some storekeeper friend in the Solomons: "Dear Ned: Odd what you say about your Doctor Harty and the good he's done. Martinsen, the trader, was here only last month and *he* said . . ."

One would come for me from a hotel man in the Pandemonium: "This Harty you speak of — is he the same we have heard about from our friend Martinsen of the *Witch*? I would investigate if I were you. If they are one and the same, you have the worst sort of scoundrel on your hands . . ."

To sum it up, Matt Martinsen had been cruelly and systematically smashing what was left of Doc's reputation as he went his rounds. And people believed him. Even his daughter believed him.

Thus I had an idea we would not see Martinsen's *Witch* at Teala again. But I was wrong.

When she dropped anchor, I turned to Pawley and Trefflan. "Do you suppose Matt *knows* the Doc is here?" I said.

"He must," said Pawley. "Then he can't be afraid —"

"Give the devil his due. He's afraid of nothing."

Our pier hadn't depth enough for a ship her size. We watched the native crew lower a dinghy. Suddenly, "There's his girl," Pawley said. "There's Ruth."

"Where's the man himself?" I asked.

"Below in the cuddy, perhaps. Loading his revolver."

The dinghy didn't wait for Martinsen to load his gun, if that was what detained him. The girl dropped into it with her bright hair blowing in the sunlight, and the little boat made for the pin.

I glanced at Trefflan and Pawley, and we went trooping down the road.

Ruth knew us, of course. She'd been to Teala before, many a time. When I gave her a hand up to the pier she thanked me with a smile, then, facing the three of us, said thickly, "Doctor Harty is here, isn't he?"

"He's here," I said.

"I must see him. My father is ill."

"What's the matter with him?" Pawley asked.

But Ruth was not one to waste time in talk. "Where is he?" she said, catching hold of my hand. "Take me to him!"

It was just after ten in the morning and Doc's yard was full of natives awaiting their turn. When I walked in with Ruth in tow, he glanced up from a job he was doing on the big toe of a wide-eyed youngster.

Doc's eyes were suddenly as wide as those of his patient.

"Ruth!" he said, staring. Whether he saw the ghost of a dead dream or the daughter of a despised enemy. I can't say.

Ruth went straight up to him. "Fred," she said. "I need your help."

"What is it? One of the crew?"

"Not one of the crew. My father."

A line of crimson crept up Doc's face. "Your father!" he said in a whisper.

"He didn't want me to come to you," the girl said. "But he's desperately ill. A hatch cover fell on his leg, days ago."

Doc took in a breath and bent to his patient again. I couldn't see his face, but I did see him stop work once to steady his hands. Done at last, he sent the boy on his way with a friendly backside slap, then thrust some things into a bag, and, facing Ruth again, informed her with a grim nod that he was ready.

MARTINSEN lay in his bunk, his once ruddy face gray and shrunken, his eyes dull with pain. But there was defiance still, in his stare.

Without a word Doc drew back the covers and knelt to peel the layers of bandage from the leg. It was the size of an elephant's leg and pretty much the same shade of gray. He squeezed it, and the grayness turned fish-belly white.

"I can't help you," Doc said, his examination finished.

Martinsen reared up on his elbows. "Of course you can help me! You're the best doctor in the islands!"

"The best in the world couldn't save you."

Martinsen's gaze filled with desperation. "I can pay whatever you ask."

"Can you?"

"Anything! A statement of truth from Loliti — that's what you want, isn't it? To clear your name. I'll get it, I swear!"

It was an odd way for sworn enemies to face each other, one erect on sound legs, the other propped on his elbows in a pool of sweat. They did it, though; Martinsen pleading, Doc Harty pinning him to the bunk with a look of hate.

"All right," Doc said then. "I'll cure you. I can't, but I will."

YOU'D say it was a miracle, I suppose. By every rule in the book, Martinsen should have died.

He didn't. He lived, and the leg lived with him. In three weeks the man was out of his bunk. In a fortnight more he was ashore, taking a daily constitutional about Teala Town to build himself up.

You think the man was grateful? Secretly he might have been, but not a hint of it ever passed his lips.

To Doc, who stopped daily to examine him, he would mutter blackly, "How much longer am I to stay penned up here in this mouse hole? Is this your revenge? I'm well, I tell you!"

"Not well enough," Doc would say.

The odd thing was that Martinsen did as the Doc told him. Despising the town, hating the hotel he lived in, mistrusting the lot of us so sorely he wouldn't permit his daughter to quit the ship and join him, he nevertheless stayed on. Even when the last, lingering twinge had left the leg and he was able to bound up and down my veranda steps at will.

"Why in heaven's name don't you give him his walking papers?" I demanded of Doc, when it seemed I was cursed with the man for all eternity. "If you had to live under the same roof with him, you'd say the word soon enough!"

"A little longer," he replied.

So Martinsen stayed, thriving on the good food and care until he was a picture of health. And what of his promise, that he would obtain a statement from Loliti to clear Doc's name? Not a word was spoken of it, except by the rest of us.

"He won't go through with it," predicted Trefflan. "He never meant to."

"He'll laugh in Doc's face," said Pawley. "Mark my words."

I thought they were right. And the waiting went on. Until . . .

Late one afternoon Doc came to the hotel. "I've sent word to your daughter on the ship," he said, "that you can pack your bag tonight. She'll be on her way here now, to lend you a hand. Mr. Martinsen, how are you feeling?"

"Right as rain," said Martinsen.

"Good. Then it's time we kept our promises — the one you made to me and the one I made to myself."

Martinsen, interrupted at a game of solitaire on the veranda, must have expected something of the sort, but even so he needed a moment to gird himself. With the utmost deliberation he turned another card and examined it. Then, "Promise?" he said softly, with an upward glance. "Why, of course. A statement from that housekeeper of yours — that's what we agreed on, isn't it? But such a thing will take time."

"I don't want a statement from the girl," Doc said. "I want one from you."

Well! Over Martinsen's round and ruddy face spread a look of such genuine incredulity as to lay bare the man's soul.

It was a lecture, that look. Plain as day it said, *Now see here: a statement from a no-account serving girl is one thing, and perhaps I'd have gone to the bother of getting it for you if an opportunity turned up. But a statement from Matt Martinsen . . . What a laugh!*

The trader laughed.

"You refuse?" Doc said quietly.

"You're out of your mind!" returned Martinsen gruffly. "I didn't file the complaint against you; the girl did. What kind of fool do you take me for?"

"A healthy one, at least," Doc said. "I've made certain of that. So —"

Say this for Martinsen: he was no man to run from a fight. He rose to meet this one with a crooked grin, and began in the age-old tradition by upending the table against his adversary's legs. And having staggered Doc with his initial thrust, he quickly pursued his advantage. In the twinkling of an eye, with a knee in his groin and an elbow under his ribs, Doc was against the rail, white of face and gasping.

But the lightning jab was not enough. Doc recovered and threw him off, and then back and forth they went, locked in a contest as primitive as an island legend. The flimsy floor heaved under them like a sea in storm. The hotel seemed likely to topple about their heads.

I hold no brief for the philosopher who says right makes might. Before our anxious eyes, first one and then the other had the upper hand. Up and down the veranda they fought, on the steps, in the dust of the road. It was either man's battle until the end.

In the end, toe to toe in the roadway, they battered each other with leaden fists until one went down and stayed. The one to go was Martinsen.

Doc Harty looked to us for help and we carried the man to a chair. And once more Doc stood before him, this time in triumph with pen and paper on the table.

"Write," said Doc.

Martinsen slowly raised a battered face. "No."

"Write, I tell you! A confession that you put Loliti up to it!"

"Why should I?" the trader retorted. "You've thrashed me. But to get a confession you'll have to hold a gun at my head and threaten to use it — and you're not the sort to make such an act convincing." Wearily he stood up, and the puffed lips turned a grin. "Go to blazes," he said amiably. So much for the philosophers!

Doc Harty stood silent. What could he do? What could any man do, short of murder? He lifted his hands and looked, puzzled, at the skinned knuckles, let them fall again and turned away. Down the steps he went. Across the road.

Martinsen, with a laugh, turned to go upstairs. And there by the staircase, awaiting him, stood his daughter.

She had come in the back way to avoid the storm on the veranda, I suppose. No matter; she had been there long enough to witness the final act of the drama. That was certain. Hands on hips, she faced him — no longer the young lady raised by a maiden aunt in Sydney, but a true daughter of Matt Martinsen himself. A less groggy Martinsen would have recognized the change and behaved accordingly.

He didn't. "Darlin'!" he cooed, advancing on her. "Run up and pack my things, like a good girl. We're leavin'."

"You're leaving. I'm not," said she, not budging.

He halted. "What did you say?"

"I said you can leave if you wish to, Matt Martinsen. I'm staying!" Tall and straight she faced him, her bright eyes hurling the challenge. "I'm staying here in Teala to marry the man I love!"

Martinsen looked and saw she meant it, and over his face for the second time that evening spread the look of incredulity. "No," he said in a hoarse whisper. "No. . . ."

"He's twice the man you are," she said, driving the knife deep with her deadly calm, "no matter what you've made of him with your lies. And if he won't have me, then I'll sit on his doorstep until the whole world knows I want him."

"I — I won't permit it," Martinsen mumbled.

"Stop me then, if you can," she said, and went past him.

He let her go.

He sat. How long? Trefflan, Pawley and I, we asked one another later how long and could not agree on an answer. How long is forever? With chin on chest and gaze fixed blankly on the floor, he sat, the lamplight dimly registering the mask of defeat that hardened like concrete on his face.

At last he looked at us. "Something to write with," he said. "If you will."

I took him pen and paper.

He wrote. He signed his name and we, as witnesses, signed ours. Rising, he read carefully what was written, then passed the paper to me.

"My wedding present," he said with a sigh. "Give it to them, if you'll be so kind."

Ten minutes later we watched him go down the road with his bag, and when last we saw him he stood on deck, gazing shoreward, as the *Witch* said farewell to Teala for the final time.

THE MAN WHO COULDN'T DIE
by HUGH B. CAVE

THE route by which Mr. Weldon Witherby arrived at Fortune Island is, to say the least, rather obscure.

He began, apparently, in Rangoon, where in some minor political post he was viewed with at least a measure of respect. What happened to him there — a woman, perhaps, or a letter from home, or the shattering of his aspirations by some bit of official chicanery — need not have been a tremendous thing. Some men are so constituted that a mere shift in the direction of a light breeze will bowl them over.

At any rate, he left Rangoon quite suddenly and appeared some months later in Darvel Bay, which is Borneo, calling himself Whitby — until an exchange of solemn letters between government officials turned the black light of his past upon him and sent him on his way again.

He paused in Balikpapan, but rebelled at the taste of petroleum in his evening gin. He bobbed up in Celebes, across the Straat Makassar, to make his way afoot from Manado to Baoe-baoe — a remarkable achievement for one without a guilder in his pocket or even a decent pocket to put one in. And then, like a lemming plunging headlong into the sea, he vanished.

Many hungerings later, this sad little man turned up in Dili, dead drunk and three-quarters starved. At that stage of his journey his pace had slowed to something less than a crawl and the digressions were many.

A year or so later he arrived at Fortune Island aboard a very ancient coastal steamer, in the capacity of assistant to the Chinese proprietor of its 'tween-decks trading store. And he was put ashore because he was ill.

Now you know as much about Weldon Witherby's search for oblivion, and the reason for it, as is known anywhere, and a good deal more than did the four inhabitants of Fortune Island when he arrived in their midst. As a matter of fact, the four were not even aware that their number had been augmented until the steamer which dumped him had departed. For though Fortune is tiny, it happens also to be a mountain-top jutting fanglike from the sea, and at the time of Witherby's coming the four occupants were industriously digging on the far side of the mountain.

They were scratching, stubbornly and angrily, for treasure.

If the truth be known, Witherby had been put ashore on Fortune to die, to save his captain the inconvenience of a burial at sea. He was sick enough to die, and by all logic he should have. But he didn't.

Having slept out the worst of his sickness on the beach, he waked as from the dead to wonder where he was, and at three o'clock of a bright, moon-silvered morning, philosophically rose and walked. He walked until he found a softer bed under the fang of the mountain, and slept again. At dawn he emerged to blink at the sea.

The island looked as though it was uninhabited. Likely it was waterless and all but barren of things to eat. No ship would stop unsignaled, and — this being a region frequented by only the most bohemian of vessels — none was likely to investigate even if signaled. So, decided Witherby, he was marooned.

This settled, he hitched up his trousers and went looking for food. He had long since ceased to be surprised by the things Fate did to him.

H E WAS discovered an hour later when one of the four inhabitants of Fortune, a black-bearded fellow named LeClair, saw him shuffling along the beach. The figure Witherby cut was not impressive. His feet were bare. Tattered khaki trousers and a frayed rag of undershirt were all the clothes he owned.

LeClair watched him for a time in amazement; then the black-bearded fellow hurried to his companions to tell the startling news. They were breakfasting, and the tidings came like a spear hurled into their midst.

"A white man, here?" echoed Morton, spitting out a mouthful of scalding tea. "You gone crazy, Frenchy?"

"It iss the heat and too much of this damn digging," declared Selinger, rocking back on his buttocks. "I haf said all along we should take a rest."

"Rest, be damned," muttered the one called Java Jones, rising high and thin to stand egg-bald in the sunlight. "I'll do my resting at Batavia, thanks, at the Hotel des Indes. Come now, Frenchy, out with it! What're you trying to tell us?"

So LeClair told it again and invited them to go with him.

When Mr. Witherby first saw them he was seated on the beach with a bit of volcanic rock in his fist, leisurely cracking open the last of a handful of clams and mussels. He was not unhappy. He felt better than he had for days. The presence of four white men on his uninhabited island puzzled him, though, and when they lined up before him he greeted them with only a cautious nod.

"Who might you be?" demanded Morton ominously. "And how'd you manage to get here to this Godforsaken spot?"

Witherby explained as best he could.

LeClair eyed him with suspicion. "What d'ye want here?"

"Why, nothing," said Witherby.

"You haf nudding and you want nudding, eh?" said Selinger. "How do you expec' to live, I should like to know, without food or water?"

"Oh, I'll try to get along."

"He's balmy," declared Java Jones. "Let him be. Or toss him to the squid and be done with him."

But Selinger, who had suffered more than the others from the toil and heat of the past weeks, thrust himself forward and planted himself before little Mr. Witherby with arms akimbo and a malignant smile upon his blistered lips. "We haf food and drink' enough to gif you some," said he, "but you will haf to earn it, my friend. You will haf to work!"

Morton did not like that. "Now wait a minute, Dutch. We can't have no stranger nosin' around —"

"He can dig, no? He does not haf to know what we dig for. And he can cook, maybe, and keep clean the camp." Selinger turned to LeClair and Java Jones for their approval, and found them nodding. Again he faced the little man on the rock.

"Well, Mister Widderby, what haf you to say?"

Mr. Witherby looked at them. All four, he observed, were cut from the same cloth, and a coarser weave would be hard to find. Moreover, he knew two of them by reputation, and what he knew was not encouraging.

The bald one, Java Jones, was owner and captain of a decrepit schooner, *Lily* by name, which had uglied the waters of every port from Serang to Samarai. By profession he was a hunter of treasure — all sorts of treasure, from the money-belt on a wreck-imprisoned corpse six fathoms deep to a wench who might fetch a price from the proprietor of some waterfront institution of pleasure.

If Jones' ship had brought them, one thing was certain: These four were on Fortune Island to harvest wealth of some sort.

Mr. Witherby knew Selinger, too, though the Dutchman would have been surprised if so informed. They had met one steaming day in Fakfak, which is a town where two whites, meeting, might be expected to display at least the mutual interest of shipwrecked sailors bumping heads in mid-Pacific. But in Fakfak Mr. Witherby had been penniless and Selinger up to his thick red neck in a scheme to acquire pearls without paying for them — and so the Dutchman's reply to the little man's pitiful plea for assistance had been a rude caress with the back of his hand.

As for LeClair and the one called Morton, Witherby did not know them, even by repute. But if their lots were cast with those of the two he did know, it was safe to assume they were blackguards also.

But could he afford to reject their offer? Supposing he did. For a time, no doubt, he might keep himself alive with shellfish and maintain a moist tongue with almost-fresh water from holes scooped in the sand. But not for long. And these four, if they possessed a camp and provisions, must also own the means of quitting the island when their work was finished.

Mr. Witherby did not relish the prospect of dying alone on a sunbaked needle of rock in the middle of a lonely sea. He chose the lesser evil. "Very well," he decided, "I'll work for my keep."

And thus for Weldon Witherby began an interlude of trial and tribulation unparalleled by anything he had previously lived through.

II

IT WAS apparent from the first that he was not to be accepted by the others as an equal, or even as a fellow human being. He had contracted to pay for his keep with labor, and labor they demanded of him from sun-up until the last bit of driftwood turned to ash in the evening fire.

He cooked for them and was cursed when the meals were not to their taste. He fashioned a broom and daily swept the camp. He managed to make a mansion of sorts out of what had been a pigsty, yet they complained of the time it took him.

He foraged for fresh delicacies to lighten their diet. Turtle-eggs he brought them, and fish and clams. And one day he returned in triumph from the hunt, with lobsters enough to go the rounds. But his own food, fresh or otherwise, was more often than not snatched and divided among his employers, while they derided him for his lack of industry.

"Y'r lazy, that's what you are!" accused LeClair. "Sneaky lazy, always slippin' off to busy y'rself with easy jobs. We ought to cut y'r rations, y' miserable monkey!"

"Dig!" said Java Jones bitterly. "That's why you were hired — to dig! And you do less of it than any of us!" Actually, he dug *more* than any of them, for when they pressed a shovel into his hands he could rest only at the risk of having a chunk of rock or bit of driftwood hurled at his head. He dug hour after hour, day after day, his hands gloved with blisters and head throbbing in the blowtorch blast of the sun.

And for what? Why, for a treasure that would not be his if he found it.

Two weeks of his servitude had passed before he learned what he dug for. Not that he lacked a normal curiosity; but the Fates had long since taught him the value of a still tongue, and so he waited patiently for his questions to be answered without his asking them.

Selinger answered them in an outburst of rage one day.

"I t'ink we are crazy!" shouted the Dutchman. "For a month now we dig, dig, dig, all over the damn island, and how do we know for sure that this drunken fellow from the *Gulbrason* was giving us the truth? How do we know this iss the right island?"

"Stow it," grumbled Java Jones. "Dig, dig, dig —"

"Shut up!"

But Selinger had spoken, and Mr. Witherby had all the information he needed. He knew about the *Gulbrason*. Who didn't? Her disappearance, months before, had been discussed in half the points through which he had wandered.

She had been a coaster, this *Gulbrason,* engaged like the rest of her humble breed in transporting commonplace cargoes and occasional passengers from one miserable port of call to another. But on this last spectacular voyage of hers she had carried, in addition to her captain and crew of four, only one man and a trunk.

The passenger's name had been McKillop, it was said, and he was a Scot, and he had come out of the black heart of Papua near Daru with diamonds. Many curious eyes had seen the diamonds with which he paid the *Gulbrason's* captain to transport him through the Arafura to Timor.

But no one had ever again seen the *Gulbrason*.

Mr. Witherby, on his leisurely journey into oblivion, had heard no end of speculation concerning the fate of the *Gulbrason* and her treasure. That she had poked her ancient nose into the year's worst storm was fairly certain, considering her date of departure from Daru and her probable route. That she had foundered with all on board was considered likely. Now, however, it was apparent that all of her crew had not perished. One, at least, had survived. And somewhere along the way Selinger or LeClair or Morton or Java Jones, or all of them together, had heard a tale to send them treasure-hunting.

MR. WITHERBY wondered idly what had happened. Perhaps the *Gulbrason* had gone down near Fortune Island, or been smashed to bits against it. Some surviving member of her crew might have dragged her treasure ashore and buried it. As for the fellow's ultimate departure from Fortune, that was not too difficult to reconstruct. He had built a raft, probably, of the ship's wreckage, and salvaged provisions enough to keep him alive on the journey.

Presumably the treasure would be safe, hidden in Fortune's lonely sands, until he chose to return for it. He need only keep his mouth shut.

But he had neglected to shut his mouth tight enough.

Mr. Witherby wondered one other thing: Where was the ship which had brought Java Jones and his three loot-seekers to Fortune? He got the answer to that a few days later, when still another of the quartet — this time Morton — flew into a rage.

"WHY don't the *Lily* come back?" bellowed Morton, turning from a long and sullen inspection of the sea. "With her here, at least we'd have fresh drinkin' water and food that's fit to eat! Who told 'em to stay away this long, anyway?"

"I did," said Java Jones. "And I'd a reason for it."

"What reason?"

"Well, several, you might say. First off, that fool from the *Gulbrason* no doubt blabbed to others beside us, and while maybe they wouldn't know Fortune Island from his description of it, they just might come close. With the *Lily* anchored here, we'd as well put up a signboard to welcome 'em. And second," said Jones over the curl of his lower lip, "I'd a hunch you'd want to quit if the diamonds didn't pop right up and kiss you. So I made certain you'd stick it out a while."

It made no difference to Witherby. He cooked and swept and dug. The sun broiled him, the shovel rubbed his hands raw, the hot sand baked his blistered feet. An ache, an agony, grew inside him, consuming him. He was nearing the end of his long, dreary march to oblivion. Even LeClair's monkey commanded more respect than he, was given more to eat. They used him, of course, as an escape valve for their own pent-up resentments, because it was a good deal safer to cuff Witherby than to snarl at one another. Seeing his exhaustion, they made him work the harder. Knowing him to be hungry, they whittled down his rations, then laughed at him when, to keep alive, he crept from the camp evenings and crawled about the island in search of purslane and gnetum seeds and other scraggly growing things to munch raw when the cramps bent him.

On these pitiful scrabblings for food, LeClair's monkey usually accompanied him. Why? They had something in common, perhaps. Witherby was at rope's end. His utter abjectness may have awakened in the monkey a feeling of kinship, for the monk was a grotesque little beast, moldy as an old hair sofa, scarred from quivering nose to twitching tail-tip by the missiles it had failed to duck during its precarious life among humans.

The monkey had no name, and for a long time Witherby sought to invent one. "We might call you Willy," he would say, limping along the shore in the moonlight with the monk perched on his shoulder and squeezing its hot little head against his pallid cheek. "I had a friend in Gorontalo once by that name, and we'd a gay time together until the constabulary nabbed him for stealing. Or Davy, now — how would that be? There was a lad name of Davy in Koepang who saw me through a sickness . . ."

But no name out of the past quite seemed to suit, and so he took to calling the monk "Little One." And many a night they sat somewhere on the black spine of rock that was Fortune Island, watching the wink of phosphorus on the empty sea while swapping monkey-squeaks and man-musings in their solitude.

Mr. Weldon Witherby, once of Rangoon, had arrived at last on the bottom rung of the ladder. He could go no lower. He was sick, friendless, and penniless. His status in life had become that of a galley-slave who, when no longer useful, would certainly be dropped over the side. And his sole companion was a monkey.

That he and the monk were still alive when the *Lily* returned to Fortune was something of a miracle, for she took her own good time, and during the last week before her return neither slave nor monkey was offered a share of the dwindling food supply. The digging had been abandoned by then. The four treasure-seekers asked only one thing more of Fortune: to be quit of the place.

THE *Lily* brought to Fortune two items of consequence: a falling barometer and a woman. The first was no surprise to the island's inhabitants. All that day their bleak prison had lain like a charred cinder in a fiery furnace, the still air so hot it scorched the lungs; yet the merciless sun was not red but a muddy saffron, the sky not blue but the exact shade of the revolver-barrel protruding from LeClair's belt. That a storm was due they were unhappily aware. The *Lily's* glass merely made it official.

As for the woman, she was a bit of extra business picked up by the *Lily's* crew as casually as other men might pluck a coin from the dust while strolling. Witherby saw her when she was brought ashore in triumph by Markey, the mate, who had captained the vessel.

"She'll fetch a fancy price at China John's," said Markey, leering. "Snatched her when she came aboard to peddle, we did. And she took some snatchin', I can tell you!"

The girl spat at him.

She was nineteen or twenty, Witherby guessed, but of course her age was of little value in judging her; in the islands it's how you live, not how long, that matters. From the looks of her she had fought them every foot of the voyage.

Under the grime, though, and the rag of flowered cotton that covered her, she was remarkable for her beauty. A *half-caste*, she was, certainly: the end product, perhaps, of a chance meeting between some vagrant white, like Witherby, and an island wench. But half-caste or no, she had the look in her eye of one who would battle the devil himself for her rights. And Mr. Witherby, having visited the place known as China John's, pitied her from the bottom of his heart.

"What's your name?" Java Jones asked as she stood glowering at them.

"It's a queer one," said the leering Markey, "so we'd best give her a new one. How would 'Sally' do!"

"No," said LeClair. "It's time there was a mam'selle in that place. Call her 'Jeanette.'"

So they made a game of naming her, while the girl faced them with lips squeezed tight and eyes flashing defiance. Until, surprisingly, Mr. Witherby interrupted.

Said Witherby thoughtfully, *"Omnia ad Dei gloriam."*

They blinked at him. "What kind of talk is that?" demanded Jones.

"Only Latin," Witherby murmured. "I once knew it rather well. It means, of course, 'All things to the glory of God.' Because she is beautiful. Surely you can see that!"

"Omnia Dei — give us it again, Worthless."

"Omnia ad Dei gloriam," repeated Witherby slowly, his solemn gaze on the girl.

"Gloriam," echoed Java Jones. "That's all right, that is. Gloriam. It's a good name." He stepped toward her, nodding. "And now that you got a name, sister, it's time you learned pretty manners to go with it, say I. Because in the morning we clear out of this rotten hole, and I've my heart set on a pleasant voyage home."

As he reached for her and grasped her wrist, she whirled on him, and white teeth flashed to his arm. With a yelp of pain, Java Jones took back his hand as though it had touched the sun. Then, bellowing, he swung a fist.

Mr. Witherby, wincing, went quickly away. He was still absent some two hours later when the storm broke.

III

THEY had expected the storm, but it took them by surprise, all the same. That was because the usual preamble was missing. No whispered warnings danced ahead of this upheaval; the first challenge was a full-voiced bellow. One moment air and sea were still as a stopped clock; then the black cask of the sky burst its seams and loosed on them a deluge, the wind sprang screaming from a hidden lair, and the sea rose up, thundering, to batter the island to which they clung. And these things occurred not one after another, in rational progression, but all in the mocking wink of a monstrous eye.

In an instant the camp at the base of Fortune's rocky fang was gone, wrenched from its moorings as if the manila lines that held it had been no stronger than the strands of a spider's web. The wind sucked it up with a noisy gulp and they saw it no more. In a moment more, they themselves were crawling like flies on the face of the mountain, or creeping crablike along its battered base, seeking shelter where they could find it, each man for himself. For even the *Lily* was gone then, scudding like a frightened wraith over the boiling sea.

LeClair was first to go. Terror sent him on hands and knees over slippery rocks to a niche in the mountain base that promised shelter, but into his refuge poured a sea that drowned him. The gay waves rolled him into the open again, made sport of him, and left him face down on the beach.

Then Morton. He sought the heights, but the wind plucked

him from his climb and, like a seaman torn screaming from the main skysail-yard of a stricken ship, he plummeted to his finish. The others, Selinger and Java John, Markey and the girl Gloriam and the *Lily's* crew fled this way and that, screaming or cursing or sobbing out their terrors.

And what of Mr. Witherby? That unhappy soul, when the typhoon arrived at Fortune, was seated with LeClair's monkey on a sheltered bit of beach some distance from the camp, pondering, as might be expected, man's inhumanity to man. The storm upon him, he merely clutched the monkey closer and sat where he was — until the sea discovered his retreat and hissed in to drive him out.

He went then along the shore, grimly battling the wind for possession of the whimpering ball of hair that clung to him for protection. *He* was frightened, but where could a man go in such a place? Not up, or the howling wind-demons would flay the flesh from his bones. Not into the rock itself, or the sea would follow and drown him. So, then, the problem was simplified. If he found a sheltered spot, he would duck into it. If not, he would keep on walking.

HE CAME presently to the remains of Morton, flattened at the base of the cliff, and transferred from the dead man's pocket to his own a half-eaten square of chocolate. And then he discovered LeClair, on the beach where the waves had tossed him, and acquired some cigarettes and a revolver — both wet but potentially usable. And then Witherby saw the boat.

Precisely what little Mr. Witherby hoped to do in such a storm with a small boat and a pair of oars is not known. Perhaps he thought to row himself and his monkey out to the *Lily* and cut her loose, on the chance of finding a way out of his servitude. He knew the *Lily* was unmanned, and at that time he was unaware she had been swept away. At any rate, he saw the boat and ran to it; he tucked the monkey into it, and, with strength he had not known he possessed, he contrived to launch the craft, during a sudden lull in the storm's fury.

She was a cork, that boat. She defied the mountainous waves to upset her. With Witherby tugging at the oars, she bore her two forlorn passengers, man and monkey, inch by straining inch past the foaming rocks at the island's tip and into the clear.

But then the storm returned with renewed vigor, and Witherby perceived the futility of his efforts. He stopped rowing. With the monkey in his arms he huddled in the bottom of the boat and let the typhoon take him. Drowning, after all, was more pleasant to contemplate than a return to his previous status of slave.

Drowning, however, was not to be his lot. The green waves bowled him along through the remainder of that devilish day, into the nightmare night that followed. His boat climbed their swollen sides with the tenacity of a crag-rat, plummeted from their crests with the grace of a plunging gull.

THEN the night was over, and the storm with it, and Witherby looked out on a watery world colored red by a friendly sun. "Little One," he said in wonderment, "look at us. We're alive!" Little One's reply was an ecstatic squeal.

But Witherby was too wise in the ways of Fate to be long fooled.

"Alive," he amended, "but for how long? Who's to lead us out of here?" There they were, in a boat on an empty ocean. The wind

had passed. The sea was calming after its orgiastic excesses. But the calm was more frightening than the tumult.

During the awful hours of storm there had been hope of ultimate salvation behind the terrors of each passing moment. The boat, after all, was being blown somewhere and might in the end fetch up against land. Now peace had fallen from heaven, but in peace lay peril. For Mr. Witherby and Little One had only half a bar of chocolate to see them through the torments of hunger. Of water they had none at all. They would perish unless they reached land in a day or two.

Where *was* land? Witherby had not the faintest notion. How far they had been blown from Fortune Island, or in what direction, he knew not. The climbing sun told him where east lay — but he had no way of knowing what lay eastward. The world about him was all water, metal-bright, blinding, and boundless. And as the hours passed, the sun grew hot.

Witherby took up the oars and began to row. Presently he gave up. What was the use of rowing?

"Little One," he said flatly, "we're done for, I'm afraid. There's not a thing we can do but sit and wait."

And so began for Weldon Witherby the last and most wretched lap of the downhill journey which had begun for him in Rangoon. Fortune Island had not, after all, been the bottom rung of the ladder. Fate had tucked another one under him, giving him, you might say, the full treatment.

He was to be broiled alive. His departure from earth was to be no mere plunge over the finish line, but spectacular as a session at the Inquisition. Fate had the tools for it — a white-hot ball of sun, a dead-calm sea, and a shadeless boat. Witherby contributed his empty belly and a parched tongue. And for good measure there was Little One, who suffered as Witherby suffered and made the hours hideous with his whining.

That day ended somehow, and during the night, when it was cooler, Witherby sat at the oars again. His efforts scarcely moved the boat, but he pulled steadily, and between the dismal creaks of the oarlocks he talked to the monkey to keep it quiet. He told Little One of his aimless wanderings along the great dark wailing-wall of the southern islands, and of the ignominies he had endured along the way. No bitterness embellished the tale; Witherby simply strung the facts together in their proper sequence, bead fashion, and dangled the necklace before the monkey in hope of amusing it for a time. He told of the cuffings he had received in Madjene and the bootings in Boetoeng, of losing his last guilder in Boeroe and eating dead fish on the beach at Ambon. He told of sickness and taunts, of hunger, of being stripped naked and tossed into gutters by irate purveyors of drinks who resented his wheedling; and of the café proprietor who had draped a live *krait* about his neck, while he was drunk, to amuse the customers. But in fairness to Fate, Witherby told also of the times along the way when, incredibly, he had stubbed his toe on luck of a better sort — as, for example, his finding of an unopened fifth of Scotch whisky on the shore near Fakfak, and his lavish two-weeks' stay in the home of a Mrs. Buxton, at Moresby, who had mistaken him for someone she once knew. "And what," Witherby asked of the monkey finally, "does it all add up to, would you say? Why, it's silly, that's all. What's a man to do if the Fates insist on dancing him up and down on a string in such fashion? What's a man meant for, d'you suppose?"

"I'LL tell you," said Witherby, becoming philosophical as he tugged that strange boat over that strange moonlit sea, on and on toward nothing and nowhere. "A man's got to take it as he finds it, and keep as steady on his feet as he's able. Because the fact is, my friend, we're put here for a purpose we know nothing about until it's accomplished — if we know it then — and there's nothing we can do to alter the plan one jot.

"Take that fellow Enrikson that I've told you about — the one whose cutter went down in the Solomons. He was put here to fill the empty cookpot of some starving aborigine, and for no other reason. But did he know it? Not until they popped him into boiling water, he didn't. Or consider my friend Davy, in Koepang, who nursed me through a sickness and got sick himself and died. He was put here to keep me going, no doubt, though God knows why.

"And what are *we* here for? Who knows? Maybe we won't ever find out, though at the moment it looks as if both of us were meant to feed the sharks. If true, we've been brought a long way, I'd say, to do a paltry little. Or don't you know we've been followed by sharks for the past hour, Little One?"

Thus he philosophized, while rowing or while resting between spells of tugging at the oars. It was a harmless diversion. As for its worth to the shriveled-up ball of matted fur that sat by his feet, whining up at him, that was questionable. The monk was hungry and thirsty, and talk was a poor substitute for food and drink.

Then came the morning and the searing sun again. And more sharks. He watched them, swimming alongside in the sunlight, and shuddered. They were so efficient, those sharks, so gruesomely sure of themselves. He hated and feared them, and the thought of being destined to fill the stomach of one, or chewed up into small bloody bits and shared among the lot of them, made his own stomach twist with revulsion.

With only a vague notion, yet, of the terrors that lay ahead, Witherby pulled from his pocket the revolver he had taken from LeClair's corpse, and examined it.

It had been thoroughly drenched and the cylinder was sticky with salt. And, obviously, LeClair had been careless about keeping it loaded, for Witherby's exploring thumb discovered only one cartridge. One bullet against so many sharks? He sighed and put the weapon back into his pocket.

So that day passed, like the previous one, the sea a boundless waste of gleaming metal made white hot by the relentless sun, the boat moving only when Witherby seized the oars and moved it, which was seldom. And with hunger gnawing like a monstrous rat at his vitals, and thirst squatting like a hot cinder in his mouth, the man abandoned even his attempts to converse with the monkey. It was the end and he knew it. And what could he do about it? Why, nothing.

Well, he could do something, perhaps. Through the hideous hours of hunger and thirst, his stiff fingers fumbled with the revolver, again and again extracting the lone cartridge and replacing it. He could not throw himself overboard to put an end to the awful suffering, for with the sharks lying there in wait, such a move would be equivalent to casting himself alive into a gigantic meat-grinder. But with LeClair's gun, if the thing would still function, he might cheat some of the agonies.

All through that day and through the long night that followed, while lying racked with pain in the bottom of the boat, little Mr. Witherby pondered the problem and worked toward a decision. And listened, with a heart full of pity, to the whimperings of his small companion.

The night passed. The sun rose from a glittering sea. Witherby put forth all his strength and struggled to his knees to look about. But nothing had changed. The sea was still shoreless and the sharks still waited.

For the last time, Witherby tucked the cartridge back into the cylinder of LeClair's revolver. He popped the muzzle of the gun into his mouth and clamped his cracked lips upon it. And then, remembering, he turned to say farewell to the monkey which for so long had been his sole companion in misery.

What he saw stopped him. The monk had crept from its tiny patch of shade under the stern seat to a point some eighteen inches from Witherby's feet, and was struggling to reach him. It no longer whimpered; it was no longer able to. All the agonies of thirst and hunger and shriveling heat that Witherby felt within his own frail body were mirrored in the poor glazed eyes that so beseechingly stared up at him.

He couldn't leave the monkey like that. It wasn't decent.

He put the revolver down and leaned forward to gather the creature into his lap. He stroked it. "I know," he said. "I know how you feel. I'd put you out of it if I could, believe me. But look. Look at them. Sharks! A dozen, at least, just waiting and waiting. If I put you overboard — even held your head under, to end the misery — they'd get you before you drowned. And I can't shoot you. You see that, don't you? There's only the one bullet."

The monkey clung to him, and the glazed eyes begged up at him.

"But then I'd have to lie here and die slow," said Witherby, and if there had been moisture enough left in him for tears, he would have wept. "I'd have to lie here hour after hour, waiting. Is that fair? I found the gun, you know — not you."

The monkey only wriggled closer against him.

Witherby sat in the broiling sun and racked his sick brain for some solution. He might throttle the poor beast or dash its head against the boat. But the thought turned his stomach. No, there was only one way out.

He lifted the quivering little animal from his lap and held it gently in the yellow glitter of the sun. With trembling hand he pressed the hot muzzle of the gun against its head and squeezed the trigger. The gun functioned. Little One's sufferings were done with. Witherby laid the corpse under the stern seat and dropped the useless gun overside. And down he flopped again to let the heat, the hunger and the terrible thirst have their way with him.

Late that afternoon he became delirious and would have cast himself overboard, sharks or no sharks, had he had the strength to rise. But he was too weak.

Toward evening, as the sun sank and a breeze stole wraithlike over the dead sea, he lost consciousness.

IV

WHAT happened to Mr. Witherby during the following eight hours has since been discussed in practically every bar from one end of the South Seas' wailing-wall to the other, by all sorts of people. Some of them consider it incredible, and seek to prove the point with elaborate diagrams of ocean currents, prevailing winds, tides, and what not. Others, on better terms with the fickle Fates who rule that region, are likely to remind you of the scores of even less believable occurrences recorded in the South Seas since Mendana first set foot in the Solomons.

At any rate, the boat in which Witherby lay unconscious was borne over the sea by bits and fragments of wind until it fetched up at an island. And what island? Why, the same jagged fang of black rock from which it had begun its eventful journey hours and hours before.

From Fortune, Witherby had fled, and to Fortune the Fates returned him, though he himself knew nothing of the return voyage, or of his safe arrival, until awakened from his long sleep by the ministering hands of an angel.

Opening his eyes, he looked upward into the angel's face and begged for water. But she had already poured water between his blackened lips, and he was only repeating a cry of despair spoken the past many hours in his delirium. And as the cooling water trickled down his throat, he recognized his benefactor.

"Why — why, you're Gloriam!" he whispered.

"If you want to call me that, I suppose you've a right to," she said. "It's the name you gave me yourself."

"Then I'm back where I started from!"

"You're on Fortune Island, if that's what you mean," said she.

"But — where are the others?"

"Dead. Every last one of them. And you'll be, too, if we're not careful. Come now" — and she bent over him again with a jagged tin can in her hand, and spooned some of its contents to his mouth — "eat this, Mr. Witherby."

Witherby ate and, incredibly, he recovered. Or perhaps not so incredibly, for in his long, slow journey to oblivion this strange little man had been knocked down so many times the business of getting up again was more or less a habit with him.

He gazed now into the girl's face and said wonderingly, reverently, "You are beautiful. Oh, but you are!" And then with a sigh of contentment, he slept.

The following day she showed him what the typhoon had done to Fortune. Or, more properly, what it had done to Fortune's inhabitants.

"They made the mistake of trying to run away," she said, shuddering. "Bullies always do when they're frightened, don't they? And, of course, that was the worst thing to do here. The Frenchman was drowned and one of them fell from the side of the mountain."

"And then the Dutchman, Selinger, found a hole in the rocks where he might have been safe, but Java Jones found him in it and tried to drag him out — there was room for only one of them. They fought like mad dogs for possession of the hole until a great wave settled the dispute by destroying them both."

"And the one called Markey, who brought you to this place," said Witherby. "What of him?"

"He tried to swim out to the ship, he and the others who were left. But there was no ship."

"Yet you survived! You — only a girl! How can that be?"

"Why, I sat. I sat and prayed to be saved. But" — and she smiled at him — "we'll die anyway, both of us, in the end. There's only a little water left, and you've eaten the last of the food. We won't last long."

"Wasn't there food in the camp?"

"Most of it the sea took. I found the water in a whisky bottle half buried in the sand, where one of the men must have dropped it."

"Well," said Witherby, "let's look." But she was right. Nothing remained of the provisions Java Jones and his crew had brought ashore from the *Lily* only a few hours before the storm's coming. The island was bare. Still, it was no barer than Witherby had thought it to be that dismal day, weeks before, when he had been put ashore to perish. And he had not planned then to die of thirst and hunger — at least not quickly. So he set out to find what was needed, leaving his companion to scoop a hole in the sand under Fortune's black overhang.

When he returned from the hunt an hour or so later, the girl had struck water. Not sweet water, but good enough to drink. And at her feet Witherby proudly laid an assortment of edibles — clams and sea-slugs, a wriggling squid, purslane and gnetum seeds and a snail or two. And he looked at her and grinned. He, Witherby, Fate's whipping-boy for so long, actually grinned.

"Why, we've everything!" he said. "We've the world at our feet, and each other too!"

Thus began their exile.

IT LASTED three weeks, for Witherby was not again eager to brave the sea without first taking all possible precautions. His biggest problem was a sail for the boat. To make one he had only poor materials — his trousers and rag of undershirt, plus his companion's flimsy cotton dress and scraps of clothing squeamishly stripped from those victims of the storm who still remained on the island. Little enough to tame an ocean wind!

But with what he had, he worked diligently, sewing the bits of cloth together with a fishbone needle and threads drawn from the fabrics themselves. And while he worked, Gloriam worked with him.

Those were idyllic days. The sun gilded Fortune's jagged peak; a gentle breeze brought scents of spice and frangipani from greener islands below the western horizon. When the work on the boat palled, Witherby and his fair companion foraged for food together, or swam, naked as babes, in the sparkling surf. Or sat and talked. When darkness dropped over their Eden, they talked sometimes for hours on end — Witherby of his varied adventures, she of hers, each with the frankness of poor, harried souls whose cards had been dealt mostly from the bottom of the deck. Only once before, when becalmed with LeClair's monkey, had Witherby reached that far back into the dark pockets of his memory; and he told her of that, too. Most surprising of all, he told of the gun and the bullet.

She only nodded. But if she had been beautiful before, when dragged ashore by Markey for Java Jones' inspection, she was beautiful now in another way. She was different, and what made her different was the wonder in her eyes as she gazed at this man who wept like a child at having slain a monkey. She had known many men in her time. In fact, she said as much, with a shrug that dismissed them as quickly as they came to mind. But never had she known a man like Witherby.

And never had Witherby known anyone quite like her.

The sail was finished. Into the little boat went every edible thing Witherby could find on Fortune — every root and nut, every scrap of bark or scraggly weed from which could be gnawed nourishment. Stored with them were the gleanings of the sea: sun-dried fish, mostly, with fresher tidbits for the first day or so. And then he dug anew for water, selecting a spot of shade high up on the beach near where Java Jones' camp had stood.

SHE stood beside him as he dug, to fill the whisky bottle and half a score other containers — shells, most of them — which she had painstakingly collected for the journey. And as he worked, she watched with a wistful smile on the soft curve of her lips, and a gaze that kept slipping off to explore the sunlit beach and high rocks where he and she had spent so much of their time together.

She was startled when, of a sudden, he stopped digging and shouted, "Look! I've found something!"

He dug again, his hands tossing up clouds of sand. The hole deepened and he reached deep into it. Then at her feet he dropped a chest, or trunk, wound round with ropes.

"It's what they were looking for!" he said. "We've found it. We've found the treasure!"

And so he had — for when his fumbling hands worked loose the ropes and raised the lid, there lay the possessions of the man named McKillop, his books and maps and clothes, and the diamonds he had brought out of the black heart of Papua months before. Java Jones and his hungry crew had heard the story aright from the *Gulbrason's* survivor.

Witherby spread the loot before him on the sand, and the girl Gloriam inspected it with him. And presently, sadly, she said to him, "You're rich now, aren't you?"

"Why, yes. I suppose I am."

"It's what you wanted — what you've sought all your life."

Witherby looked up at her and frowned. "No, I wouldn't say that. I've wanted something — but it wasn't wealth, I'm sure." He shook his head. "No, it wasn't wealth. But we'll take it, now that we've found it. We'd be fools not to."

He was stronger than he had been. Strong enough now to lift the chest in his arms and carry it to the boat without staggering. And as if to prove that wealth held no great interest for him, he returned at once to finish digging for water, and dug without rest until he found it.

"There," he said, filling the last of the containers. "Now we can go."

Thus they departed. The idyll was over, their stay on Fortune finished. A fragrant breeze filled their brave little sail, and the black fang of that isle of destiny slipped slowly behind. They turned for a last look — babes in the wood, departing their hiding place and venturing again into the forest. And both were frightened.

"Where," asked Gloriam, "are we going?"

"Why, I'm taking you home, of course."

"I have no home."

Witherby stared at her. "Then where shall I take you?"

"Why, wherever you're going."

"But I haven't given a thought to where I'm going. I really haven't." Shaken, he leaned toward her, afraid of his hopes, yet finding in her eyes the courage to let them live. "Where — where ought I to go?"

"Why, anywhere," she said. "So long as we go together."

And so they did. Everyone knows that now: how Witherby and the girl named Gloriam trudged up the road in Daru one golden morning dressed in what might have been clothing but more closely resembled the shredded sail of a Bajao outrigger — Witherby striding along proudly with a chest of sorts balanced on one sturdy shoulder, and the girl smiling at his side with her hand clasped in his. Everyone knows they were made man and wife that day before the sun set, and were on their way again next morning as happy as children.

Where they went from Daru is none of your business or mine, either, for they had new names then, to go with their new clothes, and plans, too, for leaving the past behind them. There are legends enough, Lord knows, in those parts, without prying. And truths enough to explain anything.

IT'S been said, for instance, that any man who turns to the wailing-wall of the South Seas in search of — well, in search of anything — will sooner or later discover what Fate wants of him. Maybe a king's ransom awaits him; if so, he'll find it. Or a place of honor in some cannibal's cook-pot — he'll find that, too. Or perhaps he was only meant to arrive at a certain place at an appointed time, to take his place for one brief moment in a game the gods are playing.

Witherby did that, all right. And if the gods seem to have taken their own good time about getting him there, remember that no man can play a part properly without first serving his apprenticeship.

An ordinary man, you'll admit, would have shot himself — not spent his last bullet on a dying monkey.

We don't get letters . . . at least not via the postal service, before the first issue has been published. So, to introduce the Adventure Tales letter column, staff-member Darrell Schweitzer seems to have obtained the following by, let us say, other means, perhaps related to the sort of mysterious rays and etheric forces which transported heroes to Barsoom and beyond in days of yore.

We would love to hear from readers about our first issue. Write to: Adventure Tales, c/o Wildside Press, P.O. Box 301, Holicong, PA 18928-0301. Or send an email to editor@wildsidepress.com.

Dear Editor of *Adventure Tales,*

So, it's "The Morgue," is it? That makes my cold, clay heart skip a beat. I mean . . . well, I can hope . . . (heh-heh, pant-pant) . . . after all, if the letters column in *Argosy* was called "Argonotes," and *Adventure,* a magazine devoted to wholesome, manly outdoor tales had "The Camp-Fire," and *Startling Stories,* a scientifiction magazine, had "The Ether Vibrates" (Hooray for Sergeant Saturn!), does that mean your magazine with "The Morgue" is going to be *my* kind of magazine? Are all the characters going to be *dead?*

Yours sincerely,
Norman the Necrophile
Nodding, North Dakota

Dear Norman,

Not quite. We like Sergeant Saturn too, and wish we could find out where he got his Xeno (the preferred drink of space-farers everywhere), and we hope you will like our magazine, but we're sorry if we've misled you. A "morgue," in the sense of a newspaper morgue, is a big, dark, musty room where back-files are kept, where one can spend hours or days reading through old publications in search of forgotten gems. That is what Adventure Tales is all about. We hope to find fascinating and exciting stories from back-issue magazines, many of which haven't seen the light of day in three-quarters of a century, but which need to be rediscovered. While there will no doubt be the occasional corpse in them, we cannot guarantee that all characters in all stories will be dead all the time.

— The Editor

⚑   ⚑   ⚑

Hey, You Mugs —

So there I was in a back-alley, face-to-face with the Big Operator himself, a crooked shamus who shoved his gat in my gut and said, "Who are ya callin' a shamus, Shamus?" while I tried to ex-

plain to him that the preferred term is Gumshoe, but unfortunately my shoes were glued to the gummy asphalt of these mean streets down which a man must go (even if minding his own business) and so all I could do was wobble back and forth like a punching-bag on one of those springy stands while he and his boys had their fun with me with their fists until they got tired and went away and left me appreciating through a red haze of pain that my experiences gave me a special insight into the meaning of the term *pulp.* It sounds like your magazine of pulp fiction is for me.

Yours whatever,
Sam Shovel, Detective (Deceased)
San Francisco, Calif.

Dear Sam,

We hope you will enjoy Adventure Tales during your period of recuperation, if that's what comes next. However, we should like to point out that much of the public, due to the influence of the movie Pulp Fiction, has a somewhat narrower idea of the meaning of the term "pulp" than we do. It means a lot more than just hardboiled detective fiction featuring two-fisted heroes in trenchcoats and alluring babes in little more than their cleavage, although such stories were indeed published in the original pulp magazines. "Pulp" was originally a technical term, for a kind of very cheap, high wood-pulp paper used for popular magazines in the first half of the 20th century. Pulp magazines were noted for their bright, lurid covers. Before the invention of television, or the paperback revolution, all-fiction pulp magazines were a major form of mass-entertainment, though, as is made clear in John Locke's excellent Pulp Fictioneers, Adventures in the Storytelling Business (Adventure House, 2004), a collection of old articles by pulp writers, the term "pulp magazine" didn't come into common use until the late 1920s at least.

The first pulp was Argosy, converted to an all-fic-

tion, pulp-paper format in 1896, for most of its run a weekly. Argosy was aimed at the whole family, which featured stories of all types: adventure, western detective, romance, sport, and even "fantastics" – early science fiction. Eventually publishers attempted to slice up this market with specialized magazines, of which Detective Story Magazine was the first, followed by magazines devoted to every conceivable category, including some rather bizarre freaks such as Fire Fighters, Submarine Stories, Suicide Stories, and, we kid you not, the holy grail of pulp collecting, Zeppelin Stories, of which only two copies of one of its four issues are known to exist.

Science fiction as a category was born in this type of publishing, which gave the world Amazing Stories and Astounding Stories of Super Science (now published as Analog). Also Weird Tales, for that matter. As most pulp magazines tended toward hastily-written, formulaic stories, mass-produced without a great deal of stylistic polish, the term "pulp," applied to the contents of these magazines, began to acquire connotations it has not lost today, even when most of the general public has never read or even seen a real pulp magazine, which was printed on pulp paper, with untrimmed edges, in an 7" x 10" format (the page size National Geographic uses).

This does not mean, however, that much excellent fiction was not found there. One can readily point to the classic detective tales of Dashiell Hammett and Raymond Chandler in Black Mask, Ray Bradbury's The Martian Chronicles, most of it first published in Thrilling Wonder Stories and Planet Stories, or Isaac Asimov's The Foundation Trilogy from Astounding Science Fiction, and the widely-varied and excellent content of Weird Tales (H.P. Lovecraft; Robert E. Howard's Conan series; the early Ray Bradbury of The October Country; Manly Wade Wellman's tales of Appalacian magic), not to mention Edgar Rice Burroughs' Tarzan of the Apes, which ap-

peared in All-Story *in 1912, to demonstrate that pulp magazines contained much fiction of very great and lasting interest. We intend to reprint some of the good stuff in* Adventure Tales.

Stay out of sticky back-alleys, Sam.
    — The Editor

ꢙ   ꢙ   ꢙ

Dear Sir,

Sometimes in letter-columns like this the old-time pulp writers would regale readers with thrilling accounts of their true-life adventures. In that spirit I offer you this.

It was 1919, or 1927, or one of those nineteen-somethings. I was in Zambouanga, or Port Moresby, or maybe I had been shanghaied to Shanghai. The details don't matter. I was in a dank, dirty dive of the sort frequented by the dankest, dirtiest scoundrels on Earth, eager for adventure. Well, most of them were eager for my wallet. I was the one after adventure. I found it. Several drinks, a treasure map, and a couple of kris-wielding Malay assassins later, I was on an expedition hacking my way through the jungle in the fabulous Plateau of Leng, by way of the Lost Valley of Fongo-Fongo. How a valley can actually be lost is only apparent if you've been there. I've been there. There was this crazy archeologist who came along, Indiana Something-or-Other, who carried a bullwhip and would always leap over a thousand-foot waterfall into a river full of crocodiles when there was an easy foot-bridge five miles down-stream. A show-off. But it wasn't the crocs that got him. It was the the gigantic jungle leeches the size of Volkswagons. We didn't miss him and at least he kept the leeches busy long enough for the rest of us to escape. In the end only I was left. I staggered out of the jungle into Kurdistan, which is nowhere near any jungle, so boy was I lost. I was out of my head. I hadn't eaten anything but fungus in fourteen years so I was kinda skinny. Everybody I saw looked really, really fat. When I met up with a local chieftain, whose name was something like "Muh-Fhet," I couldn't help but inquire, "Tell me Muh-Fhet, how much does the average Kurd weigh?"

Now they don't shrink heads in Kurdistan, but for me they made an exception. I look silly. The only thing I can wear to keep the rain off my noggin is a dixie cup. I went up the Amazon to try to find a witch-doctor who could help me, but the natives just laughed.

You know all about adventures. What do you think I ought to do?

Yours sincerely,
    Col. Alonzo P. Argh, Sr.

Dear Colonel Argh,
    The only things we can think of to suggest are these:
    1) Get used to it.
    2) Read our magazine to take your mind off your troubles!
    — The Editor

A NOTE FROM THE PUBLISHER
About the book paper edition you now hold . . .

Our printer has a number of requirements for book paper editions — one of which is the page count. In order to have a flat spine with lettering on it, we have to produce a magazine that's a minimum of 108 pages long. Needless to say, *Adventure Tales* wouldn't be anywhere near that long on its own, so we have to pad it out a bit with additional interesting material.

So . . . here is a *second* table of contents with lots of "padding" taken from past and future Wildside Press books, all of which I hope you will find of interest!

— John Betancourt

THE SPIDER STRAIN
by Johnston McCulley

I
Love, and Mystery

IT WAS not the first time that John Warwick had felt very thankful that his training as a member of society, and in the world at large, had been such that it enabled him successfully to talk about one thing and think of something else entirely different at the same time.

He managed to maintain the conversation with the charming young woman at his side, and while he did so, he considered that there was something taking place in which he was greatly interested, and sensed that there would be something in the nature of a climax soon.

John Warwick guided his powerful roadster along the pretty highways on the bank of the river, beneath overhanging boughs of trees dressed in their autumn foliage.

Now he allowed the great engine to drive the car at a rate of speed that almost took one's breath away — and now he throttled it down until the car crept, purring, along the highway, seeming to rest before another burst of speed.

He was driving in that fashion for a purpose. Silvia Rodney, the young woman who sat at his side, believed that it was because Warwick was nervous, and she smiled happily, for Warwick's manner led her to believe that he was about to address her on a subject a young woman always likes to hear discussed by a man she more than admires.

Warwick's real purpose, however, was to discover just why he was being followed, and by whom. He had known for the past two hours that he was being followed by somebody. He was aware that he was being watched closely as he ate luncheon with Silvia Rodney at a little inn far up the river, but he had been unable to locate the person who had him under surveillance. And John Warwick had a perfect right to feel a bit nervous about it.

Known to the world at large as the one remaining member of an old and respected family of culture and wealth, the truth of the matter was that John Warwick was a criminal of a sort, a clever member of the band controlled and commanded by The Spider, a supercriminal who had been the despair of the police of Europe in days gone by, and who still was active, though not to such a great extent.

Ruined by men who had called themselves his friends, John Warwick had joined The Spider's band at the supercriminal's suggestion, and had become a valuable man to the master crook. He maintained his position in society, for there he was of the greatest value to The Spider. He would be of value only as long as he remained free from suspicion. His successful work had antagonized criminals who were fighting The Spider, and Warwick knew that they would expose him if they ever got the opportunity.

Knowing that he was being followed and watched, John Warwick speculated as to the identity of the person or persons doing it. Were they officers of the law who had grown suspicious of him? Had he made some fatal slip that had put them on the right track? Or were they criminals antagonistic to The Spider and his band?

Warwick did not betray his nervousness and anxiety to the girl at his side, and nobody could have told from his manner that he was thinking of annoyance or trouble. He indulged in his usual brand of small talk, spoke of things to be seen along the road, chatted of the beauties of the scenery, gave the impression that he was a bit bored by it all — and, in reality, was very much alert.

"Great old season, autumn — what?" Warwick said now, glancing at Silvia.

"It is, indeed, John," the girl replied.

"True to all the forms of life — and all that sort of thing," he went on. "I always did admire a man or woman in the autumn of their existence — mellow with age, rich in experience, wise to the ways of the wicked world, and all that sort of silly rot! Live and learn — what? Quite so! A man gets really fit to live about the time he has to die. My word!"

"John Warwick, you are speaking like an old man, and you certainly are not one!"

"Thirty-four, dear lady!"

"I am twenty-six myself."

"Refuse to believe it!" Warwick declared. "Must be spoofing me, what? Don't look a day more than eighteen!"

"John Warwick, you are trying to flatter me!"

"My word! Couldn't be done, dear young lady! Not the proper sort of words in the old dictionary — none nearly strong enough. Webster chap should have met a girl like you — would have invented a lot more good adjectives!"

"John Warwick! I'll be angry in a moment!"

"Angry? My word!" Warwick gasped. "I always had a suspicion that girls liked to hear men say that sort of thing."

"But I am not a silly girl!" Silvia Rodney declared, pouting a bit — and she turned half away from him and looked at the river sparkling in the bright sunshine.

John Warwick managed to glance at her from the corners of his eyes — and sighed.

Silvia Rodney was the niece of The Spider. When Warwick first joined the supercriminal's band, he had made a pretense of paying a great deal of attention to her — it gave him an excuse for visiting so much at the mansion on American Boulevard where The Spider had his home and headquarters. This acquaintance had developed into love with a speed that was truly amazing. John Warwick, a man of society, hunter of big game, world roamer in days gone by, the man many women had sought for husband and could not capture, had fallen in love with the sweet, unassuming girl — and had been forced through circumstances to hold his tongue.

For from Silvia Rodney had been kept the knowledge of her uncle's true character. She had been taught to believe that he was the representative of a certain European power, and that he was working in the interests of humanity.

John Warwick was too honest to speak to her of love without telling her that he was a criminal of a sort — and The Spider had forbidden him doing that. He knew that Silvia Rodney returned his love, and was wondering why he did not ask her to become his wife.

Warwick had been a ruined man when he had joined The Spider's band. But, because of his excellent work, he had gathered a small fortune again; and The Spider, by way of reward, also had engineered a campaign on the Stock Exchange that had netted Warwick almost a quarter of a million dollars.

Warwick was all right financially now, yet he remained true to The Spider, not through fear of what might happen to him if he left the supercriminal's band, but out of gratitude to The Spider for his help.

There were times when John Warwick wished that he might marry Silvia Rodney and cease his nefarious work. It had not been so very nefarious at that. The Spider and his followers committed thefts, but generally on the side of right. Ill-gotten gains were what they generally took from their victims; and now and then The Spider contracted to obtain and return something that had been procured by improper means from its rightful owner. There were worse criminals than The Spider and his people, but nevertheless, what they did was outside the law.

Warwick stopped the roadster in a grove beside the highway and helped Silvia Rodney out.

"Dear young lady," he said, "we will walk about one hundred feet through these woods and come to a high place overlooking a bend in the river. It is the most beautiful spot in the entire state, especially at this time of the year."

Warwick led the way through the brush, and finally they emerged on the top of a giant rock at the river's edge. Silvia gave a little cry of delight at the scene that unfolded before them.

A great river was at their feet, curving into the distance, and the woods on both shores were dressed in red and brown and gold. In the far distance, they could see the city.

They sat down on a fallen log to watch the scene — and John Warwick sighed again.

"Why — why not say it, John?" Silvia Rodney whispered to him, after a time.

"Pardon?"

"Must I say it?" she asked.

"My word! Whatever can you mean?"

"John Warwick, there seems to be some deep and dark mystery about you," the girl said. "Perhaps it is forward of me to speak in this way, but I flatter myself that I am a modern young woman, not bound by every silly and narrow-minded convention — and I always like to have mysteries solved. John Warwick, you have been in — in love with me for a year!"

"Certainly, my dear little lady!" Warwick replied. "What man would not be?"

"John Warwick, I want you to know that I am speaking seriously. A woman always can tell when a man really is in love with her. And — and I should think — that a big, wise man — could tell when a girl — was really in love with him."

"My word!"

"And you know that I — well, that I am!" she gasped. "And yet you — you never speak of it. I suppose that it must be because I am not good enough for you."

"Oh, my word! You're a great girl — and I'm a regular rotter, really."

"I know better than that — you are nothing of the sort!" she declared. "And I'll not have you defaming yourself in that way! Perhaps it isn't at all nice for me to speak in this way, but I must have an explanation, John. I — I cannot go on in this way! Is it that you don't — want me?"

"Oh, my dear girl!"

John Warwick turned away from her and looked up the broad river. He had faced charging elephants and infuriated tigers, he had been in many a close corner during his work for The Spider, but never in his life before had he faced an ordeal such as this. The charming girl who sat at his side was more formidable, in her way, than a jungle filled with wild beasts.

"What is it, John?" she asked now. "Is it something that you cannot tell me?"

"I — I am not good enough!" he replied.

"John Warwick, I have been investigating you a bit. Alice Norton has spoken to me about you a hundred times, and she has known you from boyhood. You have been a good, clean man, John. You were a bit wild in college, and just after you graduated, but your wildness consisted mostly of globe-trotting and hunting lions, and things like that."

"I suppose so," Warwick sighed.

"There is nothing in your past life that would keep a nice girl from becoming your wife."

"My word! Regular paragon — what? Example to be held up to erring youth, and all that sort of thing!"

"Now you are trying to make me laugh and change the subject. And I refuse to do anything of the sort, John Warwick! We are going to have an explanation here this afternoon — or I never shall go riding with you again, or talk to you when you visit my uncle."

"Oh, I say! Condemn a chap, and all that?"

"I mean it, John!"

Warwick looked up the river again — and saw nothing. He was feeling very uncomfortable, to say the least. He was remembering his promise to The Spider, and he did not want to lose the sweet companionship of the girl at his side.

Silvia Rodney touched him on the arm. "Silly man!" she said.

"Beg pardon?"

"I think that I understand, John. You have wanted to speak to me for some time — I could tell. And you have not, because — well, because of my uncle, I suppose."

"But what could your jolly old uncle have to do with it?" John Warwick asked. "You mean that I am afraid he wouldn't give you to me, if I were to ask him?"

"I suppose you think that I am a silly girl who is blind and deaf and dumb," she said. "My uncle seems to think so, too. Why, John, I have known the truth for two years, at least, but never have let my uncle find out. I felt a bit badly about it at first — and then I discovered that my uncle isn't so very bad after all. He was bad in his youth, but now he and his men and women are working more in the interests of right than anything else. I know that my uncle is The Spider, the supercriminal!"

"My word!"

"It is the blood that flows through his veins," she went on. "His father was a famous criminal. My own father was associated with my uncle for some time before his death. I am resigned to those facts now, John."

"My word!"

"And you are not so very bad, you see. What have you done recently? You recovered an idol that had been taken from India. Uncle received money for that, of course, and so did you, yet it was honest in a way to have the idol returned. Then you recovered a famous painting that had been stolen, and so it found its way back to its original owner. You committed burglary to get it, and yet it was honest, in a way. So, you see, things are not so very bad."

"My word!" Warwick gasped again.

"And so, John, if that was the reason why you did not speak —"

"But I am a crook!" he protested. "Can I ask a sweet girl to become my wife when I am a criminal, when I am liable to arrest and incarceration at any moment?"

"John, if the girl loved you, she would be willing to run that risk."

"My dear lady! Since I have been working for your uncle, he has aided me in building up my shattered fortunes. I could maintain my place in society now and have a wife at my side. And I do want you, dear girl! But I cannot have you — unless The Spider releases me. If he would do that —"

"I feel sure that he will, John. He loves me, you know, and will do anything for my happiness."

"We shall ask him," Warwick said.

"You let me ask him, John. Let me tell him everything. I feel sure that it will be all right."

"You'll marry me, if The Spider releases me?"

"Of course!" she said. "So we — we are engaged, now?"

"I suppose so — provisionally."

"Well —" John Warwick faced her again, and saw her smile and her trembling lips. He took her into his arms quickly, and kissed her. "Let us hope and pray that The Spider will be merciful!" he said.

They got up and started walking back through the woods toward the roadster. Suddenly, Warwick remembered! During his conversation with Silvia, he had forgotten about his belief that he was being followed and watched.

Now he was doubly alert as they walked back through the brush. He glanced around the grove as he helped the radiant Silvia into the roadster, but he saw nothing suspicious. He started the car, turned it into the road beside the river, and drove it toward the distant city.

Once more he maintained a conversation, a more animated one this time, but he was busy thinking and planning. He was driving at a good rate of speed when they went around a sharp curve in the road; then he stopped the car suddenly, backed it up, and waited.

Presently another car shot around the curve — a roadster as big and powerful as Warwick's. Only one man was in it. His faced flushed as he caught sight of Warwick and realized that he had been caught. He bent his head and drove on furiously.

"What is it?" Silvia had asked.

"Had an idea that chap was following us," Warwick explained, "I've been feeling it for a couple of hours. Thought I'd catch him by stopping quickly and letting him drive past."

"Who was it, John?"

"I have not the slightest idea my dear," Warwick replied. "But I'll jolly well find out, you may be sure! Can't be having unknown fellows following me around, what? My word, no!"

II
Under Orders

ONE hour later, John Warwick was pacing the floor of the big living room in the residence of The Spider on American Boulevard.

Silvia Rodney was closeted with her uncle in his den on the upper floor of the house. Warwick was nervous. He dreaded his coming interview with the supercriminal, which he knew he would be forced to hold as soon as Silvia came down the stairs.

"Feel like an ass, what?" Warwick told himself. "Might be a silly college youth, and all that sort of thing! Peculiar how some things work out in this old world! Never seem to know what is going to happen next. My word!"

He paced the floor for nearly another half an hour, consuming cigarette after cigarette; and then a radiant Silvia came down the stairs and rushed into his arms.

"Everything is all right, John," she said. "And you are to go up immediately and see him."

"Think I'd better take a gun along?" Warwick asked.

"Nonsense!"

"Your jolly old uncle might turn violent, you know — me capturing his pet and only niece, and all that sort of thing. Might decide to have revenge, or something like that."

"I don't think you need fear him, John."

"Well, I'll toddle up the stairs and have the dreaded ordeal over with, at any rate. No particular use in postponing it, what?"

Warwick hurried up the stairs and knocked at the door of The Spider's den. A gruff voice bade him enter. Warwick did so and closed and bolted the door behind him, as was customary when holding a conference with the supercriminal in his office.

The Spider sat in the usual place behind his big mahogany desk, in his invalid's chair, his fat hands spread out before him, his flabby cheeks shaking, and his little, piglike eyes glittering in a peculiar fashion.

"Sit down!" the supercriminal commanded; and once more he spoke in a gruff voice.

John Warwick sat down, and the Spider looked at him until Warwick began to feel uncomfortable.

"Say it, jolly old sir, and get it out of your system!" Warwick suggested finally.

"There doesn't seem to be much for me to say, Warwick. I want to secure the happiness of my niece, of course. It was a great shock to me to learn that she was aware of the nature of my business. I had believed that she was ignorant of it."

"Deuce of a shock to me, too, sir," John Warwick admitted. "I had no idea that she had guessed the truth."

"Perhaps it is for the best that things have worked out in this manner," The Spider went on. "She tells me that you will not marry while you are continuing your career of crime."

"Certainly not, sir — never think of it!" Warwick declared. "It wouldn't be fair to her."

"I'm glad you look at it in that way. You have your fortune back now, of course, and can give her a good home. You need play criminal no longer — for you are playing at it! You are not a criminal at heart. I suppose that I shall have to release you as a member of my band, Warwick. All that you know, you will have to keep secret, of course, but I feel that I can trust you to do that. So I am going to give you your release, Warwick."

"Thank you, jolly old sir!"

"After you have attended to a couple more matters for me," The Spider added.

"Oh, I see! Something already planned — what?"

"Yes — two things. As soon as they are accomplished, you are to be a free man, and then you can marry Silvia and settle down as a respectable citizen."

"The old world isn't such a bad place after all — what?" Warwick said. "Man gets his reward in time, and all that sort of silly rot! Feel like a new man already! My word!"

"Don't be hasty, Warwick! These two things that I have mentioned are far from being trivial."

"Oh, I gathered that much!"

"You may begin work on the first just as soon as you please and do it in your own way."

"Orders, old sir and employer?"

"Exactly. I presume that you are acquainted with Mrs. Burton Barker?"

"I am," Warwick replied grimly. "Her husband was one of the group of men that robbed me of my fortune."

"Then this work should be a pleasure for you," said The Spider. "You may have observed that Mrs. Burton Barker wears a peculiar locket on a long gold chain."

"I have noticed it often, old sir and employer. No matter how she may be dressed, she always wears the silly thing. She's always twining the chain around her fingers and playing with it. I've wondered many times why she persists in wearing it when Barker could buy her all sorts of jewels, if she wished them."

"That locket happens to be an important bit of merchandise," the supercriminal said.

"I am to get the locket?"

"You are."

"As soon as possible?"

"Yes," The Spider replied. "And the sooner you can get it, so much the better!"

"It seems like a silly thing to steal!" Warwick declared. "You could buy all you wanted for about fifty dollars each."

"You couldn't purchase that particular locket at any price, and there is not another in all the world exactly like it!" declared the supercriminal.

"Some sort of history connected with the foolish thing?" Warwick wanted to know.

"Something like that, Warwick. You just get that locket as soon as you can and leave the rest to me. There will be ten thousand dollars in it for you — if you succeed."

"If I succeed!" Warwick gasped. "My word! Always succeed, don't I? Couldn't afford to fail — simply couldn't — when I am so nearly done working for you, could I? Fall down at the last moment, and all that sort of thing? Certainly not! My word, no!"

"Getting possession of that locket might not be as easy as it sounds," The Spider warned him.

"How is that, old sir?"

"It happens that there are some other persons very anxious to get their hands on it."

"Ah, I see!"

"And they are so anxious that they will go to about any length to get it, Warwick. You will have strong competition, in other words. This will amount to more than merely snipping a locket from a chain worn by a woman."

"What is the silly old locket, anyway?" Warwick wanted to know.

"I may tell you about that later," The Spider returned. "You'll have enough on your mind in planning to get it and outwit the others at the same time."

"And the others —"

"I can tell you absolutely nothing about them, Warwick. Another man is after that locket of Mrs. Burton Barker's, but he will not make an attempt to get it himself. He has assistants, however, and I do not know them. You'll have to be alert, on guard, and find out things for yourself."

"My word! Deep and dark mystery — what? And all over a silly bit of a locket that —"

"Allow me to tell you that it is not a silly locket, Warwick! It is a very important locket, and we must have it. Do you understand? We must get it!"

"Very well, old sir. I'll get the thing. I'm going to some sort of an affair at Burton Barker's place this very evening — going to take Silvia with me."

"Be careful, Warwick!"

"Invitations are already accepted, old sir and employer — and it'd look rather peculiar if she did not go. I always do my work best when everything appears natural — understand? Somebody might get suspicious if everything did not."

"But, Silvia —"

"She'll be in the way — bother me, you mean? Bless you — no! She probably will dance with a lot of chaps and give me time to do my work. I'll be more careful, too, if she is there — be afraid of making some silly mistake and wrecking our happiness. By the way, do these — er — other chaps of whom you spoke know that I am going after that locket?"

"They know that I am after it, and that you are one of my trusted men," The Spider replied. "And so, naturally, they will think that you are on the job when they see you at the Barker place."

"Suppose they will be there, too? Are they the sort that could go to a place like that?" Warwick asked.

"I haven't the slightest idea, Warwick."

"I'd better lose no time then, what? I'll get to work as soon as possible — nab the silly thing before anybody else can!"

"That would be best, I think. Do you want any help?"

"I fancy not," Warwick replied. "I'd probably work much better alone in such a case. I may use Togo, if it proves necessary. He is worth a dozen ordinary men."

"Very well; have it your own way and use your own methods," the supercriminal told him. "All I'm interested in is the proper result. I want that locket, Warwick. I must have it — and I don't want you to fail!"

"My word! You speak as though I always had failed!" Warwick complained. "Never failed yet, have I?"

"There is a first time for everything, Warwick," said the supercriminal, "and I am not eager for this to be your first failure. Keep your eyes open for the others. I am sorry that I can give you no definite information concerning them."

"Then I suppose I'll have to be suspicious of everybody — what?" Warwick said. "I'd better toddle along now, old and respected sir! I have to see Silvia again, hurry home, dress — all that sort of silly rot. 'Bye!"

"Good luck, Warwick!"

"Thanks, old sir and employer! I fancy that this will not be a very difficult job. Getting a silly locket that hangs on the end of a chain — my word!"

"Ten thousand in it for you, Warwick. That will pay for a honeymoon."

"Not for the sort that Silvia and I intend having, but it will help some," Warwick replied "'Bye!"

Warwick left the den of The Spider, and hurried down the stairs to where Silvia was waiting for him.

"Everything is jolly well all right, dear girl," he reported "I have a couple more tasks to perform for your uncle and then I am to be — er — free. Understand? And then — !"

"You'll be careful, John?"

"Of course! My word! Be jolly well careful when a mistake would mean my losing you! We are going to Mrs. Burton Barker's place tonight, remember!"

"Will you have work to do there, John?"

"Now, now! Little girls should not ask too many questions, you know!"

"But I am interested!" Silvia declared. "And perhaps I might be able to help you!"

"Heaven forbid!" Warwick exclaimed fervently. "Allow you to run into danger — what? My word!"

"Oh, perhaps you think that I am not clever enough to help you," she accused. "Please remember, sir, that The Spider is my uncle, and some of the same strain of blood that is in his veins flows through mine!"

"Why, my dear girl!"

"And I'd like to help you," she coaxed.

"But I don't fancy that you can in this — er — particular case," Warwick told her. "Perhaps you may in the other — the last one — we'll see about it later. We can't afford to take any unnecessary risks, you know. I'll tell you a bit more about it tonight. Have to toddle along now — dinner, dress, all that sort of thing. 'Bye!"

Warwick kissed her again, and then he hurried out to the curb. But he shivered as he sprang into his roadster.

"Just fancy a girl as sweet as Silvia running the danger of arrest to help me steal a silly locket," he mused as he drove rapidly up the boulevard. "My word! It isn't being done! Not the proper sort of thing at all — what?"

III
Togo Shows Emotion

TOGO was the peer of all Japanese valets, as John Warwick often had said — and yet he was more than that. Though the world in general did not suspect, Togo himself was a valued member of The Spider's band, and had been for years before John Warwick was induced to join it.

Togo had worked for the supercriminal in the old days in Paris, and he knew many things about the band that even John Warwick did not know. The deeds of The Spider and his men and women were mild now to what they had been in those days before an accident made a cripple of the supercriminal and prevented his active physical participation in the band's doings. Though he could not get about except in an invalid's chair, yet The Spider remained the brains of the band.

Warwick and some of the others knew that in the den of the house on American Boulevard there were great filing cases that held many interesting documents. Some of these related to criminals, some were of such a nature that they could have been used against prominent men, and others were documents regarding police officers and detectives.

Whereas any well-regulated police department kept a rogues' gallery of crooks, The Spider maintained his rogues' gallery of peace officers, knew their peculiarities, their weak spots, and their strong points. But only Togo and few of the old-timers knew of other things that were in those secret archives — things that related to days gone by, little accounts that the supercriminal sought to settle from time to time, in some as the creditor and in some as a debtor.

Togo was also sincerely attached to John Warwick. Several times, he had given Warwick valuable aid, and on one occasion had saved him from exposure and arrest. When Warwick returned to his rooms this day, Togo opened the door for him, stepped back, and bowed, flashing his teeth in a smile.

"Honorable Togo, I am a bit late," Warwick said. "Kindly have dinner sent up from the restaurant downstairs just as soon as possible. There is a little social affair this evening at the home of Mrs. Burton Barker, and I am obliged to attend. Beastly bore, I suppose, and all that — but it happens to be necessary."

"Yes, sar!" Togo said.

"Togo, I was driving with Miss Silvia Rodney this afternoon, and chap betrayed particular interest in me."

"Sar?"

"He appeared rather anxious and eager to know all about my comings and goings, and all that sort of thing. I maneuvered to get a glimpse of him, finally. My word! Very common-looking chap at that — very common indeed!"

"Policeman, sar?"

"If he is, he is a new one on me, Togo, old top. I fancy that he is no policeman, or anything of that sort. I have a faint idea that the chap is one of those criminal fellows. The sort that always are poking their noses into the business of other folk — you know!"

"Yes, sar!"

"It might be well, old boy, if you kept your eyes and ears open a bit around here, what? We've been bothered before now by fellows who were inclined to cause us a bit of annoyance, haven't we? Getting rather sick of it!"

"I understand, sar."

"If anybody should come prowling about —"

"I shall attend to him, sar!" Togo promised.

"There you are — always bloodthirsty! My word! Assassinate the whole world if you could, what?"

"Only if the world was against you, sar!"

"Um! Thanks!" Warwick said. "Faithful chap, and all that! Well, keep eyes and ears open, old boy. And toddle right along now and order that dinner!"

*   *   *

Half an hour later, Warwick was eating dinner in the living

room of his suite, Togo serving it. When he came to coffee, Warwick leaned back in his chair, puffed at a cigarette, and regarded Togo carefully.

"I've a bit of news for you, old top — astonishing news," he said, presently. "You are as much a comrade in arms as a valet, and so you should know."

"Thank you, sar!"

"You know our flabby-cheeked friend with whom we are associated now and then in a little enterprise? Quite so! Well, I have to tell you, honorable Japanese, that before very long I shall be leaving his band."

"Sar?" Togo cried.

A swift change came over Togo's face. For a moment the Japanese, who seldom showed emotion, revealed his feelings, and in no uncertain manner.

"Oh, everything will be quite regular, honorable Togo!" Warwick assured him. "I am not turning traitor, or bolting, or anything like that. My word, no! I'm thinking of getting married, old boy — understand?"

Togo grinned.

"I see that you do understand," John Warwick continued. "And a married man should not be doing things that might get him into trouble with the police, should he? So there you are! Our friend, whose name need not be mentioned here at this moment, has agreed to — er — release me after I accomplish two certain things. You gather that all in, honorable Togo?"

"Yes, sar!"

"Excellent! Your own future is provided for, of course. I'll need you with me as much as before, and all that. It's up to you to say whether you remain with me or go back to where you can — er — be more active in the service of our flabby-cheeked friend."

"I shall be glad to remain, sar," Togo replied.

"Good! I have to accomplish the first task of the two tonight, if I can, at the residence of Mrs. Button Barker."

"I am to help, sar?" Togo asked eagerly.

"Um! I fail to see at this moment just how you can help, old top. Sorry! Like to have you in those last two little games if I could, and all that. But this is a strictly society affair, you know — dress-suit stuff."

"I understand, sar."

"I've got to get a little locket —"

"A locket, sar?" Togo cried.

"My word! Whatever is the matter with you? Why shriek at me in that fashion?" Warwick demanded, putting down the coffee cup. "Are you beside yourself — what?"

"Your pardon, sar!"

"But I fail to understand, confound it! Never knew you to act so in the world! Have you been drinking?"

"No, sar!"

"Explain, then!"

"I — I was startled, sar."

"I should think you were! And you certainly startled me! Almost made me choke, confound it!" Warwick exclaimed. "What do you mean by such a thing?"

"You mentioned a locket, sar. I — I was wondering if it could be the locket."

"Honorable Japanese, it is merely a silly locket that a foolish woman wears on the end of a long, ridiculous chain. Why our flabby-cheeked friend wants it is more than I know — and I suppose that it is none of my business. He didn't happen to take me into his full confidence this time, confound it!"

"Then it must be the locket," Togo said.

"What locket?" Warwick demanded. "Am I always to be surrounded by riddles? My word! It's enough to make a man take to drink, and all that sort of thing!"

"I — I cannot tell you, sar, if The Spider will not," Togo said. "I am sure you will pardon me, sar."

"My word! What mystery is this? I had thought that it was just a silly locket that somebody wanted badly enough to pay for. Other chaps are after the thing, too, it appears. Jolly old Spider told me to watch out for them!"

"Then it must be the locket I mean," Togo said. "You must be very careful, sar."

"Do I happen to have a reputation for being reckless?" Warwick demanded. "My word! A man would think that I was about to abduct the sultan of Turkey, or some little thing like that."

"It seems to be only a very simple thing, sar, but, believe me, it is not!" Togo told him.

"How on Earth does it happen that a woman like Mrs. Burton Barker is wearing a locket there could be so much fuss about? Why, the woman has had the thing for years! It seems to be a sort of pet of hers. Everybody wonders why she wears the thing. Impression is abroad that she is superstitious, and all that, and thinks the fool locket brings her good luck. Can't fathom this thing at all!"

"I — I certainly wish that I could tell you, sar, but I dare not without the permission of the master," Togo declared. "But I beg of you to be most careful, sar, and to watch out for those others you have mentioned."

"It seems to me that I have accomplished tasks far more difficult than this," Warwick said. "Is the greatest diamond in the world concealed in the thing, or some silly rot like that?"

"I believe that the locket is not of very great value in itself, sar," Togo replied.

"I fancy not, since I am to receive only ten thousand if I succeed in getting the thing. Sure you can't tell me more about it?"

"I dare not, sar!"

"My word! How very disgusting! Never did like such mysteries — get on a man's nerves, what?"

"If I only could help you, sar!" Togo exclaimed. "At least, sar, please allow me to be in the neighborhood of the Barker residence this evening. You may have need of me, sar. And, if you expect to be married soon, you will want nothing bad to happen."

"I should think not!" Warwick said. "But, this is amazing! Thought it was just a silly locket!"

"It is called the Locket of Tragedy, sar!"

"My word!" Warwick exclaimed, staring at the valet. "What a perfectly silly name to give a locket — and a cheap one at that! Nothing very tragic about Mrs. Burton Barker, I'm sure. She is just a silly butterfly of a woman!"

"It is true that she may have that appearance, sar," said Togo. "But, if you will pardon me, she is nothing of the sort. She is a dangerous woman, sar!"

"You know her?"

"I know of her, sar," said Togo. "Be on your guard, sar, when you attempt this thing. She may be expecting somebody to make an attempt to get the locket. And if you are suspected —"

"I understand, honorable Togo. Thanks, too, for this surprising warning. I always considered the woman rather shallow myself. Sort of a little girl masquerading in a grown-up's costume, what? I've known her for a score of years, since she was a girl —"

"Pardon, sar!" Togo interrupted. "But, during all those years, were there no times, when you were traveling, when you did not see her and heard nothing of her for years?"

"Of course! She was in school — and then she came out and spent the usual time abroad —"

"Ah!" Togo said significantly.

"So that is it, eh? She got mixed up with The Spider while abroad — what? Why, it can't be possible! The girl had a mother who watched her like a hawk!"

"Nevertheless, sar, something happened at that time that influenced this woman's whole life."

"She never looked like a woman of tragedy to me!" Warwick declared. "Can't imagine old Barker marrying a woman of that sort — his fancy always ran to the other kind."

"Perhaps her husband knows nothing of it."

"Of what?" Warwick asked.

"Of the locket and what it means," Togo replied.

John Warwick got up and began pacing the room. Togo piled the dishes on the tray, carried them into the hall, and rang for the waiter in the restaurant below.

"Never heard of such a thing!" Warwick grumbled. "All this row about a locket and a foolish woman! I'll bet there's nothing to it after all! I'll get the thing as quickly as I can and take it to The Spider. If I can't get a locket from a woman like Mrs. Burton Barker, I must be getting old, slowing up — what? My word, yes!"

Warwick walked to a dark corner of the room, stepped to a window there, and looked down at the street. The lights were just being turned on. A stream of automobiles was passing, men of affairs going to their homes from their offices.

Warwick glanced across the street, where there was a drug store with windows brilliantly lighted. He stepped closer to the window — and looked again Standing before one of the store windows and looking at the apartment house was the man who had followed Warwick in the roadster.

"He's watching me rather closely — what?" Warwick told himself. "I'll have to look into this matter, I'm afraid. Always did detest a mystery!"

He stepped to his desk, got an automatic pistol from one of the drawers, and slipped it into the pocket of his overcoat. He put into his coat pocket a tiny pair of pincers so sharp that they would cut through strands of any ordinary metal — say, a gold chain. He called to Togo to order the chauffeur to have the limousine in front immediately and then put on his hat and coat — but not his gloves.

"You'll be careful, sar?" Togo asked.

"Naturally!" Warwick replied. "Can't understand this sudden idea that I may get reckless! Never knew me to be reckless before, did you? My word!"

"And I cannot help you, sar?" Togo implored.

"Oh, you may happen to be in the neighborhood, if that will appease you in the least," Warwick answered. "Fail to see how you can be of help to me, though."

"Thanks, sar!" Togo cried. "Perhaps I may be of service to you,

sar! It will be a difficult task, I fear. It is not the easy one you seem to think, sar."

"Nonsense!" Warwick exclaimed. "Upon my word, I never heard such utter rot before! I'll have the silly old locket before midnight — make you a good wager on it! I never saw you quite like this before, honorable Japanese! Makes me wonder what the old world is coming to, you know. Nonsense! A man would think, from your actions and words, that I was going into a battle, or something like that!"

Togo's answer rather startled him. "You are, sar!" Togo said.

IV
One Known Foe

JOHN WARWICK left the apartment house, stepped out into the street, and then walked briskly across it. He entered the drug store and purchased a package of cigarettes. There was no particular sense in that, since he had an ample supply in his rooms, and even some in his pocket, but it gave him a chance to pass within six feet of the man who had been watching him.

Warwick did not give him as much as a glance as he entered the store. The man moved down the street a dozen feet or so, and stood by the curb. Warwick walked from the drug store, stopped to light one of the cigarettes he had purchased, tossed away the burned match, and then whirled around and stepped up to the man at the curb.

"See here!" he exclaimed, in a low, tense voice. "I'd like very much to be informed just as to why you show such a remarkable and unusual interest in my affairs!"

"What's that?" the other snarled.

"I fancy that you both heard and understood me," Warwick said. "You followed me this afternoon, while I was out motoring, and now I find you loitering around the place where I live."

"Well, what about it?"

"Why, I don't fancy it at all!" Warwick told him. "I ought to have an explanation, and all that sort of thing. My word! A fellow hates to have somebody prowling around and watching him. It isn't quite the thing, you know!"

"I've no doubt that you do object to being watched," the other man said.

"Just what do you mean by that?" Warwick demanded.

"None of your business!"

"See here! I am in the habit of being addressed in a respectful manner, confound it!"

"Well, what are you going to do about it?" the other asked, sneering once more.

"Why, confound it, sir, I can break you in two with my bare hands!" Warwick declared. "Do you imagine that I am a weakling just because I happen to be wearing evening clothes? Keep a civil tongue in your head when you are speaking to me!"

"I didn't say that I wanted to speak to you, did I? You began this conversation, didn't you?"

"I did — and probably shall end it!" said Warwick. "Why have you been following me, and all that?"

"I didn't say that I had been."

"Ah! Trying to evade the question, are you? What? My word! Do you fancy that you can indulge in repartée with me? Answer me straight now!"

"Attend to your own business! I'm getting sick of your talk!" the other told him.

"I have half a notion to hand you over immediately to the police chaps!"

"You try it, and we'll mix. I think you're crazy, if anybody wants to know!"

Warwick suddenly stepped closer to the man and grinned at him. Warwick understood now. He could handle this man physically, and with ease and he knew that the other knew it. Why, then, did this man taunt him to combat?

To cause a row, probably, and make it necessary for Warwick to go to police headquarters and settle it, or make charges — to delay John Warwick, in fact, and prevent him getting to the residence of Mrs. Burton Barker on time. The fellow might even hope to mar Warwick's face early in combat, in such a manner that Warwick would not be presentable and could not go to Mrs. Burton Barker's at all.

So Warwick grinned, and stepped closer and spoke in a tone somewhat lower.

"Your work, sir, is as coarse as your manners," he said. "You will observe that there is a patrolman just across the street. He is an old friend of mine. I give him a box of cigars now and then, and always speak to him when we pass in the street. If you start anything with me, sir, I shall knock you down, order him to take you to the station, simply announce that I shall appear in court in the morning — and go on my merry way. Your little plot would not work then, what? You'd fail and look jolly well silly, and all that sort of thing. Make a regular ass of yourself! My word!"

"You think you're smart, don't you?"

"Certainly not! Smart? Oh, I am a regular stupid ass!" Warwick said. "I don't know much of anything — but I can see through your little game!"

"I guess there are a few things that you don't know, all right!"

"Perhaps — and perhaps not!" Warwick told him. "But I do know this much — if I catch you prowling around me any more, I am going to handle you, and not in a delicate manner, either. And if you happen to have a couple of friends, I'll handle them, too."

"Quite a boy, ain't you?" the other sneered.

"Enough of one to do that," Warwick answered. "Going to tell me why you have been following me and prowling about?"

"Do you think that you can bluff me just because use happen to belong to The Spider's gang?"

"Spider's gang? My word! What on Earth are you talking about?" Warwick asked blankly.

"I suppose you've heard of The Spider!"

"Are you once of those nutty fellows, off your feed, bats in the belfry — all that sort of thing?" Warwick demanded. "I never heard such nonsense! Ought to be incarcerated and held for investigation! Liable to run amuck and slay women and children!"

"Oh, I guess we understand each other!" the other said. "That line of talk doesn't get any too far with me, you want to understand. I'm wise!"

"That is fortunate," Warwick observed. "There are but few wise men remaining on Earth, and we have desperate need of them all. I am under the impression that I have been wasting valuable time talking to a silly ass. Spider's gang! My word! Whatever can that mean? However, cease following me around. I can't have a lunatic trailing me all the time — frighten my friends to death!"

"It probably will frighten some of them, all right!"

"Now you are talking in riddles again!" Warwick declared. "I see that my limousine is waiting, and so I cannot waste any more time on you. Just a friendly tip, my man — if I find you annoying me again, I shall feel compelled to deal with you personally!"

John Warwick's voice lost its light tone and became menacing as he spoke, and his eyes narrowed and glittered for an instant. The other man recoiled, but regained his composure again almost instantly and stepped nearer Warwick.

"Maybe you'd like to try to do that little thing right now!" he said.

"Ah! You'd like very much to have me, wouldn't you?" Warwick exclaimed. "But it happens that I have an engagement — a rather important engagement —"

"Yes, I know all about that!"

"You do, eh? It appears to me that you are a bit too much interested in my personal affairs. My word! You seem to know as much as my private secretary would — if I had one. I'd advise you to remember that little tip of mine!"

John Warwick glared at the man, and then hurried across the street to where his limousine was waiting. He told the chauffeur to drive him to the residence on American Boulevard, and there he picked up Silvia, who cuddled up beside him in the big car and seemed to be very happy in so doing.

"Are you going to tell me what you are going to do tonight?" she asked.

"Little girls should not ask too many questions," Warwick told her. "It isn't much of a task, really."

"I think you are mean if you don't tell me!"

"Promise to keep it a dark secret?"

"Of course!"

"And you must forget it as soon as I have told you, and keep your mind off it. You don't want me to fail, do you?"

"Certainly not, John!"

"Very well. Mrs. Burton Barker always wears a little locket on the end of a long, gold chain. I am to get that locket. Don't ask me why, for I do not know. Your jolly old uncle wants it for some purpose, and that is enough for me. Now, you forget it!"

"Very well, I'll try, only I'm not so sure that I can," Silvia said. "But I'll not bother you, John."

Warwick glanced through the window as the big car speeded toward that section of the city where pretentious residences predominated. The Burton Barkers had an imposing mansion surrounded by lawns that were fringed with big trees.

It was one of the show places of the city. Warwick knew it well, had been in almost every room of it. He often had inspected it while Burton Barker was having it constructed, and afterward he had been a guest there scores of times. That was when he had believed that Barker was his friend.

Barker still thought that he believed it. Barker was not aware that John Warwick knew he had conspired with other men to rob him in business deals. Warwick would not have known it, had not The Spider proved it to him. Warwick had no repugnance, therefore, in committing a crime in Burton Barker's residence while he was a guest there. He remembered that Barker had robbed him in his own house, while pretending deep friendship.

The limousine turned into the driveway and came to a stop before the house. Warwick helped Silvia out, and they entered.

Many guests already had arrived, the orchestra was playing, and the scene was one of wealth and splendor.

They greeted their host and hostess, and for an instant Warwick's eyes rested on the locket he was to get. It still hung on the end of the long heavy gold chain, and Mrs. Burton Barker was twisting the chain around the fingers of her left hand, as she seemed always to be doing.

John Warwick danced once with Silvia Rodney, and then handed her over to another partner, and walked slowly through the rooms, nodding to his friends and acquaintances, acting as though he were searching for somebody, but, in reality, spotting any strangers who might happen to be present.

If it was to be his lot to face foes, he wanted to know their identities, if possible. From what had been told him, he did not know whether his antagonists would be strangers or persons with whom he was well acquainted.

One thought dominated his mind — that The Spider expected success and would not countenance failure. John Warwick had been ordered to get the locket worn by Mrs. Burton Barker, and the supercriminal expected him to get it.

Warwick passed on through the rooms, went to the veranda, strolled there and smoked a cigarette, and retraced his steps to the house again. Some belated guests were arriving. Warwick wandered toward the foot of the stairs to inspect these late-comers.

And then he almost lost his composure for a moment and stepped quickly aside, where he would not be observed. Greeting the hostess was the man who had followed him in the roadster in the afternoon, and with whom he had talked in the street before the apartment house just before starting for the Barker residence.

The man was in proper evening dress, and he greeted Mrs. Burton Barker in the approved manner.

John Warwick was puzzled to a certain extent. Mrs. Burton Barker was talking to the man as if she had been acquainted with him for some time. Was he in her employ, trying to protect the locket, and did he suspect John Warwick of planning to purloin it? The thought almost made Warwick shudder, especially when he remembered how the man had spoken regarding The Spider, for Warwick lived in continual fear of the day when suspicion would be cast upon him.

Or, was the man talking to Mrs. Burton Barker merely one of those others who were making an attempt to get possession of the locket before The Spider's people could?

While fussing around and pretending to be bored, Warwick watched the pair closely. To all appearances, the man was merely exchanging polite greetings with his hostess, but John Warwick knew that they might be speaking of important things that had to do with him. Mrs. Burton Barker was a clever woman in a way — she was able to smile and laugh, and at the same time speak of serious affairs and let those near think she was indulging in small talk, and Warwick knew it well. He had been trained in the same social school.

"Have to make sure of my ground — what?" Warwick told himself. "Must use strategy, and all that sort of thing! Can't be making some silly mistake and getting into trouble at this stage of the game. It wouldn't do at all! My word, no!"

He wandered down the corridor and approached them from another direction. He watched the man's face, made an ineffectual attempt to read his lips and ascertain what he was saying, regarded Mrs. Burton Barker carefully, and tried to imagine what she was replying.

Warwick noted that this man spent more time with his hostess than any of the other guests, and that increased his suspicions.

"No use working in the dark — what?" he told himself. "Have to ascertain a few things, I fancy!"

Warwick straightened his shoulders, managed to get a smile on his face, and then started walking directly toward Mrs. Burton Barker and the man with whom she was talking.

V

Into a Trap

MRS. BURTON BARKER smiled a welcome as John Warwick approached, for she always had admired him, but Warwick was not certain at the present time whether the welcome was sincere. The man standing beside her glared at Warwick for an instant, and then quickly regained his composure and got a blank expression into his countenance. Mrs. Burton Barker introduced him to Warwick as Mr. Marlowe, and the two men bowed coldly.

"This world is a queer old place — what?" Warwick said. "For instance, Mr. Marlowe is almost the exact image of a chap with whom I had a peculiar controversy today."

"Why, how was that, John?" Mrs. Barker asked.

"I was out motoring with Miss Rodney," Warwick explained. "A chap seemed to be following us. I managed to get a good look at him. And this evening, just before I started here, I caught the same chap watching the place where I live. Made me a bit angry, don't you know — went across the street and protested to him about it. Chap talked to me like a silly ass!"

"But why on Earth should he have been watching you, of all persons?" Mrs. Barker asked.

"Don't know, I'm sure."

"And you say that I resemble him?" Marlowe queried, a smile twitching his lips.

"Enough to be a twin of his," John Warwick replied. "I refer to looks, of course — face and form and all that. Voice somewhat similar, too."

"Of course it wasn't Mr. Marlowe?" Mrs. Barker said.

"My word! Never said that it was!" John Warwick protested. "I meant that it is peculiar how you'll meet a chap and think how much he looks like somebody else you have met. Only a certain number of types in the world, I fancy! Deuced peculiar, isn't it? Always seeing somebody who looks like somebody else!"

John Warwick grinned, and for an instant his eyes met those of Marlowe squarely.

Mrs. Burton Barker turned away then, to greet some of her other guests, and Warwick and Marlowe stepped to one side, and started walking toward the den that had been set aside as a lounging and smoking room for the male guests. There happened to be nobody in the den when they reached it.

"So you followed me here!" Warwick said, in a low voice, as soon as they were alone. "I'll have to ask you for some sort of an explanation, I fancy!"

"It happens that I am here as an invited guest," Marlowe told him. "Are you the social censor hereabouts?"

"My word, no!" Warwick exclaimed. "It is nothing in my life

what sort of person Mrs. Barker wishes to invite to her residence. But you followed me — that's the point!"

"And why should I follow you?"

"That is precisely what I am eager to know," Warwick told him. "There's no confounded sense in it! It annoys me, really! I can't be having it, you know."

"And just how are you going to stop it?" Marlowe asked.

"Why, confound it, I'll simply handle you, if this thing continues! Don't you think you'd better give me some sort of an explanation?" Warwick said.

"Explanations are not necessary," replied Marlowe. "They'd be a waste of time and breath. I guess we understand each other, all right. Yes, I guess we do!"

"You are a very poor guesser," Warwick told him. "My word! Follow a chap around all day, and then refuse to tell him the reason for it! It isn't done, you know! It isn't right at all!"

"Stop trying to throw a bluff, Warwick! I happen to be wise, you know."

"I know nothing of the sort! You may be old man Wisdom himself, for all I know — or merely a silly ass! Come, now — give me an explanation. I think that I am entitled to it."

"Why not ask The Spider what you want to know?"

"There is some more of that Spider stuff!" said Warwick. "What on Earth does that mean? Are you dippy, and all that sort of thing? Bats in the belfry — what? My word!"

Marlowe stepped nearer to him and spoke in a lower voice. "Suppose, Mr. Warwick, that we walk out on the veranda, or around the lawn, where it will be possible for us to talk without running a chance of being overheard," he said. "We may be able to arrive at an understanding of some sort."

"Very well," Warwick replied. "I certainly must have some sort of an explanation!"

They made their way through the corridor and to the veranda, where there were several couples sitting around in the semi-gloom between dances, and Marlowe went slowly down the steps to the lawn and started following a walk that curved around the house toward the flower gardens at the back.

Warwick, smiling faintly, followed at his heels. Streaks of light came through the branches of the trees here and there, and yet there were plenty of dark and shadowy places where an assault could be staged without much trouble. John Warwick was alert and cautious. He did not intend to have this fellow, Marlowe, catch him off guard and eliminate him for the time being.

"Well, talk!" he said, after a time. "I fancy that we'll not be overheard around here — what?"

"Warwick, as I said, I am wise to you," Marlowe began. "I happen to know that you are The Spider's trusted right-hand man. Don't take the trouble to deny it — for I know! And I know, also, that you are under orders right now."

"Orders? My word!"

"Orders to get possession of a certain something that is at present in the residence of Mrs. Burton Barker."

"Oh, I say!"

"That is attached to the person of Mrs. Burton Barker. I'll go as far as to specify. So you see, I understand the affair perfectly, Warwick. I happen to be connected with certain persons who do not care to have you succeed in your little undertaking. In fact, it is my particular business to see that you do not succeed. Now you

understand fully why I have been following and watching you."

"My word!" Warwick gasped. "I never heard such utter piffle in all my life before. Cannot understand it at all! Quite beyond me, and all that sort of thing!"

"Yeah? Well, that kind of talk doesn't fool me a bit, Warwick!" Marlowe told him. "You might as well save your breath. And you might as well give up all intention of trying to do as you have been ordered. For you are not going to succeed this time, Warwick, though you have done some clever things before."

John Warwick threw back his head and laughed.

"Most remarkable conversation!" he said. "It's all utter rot, of course; but allow me to tell you that, any time I set out to do a thing, that thing is done! I always succeed, old chap! Understand? There's no such word as failure in my personal vocabulary. My word, no! However, I am glad that you have told me this interesting little tale."

"Are you going to keep on trying to throw that bluff?" Marlowe demanded. "Maybe you think that I don't know a thing or two. The best thing for you to do is to forget your orders. You'll run into trouble if you try to carry them out!"

John Warwick laughed again, softly, as if at an excellent jest, and then turned back toward the house.

"I fancy that this conversation has been quite a waste of time," he said. "I might have been dancing, and all that sort of thing. Silly ass to listen to you — what?"

"You'll be a silly ass if you don't take the advice I gave you," Marlowe said. "You may not think that you are up against a tough game, but you are!"

Now they were passing a clump of brush that grew close to the walk and threw a deep shadow over it. Warwick had noticed it as they passed it before, had watched it searchingly for a moment or so, but had seen nothing that looked suspicious. He glanced at Marlowe now, but Marlowe was walking half a pace ahead of him and seemed to be giving the brush no attention at all.

"Well, Warwick, are you going to give it up?" Marlowe asked. "Are you going to take my advice?"

"Advice is something I rarely accept from a chance acquaintance," Warwick replied.

He chuckled again. And suddenly two men sprang from the dark near the clump of brush, and launched themselves upon him. At the same instant, Marlowe whirled around and sprang.

Warwick darted backward, and his chuckle died in his throat. He had been half expecting such an attack at first, but had grown to think that it would not materialize. Now he found himself fighting against overwhelming odds. He had an automatic in his pocket, but he had no chance to draw it, and, furthermore, he did not care to fire. He wanted publicity no more than these other men.

One of the men was throttling him now, preventing an outcry; another was trying to trip him and hurl him to the ground; Marlowe was gripping one of his arms, and also watching the walk ahead. Two more men came from the darkness and joined in the fray.

Warwick, his back against the clump of brush, fought as well as he could. He tried to hold off his antagonists, to clear a space through which he could dart to the walk and run down it toward the veranda. But he found that they were too many for him.

"Quiet as possible, men!" he heard Marlowe command. "We

don't want a row that will attract any of the guests! Do your work quickly! Clever, is he? He walked right into the trap!"

The pungent odor of chloroform assailed Warwick's nostrils. He tried to fight furiously, to hold off unconsciousness, to keep from being a prisoner in the hands of these men, but they held him in such manner that he scarcely could put up a struggle.

Their voices seemed to come to him from a great distance. He felt his senses going, tried to strike and kick. He called himself a fool for not guarding against surprise better while taking that walk with Marlowe, when he might have known there would be some sort of a trap.

And then the drug had its way, and Warwick ceased to call himself anything.

*   *   *

As the limp form dropped to the ground, Marlowe issued his orders quickly and in a low voice.

"Get him across the lawn and into the machine! Take him away as quickly as you can — and for Heaven's sake, don't make any mistakes! Watch him carefully! I'll let you know when to release him — when my work is done!"

One of the men grunted in reply, and then two of them picked up the unconscious Warwick and carried him across the Barker lawn, from shadow to shadow, dark spot to dark spot, careful not to be observed. Close to the curb, on the side street, a limousine was waiting, its curtains drawn, its engine purring, a chauffeur sitting behind the wheel.

John Warwick was tossed into the limousine, and it left the curb and ran down the street, gathering speed. Two of the men had entered it with Warwick; the two others hurried down the street in the opposite direction.

And Marlowe, grinning like a fiend, walked slowly through the grounds and approached the veranda from the opposite direction. He went along the railing, tossed away a half-smoked cigarette, and passed through the open front door. Ten minutes later he was being introduced to a certain young woman guest and was asking her to dance with him.

The young woman was Silvia Rodney.

VI

Togo Takes a Hand

THAT particular brand of nausea which follows a dose of chloroform had been experienced by John Warwick before; and when he regained consciousness now, and experienced it again, he kept his eyes closed, pretending to be under the influence of the drug and waiting for his brain to clear, Warwick realized that he was stretched on a couch of some sort; and he heard the voices of two men in conversation. His wrists were lashed together in front of him, but his ankles were not bound and there was no gag in his mouth. After a time, he opened one eye and glanced around the room.

It was a medium-sized room furnished in quite an ordinary manner. There were half a dozen chairs, a table, and a buffet. Warwick could see a closed door and two windows at which the shades had been drawn. Two incandescent lights burned in a chandelier.

The men were still conversing. Warwick could not see them, for they were beyond his feet, and he did not want to turn his body

yet and let them know that he was conscious.

"Ain't nothin' much to it," one of the men was saying. "We keep this bird here until Marlowe telephones that he's turned the trick, and then we give him another dose of chloroform, take him in the car out to the edge of the park, and drop him there. When he comes back to Earth, he can go home — and he won't know where we kept him. That's all."

"I thought he was one of these clever ones."

"He is — but he ain't as clever as Marlowe, I reckon. We haven't anything to worry about, anyway — we do as we're told and cash in on the coin."

"What's all this about a locket, anyway?" the other asked.

"You can search me! All I know is that Marlowe is crazy to get his hands on it — some secret, I suppose. None of our business! The big idea is to keep this man Warwick from getting it for The Spider — understand?"

"I don't believe there is any Spider!"

"Don't fool yourself! I guess Marlowe used to know all about him over in the old country. There's a Spider, all right, and he's a tough bird to go up against! I don't want him and his gang after me any — not any!"

Warwick groaned and turned his head, and then sat up weakly and held his lashed hands to his face. He heard the two men get out of their chairs and start toward him. So they were as much in the dark regarding the locket as he was, were they? They were merely engaged to detain him until Marlowe had obtained possession of the thing, and then were to release him.

"Alive again, are yuh?" one of the men asked.

"What — what is the meaning of this?" Warwick gasped. "Oh, yes — there was a fight —"

"It wasn't much of a fight, I guess — you didn't have a chance!" said the other, laughing.

"Where am I?"

"That's somethin' you ain't supposed to know, Mr. Warwick. Here you are, and here you stay for the time bein' — and if you try any funny tricks, you'll wish that you hadn't."

"But — what is the idea?" Warwick demanded.

"I guess you know all about that. Anyway, we ain't prepared to answer any questions," one of the men told him. "We're just here to see that you remain for a time."

"How long?"

"Until we get orders to let you go — and let that be an end of your questions," the other growled.

Warwick looked at them more carefully — and two precious thugs they were. He glanced rapidly around the room. He had been in corners as close as this before, and had escaped. He realized that these men meant him no real harm physically — but they were interfering with his work. The Spider had told him to get that locket from Mrs. Burton Barker, and had warned him to be on guard against foes — and the supercriminal expected nothing except success.

"Better just take it easy, Mr. Warwick," one of the men told him. "We don't want to muss up a gent like you, as has done some nervy things in his time, but we'll have to do it, if you try any tricks. We got our orders."

"I don't fancy this at all, my men," Warwick said. "Confound it, I escorted a young lady to an affair this evening, and I should be there dancing with her now. What'll she think of me if I desert her in this manner?"

"It's hard luck, but it can't be helped."

"If you men aid me to get back there, I'll make it worth your while — and forget all about this."

"Well, we need the money, but it wouldn't be healthy for us to let you you go," one of his captors replied. "We'd get ours, if we did! So we can't talk along them lines, Mr. Warwick."

"I'll pay your own figure," Warwick said.

"Nothin' doin', sir!"

Warwick knew that the decision was final. He got slowly to his feet and paced around the room. But when he tried to get near the door or one of the windows, one of his captors always got in front of him. He tried the cords that lashed his wrists, and realized that they had been tied well. There seemed to be no present way of escape.

"Might as well take it easy," one of the men assured him. "A little wait won't hurt you any — and maybe you can get back there in time to take your young lady home. You can make up some whale of a story and be a hero." The man laughed raucously, and the other joined in.

"I suppose you realize," said Warwick, "that you could be sent to prison for doing such a thing as this."

"Oh, we ain't worryin' any about that, sir. This scrap is strictly between ourselves, and neither side is goin' to call in the police. If we go to prison, a certain gent of The Spider's gang will go right along with us!"

"What do you mean by speaking of The Spider's gang?" Warwick asked.

"I suppose you don't know — oh, no! You never heard of The Spider and his gang, you didn't. You ain't been workin' for him for more than a year — oh, no!"

"My word! Never heard such nonsense in my life!" Warwick gasped. "Can it be that you have made a mistake, got the wrong man, and all that sort of thing?"

"Not any, we ain't — and you might as well cut out the bluff!" came the reply.

Warwick continued walking around the room, and after a while he sat down on the couch again.

"What time is it?" he asked.

"A few minutes to eleven," one of his captors told him. "I guess you'll be turned loose about midnight — so you ain't got long to wait. Better just take it easy!"

Warwick engaged in no further conversation. He felt his bonds whenever he had a chance, and convinced himself that they could not be removed easily. He thought of dashing to a window, but he knew that the two men would be upon him before he could accomplish his purpose And the window might be in the second or third floor — he could not tell. This might be a cottage, or a cheap lodging house. Warwick did not even know in what part of the city it was located.

To all appearances, he had resigned himself to his fate. He yawned once or twice, and asked for a drink of water. One of the men went out of the room, and returned with the drink within a short time While he was gone the other watched Warwick closely, a revolver held ready in his hand.

Though he did not show it in his countenance, John Warwick was beginning to get frantic. He would fail — and from The Spider there would be no forgiveness. The supercriminal had warned him

that he did not want failure this time. Warwick could not imagine why he had not been more careful. Here he was, a prisoner, and Marlowe and the others having every opportunity to achieve their desire.

He thought of Silvia Rodney, too, and knew that she was worrying because of his absence. Was he to lose Silvia because of failure to get the locket from Mrs. Burton Barker? Would The Spider, angry at his failure, keep him as a member of the band instead of granting him his release?

But there seemed to be no way of escape. The two men watched him closely, and if he got up to walk around the room, they left their chairs and remained close to him. A wrong move, a shriek for help, would cause them to spring upon him. They might even render him unconscious again — and then he would, indeed, be helpless and unable to carry out the orders of The Spider.

He wondered whether Marlowe had the locket already. For the hundredth time, he asked himself what that locket could be, and what secret it held.

"Well, are you going to keep me here all night?" he growled.

"Until we get orders to turn you loose."

"My word! This is disgusting — what? Liable to make you chaps pay for it in the end!"

"We ain't scared much!"

"Fancy I'll square accounts with you before we're done!" Warwick said.

He began pacing the floor again, walking from one corner of the room to the other, while they drew nearer and watched him carefully. He glanced toward the door — and saw that the knob was turning slowly!

Warwick's heart almost stood still. He guessed that the man on the other side of the door was a friend instead of a new foe, else he would not be so furtive about his entrance. He glanced at the door now and then, maintaining a conversation with the two men, at the same time edging toward the window, and acting as if he were about to make a break for liberty, thus causing them to watch him closely. Their attention was attracted from the door.

Warwick glanced that way again — and saw that the door had been opened a crack. Suddenly it was hurled wide open, and a form darted into the room. The door slammed shut.

"Hands up!" a stern voice commanded.

Warwick's captors whirled around. They found themselves menaced by an automatic. And they beheld the malevolent, glittering eyes of one Togo, John Warwick's Japanese valet.

VII
In the Conservatory

WARWICK gave a glad cry and darted to the wall, following it until he reached Togo's side, keeping from getting between Togo and the other two.

"You are all right, sar?" Togo asked.

"Quite all right, thanks," Warwick replied. "Hand me that weapon, old boy, and I'll keep these two thugs covered while you take these confounded cords off my wrists. And, if they lower their hands or make a move —"

He left the sentence unfinished. There was no need to finish it. The two men before him knew what he meant, and they did not relish the look in John Warwick's face.

He held the automatic, and Togo unfastened his wrists. Warwick motioned toward one of the men.

"He has a revolver, Togo — get it!" he ordered. "And then you may search the other. We can't be letting them retain weapons — what? My word, no!"

Togo carried out the command with alacrity, and returned to Warwick's side with two revolvers and one knife. The two men had backed against one of the walls of the room, and still held their hands above their heads.

"Sar, may I attend to them?" Togo asked.

"My word! Always bloodthirsty, aren't you?" Warwick said. "What would you do with them, old top?"

"I shall teach them never to annoy a gentleman again, sar!"

"This gentleman would not have been annoyed, Togo, old boy, if he had been thoroughly awake," Warwick said. "Serves me right — what? Teach me to keep my eyes open, and all that sort of thing!"

"But, sar —"

"Besides, Togo, we haven't time to play with these two precious thugs. And they treated me decently, at that. Just where are we, Togo, by the way?"

"In a little cottage, sar, at the edge of the city."

"Um! And how do you happen to be here?"

"I was about the grounds at the Barker residence, sar," Togo explained, "and saw the attack on you. I could not interfere at that time because there were so many, and because — it would not have done to create too much of a disturbance, sar."

"Quite correct!" Warwick said.

"When they took you away in the limousine, sar, I engaged a taxicab that happened to be passing the corner, and followed. I have the cab waiting near here, sar."

"Excellent, Togo, old top! We'll use that cab in short order. And these men —"

"Please let me handle them, sar."

"You may use that peculiar method of which you are a master and put them to sleep," Warwick said. "Take the largest one first — he has the ugliest face. If the other makes a move, I'll indulge in a bit of target practice — what?"

Togo sprang to do Warwick's bidding. His hands found the man's throat, his thumbs pressed against certain spots in the back of the neck, there came a groan and a gasp — and one of their foes was unconscious on the floor.

The other had watched from the corners of his eyes. He gave a shriek of fear as Togo turned toward him — but the shriek died in his throat as Togo turned toward him — but the shriek died in his throat when Togo's thumbs pressed home. He, too, was allowed to sink to the floor.

"We must hurry, Togo!" Warwick exclaimed. "This delay may mean failure, you know."

Togo led the way through the front of the little cottage, and out into the open air. He ran down the walk to the street, Warwick at his heels, and came to the taxicab. Warwick commanded that they be driven to the Barker residence, and he promised rich reward if the journey was made in record time.

"Feel like an ass, Togo!" he said, as the taxicab lurched along the street. "Got caught napping — what?"

"I told you that this was a dangerous adventure, sar."

"So you did! Never imagined I'd run into such violence while trying to get a silly locket from a foolish woman!"

"But that locket is no common one, sar."

"Can't be! Other chaps seem determined to get it," Warwick said. "Mighty glad you were Johnnie-on-the-spot, old boy! Feel gratitude, and all that! Must reward you someday."

"I was glad to help, sar."

"Always glad to be of service when there is a promise of a row, eh?" Warwick said.

"Yes, sar," said Togo, grinning.

"Togo, old top, this night may be my Waterloo. Wouldn't be a bit surprised if I fail to carry out the orders of our flabby-cheeked old friend, what? Other chaps have had an hour or more to get away with that locket."

"It is possible, sar, that they will take ample time and work slowly, thinking you are being held a prisoner," Togo said.

"Hope you're a good prophet! Dislike very much to fail at this juncture — might cause me all sorts of troubles and disappointments, old top."

"Pardon me, sar, but you have not failed yet. Even if they have it by the time we reach the Barker place, sar, we may be able to recover it."

"How's that?"

"That man Marlowe — I know of him sar."

"You do, eh? What about the chap?"

"He is an old foe of The Spider's, sar."

"Is, eh? Then the jolly old Spider will be more than angry if we do not succeed tonight. My word! Have to make every possible effort, and all that sort of thing!"

"If this Marlowe gets away with the locket, sar, we might follow him and get it ourselves."

"Might, certainly. Rather get it from Mrs. Barker, however. Like to outwit the chap instead of using violence. Silly ass of a thing — that locket! Can't imagine what The Spider wants with it. Buy all you want for fifty dollars each. Locket of Tragedy, eh? Rot! Utter rot, I say!"

The taxicab stopped on the corner nearest the residence of Burton Barker, and John Warwick and Togo got out, and the former rewarded the chauffeur handsomely. And then he led the way across the velvety lawn, keeping well in the shadows.

"I'll have to make it appear that I've been wandering around the grounds and smoking — what?" Warwick whispered. "I'm going inside immediately, old top. Can't endure the uncertainty, and all that sort of thing."

"I'll remain in the neighborhood, sar," Togo said. "You may have some need of me."

"Good enough!" Warwick replied. "Be somewhere along this walk, so I can locale you quickly, if it is necessary. Luckily, those chaps didn't muss me up much. 'Bye!"

Warwick went into the residence of Burton Barker through a side entrance, dodged the others, went to the room that had been set aside for the gentlemen guests, and there brushed his clothing. His linen had not been soiled, he was glad to observe. He was still fairly presentable.

And then he made his way slowly down the broad stairs and came to the hall below. The orchestra was playing, couples were in the mazes of a dance, others were chatting in the conservatory and in the refreshment rooms.

Warwick stood at the entrance of the ballroom as if bored by the scene, and watched the dancers. His eye caught Silvia's; he nodded, and she flushed with pleasure. Then his eyes moved on — and presently he had located Mrs. Burton Barker.

He was glad to find that she still wore the locket at the end of the long chain. So Marlowe had not had the opportunity to get it yet — else he was waiting for an appropriate moment. John Warwick felt hope bubbling in his breast again. There still was a chance of carrying out The Spider's orders.

Another dance began, and Warwick noticed that Marlowe was dancing it with Mrs. Burton Barker. He stood back a short distance from the door, so that he could watch them without being observed. Silvia also was dancing, so Warwick did not have to give her his present attention, and was free to attend to The Spider's business.

"Must get that silly locket!" Warwick told himself. "Never do to fail now — what? Marlowe chap had his chance and didn't make the most of it. Have a try at it myself now, I fancy. Have to keep my eye on him, though. Wonder if he has any more assistants about? Must be alert, and all that sort of thing!"

The dance came to an end, and Marlowe and Mrs. Burton Barker passed within a short distance of Warwick as they walked into the hall. Warwick watched closely as Marlowe took his hostess to the refreshment room. It was evident that the man was trying to flirt with her — and she was the sort of woman who always is ready for a flirtation with any presentable man.

They went toward the conservatory. John Warwick guessed that Marlowe might make an attempt to get the locket there. He could engage Mrs. Burton Barker's attention and snip the thing from the end of its chain easily. Perhaps he would be able to make her believe that she had dropped it while they were walking through the hall and thus escape suspicion.

Warwick followed them into the conservatory, where there were many couples walking about. He dodged those he knew, and made his way behind a bank of foliage and bloom. Marlowe and Mrs. Burton Barker were on the other side of it, just sitting down. From where he stood, Warwick could watch them closely without being seen by them. They were indulging in small talk that meant nothing, and Warwick sensed that Marlowe was merely waiting for an opportunity.

Suddenly Marlowe bent closer to Mrs. Burton Barker, and the tone of his voice changed.

"Do you know, you are the sort of woman that fascinates me," he said.

Mrs. Burton Barker laughed lightly and bent away from him, and once more Marlowe moved closer to her.

"I mean it!" he said. "You are a wonderful sort of woman — quite beyond the ordinary a man meets every day."

"You are good at flattery," Mrs. Barker observed, thus asking for more of it.

"It is not flattery, but the truth!" Marlowe declared. "Didn't you notice that I was interested more than usual? Trust a woman to know when a man is interested!"

Warwick saw him bend toward her again — and smiled. He knew what Marlowe was doing. In a moment, he would become too enthusiastic, Mrs. Barker would put up her hands to ward him off, and then Marlowe would —

"Don't be foolish, please!" Mrs. Barker was saying, but in a tone that said she liked to have him foolish.

"I'd rather spend five minutes with you than hours with a silly, flighty girl," Marlowe went on. "When a man finds a woman who combines beauty with intelligence, he has found a treasure. Your husband is a very lucky man."

"I fear that there are times when he does not believe that," Mrs. Burton Barker said.

Marlowe suddenly bent nearer to her — and she did exactly what John Warwick had known she would do, she put up her hands, and turned her face away, trying to act the timid, modest, half-frightened girl, making an attempt to avoid a caress.

Warwick watched more closely now. He saw Marlowe lean forward again, put his face close to hers and whisper some foolishness — and while he did it, his left hand went forward, a bit of metal flashed in the uncertain light of the conservatory as the gold chain was snipped, and the locket was in Marlowe's hand and being conveyed to his pocket.

VIII
Another Attempt

JOHN WARWICK stepped back silently, walked around the bank of foliage and bloom, and confronted them.

"Pardon," he said, "but I believe I have a dance with our charming hostess."

Marlowe already was upon his feet, his eyes bulging, regarding Warwick as he might have looked at a man from the grave. Warwick smiled at him peculiarly.

"Must not monopolize Mrs. Barker," he said "My word! Haven't danced with her for quite some time! Pleasure I cannot miss this evening — what? Must assert my rights, and all that sort of thing!"

"Of course I'll dance with you, John," Mrs. Barker said.

"My word! You've lost your precious locket!" Warwick exclaimed.

Mrs. Burton Barker gave a gasp of dismay and felt at the end of the chain. Instantly, she was in a panic.

"Oh! I must find it!" she cried. "See — the chain is broken!"

"Probably caught it against something and snapped it," Warwick said lightly.

But he gave Marlowe another look, and Marlowe realized that Warwick knew what had happened.

"Imagine you'll find it without much difficulty," Warwick went on to his hostess. "Saw you come in here — and you had the locket on the chain then."

"You're sure?"

"Absolutely!" Warwick replied. "Probably dropped it around here some place. Easy to find, what? Just close the conservatory door — and then we know the locket is somewhere inside."

Marlowe glared at him, and Warwick chuckled. Mrs. Burton Barker was looking around the floor, her hands clasped before her.

"I must find it — must find it!" she repeated.

"Good-luck locket — what?"

"Yes — a talisman," the woman replied. "Why don't you help me find it?"

"No doubt it'll be found almost instantly," John Warwick observed, meeting Marlowe's eyes again. "Locket can't run away — what? My word, no! Have to be right around here some place! Let's look!"

They pretended to search. Warwick watched Marlowe closely horn the corners of his eyes. He saw Marlowe drop the locket against the bank of flowers and then pretend to stoop and recover it.

"Here it is, Mrs. Barker," he announced.

"Oh, thank you!"

"Chain probably worn through," Warwick observed. "Fine gold, you know — little jerk would break it. Better have it repaired, dear lady — what?"

"I shall have it repaired in the morning," she said.

A servant approached with the intelligence that some guest wished to see the hostess, and Mrs. Burton Barker, promising to dance with Warwick later, took her leave. The two men were left alone.

Warwick stood before Marlowe, his hands upon his hips, and chuckled at the other man, whose face depicted his rage.

"Coarse work, what?" Warwick said.

"Think you're smart, don't you?"

"Why didn't you bluff it out, old chap? Didn't have the nerve? My word! I was standing behind the plants, you know, and saw you snip the thing."

"This isn't the end, Warwick!"

"Trying to threaten me now? Oh, I say! Doesn't ruffle a single feather of mine, really! My word, no! Calm in the face of danger, and all that sort of thing. By the way, better engage a new crowd of thugs. Those you have at present aren't quite up to the standard. Managed to get away from them, you see."

"I see!" Marlowe exclaimed. "May I ask how you did it?"

"Quite simple. Friend of mine saw me being abducted, followed, got into the cottage, overpowered the chaps, and rescued me."

"That damned Jap, I suppose."

"Wouldn't curse him, if I were you!"

Warwick warned. "He's quite the man, you know — been no end of help to me on several occasions. Don't like to hear him spoken of in that tone."

"Suppose we just put aside this high-falutin' talk," Marlowe said. "We understand each other — it's war between us. We're both after that locket. And I'm going to get it!"

"You had it a moment since and didn't retain it," Warwick reminded him. "My turn now, what?"

"Not if I know it! If you get that locket, Warwick, you'll be a very clever man!"

"Oh, I say! Not that, surely! Well, can't stand here talking to you all evening. Have to toddle along!"

"And I'll toddle right along in your wake," Marlowe informed him, angrily.

"Still following and watching me — what?"

"You can bet that I am!"

"And a lot of good it will do you!" John Warwick said. "Making a regular ass of yourself — you are! Have to toddle. 'Bye!"

He whirled around, walked through the conservatory and entered the wide hall. He saw Mrs. Burton Barker at the foot of the stairs, talking to a couple of guests forced to take leave early, and went toward her.

"Sure you have your locket?" he asked, when the others had gone.

"I have it in my hand," she answered. "It gave me quite a start to find it missing. I'm glad that you noticed it, John."

"You make quite a fuss over that locket, what?"

"It — it is a good-luck thing, John. I'm a bit superstitious, you know — always was, in fact."

"Don't seem to remember anything of the sort," Warwick told her. "Always regarded you as an ultramodern young woman who didn't believe in rot."

"It is just a fad of mine," she said.

"Let's see the locket a moment — maybe I can fix it."

"I'll have it repaired in the morning, John; you needn't bother now."

"You'll be dropping it somewhere, and then you surely will lose it," he told her. "Better let me tie it on the end of the chain."

He lifted the chain and looked at it closely. She handed the locket to him, and he started fastening it to the end of the chain. He knew that was the only way. If she took the locket upstairs, she probably would hide it some place where it could not be found easily. There was a chance of getting it while she was wearing it.

Silvia Rodney approached at that moment with a man with whom she had been dancing, and stopped to speak to Mrs. Burton Barker.

"Dear hostess almost lost a locket," Warwick said. "Found it again, however. Trying to fasten it to the chain again."

His eyes met Silvia's for an instant, and the girl smiled at him. Marlowe approached and joined the group.

Warwick finished attaching the locket to the chain, and stood back. Mrs. Barker was making an attempt to show that she was not agitated, that she had almost forgotten about the locket. But she was watching it closely, Warwick knew. Her fingers played with the chain continually, and now and then ran down it and touched the locket at the bottom.

"Shall we dance?" Warwick asked.

They entered the ballroom and danced. He had no chance to get the locket. He wished he might detach it in such a manner that he could kick it into a corner and pick it up afterward. But he knew that he would have to wait until Mrs. Burton Barker's mind was centered on something else. It might be disastrous to make an attempt to get the locket now.

They finished the dance, and walked into the wide hall again. Marlowe was talking to Silvia and the man who had been dancing with her, and Warwick led Mrs. Barker toward them.

"Why not the veranda and smokes?" Marlowe asked lightly.

Warwick flashed a look at him, but agreed. They all moved out to the veranda, walked toward one end of it where there were easy chairs. They seated themselves and lighted cigarettes, and indulged in some more small talk. Warwick and Marlowe were watching each other carefully, each fearing that the other would make an unexpected move.

Warwick began wondering how the thing was to be accomplished. It had seemed so simple compared to some things he had done — merely snipping a locket from a chain and getting away with it without arousing suspicion. He began to tell himself that he must be slowing up, to let such a man as Marlowe prevent him from carrying out the orders of The Spider. He would have to be doubly careful about it now. He wasn't quite sure that Mrs. Barker believed the locket had been lost accidentally in the conservatory. He couldn't afford to run any grave risk, when his future happiness and that of Silvia Rodney depended upon his success.

Mrs. Barker addressed a remark to him, and he bent forward to reply. At that instant, the lights in the house went out.

There came a chorus of exclamations from the ballroom. Chairs scraped on the veranda as guests got to their feet. Mrs. Burton Barker started to say something, and the sentence was broken off in the middle.

John Warwick sprang to his feet, for he suspected a trap of some sort. It would be like Marlowe to have a confederate snap off the lights so that he could work in the dark.

Then there came a sudden rush of men over the railing. Warwick felt himself hurled to one side. He heard an exclamation of fear, and Marlowe's whispered commands.

Warwick realized what was taking place, then. They were kidnaping Mrs. Burton Barker. They probably would carry her a short distance across the lawn, tear the locket from the chain and get away with it. Marlowe would remain behind, and probably take part in the search for the assailants, thus freeing himself of any suspicion.

It all occurred in a short space of time. Warwick sensed that Marlowe would have him attended to, also. And so he darted noiselessly to the railing and vaulted over it to the ground. He brushed against another man, who instantly grappled with him. Warwick started to fight. He felt his throat gripped, felt a peculiar pressure —

"Togo!" he whispered hoarsely.

"That you, sar? I thought it was one of the others," Togo gasped. "Did I hurt you, sar?"

"No! Silence, old top! Let's see what's going on here!"

Those inside the house were crying for lights. Servants were calling to one another, and Warwick heard something said about a fuse burning out.

He crouched at the end of the veranda with Togo He realized that Mrs. Burton Barker was being lifted over the railing, and a whiff of chloroform came to his nostrils. Marlowe was talking loudly now, as if to cover the confusion. Warwick heard Silvia's voice, asking what had happened.

And then he gripped Togo by the arm and led the way around the end of the veranda. He knew that Marlowe's men were ahead of them. He watched and saw them cross a space between two dark spots — four of them carrying a woman.

He darted forward again, with Togo at his heels, whispering explanations and orders.

"Taxi still at corner, sar," Togo whispered in reply.

Across the lawn they followed the men, careful to avoid being seen. The odds were great, and Warwick did not care to attempt a combat and come from it vanquished. The men ahead were running now. They dropped the unconscious form of Mrs. Burton Barker beside a clump of brush.

Warwick stopped there just an instant. It was as he had expected — the locket was gone.

IX

A Lost Locket

AGAIN, John Warwick darted forward, Togo close behind. Warwick was in a rage now. He did not believe in using violence toward women. He always had prided himself on avoiding the use of it whenever the orders of The Spider compelled him to deal with those of the gentler sex. And he did not intend to let four thugs assault a woman in that manner, chloroform her, and steal something that he himself wished to get into his possession.

He stopped behind a tree. The four men were at the curb, mumbling among themselves. It was evident that they were waiting for a motor car, and that the driver had missed his calculations.

"Let us get at them, sar," Togo whispered.

Warwick was just angry enough to agree. He gave the signal and, with Togo, rushed forward.

They hurled themselves upon the four like twin hurricanes. John Warwick went into action like a battleship, showering blows on all sides, but he worked silently, conserving his breath and strength as well as he could.

Togo sprang for the throat of the nearest man, and had him stretched unconscious on the ground in an instant. Then he reached for the second. But the others were putting up a fight, now that the first shock of surprise was over. Warwick and Togo found that the three of them were a match, a little more than a match. With his back against a tree, Warwick fought as well as he could, and Togo tried in vain to clutch one of his antagonists by the throat and put him out of the combat.

Warwick sent a second man lurching to the ground with a well-directed blow. The odds were even now. Togo screeched once and hurled himself at one of the thugs, and the man turned and ran. Warwick made short work of the other.

It took Warwick only a few seconds to search the three men on the ground — and he did not find the locket. Lights were blazing up in the house again, and male guests were rushing toward him. They crowded about him, demanding to know what had happened.

Warwick explained in a few words. Some men had attacked Mrs. Burton Barker on the veranda as the lights went out. She was beside the clump of brush now, unconscious from chloroform. He had taken after the men. Here were three of them — and another had got away. Togo, the Japanese valet, was after that fourth man.

The male guests made short work of the three on the ground. They were picked up and taken to the house, to be held there until the polite could be called. Mrs. Burton Barker was carried inside, too, where the frantic guests were huddling together and talking in whispers of what had occurred. They supposed it was an attempt at robbery; they felt of their necklaces and rings, to be sure that they had not suffered loss.

Warwick remained on the lawn for a quarter of an hour, and at the end of that time Togo returned.

"He got away from me, sar," Togo reported.

"Well, it can't be helped, old chap."

"They — they got it, sar?"

"I imagine that they did, Togo, honorable chap. That was the scheme of course. The man who escaped evidently had it."

"And now, sar —"

"Now, old top, I shall be compelled, for the first time in my life, to report to The Spider that I have failed. And he was particular to tell me, too, that he didn't care to have me fail in this case. He will rave and roar, I doubt not — almost have a fit, and all that sort of thing."

"You are not going to give up, sar?"

"I am not, honorable Jap. Marlowe is the head of this gang, and you can wager that Marlowe remains in the house so that nobody will suspect him. Sooner or later, Marlowe will get that locket from the man who has it."

"Then we watch this Marlowe, sar?"

"We do," Warwick said. "I have to go into the house now, of course. You may remain outside, Togo, and use your own judgment."

"I understand, sar."

"Never heard of such a fuss — all this row over a silly locket! Wonder what the thing is, anyway!"

"I feared there would be trouble, sar,"

"Spider told me as much, but I scarcely believed him," Warwick said. "Imagine I look a pretty specimen now. One of those beggars caught me a clip under the eye — be black in the morning. I'll go into the house now, old top!"

Warwick made his way to the veranda. He discovered that he was a hero. The male guests had told their fair companions that John Warwick had followed the four men who had assaulted and robbed Mrs. Button Barker and accounted for three of them.

Warwick pushed his way to the stairs and up them to the second floor. Servants rushed to his aid. In a bathroom he inspected himself. There was a cut beneath one eye. His collar was torn, his tie soiled, and there was dust on his clothes.

"Pretty sight!" he complained as he bathed his bruised knuckles. "My word, yes! A bit of a row, and all that, but one of the chaps got away!"

Burton Barker rushed into the room, bubbling his thanks and reporting that his wife was all right again — and would descend and order the dance continued.

Then Marlowe stepped into the room.

"Good boy, Warwick!" he said, grinning. "You certainly handled those fellows!"

"Where were you?" Warwick asked nastily.

"It happened so quickly, I didn't realize what was taking place," Marlowe lied. "One of the fellows hurled me back along the railing, and by the time I could get to my feet, they were gone with Mrs. Barker — and you were gone, too. Miss Rodney was nervous — I escorted her inside as soon as the lights came on again."

"Very kind of you — thanks," Warwick said.

"You certainly battered up those three prisoners. They are saying that half a dozen men jumped on them."

"Silly asses! Ought to go to jail!" Warwick said.

"They'll go to jail, all right!" Barker declared.

A servant pushed in and called him, and Barker hurried away. The others could hear a woman wailing in one of the other rooms — Mrs. Burton Barker had discovered that her locket was missing. They could hear her shriek that it must be recovered, could hear Barker giving orders to his servants.

Warwick dismissed the servants who had been helping him, and began putting on a fresh collar one of them had brought. The cut beneath his eye had been bathed and court-plaster applied, but Warwick knew that it would be a bad sight in the morning. He turned from the mirror and saw Marlowe watching him.

"Well?" Marlowe asked.

"Three of your men are going to jail," Warwick said in a low tone.

"That's their fault."

"They are liable to talk, aren't they?"

"I'm not a bit afraid of that," Marlowe said. "They'll take their medicine, and they'll be paid for doing it. They did their work well, you know."

"I suppose so."

"You didn't have a chance, Warwick! It was a good fight while it lasted, but it didn't last long. It might have been different if you had been given plenty of help. I don't understand why The Spider didn't give you help."

"There goes that Spider stuff again!"

"Oh, stop the bluff, Warwick! I'm wise, and you know that I am wise! I say it is a wonder that he didn't give you help."

Warwick stepped close to him. "Very well — since you know so much!" he said. "If I am working for some chap you call The Spider, let it be known that I never need much help!"

"This was the time you needed it, Warwick!"

"Got three of your men, at any rate!"

"But one got away, eh? And so you didn't get the locket!" Marlowe laughed, sneered, and turned toward the door.

"Lots of time yet to get that," Warwick hurled after him.

"Not a chance, Warwick — not a chance in the world! You've had your last look at that little trinket. And what you'll get from that boss of yours will be plenty — don't forget that for a moment. He could not have taken you into his confidence, or you'd have made a better attempt to win out. This was a mighty important deal."

"Don't know what you're talking about, I'm sure!" Warwick said.

"Well, you've lost, Warwick!"

"Game isn't over yet!" John Warwick observed. "Seen lots of them won in the last half of the ninth inning, you know. Rally — all that sort of thing!"

He passed Marlowe and went down the stairs. He intended to keep his eyes on Marlowe, even if he had to send Silvia Rodney home in the limousine alone. Marlowe, he knew, would get possession of that locket sometime. He would find Togo out on the lawn and tell him to hold the taxicab in readiness.

But Togo had disappeared for the time being. Servants with electric torches were searching the lawn for Mrs. Burton Barker's locket. That lady was trying to force herself to believe that it had been torn from her while she was being carried across the lawn — when, in reality, she knew that the assault had been for the purpose of getting the locket.

Mrs. Barker was on the veranda herself, almost hysterical, directing the search, refusing to go to her room. Some of the guests were taking their departure. The orchestra was still playing, and some of the couples were dancing as if nothing had happened. It was a tribute to their hostess.

Warwick went down among the others and pretended to join in the search. For the first time since he had joined The Spider's band, he felt a dread of the supercriminal. He almost feared the interview that he knew he would be forced to hold with him. The Spider did not countenance failure. He had instructed Warwick to get that locket, and he expected success.

It would be like The Spider to refuse to release him from the band and allow him to marry Silvia, and Warwick told himself that he never would marry her unless he was released. He would get the locket yet, he told himself. He would follow Marlowe day and night, with only Togo to help him — he'd get that locket if he was forced to use violence against Marlowe and his men, if he had to turn burglar or highwayman! He never had failed The Spider before, and he did not intend to fail now!

The search came to an end — and the locket had not been found. Warwick went back into the house, and received thanks from a pale Mrs. Burton Barker. He saw that she was making a brave fight to retain her composure, and he wondered again what the locket meant to her, what it meant to others. Locket of Tragedy, Togo had called it, but John Warwick didn't see any sense in that.

He met Silvia in the hall, and they stepped to one side.

"You'll be a handsome man in the morning," she said, laughing a little.

"Do not rub it in, dear lady!" Warwick told her.

"Aren't you ashamed of yourself, getting into a brawl while acting as my escort?"

"It is a serious matter!" Warwick whispered. "Dear lady, I have failed for the time being — they got away with the locket."

"How did it happen, John?"

"Marlowe — that chap you danced with — is at the bottom of it. He got Mrs. Barker to the veranda purposely. Those chaps sprang over the railing when the lights went out, grasped her and chloroformed her, rushed across the lawn with her, took the locket and left her there. My luck, I suppose, that the man who had the locket in his possession escaped.

"Then there is no chance of getting it, John?"

"I haven't quite given up yet. Going to watch this Marlowe chap. Old Togo's about, ready to help. Have to get the thing, or your jolly old uncle will be furious. Might force me to remain in — er — his employ, and all that."

"Perhaps it will all come out right, John."

"Let us hope so!" Warwick said.

Marlowe stepped up to them. "Pardon me, but I believe that I have this dance with Miss Rodney," he said pleasantly. "Our hostess wishes the ball to continue, despite the annoyance she has experienced. As a compliment to her —"

"Of course! Naturally!" Warwick said.

He surrendered Silvia and watched them as they started dancing. He felt a twinge of jealousy, but told himself it was because Marlowe was the man and because Marlowe had bested him for the time being.

He could not help admiring Marlowe's courage. The fellow was carrying it off well. He was an excellent foe, John Warwick thought. And he became more determined to get the locket, if it took him weeks!

X
A Surprise

SILVIA RODNEY danced the encore with Marlowe, while Warwick walked up and down the hall and now and then stopped to speak to some acquaintance and dodge hero worship.

Warwick was wondering just who Marlowe might be and how Mrs. Burton Barker had become acquainted with him. He intended to get a line on Marlowe and keep in touch with the man. He simply had to get the locket! Everything depended upon it —

his future standing with The Spider, his own happiness, and that of Silvia.

He wondered why Silvia was dancing with Marlowe so much, since she knew now that Marlowe was a foe to them all. Her face was radiant when Marlowe returned with her and handed her over to Warwick.

"Now I'll dance with you, John, and then, I think, we'd better go," Silvia said.

Warwick could do nothing but go out upon the floor with her, but he managed a whisper.

"Please make it short, Silvia. I want to watch Marlowe and follow him. A great deal depends on it, you know. Simply must get that locket, what? He'll lead me to it, and all that sort of thing. Have to triumph in the end, or your jolly old uncle will walk around my collar. My word, yes!"

"Aren't you going to take me home, John?"

"Will it make you very angry if I send you alone?" Warwick asked.

"Of course!"

"But, in such a case —"

"I'll be angry, nevertheless. And how will it look to the others, John? Will they not suspect something?"

"Have to cover it up in some manner," Warwick said. "Might get out at the first corner and return."

"Oh, let the old locket go!"

"Dear girl! Your jolly old uncle will be enraged."

"I'll smooth it over for you, John."

"Afraid it would be a difficult task in such a case. Uncle seemed very keen on getting the thing, remember. Some sort of a secret connected with it, and all that. Appears to be vastly important, though for the life of me I cannot understand why."

"Well, you let it go and take me home!"

"Just as you say, dear girl, but I fear that we are making a mistake," Warwick told her, sighing. "Take all the blame myself, of course, and all that. My word! Jolly old uncle probably will roar like a lion. May refuse to — well, you know, dear girl!"

"You leave it to me, John. You've never failed before, have you?"

"Never!"

"Well, uncle cannot raise so very much of a row, then."

"Can't he? I've seen him angry!" Warwick said. "Rather face a tiger unarmed. My word!"

They finished the dance and went toward the hall. Marlowe was just taking leave of Mrs. Burton Barker, and he grinned at John Warwick as he approached. Silvia went for her wraps, and Warwick stepped out on the veranda for an instant.

He walked along the railing, until there came to him from the darkness a peculiar hiss that he recognized.

"That you, Togo?" he asked.

"Yes, sar."

"Follow our man when he leaves — I cannot."

"Yes, sar."

Warwick walked back to the doorway, entered, and continued along the hall toward the stairs.

"Better luck next time," Marlowe whispered as he passed.

"Hope so!" Warwick growled.

"Should have had help, you know. You were up against a tough proposition."

"A proposition of toughs, you mean."

Marlowe's face flushed. "Bad loser, are you?" he sneered.

"Haven't lost yet, you know," Warwick retorted.

"You haven't? Don't fool yourself!"

"Lots of time yet — game's young."

"Not this particular game!" Marlowe said.

"May find out different," Warwick told him. "Rally, you know — all that sort of thing. Seen it lots of times. Advise you to keep your eyes and ears open."

"Oh, I'll be watching out for you!"

"That's an excellent idea," Warwick observed.

He went on up the stairs for his things. He met Silvia; they spoke to Mrs. Burton Barker, and went out to the limousine. Soon they were speeding down the avenue and across the city.

"Oh, cheer up, John!" the girl said.

"Don't feel like it, dear lady. Not used to failure — what? Rather gets me, you know, and all that. My word, yes!"

"It will be all right, John."

"Not so sure about that. Have to report to your jolly old uncle as soon as we reach the house, I suppose, and take what is coming to me."

"Why not put it off?" she asked.

"Never do in the world. Make a full report, and maybe he can get the silly locket by sending somebody else after it — somebody who is not a bungler,"

"But you were fighting against odds!"

"Makes no difference," he declared, "Always fought against odds before and won. Makes no difference at all!"

They rode for a time in silence, Silvia snuggling close to his side.

"When we get home," she said presently, "you wait until I talk to uncle."

"Afraid it'll do no good," Warwick replied.

"Nevertheless, John Warwick, you wait until I have talked to him, and then you can go up and — er — take what is coming to you."

"Very well. Put off the evil hour a few minutes, at any rate," he said. "Imagine I'll get an awful wigging! My word, yes! Probably be told I'm a worthless beggar, and all that sort of thing. First time I've failed, you know — not used to it!"

"Perhaps there'll be a chance yet."

"A slight one," Warwick admitted. "I gave Togo orders to follow that Marlowe chap. By the way, you seemed to like to dance with him."

"John Warwick, are you jealous?"

"My word — no! Just remarked it!" Warwick said.

"Well, you'd better not be jealous, sir! That is something I'll not endure! Here we are at home!"

Warwick told the chauffeur to wait and escorted Silvia inside the house. She left him in the big living room and went up the stairs to The Spider's den. She knew that he would not have retired, that he would wait to tell her good-night.

John Warwick spent a bad quarter of an hour. He paced back and forth across the room, fearful one moment, defiant the next, wondering what he could say to The Spider to justify himself. He decided that he could only explain and ask the supercriminal to be merciful.

And then Silvia came back down the stairs.

"How did he take it?" Warwick asked.

"Oh, I scarcely think he will have you shot John."

"Angry, I suppose?"

"You'll find out soon enough — you are to go right up and see him," she replied.

"Hope the old chap isn't too hard on me," Warwick said. "Can't dare to think of losing you, little lady."

He held her in his arms for an instant, kissed her, and then started slowly up the stairs.

Outside the door of the supercriminal's den, he paused for a moment to gather his courage. Warwick was a man who did not like to confess failure. He knew that The Spider probably had spoken kindly to Silvia, but he would not let that affect the manner in which he received John Warwick.

Finally, he opened the door, entered, closed and bolted it behind him as was the custom, and then whirled around to find The Spider in his usual place behind the big mahogany desk.

"Sit down, Warwick!" The Spider said. "And give me your close attention while I explain something about that locket."

"I regret —"

"Silence — and listen! It is getting late, and I am a tired man. I just want to tell you, Warwick, of the importance of that locket. Several years ago, the woman you know as Mrs. Burton Barker was spending her first season abroad. Her mother was with her. In a peculiar manner, the girl saw a crime committed. She was young and romantic, and she took a fancy to the man who committed it — one of my men."

"I understand, sir."

"Without her mother's knowledge, she kept engagements with this man. He saw in her only a foolish and romantic girl, and he kept up the acquaintance to get information. Her mother was rich, as you know. This man of mine intended to get all the information he could and probably lift the mother's jewels,"

"I understand."

"He let the girl know that he belonged to a famous band of criminals. He let her know too much. The Locket of Tragedy was the property of a famous Parisian, and this man of mine got it one night while looting an apartment. It was called that because it had been owned by persons who met violent ends. It had quite a history, and many a collector stood ready to pay a handsome price for it."

"I see," said Warwick.

"A queen who poisoned herself owned it once, and then a famous courtesan who was tried for murder and executed. Almost every owner of the locket met with violence. My man got it as I have said, and he showed some of the loot to the girl who now is Mrs. Barker. She wanted the locket, and he let her have it, thinking he could steal it from her later. He didn't dare refuse at the time, for he needed more information before attempting to rob her mother of a fortune in jewels.

"Before he could regain the locket her mother took a sudden notion to return to the States, bringing her daughter with her, of course. The night before they departed, this slip of a girl got possession of a bit of tissue paper. That paper is still in existence, and is enough to send me to prison for the rest of my life, and to send other men there. The authorities of Paris would pay a fortune for it.

"She returned to the States, and I sent my man after her with instructions to get the locket and the paper, which she kept in it. He failed, and returned, and I sent two other men. She did not wear the locket in those days — she had it hidden somewhere. I sent her word that, unless she returned the locket and the bit of tissue, I'd have her criminal sweetheart slain. She had spunk — replied that if I did she would hand the paper over to the police.

"She had us there — understand? She threatened to hand the things over the first month she did not receive a letter from this man she admired. We were safe as long as he wrote those letters — and I saw that he did write them.

"Then she got married, and began wearing the locket. It had grown to be a sort of duel between us by that time. She did not surrender the things even after being married, I tried a score of times to get the locket and what it contained, and I failed. I let the thing slide, as the saying is, let her hold the sword over my head.

"Last month, Warwick, she got no communication, for the simple reason that this man of mine had died. I ascertained that she was making investigation — she thought that I had made away with him, understand? She was ready to hand that locket to the police and tell her story."

"And the others —" Warwick asked.

"Members of a band antagonistic to me. They learned of the locket and its secret. They wanted to get it and send it to the authorities of Paris themselves — wanted to see me and some others sent to prison. Do you understand what that locket meant to me, Warwick? If those others got it, if Mrs. Barker retained it, I was doomed. That is how important that locket was to me!"

Warwick gave an exclamation of horror. So he, by his failure, had doomed The Spider — and perhaps himself. For, if an investigation were made, it might lead to Warwick and other new members of the band, too. And, as for Silvia — why, her life would be ruined! She would be pointed out as the niece of a supercriminal.

"It would be a case of chickens coming home to roost!" The Spider continued. "My crimes the last few years, since that accident that made me a cripple, have not been what the world would call extra bad. I have reformed to an extent, as you know. But in the old days, I did many things for which I still could be punished."

"Sir, I —" Warwick began.

The Spider silenced him with a gesture.

"So you can see the importance of that locket," the supercriminal went on, "And when you sent it to me just now, by Silvia —"

"Sir?" Warwick gasped.

"It was a great relief to me. It meant everything. It meant that I shall not have to spend my last days in some prison. And I am so thankful, Warwick, that I am going to quit. I have one thing more to do, and then I am going to disband my people. That one thing is good instead of evil — I'll explain it to you later. And I'm going to give my ill-gotten gains to certain charities and retain just enough to live on. Silvia will marry you — and be happy. Go to her now, John Warwick, and leave me alone with my happiness."

Warwick unbolted the door and hurried out. He almost rushed down the stairs, to where Silvia was waiting for him in the big living room. She laughed as she saw the expression in his face.

"Was it all right?" she asked saucily.

"Dear lady, suppose that you give me some sort of an explanation," he said.

"Regarding what?"

"Your jolly old uncle has just told me that I sent the locket up to him by you — thanked me for it. Knew nothing about it, I assure you! Imagined that thug fellow had it — sent Togo chasing after Marlowe to watch the chap —"

Silvia's laugh interrupted him.

"I told you that perhaps I could help, John," she said.

"My word! Can't understand it at all!"

"Why, John Warwick! When the lights went out and those men came over the railing, I suspected that it was a trick to get the locket. I slipped to one side and finally got right behind that man Marlowe I heard him whispering to the other men as they were using the chloroform. He took the locket himself, John, at that moment. There was a hit of light from the arc on the corner, and I could see by crouching against the wall. He took the locket and slipped it into his waistcoat pocket."

"But that was dangerous —"

"Silly! If there had been a search, he would have pretended that he had just picked it up."

"I suppose so. But how did *you* get the locket?"

"I got it while I was dancing with him, John — picked his pocket, you see."

"My word!" Warwick gasped. "You picked a chap's pocket?"

"Yes. It wasn't at all difficult, John. Remember, you foolish boy, I have a strain of The Spider's blood in my veins. It was that Spider strain that called upon me to do it. I wanted to help you — and it was a sort of adventure —"

"See here!" Warwick exclaimed. "You were deuced lucky, and you must never do such a thing again. Suppose he had felt in his pocket afterward and found the thing gone? He would have suspected you at once."

"Oh, he did feel in his pocket!"

"But —"

"But, you see, John, when I took the locket. I slipped in its place a small portiere ring that I had taken from the draperies in the hall. He merely felt the ring and thought that it was the locket. See?"

"My word!"

"And then, John —"

But she did not finish the sentence. She could not with his lips pressed against hers.

Note for collectors: "The Spider Strain" will be included in *The Spider Strain and Other Stories*, by Johnston McCulley. It's due out in September, 2004. Please see the publisher's website <www.wildsidepress.com> for information. It can be ordered for $14.99 (plus $3.95 shipping in the U.S.) from: Wildside Press, P.O. Box 301, Holicong, PA 18928-0301.

MAN OVERBOARD!
by F. Marion Crawford

YES—I HAVE heard "Man overboard!" a good many times since I was a boy, and once or twice I have seen the man go. There are more men lost in that way than passengers on ocean steamers ever learn of. I have stood looking over the rail on a dark night, when there was a step beside me, and something flew past my head like a big black bat—and then there was a splash! Stokers often go like that. They go mad with the heat, and they slip up on deck and are gone before anybody can stop them, often without being seen or heard. Now and then a passenger will do it, but he generally has what he thinks a pretty good reason. I have seen a man empty his revolver into a crowd of emigrants forward, and then go over like a rocket. Of course, any officer who respects himself will do what he can to pick a man up, if the weather is not so heavy that he would have to risk his ship; but I don't think I remember seeing a man come back when he was once fairly gone more than two or three times in all my life, though we have often picked up the life-buoy, and sometimes the fellow's cap. Stokers and passengers jump over; I never knew a sailor to do that, drunk or sober. Yes, they say it has happened on hard ships, but I never knew a case myself. Once in a long time a man is fished out when it is just too late, and dies in the boat before you can get him aboard, and—well, I don't know that I ever told that story since it happened—I knew a fellow who went over, and came back dead. I didn't see him after he came back; only one of us did, but we all knew he was there.

No, I am not giving you "sharks." There isn't a shark in this story, and I don't know that I would tell it at all if we weren't alone, just you and I. But you and I have seen things in various parts, and maybe you will understand. Anyhow, you know that I am telling what I know about, and nothing else; and it has been on my mind to tell you ever since it happened, only there hasn't been a chance.

It's a long story, and it took some time to happen; and it began a good many years ago, in October, as well as I can remember. I was mate then; I passed the local Marine Board for master about three years later. She was the *Helen B. Jackson*, of New York, with lumber for the West Indies, four-masted schooner, Captain Hackstaff. She was an old-fashioned one, even then—no steam donkey, and all to do by hand. There were still sailors in the coasting trade in those days, you remember. She wasn't a hard ship, for the old man was better than most of them, though he kept to himself and had a face like a monkey-wrench. We were thirteen, all told, in the ship's company; and some of them afterwards thought that might have had something to do with it, but I had all that nonsense knocked out of me when I was a boy. I don't mean to say that I like to go to sea on a Friday, but I *have* gone to sea on a Friday, and nothing has happened; and twice before that we have been thirteen, because one of the hands didn't turn up at the last minute, and nothing ever happened either—nothing worse than the loss of a light spar or two, or a little canvas. Whenever I have been wrecked, we had sailed as cheerily as you please—no thirteens, no Fridays, no dead

men in the hold. I believe it generally happens that way.

I dare say you remember those two Benton boys that were so much alike? It is no wonder, for they were twin brothers. They shipped with us as boys on the old *Boston Belle*, when you were mate and I was before the mast. I never was quite sure which was which of those two, even then; and when they both had beards it was harder than ever to tell them apart. One was Jim, and the other was Jack; James Benton and John Benton. The only difference I ever could see was, that one seemed to be rather more cheerful and inclined to talk than the other; but one couldn't even be sure of that. Perhaps, they had moods. Anyhow, there was one of them that used to whistle when he was alone. He only knew one tune, and that was "Nancy Lee," and the other didn't know any tune at all; but I may be mistaken about that, too. Perhaps they both knew it.

Well, those two Benton boys turned up on board the *Helen B. Jackson*. They had been on half a dozen ships since the *Boston Belle*, and they had grown up and were good seamen. They had reddish beards and bright blue eyes and freckled faces; and they were quiet fellows, good workmen on rigging, pretty willing, and both good men at the wheel. They managed to be in the same watch—it was the port watch on the *Helen B.*, and that was mine, and I had great confidence in them both. If there was any job aloft that needed two hands, they were always the first to jump into the rigging; but that doesn't often happen on a fore-and-aft schooner. If it breezed up, and the jib-topsail was to be taken in, they never minded a wetting, and they would be out at the bowsprit end before there was a hand at the downhaul. The men liked them for that, and because they didn't blow about what they could do. I remember one day in a reefing job, the downhaul parted and came down on deck from the peak of the spanker. When the weather moderated, and we shook the reefs out, the downhaul was forgotten until we happened to think we might soon need it again. There was some sea on, and the boom was off and the gaff was slamming. One of those Benton boys was at the wheel, and before I knew what he was doing, the other was out on the gaff with the end of the new downhaul, trying to reeve it through its block. The one who was steering watched him, and got as white as cheese. The other one was swinging about on the gaff end, and every time she rolled to leeward he brought up with a jerk that would have sent anything but a monkey flying into space. But he didn't leave it until he had rove the new rope, and he got back all right. I think it was Jack at the wheel; the one that seemed more cheerful, the one that whistled "Nancy Lee." He had rather have been doing the job himself than watch his brother do it, and he had a scared look; but he kept her as steady as he could in the swell, and he drew a long breath when Jim had worked his way back to the peak-halliard block, and had something to hold on to. I think it was Jim.

They had good togs, too, and they were neat and clean men in the forecastle. I knew they had nobody belonging to them ashore, no mother, no sisters, and no wives; but somehow they both looked as if a woman overhauled them now and then. I remember that they had one ditty bag between them, and they had a woman's thimble in it. One of the men said something about it to them, and they looked at each other; and one smiled, but the other didn't. Most of their clothes were alike, but they had one red guernsey between them. For some time I used to think it was always the same one that wore it, and I thought that might be a way to tell them apart. But then I heard one asking the other for it, and saying that the other had worn it last. So that was no sign either. The cook was a West Indiaman, called James Lawley; his father had been hanged for putting lights in cocoanut trees where they didn't belong. But he was a good cook, and knew his business; and it wasn't soup-and-bully and dog's-body every Sunday. That's what I meant to say. On Sunday the cook called both those boys Jim, and on week-days he called them Jack. He used to say he must be right sometimes if he did that, because even the hands on a painted clock point right twice a day.

What started me to trying for some way of telling the Bentons apart was this. I heard them talking about a girl. It was at night, in our watch, and the wind had headed us off a little rather suddenly, and when we had flattened in the jibs, we clewed down the top-sails, while the two Benton boys got the spanker sheet aft. One of them was at the helm. I coiled down the mizzen-topsail downhaul myself, and was going aft to see how she headed up, when I stopped to look at a light, and leaned against the deck-house. While I was standing there I heard the two boys talking. It sounded as if they had talked of the same thing before, and as far as I could tell, the voice I heard first belonged to the one who wasn't quite so cheerful as the other—the one who was Jim when one knew which he was.

"Does Mamie know?" Jim asked.

"Not yet," Jack answered quietly. He was at the wheel. "I mean to tell her next time we get home."

"All right."

That was all I heard, because I didn't care to stand there listening while they were talking about their own affairs; so I went aft to look into the binnacle, and I told the one at the wheel to keep her so as long as she had way on her, for I thought the wind would back up again before long, and there was land to leeward. When he answered, his voice, somehow, didn't sound like the cheerful one. Perhaps his brother had relieved the wheel while they had been speaking, but what I had heard set me wondering which of them it was that had a girl at home. There's lots of time for wondering on a schooner in fair weather.

After that I thought I noticed that the two brothers were more silent when they were together. Perhaps they guessed that I had overheard something that night, and kept quiet when I was about. Some men would have amused themselves by trying to chaff them separately about the girl at home, and I suppose whichever one it was would have let the cat out of the bag if I had done that. But, somehow, I didn't like to. Yes, I was thinking of getting married myself at that time, so I had a sort of fellow-feeling for whichever one it was, that made me not want to chaff him.

They didn't talk much, it seemed to me; but in fair weather, when there was nothing to do at night, and one was steering, the other was everlastingly hanging round as if he were waiting to relieve the wheel, though he might have been enjoying a quiet nap for all I cared in such weather. Or else, when one was taking his turn at the lookout, the other would be sitting on an anchor beside him. One kept near the other, at night more than in the daytime. I noticed that. They were fond of sitting on that anchor, and they generally tucked away their pipes under it for the *Helen B.* was a dry boat in most weather, and like most fore-and-afters was better on a wind than going free. With a beam sea we sometimes shipped a little water aft. We were by the stern, anyhow, on that voyage, and that is one reason why we lost the man.

We fell in with a southerly gale, southeast at first; and then the barometer began to fall while you could watch it, and a long swell began to come up from the south'ard. A couple of months earlier we might have been in for a cyclone, but it's "October all over" in those waters, as you know better than I. It was just going to blow, and then it was going to rain, that was all; and we had plenty of time to make everything snug before it breezed up much. It blew harder after sunset, and by the time it was quite dark it was a full gale. We had shortened sail for it, but as we were by the stern we were carrying the spanker close reefed instead of the storm trysail. She steered better so, as long as we didn't have to heave to. I had the first watch with the Benton boys, and we had not been on deck an hour when a child might have seen that the weather meant business.

The Old Man came up on deck and looked round, and in less than a minute he told us to give her the trysail. That meant heaving to, and I was glad of it; for though the *Helen B.* was a good vessel enough, she wasn't a new ship by a long way, and it did her no good to drive her in that weather. I asked whether I should call all hands, but just then the cook came aft, and the Old Man said he thought we could manage the job without waking the sleepers, and the trysail was handy on deck already, for we hadn't been expecting anything better. We were all in oilskins, of course, and the night was as black as a coal mine, with only a ray of light from the slit in the binnacle shield, and you couldn't tell one man from another except by his voice. The Old Man took the wheel; we got the boom amidships, and he jammed her into the wind until she had hardly any way. It was blowing now, and it was all that I and two others could do to get in the slack of the downhaul, while the others lowered away at the peak and throat, and we had our hands full to get a couple of turns round the wet sail. It's all child's play on a fore-and-after compared with reefing topsails in anything like weather, but the gear of a schooner sometimes does unhandy things that you don't expect, and those everlasting long halliards get foul of everything if they get adrift. I remember thinking how unhandy that particular job was. Somebody unhooked the throat-halliard block, and thought he had hooked it into the head-cringle of the trysail, and sang out to hoist away, but he had missed it in the dark, and the heavy block went flying into the lee rigging, and nearly killed him when it swung back with the weather roll. Then the Old Man got her up in the wind until the jib was shaking like thunder; then he held her off, and she went off as soon as the head-sails filled, and he couldn't get her back again without the spanker. Then the *Helen B.* did her favourite trick, and before we had time to say much we had a sea over the quarter and were up to our waists, with the parrels of the trysail only half becketed round the mast, and the deck so full of gear that you couldn't put your foot on a plank, and the spanker beginning to get adrift again, being badly stopped, and the general confusion and hell's delight that you can only have on a fore-and-after when there's nothing really serious the matter. Of course, I don't mean to say that the Old Man couldn't have steered his trick as well as you or I or any other seaman; but I don't believe he had ever been on board the *Helen B.* before, or had his hand on her wheel till then; and he didn't know her ways. I don't mean to say that what happened was his fault. I don't know whose fault it was. Perhaps nobody was to blame. But I knew something happened somewhere on board when we shipped that sea, and you'll never get it out of my head. I hadn't any spare time myself, for I was becketing the rest of the trysail to the mast. We were on the starboard tack, and the throat-halliard came down to port as usual, and I suppose there were at least three men at it, hoisting away, while I was at the beckets.

Now I am going to tell you something. You have known me, man and boy, several voyages; and you are older than I am; and you have always been a good friend to me. Now, do you think I am the sort of man to think I hear things where there isn't anything to hear, or to think I see things when there is nothing to see? No, you don't. Thank you. Well now, I had passed the last becket, and I sang out to the men to sway away, and I was standing on the jaws of the spanker-gaff, with my left hand on the bolt-rope of the trysail, so that I could feel when it was board-taut, and I wasn't thinking of anything except being glad the job was over, and that we were going to heave her to. It was as black as a coal-pocket, except that you could see the streaks on the seas as they went by, and abaft the deck-house I could see the ray of light from the binnacle on the captain's yellow oilskin as he stood at the wheel—or rather I might have seen it if I had looked round at that minute. But I didn't look round. I heard a man whistling. It was "Nancy Lee," and I could have sworn that the man was right over my head in the crosstrees. Only somehow I knew very well that if anybody could have been up there, and could have whistled a tune, there were no living ears sharp enough to hear it on deck then. I heard it distinctly, and at the same time I heard the real whistling of the wind in the weather rigging, sharp and clear as the steam-whistle on a Dago's peanut-cart in New York. That was all right, that was as it should be; but the other wasn't right; and I felt queer and stiff, as if I couldn't move, and my hair was curling against the flannel lining of my sou'wester, and I thought somebody had dropped a lump of ice down my back.

I said that the noise of the wind in the rigging was real, as if the other wasn't, for I felt that it wasn't, though I heard it. But it was, all the same; for the captain heard it, too. When I came to relieve the wheel, while the men were clearing up decks, he was swearing. He was a quiet man, and I hadn't heard him swear before, and I don't think I did again, though several odd things happened after that. Perhaps he said all he had to say then; I don't see how he could have said anything more. I used to think nobody could swear like a Dane, except a Neapolitan or a South American; but when I had heard the Old Man I changed my mind. There's nothing afloat or ashore that can beat one of your quiet American skippers, if he gets off on that tack. I didn't need to ask him what was the matter, for I knew he had heard "Nancy Lee," as I had, only it affected us differently.

He did not give me the wheel, but told me to go forward and get the second bonnet off the staysail, so as to keep her up better. As we tailed on to the sheet when it was done, the man next to me knocked his sou'wester off against my shoulder, and his face came so close to me that I could see it in the dark. It must have been very

white for me to see it, but I only thought of that afterwards. I don't see how any light could have fallen upon it, but I knew it was one of the Benton boys. I don't know what made me speak to him. "Hullo, Jim! Is that you?" I asked. I don't know why I said Jim, rather than Jack.

"I am Jack," he answered.

We made all fast, and things were much quieter.

"The Old Man heard you whistling 'Nancy Lee,' just now," I said, "and he didn't like it."

It was as if there were a white light inside his face, and it was ghastly. I know his teeth chattered. But he didn't say anything, and the next minute he was somewhere in the dark trying to find his sou'wester at the foot of the mast.

When all was quiet, and she was hove to, coming to and falling off her four points as regularly as a pendulum, and the helm lashed a little to the lee, the Old Man turned in again, and I managed to light a pipe in the lee of the deckhouse, for there was nothing more to be done till the gale chose to moderate, and the ship was as easy as a baby in its cradle. Of course the cook had gone below, as he might have done an hour earlier; so there were supposed to be four of us in the watch. There was a man at the lookout, and there was a hand by the wheel, though there was no steering to be done, and I was having my pipe in the lee of the deck-house, and the fourth man was somewhere about decks, probably having a smoke too. I thought some skippers I had sailed with would have called the watch aft, and given them a drink after that job, but it wasn't cold, and I guessed that our Old Man wouldn't be particularly generous in that way. My hands and feet were red-hot, and it would be time enough to get into dry clothes when it was my watch below; so I stayed where I was, and smoked. But by and by, things being so quiet, I began to wonder why nobody moved on deck; just that sort of restless wanting to know where every man is that one sometimes feels in a gale of wind on a dark night. So when I had finished my pipe I began to move about. I went aft, and there was a man leaning over the wheel, with his legs apart and both hands hanging down in the light from the binnacle, and his sou'wester over his eyes. Then I went forward, and there was a man at the lookout, with his back against the foremast, getting what shelter he could from the staysail. I knew by his small height that he was not one of the Benton boys. Then I went round by the weather side, and poked about in the dark, for I began to wonder where the other man was. But I couldn't find him, though I searched the decks until I got right aft again. It was certainly one of the Benton boys that was missing, but it wasn't like either of them to go below to change his clothes in such warm weather. The man at the wheel was the other, of course. I spoke to him.

"Jim, what's become of your brother?"

"I am Jack, sir."

"Well, then, Jack, where's Jim? He's not on deck."

"I don't know, sir."

When I had come up to him he had stood up from force of instinct, and had laid his hands on the spokes as if he were steering, though the wheel was lashed; but he still bent his face down, and it was half hidden by the edge of his sou'wester, while he seemed to be staring at the compass. He spoke in a very low voice, but that was natural, for the captain had left his door open when he turned in, as it was a warm night in spite of the storm, and there was no fear of shipping any more water now.

"What put it into your head to whistle like that, Jack? You've been at sea long enough to know better."

He said something, but I couldn't hear the words; it sounded as if he were denying the charge.

"Somebody whistled," I said.

He didn't answer, and then, I don't know why, perhaps because the Old Man hadn't given us a drink, I cut half an inch off the plug of tobacco I had in my oilskin pocket, and gave it to him. He knew my tobacco was good, and he shoved it into his mouth with a word of thanks. I was on the weather side of the wheel.

"Go forward and see if you can find Jim," I said.

He started a little, and then stepped back and passed behind me, and was going along the weather side. Maybe his silence about the whistling had irritated me, and his taking it for granted that because we were hove to and it was a dark night, he might go forward any way he pleased. Anyhow, I stopped him, though I spoke good-naturedly enough.

"Pass to leeward, Jack," I said.

He didn't answer, but crossed the deck between the binnacle and the deckhouse to the lee side. She was only falling off and coming to, and riding the big seas as easily as possible, but the man was not steady on his feet and reeled against the corner of the deckhouse and then against the lee rail. I was quite sure he couldn't have had anything to drink, for neither of the brothers were the kind to hide rum from their shipmates, if they had any, and the only spirits that were aboard were locked up in the captain's cabin. I wondered whether he had been hit by the throat-halliard block and was hurt.

I left the wheel and went after him, but when I got to the corner of the deck-house I saw that he was on a full run forward, so I went back. I watched the compass for a while, to see how far she went off, and she must have come to again half a dozen times before I heard voices, more than three or four, forward; and then I heard the little West Indies cook's voice, high and shrill above the rest:

"Man overboard!"

There wasn't anything to be done, with the ship hove to and the wheel lashed. If there was a man overboard, he must be in the water right alongside. I couldn't imagine how it could have happened, but I ran forward instinctively. I came upon the cook first, half-dressed in his shirt and trousers, just as he had tumbled out of his bunk. He was jumping into the main rigging, evidently hoping to see the man, as if any one could have seen anything on such a night, except the foam-streaks on the black water, and now and then the curl of a breaking sea as it went away to leeward. Several of the men were peering over the rail into the dark. I caught the cook by the foot, and asked who was gone.

"It's Jim Benton," he shouted down to me. "He's not aboard this ship!"

There was no doubt about that Jim Benton was gone; and I knew in a flash that he had been taken off by that sea when we were setting the storm trysail. It was nearly half an hour since then; she had run like wild for a few minutes until we got her hove to, and no swimmer that ever swam could have lived as long as that in such a sea. The men knew it as well as I, but still they stared into the foam as if they had any chance of seeing the lost man. I let the cook get into the rigging and joined the men, and asked if they had made a thorough search on board, though I knew they had

and that it could not take long, for he wasn't on deck, and there was only the forecastle below.

"That sea took him over, sir, as sure as you're born," said one of the men close beside me.

We had no boat that could have lived in that sea, of course, and we all knew it. I offered to put one over, and let her drift astern two or three cable's-lengths by a line, if the men thought they could haul me aboard again; but none of them would listen to that, and I should probably have been drowned if I had tried it, even with a life-belt; for it was a breaking sea. Besides, they all knew as well as I did that the man could not be right in our wake. I don't know why I spoke again.

"Jack Benton, are you there? Will you go if I will?"

"No, sir," answered a voice; and that was all.

By that time the Old Man was on deck, and I felt his hand on my shoulder rather roughly, as if he meant to shake me.

"I'd reckoned you had more sense, Mr. Torkeldsen," he said. "God knows I would risk my ship to look for him, if it were any use; but he must have gone half an hour ago."

He was a quiet man, and the men knew he was right, and that they had seen the last of Jim Benton when they were bending the trysail—if anybody had seen him then. The captain went below again, and for some time the men stood around Jack, quite near him, without saying anything, as sailors do when they are sorry for a man and can't help him; and then the watch below turned in again, and we were three on deck.

Nobody can understand that there can be much consolation in a funeral, unless he has felt that blank feeling there is when a man's gone overboard whom everybody likes. I suppose landsmen think it would be easier if they didn't have to bury their fathers and mothers and friends; but it wouldn't be. Somehow the funeral keeps up the idea of something beyond. You may believe in that something just the same; but a man who has gone in the dark, between two seas, without a cry, seems much more beyond reach than if he were still lying on his bed, and had only just stopped breathing. Perhaps Jim Benton knew that, and wanted to come back to us. I don't know, and I am only telling you what happened, and you may think what you like.

Jack stuck by the wheel that night until the watch was over. I don't know whether he slept afterwards, but when I came on deck four hours later, there he was again, in his oilskins, with his sou'-wester over his eyes, staring into the binnacle. We saw that he would rather stand there, and we left him alone. Perhaps it was some consolation to him to get that ray of light when everything was so dark. It began to rain, too, as it can when a southerly gale is going to break up, and we got every bucket and tub on board, and set them under the booms to catch the fresh water for washing our clothes. The rain made it very thick, and I went and stood under the lee of the staysail, looking out. I could tell that day was breaking, because the foam was whiter in the dark where the seas crested, and little by little the black rain grew grey and steamy, and I couldn't see the red glare of the port light on the water when she went off and rolled to leeward. The gale had moderated considerably, and in another hour we should be under way again. I was still standing there when Jack Benton came forward. He stood still a few minutes near me. The rain came down in a solid sheet, and I could see his wet beard and a corner of his cheek, too, grey in the dawn. Then he stooped down and began feeling under the anchor for his pipe. We had hardly shipped any water forward, and I suppose he had some way of tucking the pipe in, so that the rain hadn't floated it off. Presently he got on his legs again, and I saw that he had two pipes in his hand. One of them had belonged to his brother, and after looking at them a moment I suppose he recognised his own, for he put it in his mouth, dripping with water. Then he looked at the other fully a minute without moving. When he had made up his mind, I suppose, he quietly chucked it over the lee rail, without even looking round to see whether I was watching him. I thought it was a pity, for it was a good wooden pipe, with a nickel ferrule, and somebody would have been glad to have it. But I didn't like to make any remark, for he had a right to do what he pleased with what had belonged to his dead brother. He blew the water out of his own pipe, and dried it against his jacket, putting his hand inside his oilskin; he filled it, standing under the lee of the foremast, got a light after wasting two or three matches, and turned the pipe upside down in his teeth, to keep the rain out of the bowl. I don't know why I noticed everything he did, and remember it now; but somehow I felt sorry for him, and I kept wondering whether there was anything I could say that would make him feel better. But I didn't think of anything, and as it was broad daylight I went aft again, for I guessed that the Old Man would turn out before long and order the spanker set and the helm up. But he didn't turn out before seven bells, just as the clouds broke and showed blue sky to leeward—"the Frenchman's barometer," you used to call it.

Some people don't seem to be so dead, when they are dead, as others are. Jim Benton was like that. He had been on my watch, and I couldn't get used to the idea that he wasn't about decks with me. I was always expecting to see him, and his brother was so exactly like him that I often felt as if I did see him and forgot he was dead, and made the mistake of calling Jack by his name; though I tried not to, because I knew it must hurt. If ever Jack had been the cheerful one of the two, as I had always supposed he had been, he had changed very much, for he grew to be more silent than Jim had ever been.

One fine afternoon I was sitting on the main-hatch, overhauling the clockwork of the taffrail-log, which hadn't been registering very well of late, and I had got the cook to bring me a coffeecup to hold the small screws as I took them out, and a saucer for the sperm-oil I was going to use. I noticed that he didn't go away, but hung round without exactly watching what I was doing, as if he wanted to say something to me. I thought if it were worth much he would say it anyhow, so I didn't ask him questions; and sure enough he began of his own accord before long. There was nobody on deck but the man at the wheel, and the other man away forward.

"Mr. Torkeldsen," the cook began, and then stopped.

I supposed he was going to ask me to let the watch break out a barrel of flour, or some salt horse.

"Well, doctor?" I asked, as he didn't go on.

"Well, Mr. Torkeldsen," he answered, "I somehow want to ask you whether you think I am giving satisfaction on this ship, or not?"

"So far as I know, you are, doctor. I haven't heard any complaints from the forecastle, and the captain has said nothing, and I think you know your business, and the cabin-boy is bursting out of his clothes. That looks as if you are giving satisfaction. What makes you think you are not?"

I am not good at giving you that West Indies talk, and shan't try; but the doctor beat about the bush awhile, and then he told me he thought the men were beginning to play tricks on him, and he didn't like it, and thought he hadn't deserved it, and would like his discharge at our next port. I told him he was a damned fool, of course, to begin with; and that men were more apt to try a joke with a chap they liked than with anybody they wanted to get rid of; unless it was a bad joke, like flooding his bunk, or filling his boots with tar. But it wasn't that kind of practical joke. The doctor said that the men were trying to frighten him, and he didn't like it, and that they put things in his way that frightened him. So I told him he was a damned fool to be frightened, anyway, and I wanted to know what things they put in his way. He gave me a strange answer. He said they were spoons and forks, and odd plates, and a cup now and then, and such things.

I set down the taffrail-log on the bit of canvas I had put under it, and looked at the doctor. He was uneasy, and his eyes had a sort of hunted look, and his yellow face looked grey. He wasn't trying to make trouble. He was in trouble. So I asked him questions.

He said he could count as well as anybody, and do sums without using his fingers, but that when he couldn't count any other way he did use his fingers, and it always came out the same. He said that when he and the cabin-boy cleared up after the men's meals there were more things to wash than he had given out. There'd be a fork more, or there'd be a spoon more, and sometimes there'd be a spoon and a fork, and there was always a plate more. It wasn't that he complained of that. Before poor Jim Benton was lost they had a man more to feed, and his gear to wash up after meals, and that was in the contract, the doctor said. It would have been if there were twenty in the ship's company; but he didn't think it was right for the men to play tricks like that. He kept his things in good order, and he counted them, and he was responsible for them, and it wasn't right that the men should take more things than they needed when his back was turned, and just soil them and mix them up with their own, so as to make him think—

He stopped there, and looked at me, and I looked at him. I didn't know what he thought, but I began to guess. I wasn't going to humour any such nonsense as that, so I told him to speak to the men himself, and not come bothering me about such things.

"Count the plates and forks and spoons before them when they sit down to table, and tell them that's all they'll get; and when they have finished, count the things again, and if the count isn't right, find out who did it. You know it must be one of them. You're not a green hand; you've been going to sea ten or eleven years, and don't want any lesson about how to behave if the boys play a trick on you."

"If I could catch him," said the cook, "I'd have a knife into him before he could say his prayers."

Those West India men are always talking about knives, especially when they are badly frightened. I knew what he meant, and didn't ask him, but went on cleaning the brass cogwheels of the patent log and oiling the bearings with a feather. "Wouldn't it be better to wash it out with boiling water, sir?" asked the cook, in an insinuating tone. He knew that he had made a fool of himself, and was anxious to make it right again.

I heard no more about the odd platter and gear for two or three days, though I thought about his story a good deal. The doctor evidently believed that Jim Benton had come back, though he didn't quite like to say so. His story had sounded silly enough on a bright afternoon, in fair weather, when the sun was on the water, and every rag was drawing in the breeze, and the sea looked as pleasant and harmless as a cat that has just eaten a canary. But when it was toward the end of the first watch, and the waning moon had not risen yet, and the water was like still oil, and the jibs hung down flat and helpless like the wings of a dead bird—it wasn't the same then. More than once I have started then, and looked round when a fish jumped, expecting to see a face sticking up out of the water with its eyes shut. I think we all felt something like that at the time.

One afternoon we were putting a fresh service on the jib-sheet-pennant. It wasn't my watch, but I was standing by looking on. Just then Jack Benton came up from below, and went to look for his pipe under the anchor. His face was hard and drawn, and his eyes were cold like steel balls. He hardly ever spoke now, but he did his duty as usual and nobody had to complain of him, though we were all beginning to wonder how long his grief for his dead brother was going to last like that. I watched him as he crouched down, and ran his hand into the hiding-place for the pipe. When he stood up, he had two pipes in his hand.

Now, I remembered very well seeing him throw one of those pipes away, early in the morning after the gale; and it came to me now, and I didn't suppose he kept a stock of them under the anchor. I caught sight of his face, and it was greenish white, like the foam on shallow water, and he stood a long time looking at the two pipes. He wasn't looking to see which was his, for I wasn't five yards from him as he stood, and one of those pipes had been smoked that day, and was shiny where his hand had rubbed it, and the bone mouthpiece was chafed white where his teeth had bitten it. The other was water-logged. It was swelled and cracking with wet, and it looked to me as if there were a little green weed on it.

Jack Benton turned his head rather stealthily as I looked away, and then he hid the thing in his trousers pocket, and went aft on the lee side, out of sight. The men had got the sheet pennant on a stretch to serve it, but I ducked under it and stood where I could see what Jack did, just under the fore-staysail. He couldn't see me, and he was looking about for something. His hand shook as he picked up a bit of half-bent iron rod, about a foot long, that had been used for turning an eyebolt, and had been left on the mainhatch. His hand shook as he got a piece of marline out of his pocket, and made the water-logged pipe fast to the iron. He didn't mean it to get adrift, either, for he took his turns carefully, and hove them taut and then rode them, so that they couldn't slip, and made the end fast with two half-hitches round the iron, and hitched it back on itself. Then he tried it with his hands, and looked up and down the deck furtively, and then quietly dropped the pipe and iron over the rail, so that I didn't even hear the splash. If anybody was playing tricks on board, they weren't meant for the cook.

I asked some questions about Jack Benton, and one of the men told me that he was off his feed, and hardly ate anything, and swallowed all the coffee he could lay his hands on, and had used up all his own tobacco and had begun on what his brother had left.

"The doctor says it ain't so, sir," said the man, looking at me shyly, as if he didn't expect to be believed; "the doctor says there's as much eaten from breakfast to breakfast as there was before Jim fell overboard, though there's a mouth less and another that eats

nothing. I says it's the cabin-boy that gets it. He's bu'sting."

I told him that if the cabin-boy ate more than his share, he must work more than his share, so as to balance things. But the man laughed strangely, and looked at me again.

"I only said that, sir, just like that. We all know it ain't so."

"Well, how is it?"

"How is it?" asked the man, half-angry all at once. "I don't know how it is, but there's a hand on board that's getting his whack along with us as regular as the bells."

"Does he use tobacco?" I asked, meaning to laugh it out of him, but as I spoke I remembered the water-logged pipe.

"I guess he's using his own still," the man answered, in a strange, low voice. "Perhaps he'll take some one else's when his is all gone."

It was about nine o'clock in the morning, I remember, for just then the captain called to me to stand by the chronometer while he took his fore observation. Captain Hackstaff wasn't one of those old skippers who do everything themselves with a pocket watch, and keep the key of the chronometer in their waistcoat pocket, and won't tell the mate how far the dead reckoning is out. He was rather the other way, and I was glad of it, for he generally let me work the sights he took, and just ran his eye over my figures afterwards. I am bound to say his eye was pretty good, for he would pick out a mistake in a logarithm, or tell me that I had worked the "Equation of Time" with the wrong sign, before it seemed to me that he could have got as far as "half the sum, minus the altitude." He was always right, too, and besides he knew a lot about iron ships and local deviation, and adjusting the compass, and all that sort of thing. I don't know how he came to be in command of a fore-and-aft schooner. He never talked about himself, and maybe he had just been mate on one of those big steel square-riggers, and something had put him back. Perhaps he had been captain, and had got his ship aground, through no particular fault of his, and had to begin over again. Sometimes he talked just like you and me, and sometimes he would speak more like books do, or some of those Boston people I have heard. I don't know. We have all been shipmates now and then with men who have seen better days. Perhaps he had been in the Navy, but what makes me think he couldn't have been, was that he was a thorough good seaman, a regular old wind-jammer, and understood sail, which those Navy chaps rarely do. Why, you and I have sailed with men before the mast who had their master's certificates in their pockets—English Board of Trade certificates, too—who could work a double altitude if you would lend them a sextant and give them a look at the chronometer, as well as many a man who commands a big square-rigger. Navigation ain't everything, nor seamanship, either. You've got to have it in you, if you mean to get there.

I don't know how our captain heard that there was trouble forward. The cabin-boy may have told him, or the men may have talked outside his door when they relieved the wheel at night. Anyhow, he got wind of it, and when he had got his sight that morning he had all hands aft, and gave them a lecture. It was just the kind of talk you might have expected from him. He said he hadn't any complaint to make, and that so far as he knew everybody on board was doing his duty, and that he was given to understand that the men got their whack, and were satisfied. He said his ship was never a hard ship, and that he liked quiet, and that was the reason he didn't mean to have any nonsense, and the men might just as well understand that, too. We'd had a great misfortune, he said, and it was nobody's fault. We had lost a man we all liked and respected, and he felt that everybody in the ship ought to be sorry for the man's brother, who was left behind, and that it was rotten lubberly childishness, and unjust and unmanly and cowardly, to be playing schoolboy tricks with forks and spoons and pipes, and that sort of gear. He said it had got to stop right now, and that was all, and the men might go forward. And so they did.

It got worse after that, and the men watched the cook, and the cook watched the men, as if they were trying to catch each other; but I think everybody felt that there was something else. One evening, at supper-time, I was on deck, and Jack came aft to relieve the wheel while the man who was steering got his supper. He hadn't got past the main-hatch on the lee side, when I heard a man running in slippers that slapped on the deck, and there was a sort of a yell and I saw the coloured cook going for Jack, with a carving-knife in his hand. I jumped to get between them, and Jack turned round short, and put out his hand. I was too far to reach them, and the cook jabbed out with his knife. But the blade didn't get anywhere near Benton. The cook seemed to be jabbing it into the air again and again, at least four feet short of the mark. Then he dropped his right hand, and I saw the whites of his eyes in the dusk, and he reeled up against the pin-rail, and caught hold of a belaying-pin with his left. I had reached him by that time, and grabbed hold of his knife-hand and the other too, for I thought he was going to use the pin; but Jack Benton was standing staring stupidly at him, as if he didn't understand. But instead, the cook was holding on because he couldn't stand, and his teeth were chattering, and he let go of the knife, and the point stuck into the deck.

"He's crazy!" said Jack Benton, and that was all he said and he went aft.

When he was gone, the cook began to come to, and he spoke quite low, near my ear.

"There were two of them! So help me God, there were two of them!"

I don't know why I didn't take him by the collar, and give him a good shaking; but I didn't. I just picked up the knife and gave it to him, and told him to go back to his galley, and not to make a fool of himself. You see, he hadn't struck at Jack, but at something he thought he saw, and I knew what it was, and I felt that same thing, like a lump of ice sliding down my back, that I felt that night when we were bending the trysail.

When the men had seen him running aft, they jumped up after him, but they held off when they saw that I had caught him. By and by, the man who had spoken to me before told me what had happened. He was a stocky little chap, with a red head.

"Well," he said, "there isn't much to tell. Jack Benton had been eating his supper with the rest of us. He always sits at the after corner of the table, on the port side. His brother used to sit at the end, next him. The doctor gave him a thundering big piece of pie to finish up with, and when he had finished he didn't stop for a smoke, but went off quick to relieve the wheel. Just as he had gone, the doctor came in from the galley, and when he saw Jack's empty plate he stood stock still staring at it; and we all wondered what was the matter, till we looked at the plate. There were two forks in it, sir, lying side by side. Then the doctor grabbed his knife, and flew up through the hatch like a rocket. The other fork was there all right, Mr. Torkeldsen, for we all saw it and handled it; and we all

had our own. That's all I know."

I didn't feel that I wanted to laugh when he told me that story; but I hoped the Old Man wouldn't hear it, for I knew he wouldn't believe it, and no captain that ever sailed likes to have stories like that going round about his ship. It gives her a bad name. But that was all anybody ever saw except the cook, and he isn't the first man who has thought he saw things without having any drink in him. I think, if the doctor had been weak in the head as he was afterwards, he might have done something foolish again, and there might have been serious trouble. But he didn't. Only, two or three times I saw him looking at Jack Benton in a funny, scared way, and once, I heard him talking to himself.

"There's two of them! So help me God, there's two of them!"

He didn't say anything more about asking for his discharge, but I knew well enough that if he got ashore at the next port we should never see him again, if he had to leave his kit behind him, and his money, too. He was scared all through, for good and all; and he wouldn't be right again till he got another ship. It's no use to talk to a man when he gets like that, any more than it is to send a boy to the main truck when he has lost his nerve.

Jack Benton never spoke of what happened that evening. I don't know whether he knew about the two forks, or not; or whether he understood what the trouble was. Whatever he knew from the other men, he was evidently living under a hard strain. He was quiet enough, and too quiet; but his face was set, and sometimes it twitched oddly when he was at the wheel, and he would turn his head round sharp to look behind him. A man doesn't do that naturally, unless there's a vessel that he thinks is creeping up on the quarter. When that happens, if the man at the wheel takes a pride in his ship, he will almost always keep glancing over his shoulder to see whether the other fellow is gaining. But Jack Benton used to look round when there was nothing there; and what is curious, the other men seemed to catch the trick when they were steering. One day the Old Man turned out just as the man at the wheel looked behind him.

"What are you looking at?" asked the captain.

"Nothing, sir," answered the man.

"Then keep your eye on the mizzenroyal," said the Old Man, as if he were forgetting that we weren't a squarerigger.

"Ay, ay, sir," said the man.

The captain told me to go below and work up the latitude from the dead-reckoning, and he went forward of the deckhouse and sat down to read, as he often did. When I came up, the man at the wheel was looking round again, and I stood beside him and just asked him quietly what everybody was looking at, for it was getting to be a general habit. He wouldn't say anything at first, but just answered that it was nothing. But when he saw that I didn't seem to care, and just stood there as if there were nothing more to be said, he naturally began to talk.

He said that it wasn't that he saw anything, because there wasn't anything to see except the spanker sheet just straining a little, and working in the sheaves of the blocks as the schooner rose to the short seas. There wasn't anything to be seen, but it seemed to him that the sheet made a strange noise in the blocks. It was a new manilla sheet; and in dry weather it did make a little noise, something between a creak and a wheeze. I looked at it and looked at the man, and said nothing; and presently he went on. He asked me if I didn't notice anything peculiar about the noise. I listened awhile, and said I didn't notice anything. Then he looked rather sheepish, but said he didn't think it could be his own ears, because every man who steered his trick heard the same thing now and then, sometimes once in a day, sometimes once in a night, sometimes it would go on a whole hour.

"It sounds like sawing wood," I said, just like that.

"To us it sounds a good deal more like a man whistling 'Nancy Lee.'" He started nervously as he spoke the last words. "There, sir, don't you hear it?" he asked suddenly.

I heard nothing but the creaking of the manilla sheet. It was getting near noon, and fine, clear weather in southern waters, just the sort of day and the time when you would least expect to feel creepy. But I remembered how I had heard that same tune overhead at night in a gale of wind a fortnight earlier, and I am not ashamed to say that the same sensation came over me now, and I wished myself well out of the *Helen B.*, and aboard of any old cargo-dragger, with a windmill on deck, and an eighty-nine-forty-eighter for captain, and a fresh leak whenever it breezed up.

Little by little during the next few days life on board that vessel came to be about as unbearable as you can imagine. It wasn't that there was much talk, for I think the men were shy even of speaking to each other freely about what they thought. The whole ship's company grew silent, until one hardly ever heard a voice, except giving an order and the answer. The men didn't sit over their meals when their watch was below, but either turned in at once or sat about on the forecastle smoking their pipes without saying a word. We were all thinking of the same thing. We all felt as if there were a hand on board, sometimes below, sometimes about decks, sometimes aloft, sometimes on the boom end; taking his full share of what the others got, but doing no work for it. We didn't only feel it, we knew it. He took up no room, he cast no shadow, and we never heard his footfall on deck; but he took his whack with the rest as regular as the bells, and he whistled "Nancy Lee." It was like the worst sort of dream you can imagine; and I dare say a good many of us tried to believe it was nothing else sometimes, when we stood looking over the weather rail in fine weather with the breeze in our faces; but if we happened to turn round and look into each other's eyes, we knew it was something worse than any dream could be; and we would turn away from each other with a queer, sick feeling, wishing that we could just for once see somebody who didn't know what we knew.

There's not much more to tell about the *Helen B. Jackson* so far as I am concerned. We were more like a shipload of lunatics than anything else when we ran in under Morro Castle, and anchored in Havana. The cook had brain fever and was raving mad in his delirium; and the rest of the men weren't far from the same state. The last three or four days had been awful, and we had been as near to having a mutiny on board as I ever want to be. The men didn't want to hurt anybody; but they wanted to get away out of that ship, if they had to swim for it; to get away from that whistling, from that dead shipmate who had come back, and who filled the ship with his unseen self. I know that if the Old Man and I hadn't kept a sharp lookout the men would have put a boat over quietly on one of those calm nights, and pulled away, leaving the captain and me and the mad cook to work the schooner into harbour. We should have done it somehow, of course, for we hadn't far to run if we could get a breeze; and once or twice I found myself wishing that the crew were really gone, for the awful state of fright in which

they lived was beginning to work on me too. You see I partly believed and partly didn't; but anyhow I didn't mean to let the thing get the better of me, whatever it was. I turned crusty, too, and kept the men at work on all sorts of jobs, and drove them to it until they wished I was overboard, too. It wasn't that the Old Man and I were trying to drive them to desert without their pay, as I am sorry to say a good many skippers and mates do, even now. Captain Hackstaff was as straight as a string, and I didn't mean those poor fellows should be cheated out of a single cent; and I didn't blame them for wanting to leave the ship, but it seemed to me that the only chance to keep everybody sane through those last days was to work the men till they dropped. When they were dead tired they slept a little, and forgot the thing until they had to tumble up on deck and face it again. That was a good many years ago. Do you believe that I can't hear "Nancy Lee" now, without feeling cold down my back? For I heard it too, now and then, after the man had explained why he was always looking over his shoulder. Perhaps it was imagination. I don't know. When I look back it seems to me that I only remember a long fight against something I couldn't see, against an appalling presence, against something worse than cholera or Yellow Jack or the plague—and goodness knows the mildest of them is bad enough when it breaks out at sea. The men got as white as chalk, and wouldn't go about decks alone at night, no matter what I said to them. With the cook raving in his bunk the forecastle would have been a perfect hell, and there wasn't a spare cabin on board. There never is on a fore-and-after. So I put him into mine, and he was more quiet there, and at last fell into a sort of stupor as if he were going to die. I don't know what became of him, for we put him ashore alive and left him in the hospital.

The men came aft in a body, quiet enough, and asked the captain if he wouldn't pay them off, and let them go ashore. Some men wouldn't have done it, for they had shipped for the voyage, and had signed articles. But the captain knew that when sailors get an idea into their heads they're no better than children; and if he forced them to stay aboard he wouldn't get much work out of them, and couldn't rely on them in a difficulty. So he paid them off, and let them go. When they had gone forward to get their kits, he asked me whether I wanted to go too, and for a minute I had a sort of weak feeling that I might just as well. But I didn't, and he was a good friend to me afterwards. Perhaps he was grateful to me for sticking to him.

When the men went off he didn't come on deck; but it was my duty to stand by while they left the ship. They owed me a grudge for making them work during the last few days, and most of them dropped into the boat without so much as a word or a look, as sailors will. Jack Benton was the last to go over the side, and he stood still a minute and looked at me, and his white face twitched. I thought he wanted to say something.

"Take care of yourself, Jack," said I. "So long!"

It seemed as if he couldn't speak for two or three seconds; then his words came thick.

"It wasn't my fault, Mr. Torkeldsen. I swear it wasn't my fault!"

That was all; and he dropped over the side, leaving me to wonder what he meant.

The captain and I stayed on board, and the ship-chandler got a West India boy to cook for us.

That evening, before turning in, we were standing by the rail having a quiet smoke, watching the lights of the city, a quarter of a mile off, reflected in the still water. There was music of some sort ashore, in a sailors' dance-house, I dare say; and I had no doubt that most of the men who had left the ship were there, and already full of jiggy-jiggy. The music played a lot of sailors' tunes that ran into each other, and we could hear the men's voices in the chorus now and then. One followed another, and then it was "Nancy Lee," loud and clear, and the men singing "Yo-ho, heave-ho!"

"I have no ear for music," said Captain Hackstaff, "but it appears to me that's the tune that man was whistling the night we lost the man overboard. I don't know why it has stuck in my head, and of course it's all nonsense; but it seems to me that I have heard it all the rest of the trip."

I didn't say anything to that, but I wondered just how much the Old Man had understood. Then we turned in, and I slept ten hours without opening my eyes.

I stuck to the *Helen B. Jackson* after that as long as I could stand a fore-and-after; but that night when we lay in Havana was the last time I ever heard "Nancy Lee" on board of her. The spare hand had gone ashore with the rest, and he never came back, and he took his tune with him; but all those things are just as clear in my memory as if they had happened yesterday. After that I was in deep water for a year or more, and after I came home I got my certificate, and what with having friends and having saved a little money, and having had a small legacy from an uncle in Norway, I got the command of a coastwise vessel, with a small share in her. I was at home three weeks before going to sea, and Jack Benton saw my name in the local papers, and wrote to me.

He said that he had left the sea, and was trying farming, and he was going to be married, and he asked if I wouldn't come over for that, for it wasn't more than forty minutes by train; and he and Mamie would be proud to have me at the wedding. I remembered how I had heard one brother ask the other whether Mamie knew. That meant, whether she knew, he wanted to marry her, I suppose. She had taken her time about it, for it was pretty nearly three years then since we had lost Jim Benton overboard.

I had nothing particular to do while we were getting ready for sea; nothing to prevent me from going over for a day, I mean; and I thought I'd like to see Jack Benton, and have a look at the girl he was going to marry. I wondered whether he had grown cheerful again, and had got rid of that drawn look he had when he told me it wasn't his fault. How could it have been his fault, anyhow? So I wrote to Jack that I would come down and see him married; and when the day came I took the train, and got there about ten o'clock in the morning. I wish I hadn't. Jack met me at the station, and he told me that the wedding was to be late in the afternoon, and that they weren't going off on any silly wedding trip, he and Mamie, but were just going to walk home from her mother's house to his cottage. That was good enough for him, he said. I looked at him hard for a minute after we met. When we had parted I had a sort of idea that he might take to drink, but he hadn't. He looked very respectable and well-to-do in his black coat and high city collar; but he was thinner and bonier than when I had known him, and there were lines in his face, and I thought his eyes had a funny look in them, half shifty, half scared. He needn't have been afraid of me, for I didn't mean to talk to his bride about the *Helen B. Jackson.*

He took me to his cottage first, and I could see that he was proud of it. It wasn't above a cable's-length from highwater mark, but the tide was running out, and there was already a broad stretch of hard wet sand on the other side of the beach road. Jack's bit of land ran back behind the cottage about a quarter of a mile, and he said that some of the trees we saw were his. The fences were neat and well kept, and there was a fair-sized barn a little way from the cottage, and I saw some nice-looking cattle in the meadows; but it didn't look to me to be much of a farm, and I thought that before long Jack would have to leave his wife to take care of it, and go to sea again. But I said it was a nice farm, so as to seem pleasant, and as I don't know much about these things I dare say it was, all the same. I never saw it but that once. Jack told me that he and his brother had been born in the cottage, and that when their father and mother died they leased the land to Mamie's father, but had kept the cottage to live in when they came home from sea for a spell. It was as neat a little place as you would care to see: the floors as clean as the decks of a yacht, and the paint as fresh as a man-o'-war. Jack always was a good painter. There was a nice parlour on the ground floor, and Jack had papered it and had hung the walls with photographs of ships and foreign ports, and with things he had brought home from his voyages: a boomerang, a South Sea club, Japanese straw hats and a Gibraltar fan with a bull-fight on it, and all that sort of gear. It looked to me as if Miss Mamie had taken a hand in arranging it. There was a brand-new polished iron Franklin stove set into the old fireplace, and a red table-cloth from Alexandria, embroidered with those outlandish Egyptian letters. It was all as bright and homelike as possible, and he showed me everything, and was proud of everything, and I liked him the better for it. But I wished that his voice would sound more cheerful, as it did when we first sailed in the *Helen B.*, and that the drawn look would go out of his face for a minute. Jack showed me everything, and took me upstairs, and it was all the same: bright and fresh and ready for the bride. But on the upper landing there was a door that Jack didn't open. When we came out of the bedroom I noticed that it was ajar, and Jack shut it quickly and turned the key.

"That lock's no good," he said, half to himself. "The door is always open."

I didn't pay much attention to what he said, but as we went down the short stairs, freshly painted and varnished so that I was almost afraid to step on them, he spoke again.

"That was his room, sir. I have made a sort of store-room of it."

"You may be wanting it in a year or so," I said, wishing to be pleasant.

"I guess we won't use his room for that," Jack answered in a low voice.

Then he offered me a cigar from a fresh box in the parlour, and he took one, and we lit them, and went out; and as we opened the front door there was Mamie Brewster standing in the path as if she were waiting for us. She was a fine-looking girl, and I didn't wonder that Jack had been willing to wait three years for her. I could see that she hadn't been brought up on steam-heat and cold storage, but had grown into a woman by the sea-shore. She had brown eyes, and fine brown hair, and a good figure.

"This is Captain Torkeldsen," said Jack. "This is Miss Brewster, captain; and she is glad to see you."

"Well, I am," said Miss Mamie, "for Jack has often talked to us about you, captain."

She put out her hand, and took mine and shook it heartily, and I suppose I said something, but I know I didn't say much.

The front door of the cottage looked toward the sea, and there was a straight path leading to the gate on the beach road. There was another path from the steps of the cottage that turned to the right, broad enough for two people to walk easily, and it led straight across the fields through gates to a larger house about a quarter of a mile away. That was where Mamie's mother lived, and the wedding was to be there. Jack asked me whether I would like to look round the farm before dinner, but I told him I didn't know much about farms. Then he said he just wanted to look round himself a bit, as he mightn't have much more chance that day; and he smiled, and Mamie laughed.

"Show the captain the way to the house, Mamie," he said. "I'll be along in a minute."

So Mamie and I began to walk along the path, and Jack went up toward the barn.

"It was sweet of you to come, captain," Miss Mamie began, "for I have always wanted to see you."

"Yes," I said, expecting something more.

"You see, I always knew them both," she went on. "They used to take me out in a dory to catch codfish when I was a little girl, and I liked them both," she added thoughtfully. "Jack doesn't care to talk about his brother now. That's natural. But you won't mind telling me how it happened, will you? I should so much like to know."

Well, I told her about the voyage and what happened that night when we fell in with a gale of wind, and that it hadn't been anybody's fault, for I wasn't going to admit that it was my old captain's, if it was. But I didn't tell her anything about what happened afterwards. As she didn't speak, I just went on talking about the two brothers, and how like they had been, and how when poor Jim was drowned and Jack was left, I took Jack for him. I told her that none of us had ever been sure which was which.

"I wasn't always sure myself," she said, "unless they were together. Leastways, not for a day or two after they came home from sea. And now it seems to me that Jack is more like poor Jim, as I remember him, than he ever was, for Jim was always more quiet, as if he were thinking."

I told her I thought so, too. We passed the gate and went into the next field, walking side by side. Then she turned her head to look for Jack, but he wasn't in sight. I shan't forget what she said next.

"Are you sure now?" she asked.

I stood stock-still, and she went on a step, and then turned and looked at me. We must have looked at each other while you could count five or six.

"I know it's silly," she went on, "it's silly, and it's awful, too, and I have got no right to think it, but sometimes I can't help it. You see it was always Jack I meant to marry."

"Yes," I said stupidly, "I suppose so."

She waited a minute, and began walking on slowly before she went on again.

"I am talking to you as if you were an old friend, captain, and I have only known you five minutes. It was Jack I meant to marry, but now he is so like the other one."

When a woman gets a wrong idea into her head, there is only one way to make her tired of it, and that is to agree with her. That's what I did, and she went on, talking the same way for a little while, and I kept on agreeing and agreeing until she turned round on me.

"You know you don't believe what you say," she said, and laughed. "You know that Jack is Jack, right enough; and it's Jack I am going to marry."

Of course I said so, for I didn't care whether she thought me a weak creature or not. I wasn't going to say a word that could interfere with her happiness, and I didn't intend to go back on Jack Benton; but I remembered what he had said when he left the ship in Havana: that it wasn't his fault.

"All the same," Miss Mamie went on, as a woman will, without realising what she was saying, "all the same, I wish I had seen it happen. Then I should know."

Next minute she knew that she didn't mean that, and was afraid that I would think her heartless, and began to explain that she would really rather have died herself than have seen poor Jim go overboard. Women haven't got much sense, anyhow. All the same, I wondered how she could marry Jack if she had a doubt that he might be Jim after all. I suppose she had really got used to him since he had given up the sea and had stayed ashore, and she cared for him.

Before long we heard Jack coming up behind us, for we had walked very slowly to wait for him.

"Promise not to tell anybody what I said, captain," said Mamie, as girls do as soon as they have told their secrets.

Anyhow, I know I never did tell any one but you. This is the first time I have talked of all that, the first time since I took the train from that place. I am not going to tell you all about the day. Miss Mamie introduced me to her mother, who was a quiet, hard-faced old New England farmer's widow, and to her cousins and relations; and there were plenty of them too at dinner, and there was the parson besides. He was what they call a Hard-shell Baptist in those parts, with a long, shaven upper lip and a whacking appetite, and a sort of superior look, as if he didn't expect to see many of us hereafter—the way a New York pilot looks round, and orders things about when he boards an Italian cargo-dragger, as if the ship weren't up to much anyway, though it was his business to see that she didn't get aground. That's the way a good many parsons look, I think. He said grace as if he were ordering the men to sheet home the topgallant-sail and get the helm up. After dinner we went out on the piazza, for it was warm autumn weather; and the young folks went off in pairs along the beach road, and the tide had turned and was beginning to come in. The morning had been clear and fine, but by four o'clock it began to look like a fog, and the damp came up out of the sea and settled on everything. Jack said he'd go down to his cottage and have a last look, for the wedding was to be at five o'clock, or soon after, and he wanted to light the lights, so as to have things look cheerful.

"I will just take a last look," he said again, as we reached the house. We went in, and he offered me another cigar, and I lit it and sat down in the parlour. I could hear him moving about, first in the kitchen and then upstairs, and then I heard him in the kitchen again; and then before I knew anything I heard somebody moving upstairs again. I knew he couldn't have got up those stairs as quick as that. He came into the parlour, and he took a cigar himself, and while he was lighting it I heard those steps again overhead. His hand shook, and he dropped the match.

"Have you got in somebody to help?" I asked.

"No," Jack answered sharply, and struck another match.

"There's somebody upstairs, Jack," I said. "Don't you hear

footsteps?"

"It's the wind, captain," Jack answered; but I could see he was trembling.

"That isn't any wind, Jack," I said; "it's still and foggy. I'm sure there's somebody upstairs."

"If you are so sure of it, you'd better go and see for yourself, captain," Jack answered, almost angrily.

He was angry because he was frightened. I left him before the fireplace, and went upstairs. There was no power on earth that could make me believe I hadn't heard a man's footsteps over-head. I knew there was somebody there. But there wasn't. I went into the bedroom, and it was all quiet, and the evening light was streaming in, reddish through the foggy air; and I went out on the landing and looked in the little back room that was meant for a servant girl or a child. And as I came back again I saw that the door of the other room was wide open, though I knew Jack had locked it. He had said the lock was no good. I looked in. It was a room as big as the bedroom, but almost dark, for it had shutters, and they were closed. There was a musty smell, as of old gear, and I could make out that the floor was littered with sea chests, and that there were oilskins and such stuff piled on the bed. But I still believed that there was somebody upstairs, and I went in and struck a match and looked round. I could see the four walls and the shabby old paper, an iron bed and a cracked looking-glass, and the stuff on the floor. But there was nobody there. So I put out the match, and came out and shut the door and turned the key. Now, what I am telling you is the truth. When I had turned the key, I heard footsteps walking away from the door inside the room. Then I felt strange for a minute, and when I went downstairs I looked behind me, as the men at the wheel used to look behind them on board the *Helen B.*

Jack was already outside on the steps, smoking. I have an idea that he didn't like to stay inside alone.

"Well?" he asked, trying to seem careless.

"I didn't find anybody," I answered, "but I heard somebody moving about."

"I told you it was the wind," said Jack, contemptuously. "I ought to know, for I live here, and I hear it often."

There was nothing to be said to that, so we began to walk down toward the beach. Jack said there wasn't any hurry, as it would take Miss Mamie some time to dress for the wedding. So we strolled along, and the sun was setting through the fog, and the tide was coming in. I knew the moon was full, and that when she rose the fog would roll away from the land, as it does sometimes. I felt that Jack didn't like my having heard that noise, so I talked of other things, and asked him about his prospects, and before long we were chatting as pleasantly as possible. I haven't been at many weddings in my life, and I don't suppose you have, but that one seemed to me to be all right until it was pretty near over; and then, I don't know whether it was part of the ceremony or not, but Jack put out his hand and took Mamie's and held it a minute, and looked at her, while the parson was still speaking.

Mamie turned as white as a sheet and screamed. It wasn't a loud scream, but just a sort of stifled little shriek, as if she were half frightened to death; and the parson stopped, and asked her what was the matter, and the family gathered round.

"Your hand's like ice," said Mamie to Jack, "and it's all wet!" She kept looking at it, as she got hold of herself again.

"It don't feel cold to me," said Jack, and he held the back of his hand against his cheek. "Try it again."

Mamie held out hers, and touched the back of his hand, timidly at first, and then took hold of it.

"Why, that's funny," she said.

"She's been as nervous as a witch all day," said Mrs. Brewster, severely.

"It is natural," said the parson, "that young Mrs. Benton should experience a little agitation at such a moment."

Most of the bride's relations lived at a distance, and were busy people, so it had been arranged that the dinner we'd had in the middle of the day was to take the place of a dinner afterwards, and that we should just have a bite after the wedding was over, and then that everybody should go home, and the young couple would walk down to the cottage by themselves. When I looked out I could see the light burning brightly in Jack's cottage, a quarter of a mile away. I said I didn't think I could get any train to take me back before half-past nine, but Mrs. Brewster begged me to stay until it was time, as she said her daughter would want to take off her wedding dress before she went home; for she had put on something white with a wreath, that was very pretty, and she couldn't walk home like that, could she?

So when we had all had a little supper the party began to break up, and when they were all gone Mrs. Brewster and Mamie went upstairs, and Jack and I went out on the piazza to have a smoke, as the old lady didn't like tobacco in the house.

The full moon had risen now, and it was behind me as I looked down toward Jack's cottage, so that everything was clear and white, and there was only the light burning in the window. The fog had rolled down to the water's edge, and a little beyond, for the tide was high, or nearly, and was lapping up over the last reach of sand, within fifty feet of the beach road.

Jack didn't say much as we sat smoking, but he thanked me for coming to his wedding, and I told him I hoped he would be happy; and so I did. I dare say both of us were thinking of those footsteps upstairs, just then, and that the house wouldn't seem so lonely with a woman in it. By and by we heard Mamie's voice talking to her mother on the stairs, and in a minute she was ready to go. She had put on again the dress she had worn in the morning, and it looked black at night, almost as black as Jack's coat.

Well, they were ready to go now. It was all very quiet after the day's excitement, and I knew they would like to walk down that path alone now that they were man and wife at last. I bade them good-night, although Jack made a show of pressing me to go with them by the path as far as the cottage, instead of going to the station by the beach road. It was all very quiet, and it seemed to me a sensible way of getting married; and when Mamie kissed her mother good-night I just looked the other way, and knocked my ashes over the rail of the piazza. So they started down the straight path to Jack's cottage, and I waited a minute with Mrs. Brewster, looking after them, before taking my hat to go. They walked side by side, a little shyly at first, and then I saw Jack put his arm round her waist. As I looked he was on her left, and I saw the outline of the two figures very distinctly against the moonlight on the path; and the shadow on Mamie's right was broad and black as ink, and it moved along, lengthening and shortening with the unevenness of the ground beside the path.

I thanked Mrs. Brewster, and bade her good-night; and though she was a hard New England woman her voice trembled a little as she answered, but being a sensible person she went in and shut the door behind her as I stepped out on the path. I looked after the couple in the distance a last time, meaning to go down to the road, so as not to overtake them; but when I had made a few steps I stopped and looked again, for I knew I had seen something strange, though I had only realised it afterwards. I looked again, and it was plain enough now; and I stood stock-still, staring at what I saw. Mamie was walking between two men. The second man was just the same height as Jack, both being about a half ahead taller than she; Jack on her left in his black tail-coat and round hat, and the other man on her right—well, he was a sailor-man in wet oilskins. I could see the moonlight shining on the water that ran down him, and on the little puddle that had settled where the flap of his sou'wester was turned up behind: and one of his wet, shiny arms was round Mamie's waist, just above Jack's. I was fast to the spot where I stood, and for a minute I thought I was crazy. We'd had nothing but some cider for dinner, and tea in the evening, otherwise I'd have thought something had got into my head, though I was never drunk in my life. It was more like a bad dream after that.

I was glad Mrs. Brewster had gone in. As for me, I couldn't help following the three, in a sort of wonder to see what would happen, to see whether the sailorman in his wet togs would just melt away into the moonshine. But he didn't.

I moved slowly, and I remembered afterwards that I walked on the grass, instead of on the path, as if I were afraid they might hear me coming. I suppose it all happened in less than five minutes after that, but it seemed as if it must have taken an hour. Neither Jack nor Mamie seemed to notice the sailor. She didn't seem to know that his wet arm was round her, and little by little they got near the cottage, and I wasn't a hundred yards from them when they reached the door. Something made me stand still then. Perhaps it was fright, for I saw everything that happened just as I see you now.

Mamie set her foot on the step to go up, and as she went forward I saw the sailor slowly lock his arm in Jack's, and Jack didn't move to go up. Then Mamie turned round on the step, and they all three stood that way for a second or two. She cried out then—I heard a man cry like that once, when his arm was taken off by a steam-crane—and she fell back in a heap on the little piazza.

I tried to jump forward, but I couldn't move, and I felt my hair rising under my hat. The sailor turned slowly where he stood, and swung Jack round by the arm steadily and easily, and began to walk him down the pathway from the house. He walked him straight down that path, as steadily as Fate; and all the time I saw the moonlight shining on his wet oilskins. He walked him through the gate, and across the beach road, and out upon the wet sand, where the tide was high. Then I got my breath with a gulp, and ran for them across the grass, and vaulted over the fence, and stumbled across the road. But when I felt the sand under my feet, the two were at the water's edge; and when I reached the water they were far out, and up to their waists; and I saw that Jack Benton's head had fallen forward on his breast, and his free arm hung limp beside him, while his dead brother steadily marched him to his death. The moonlight was on the dark water, but the fog-bank was white beyond, and I saw them against it; and they went slowly and steadily down. The water was up to their armpits, and then up to their shoulders, and then I saw it rise up to the black rim of Jack's hat. But they never wavered; and the two heads went straight on, straight on, till they were under, and there was just a ripple in the moonlight where Jack had been.

It has been on my mind to tell you that story, whenever I got a chance. You have known me, man and boy, a good many years; and I thought I would like to hear your opinion. Yes, that's what I always thought. It wasn't Jim that went overboard; it was Jack, and Jim just let him go when he might have saved him; and then Jim passed himself off for Jack with us, and with the girl. If that's what happened, he got what he deserved. People said the next day that Mamie found it out as they reached the house, and that her husband just walked out into the sea, and drowned himself; and they would have blamed me for not stopping him if they'd known that I was there. But I never told what I had seen, for they wouldn't have believed me. I just let them think I had come too late.

When I reached the cottage and lifted Mamie up, she was raving mad. She got better afterwards, but she was never right in her head again.

Oh, you want to know if they found Jack's body? I don't know whether it was his, but I read in a paper at a Southern port where I was with my new ship that two dead bodies had come ashore in a gale down East, in pretty bad shape. They were locked together, and one was a skeleton in oilskins.

TOBERBORY
by Saki

IT WAS a chill, rain-washed afternoon of a late August day, that indefinite season when partridges are still in security or cold storage, and there is nothing to hunt—unless one is bounded on the north by the Bristol Channel, in which case one may lawfully gallop after fat red stags. Lady Blemley's house-party was not bounded on the north by the Bristol Channel, hence there was a full gathering of her guests round the tea-table on this particular afternoon. And, in spite of the blankness of the season and the triteness of the occasion, there was no trace in the company of that fatigued restlessness which means a dread of the pianola and a subdued hankering for auction bridge. The undisguised open-mouthed attention of the entire party was fixed on the homely negative personality of Mr. Cornelius Appin. Of all her guests, he was the one who had come to Lady Blemley with the vaguest reputation. Some one had said he was "clever," and he had got his invitation in the moderate expectation, on the part of his hostess, that some portion at least of his cleverness would be contributed to the general entertainment. Until tea-time that day she had been unable to discover in what direction, if any, his cleverness lay. He was neither a wit nor a croquet champion, a hypnotic force nor a begetter of amateur theatricals. Neither did his exterior suggest the sort of man in whom women are willing to pardon a generous measure of mental deficiency. He had subsided into mere Mr. Appin, and the Cornelius seemed a piece of transparent baptismal bluff. And now he was claiming to have launched on the world a discovery beside which the invention of gunpowder, of the printing-press, and of steam locomotion were inconsiderable trifles. Science had made bewildering strides in many directions during recent decades, but this thing seemed to belong to the domain of miracle rather than to scientific achievement.

"And do you really ask us to believe," Sir Wilfrid was saying, "that you have discovered a means for instructing animals in the art of human speech, and that dear old Tobermory has proved your first successful pupil?"

"It is a problem at which I have worked for the last seventeen years," said Mr. Appin, "but only during the last eight or nine months have I been rewarded with glimmerings of success. Of course I have experimented with thousands of animals, but latterly only with cats, those wonderful creatures which have assimilated themselves so marvellously with our civilization while retaining all their highly developed feral instincts. Here and there among cats one comes across an outstanding superior intellect, just as one does among the ruck of human beings, and when I made the acquaintance of Tobermory a week ago I saw at once that I was in contact with a "Beyond-cat" of extraordinary intelligence. I had gone far along the road to success in recent experiments; with Tobermory, as you call him, I have reached the goal."

Mr. Appin concluded his remarkable statement in a voice which he strove to divest of a triumphant inflection. No one said "Rats," though Clovis's lips moved in a monosyllabic contortion, which probably invoked those rodents of disbelief.

"And do you mean to say," asked Miss Resker, after a slight pause, "that you have taught Tobermory to say and understand easy sentences of one syllable?"

"My dear Miss Resker," said the wonder-worker patiently, "one teaches little children and savages and backward adults in that piecemeal fashion; when one has once solved the problem of making a beginning with an animal of highly developed intelligence one has no need for those halting methods. Tobermory can speak our language with perfect correctness."

This time Clovis very distinctly said, "Beyond-rats!" Sir Wilfred was more polite but equally sceptical.

"Hadn't we better have the cat in and judge for ourselves?" suggested Lady Blemley.

Sir Wilfred went in search of the animal, and the company settled themselves down to the languid expectation of witnessing some more or less adroit drawing-room ventriloquism.

In a minute Sir Wilfred was back in the room, his face white beneath its tan and his eyes dilated with excitement.

"By Gad, it's true!"

His agitation was unmistakably genuine, and his hearers started forward in a thrill of wakened interest.

Collapsing into an armchair he continued breathlessly:

"I found him dozing in the smoking-room, and called out to him to come for his tea. He blinked at me in his usual way, and I said, 'Come on, Toby; don't keep us waiting' and, by Gad! he drawled out in a most horribly natural voice that he'd come when he dashed well pleased! I nearly jumped out of my skin!"

Appin had preached to absolutely incredulous hearers; Sir Wilfred's statement carried instant conviction. A Babel-like chorus of startled exclamation arose, amid which the scientist sat mutely enjoying the first fruit of his stupendous discovery.

In the midst of the clamour Tobermory entered the room and made his way with velvet tread and studied unconcern across the group seated round the tea-table.

A sudden hush of awkwardness and constraint fell on the company. Somehow there seemed an element of embarrassment in addressing on equal terms a domestic cat of acknowledged dental ability.

"Will you have some milk, Tobermory?" asked Lady Blemley in a rather strained voice.

"I don't mind if I do," was the response, couched in a tone of even indifference. A shiver of suppressed excitement went through the listeners, and Lady Blemley might be excused for pouring out the saucerful of milk rather unsteadily.

"I'm afraid I've spilt a good deal of it," she said apologetically.

"After all, it's not my Axminster," was Tobermory's rejoinder.

Another silence fell on the group, and then Miss Resker, in her best district-visitor manner, asked if the human language had been difficult to learn. Tobermory looked squarely at her for a moment and then fixed his gaze serenely on the middle distance. It was obvious that boring questions lay outside his scheme of life.

"What do you think of human intelligence?" asked Mavis Pellington lamely.

"Of whose intelligence in particular?" asked Tobermory coldly.

"Oh, well, mine for instance," said Mavis with a feeble laugh.

"You put me in an embarrassing position," said Tobermory, whose tone and attitude certainly did not suggest a shred of embarrassment. "When your inclusion in this house-party was suggested Sir Wilfrid protested that you were the most brainless woman of his acquaintance, and that there was a wide distinction between hospitality and the care of the feeble-minded. Lady Blemley replied that your lack of brain-power was the precise quality which had earned you your invitation, as you were the only person she could think of who might be idiotic enough to buy their old car. You know, the one they call 'The Envy of Sisyphus,' because it goes quite nicely up-hill if you push it."

Lady Blemley's protestations would have had greater effect if she had not casually suggested to Mavis only that morning that the car in question would be just the thing for her down at her Devonshire home.

Major Barfield plunged in heavily to effect a diversion.

"How about your carryings-on with the tortoise-shell puss up at the stables, eh?"

The moment he had said it every one realized the blunder.

"One does not usually discuss these matters in public," said Tobermory frigidly. "From a slight observation of your ways since you've been in this house I should imagine you'd find it inconvenient if I were to shift the conversation to your own little affairs."

The panic which ensued was not confined to the Major.

"Would you like to go and see if cook has got your dinner ready?" suggested Lady Blemley hurriedly, affecting to ignore the fact that it wanted at least two hours to Tobermory's dinner-time.

"Thanks," said Tobermory, "not quite so soon after my tea. I don't want to die of indigestion."

"Cats have nine lives, you know," said Sir Wilfred heartily.

"Possibly," answered Tobermory; "but only one liver."

"Adelaide!" said Mrs. Cornett, "do you mean to encourage that cat to go out and gossip about us in the servants' hall?"

The panic had indeed become general. A narrow ornamental balustrade ran in front of most of the bedroom windows at the Towers, and it was recalled with dismay that this had formed a favourite promenade for Tobermory at all hours, whence he could watch the pigeons—and heaven knew what else besides. If he intended to become reminiscent in his present outspoken strain the effect would be something more than disconcerting. Mrs. Cornett, who spent much time at her toilet table, and whose complexion was reputed to be of a nomadic though punctual disposition, looked as ill at ease as the Major. Miss Scrawen, who wrote fiercely sensuous poetry and led a blameless life, merely displayed irritation; if you are methodical and virtuous in private you don't nec-

essarily want everyone to know it. Bertie van Tahn, who was so depraved at 17 that he had long ago given up trying to be any worse, turned a dull shade of gardenia white, but he did not commit the error of dashing out of the room like Odo Finsberry, a young gentleman who was understood to be reading for the Church and who was possibly disturbed at the thought of scandals he might hear concerning other people. Clovis had the presence of mind to maintain a composed exterior; privately he was calculating how long it would take to procure a box of fancy mice through the agency of the *Exchange and Mart* as a species of hush-money.

Even in a delicate situation like the present, Agnes Resker could not endure to remain long in the background.

"Why did I ever come down here?" she asked dramatically.

Tobermory immediately accepted the opening.

"Judging by what you said to Mrs. Cornett on the croquet-lawn yesterday, you were out of food. You described the Blemleys as the dullest people to stay with that you knew, but said they were clever enough to employ a first-rate cook; otherwise they'd find it difficult to get any one to come down a second time."

"There's not a word of truth in it! I appeal to Mrs. Cornett—" exclaimed the discomfited Agnes.

"Mrs. Cornett repeated your remark afterwards to Bertie van Tahn," continued Tobermory, "and said, 'That woman is a regular Hunger Marcher; she'd go anywhere for four square meals a day,' and Bertie van Tahn said—"

At this point the chronicle mercifully ceased. Tobermory had caught a glimpse of the big yellow tom from the Rectory working his way through the shrubbery towards the stable wing. In a flash he had vanished through the open French window.

With the disappearance of his too brilliant pupil Cornelius Appin found himself beset by a hurricane of bitter upbraiding, anxious inquiry, and frightened entreaty. The responsibility for the situation lay with him, and he must prevent matters from becoming worse. Could Tobermory impart his dangerous gift to other cats? was the first question he had to answer. It was possible, he replied, that he might have initiated his intimate friend the stable puss into his new accomplishment, but it was unlikely that his teaching could have taken a wider range as yet.

"Then," said Mrs. Cornett, "Tobermory may be a valuable cat and a great pet; but I'm sure you'll agree, Adelaide, that both he and the stable cat must be done away with without delay."

"You don't suppose I've enjoyed the last quarter of an hour, do you?" said Lady Blemley bitterly. "My husband and I are very fond of Tobermory—at least, we were before this horrible accomplishment was infused into him; but now, of course, the only thing is to have him destroyed as soon as possible."

"We can put some strychnine in the scraps he always gets at dinner-time," said Sir Wilfred, "and I will go and drown the stable cat myself. The coachman will be very sore at losing his pet, but I'll say a very catching form of mange has broken out in both cats and we're afraid of it spreading to the kennels."

"But my great discovery!" expostulated Mr. Appin; "after all my years of research and experiment—"

"You can go and experiment on the short-horns at the farm, who are under proper control," said Mrs. Cornett, "or the elephants at the Zoological Gardens. They're said to be highly intelligent, and they have this recommendation, that they don't come creeping about our bedrooms and under chairs, and so forth."

An archangel ecstatically proclaiming the Millennium, and then finding that it clashed unpardonably with Henley and would have to be indefinitely postponed, could hardly have felt more crestfallen than Cornelius Appin at the reception of his wonderful achievement. Public opinion, however, was against him—in fact, had the general voice been consulted on the subject it is probable that a strong minority vote would have been in favour of including him in the strychnine diet.

Defective train arrangements and a nervous desire to see matters brought to a finish prevented an immediate dispersal of the party, but dinner that evening was not a social success. Sir Wilfred had had rather a trying time with the stable cat and subsequently with the coachman. Agnes Resker ostentatiously limited her repast to a morsel of dry toast, which she bit as though it were a personal enemy; while Mavis Pellington maintained a vindictive silence throughout the meal. Lady Blemley kept up a flow of what she hoped was conversation, but her attention was fixed on the doorway. A plateful of carefully dosed fish scraps was in readiness on the sideboard, but the sweets and savoury and dessert went their way, and no Tobermory appeared in the dining-room or kitchen.

The sepulchral dinner was cheerful compared with the subsequent vigil in the smoking-room. Eating and drinking had at least supplied a distraction and cloak to the prevailing embarrassment. Bridge was out of the question in the general tension of nerves and tempers, and after Odo Finsberry had given a lugubrious rendering of 'Melisande in the Wood' to a frigid audience, music was tacitly avoided. At eleven the servants went to bed, announcing that the small window in the pantry had been left open as usual for Tobermory's private use. The guests read steadily through the current batch of magazines, and fell back gradually on the "Badminton Library" and bound volumes of Punch. Lady Blemley made periodic visits to the pantry, returning each time with an ex-

pression of listless depression which forestalled questioning.

At two o'clock Clovis broke the dominating silence.

"He won't turn up tonight. He's probably in the local newspaper office at the present moment, dictating the first installment of his reminiscences. Lady What's-her-name's book won't be in it. It will be the event of the day."

Having made this contribution to the general cheerfulness, Clovis went to bed. At long intervals the various members of the house-party followed his example.

The servants taking round the early tea made a uniform announcement in reply to a uniform question. Tobermory had not returned.

Breakfast was, if anything, a more unpleasant function than dinner had been, but before its conclusion the situation was relieved. Tobermory's corpse was brought in from the shrubbery, where a gardener had just discovered it. From the bites on his throat and the yellow fur which coated his claws it was evident that he had fallen in unequal combat with the big Tom from the Rectory.

By midday most of the guests had quitted the Towers, and after lunch Lady Blemley had sufficiently recovered her spirits to write an extremely nasty letter to the Rectory about the loss of her valuable pet.

Tobermory had been Appin's one successful pupil, and he was destined to have no successor. A few weeks later an elephant in the Dresden Zoological Garden, which had shown no previous signs of irritability, broke loose and killed an Englishman who had apparently been teasing it. The victim's name was variously reported in the papers as Oppin and Eppelin, but his front name was faithfully rendered Cornelius.

"If he was trying German irregular verbs on the poor beast," said Clovis, "he deserved all he got."

RAFFLES HOLMES
by John Kendrick Bangs

I
INTRODUCING MR. RAFFLES HOLMES

It was a blistering night in August. All day long the mercury in the thermometer had been flirting with the figures at the top of the tube, and the promised shower at night which a mendacious Weather Bureau had been prophesying as a slight mitigation of our sufferings was conspicuous wholly by its absence. I had but one comfort in the sweltering hours of the day, afternoon and evening, and that was that my family were away in the mountains, and there was no law against my sitting around all day clad only in my pajamas, and otherwise concealed from possibly intruding eyes by the wreaths of smoke that I extracted from the nineteen or twenty cigars which, when there is no protesting eye to suggest otherwise, form my daily allowance. I had tried every method known to the resourceful flat-dweller of modern times to get cool and to stay so, but alas, it was impossible. Even the radiators, which all winter long had never once given forth a spark of heat, now hissed to the touch of my moistened finger. Enough cooling drinks to float an ocean greyhound had passed into my inner man, with no other result than to make me perspire more profusely than ever, and in so far as sensations went, to make me feel hotter than before.

Finally, as a last resource, along about midnight, its gridiron floor having had a chance to lose some of its stored-up warmth, I climbed out upon the fire-escape at the rear of the Richmere, hitched my hammock from one of the railings thereof to the leader running from the roof to the area, and swung myself therein some eighty feet above the concealed pavement of our backyard—so called, perhaps, because of its dimensions which were just about that square.

It was a little improvement, though nothing to brag of. What fitful zephyrs there might be, caused no doubt by the rapid passage to and fro on the roof above and fence-tops below of vagrant felines on Cupid's contentious battles bent, to the disturbance of the still air, soughed softly through the meshes of my hammock and gave some measure of relief, grateful enough for which I ceased the perfervid language I had been using practically since sunrise, and dozed off. And then there entered upon the scene that marvelous man, Raffles Holmes, of whose exploits it is the purpose of these papers to tell.

I had dozed perhaps for a full hour when the first strange sounds grated upon my ear. Somebody had opened a window in the kitchen of the first-floor apartment below, and with a dark lantern was inspecting the iron platform of the fire escape without. A moment later this somebody crawled out of the window, and with movements that in themselves were a sufficient indication of the questionable character of his proceedings, made for the ladder leading to the floor above, upon which many a time and oft had I too climbed to home and safety when an inconsiderate janitor had locked me out. Every step that he took was stealthy—that much I

could see by the dim starlight. His lantern he had turned dark again, evidently lest he should attract attention in the apartments below as he passed their windows in his upward flight.

"Ha! ha!" thought I to myself. "It's never too hot for Mr. Sneak to get in his fine work. I wonder whose stuff he is after?"

Turning over flat on my stomach so that I might the more readily observe the man's movements, and breathing *pianissimo* lest he in turn should observe mine, I watched him as he climbed. Up he came as silently as the midnight mouse upon a soft carpet—up past the Jorkins' apartments on the second floor; up stealthily by the Tinkletons' abode on the third; up past the fire escape Italian garden of little Mrs. Persimmon on the fourth; up past the windows of the disagreeable Garraways' kitchen below mine, and then, with the easy grace of a feline, zip! he silently landed within reach of my hand on my own little iron veranda, and craning his neck to one side peered in through the open window and listened intently for two full minutes.

"Humph!" whispered my inner consciousness to itself. "He is the coolest thing I've seen since last Christmas left town. I wonder what he is up to? There's nothing in my apartment worth stealing, now that my wife and children are away, unless it be my Jap valet, Nogi, who might make a very excellent cab driver if I could only find words to convey to his mind the idea that he is discharged."

And then the visitor, apparently having correctly assured himself that there was no one within, stepped across the window sill and vanished into the darkness of my kitchen. A moment later I too entered the window in pursuit—not so close a one, however, as to acquaint him with my proximity. I wanted to see what the chap was up to; and also being totally unarmed and ignorant as to whether or not he carried dangerous weapons, I determined to go slow for a little while. Moreover, the situation was not wholly devoid of novelty, and it seemed to me that here at last was abundant opportunity for a new sensation.

As he had entered, so did he walk cautiously along the narrow bowling alley that serves for a hallway connecting my drawing room and library with the dining room, until he came to the library, into which he disappeared. This was not reassuring to me, because, to tell the truth, I value my books more than I do my plate, and if I were to be robbed I should much have preferred his taking my plated plate from the dining room than any one of my editions-deluxe sets of the works of Marie Corelli, Hall Caine, and other standard authors from the library shelves.

Once in the library, he quietly drew the shades at the windows thereof to bar possible intruding eyes from without, turned on the electric lights, and proceeded to go through my papers as calmly and coolly as though they were his own. In a short time, apparently, he found what he wanted in the shape of a royalty statement recently received by me from my publishers, and, lighting one of my cigars from a bundle of brevas in front of him, took off his coat and sat down to peruse the statement of my returns.

Simple though it was, this act aroused the first feeling of resentment in my breast, for the relations between the author and his publishers are among the most sacred confidences of life, and the peeping Tom who peers through a keyhole at the courtship of a young man engaged in wooing his *fiancée* is no worse an intruder than he who would tear aside the veil of secrecy which screens the official returns of a "best seller" from the public eye.

Feeling, therefore, that I had permitted matters to proceed as far as they might with propriety, I instantly entered the room and confronted my uninvited guest, bracing myself, of course, for the defensive onslaught which I naturally expected to sustain. But nothing of the sort occurred, for the intruder, with a composure that was nothing short of marvelous under the circumstances, instead of rising hurriedly like one caught in some disreputable act, merely leaned farther back in the chair, took the cigar from his mouth, and greeted me with:

"Howdy do, sir. What can I do for you this beastly hot night?"

The cold rim of a revolver-barrel placed at my temple could not more effectually have put me out of business than this nonchalant reception. Consequently I gasped out something about its being the sultriest 47th of August in eighteen years, and plumped back into a chair opposite him.

"I wouldn't mind a Remsen cooler myself," he went on, "but the fact is your butler is off for tonight, and I'm hanged if I can find a lemon in the house. Maybe you'll join me in a smoke?" he added, shoving my own bundle of brevas across the table. "Help yourself."

"I guess I know where the lemons are," said I. "But how did you know my butler was out?"

"I telephoned him to go to Philadelphia this afternoon to see his brother Yoku, who is ill there," said my visitor. "You see, I didn't want him around tonight when I called. I knew I could manage you alone in case you turned up, as you see you have, but two of you, and one a Jap, I was afraid might involve us all in ugly complications. Between you and me, Jenkins, these Orientals are pretty lively fighters, and your man Nogi particularly has got jiujitsu down to a pretty fine point, so I had to do something to get rid of him. Our arrangement is a matter for two, not three, anyhow."

"So," said I, coldly. "You and I have an arrangement, have we? I wasn't aware of it."

"Not yet," he answered. "But there's a chance that we may have. If I can only satisfy myself that you are the man I'm looking for, there is no earthly reason that I can see why we should not come to terms. Go on out and get the lemons and the gin and soda, and let's talk this thing over man to man like a couple of good fellows at the club. I mean you no harm, and you certainly don't wish to do any kind of injury to a chap who, even though appearances are against him, really means to do you a good turn."

"Appearances certainly are against you, sir," said I, a trifle warmly, for the man's composure was irritating. "A disappearance would be more likely to do you credit at this moment,"

"Tush, Jenkins!" he answered. "Why waste breath saying self-evident things? Here you are on the verge of a big transaction, and you delay proceedings by making statements of fact, mixed in with a cheap wit which, I must confess, I find surprising, and so obvious as to be visible even to the blind. You don't talk like an author whose stuff is worth ten cents a word—more like a penny-a-liner, in fact, with whom words are of such small value that no

one's the loser if he throws away a whole dictionary. Go out and mix a couple of your best Remsen coolers, and by the time you get back I'll have got to the gist of this royalty statement of yours, which is all I've come for. Your silver and books and love letters and manuscripts are safe from me. I wouldn't have 'em as a gift."

"What concern have you with my royalties?" I demanded.

"A vital one," said he. "Mix the coolers, and when you get back I'll tell you. Go on. There's a good chap. It'll be daylight before long, and I want to close up this job if I can before sunrise."

What there was in the man's manner to persuade me to compliance with his wishes, I am sure I cannot say definitely. There was a cold, steely glitter in his eye, for one thing. With it, however, was a strengthfulness of purpose, a certain pleasant masterfulness, that made me feel that I could trust him, and it was to this aspect of his nature that I yielded. There was something frankly appealing in his long, thin, ascetic looking face, and I found it irresistible.

"All right," said I with a smile and a frown to express the conflicting quality of my emotions. "So be it. I'll get the coolers, but you must remember, my friend, that there are coolers and coolers, just as there are jugs and jugs. The kind of jug that remains for you will depend upon the story you have to tell when I get back, so you'd better see that it's a good one."

"I am not afraid, Jenkins, old chap," he said with a hearty laugh as I rose. "If this royalty statement can prove to me that you are the literary partner I need in my business, I can prove to you that I'm a good man to tie up to—so go along with you."

With this he lighted a fresh cigar and turned to a perusal of my statement, which, I am glad to say, was a good one, owing to the great success of my book, *Wild Animals I Have Never Met*—the seventh-best seller at Rochester, Watertown, and Miami in June and July, 1905.

I went out into the dining room and mixed the coolers. As you may imagine, I was not long at it, for my curiosity over my visitor lent wings to my corkscrew, and in five minutes I was back with the tempting beverages in the tall glasses, the lemon curl giving it the vertebrate appearance that all stiff drinks should have, and the ice tinkling refreshingly upon the sultry air.

"There," said I, placing his glass before him. "Drink hearty, and then to business. Who are you?"

"There is my card," he replied, swallowing a goodly half of the cooler and smacking his lips appreciatively, and tossing a visiting card across to me on the other side of the table. I picked up the card and read as follows: "Mr. Raffles Holmes, London and New York."

"Raffles Holmes?" I cried in amazement.

"The same, Mr. Jenkins," said he. "I am the son of Sherlock Holmes, the famous detective, and grandson of A. J. Raffles, the distinguished—er—ah—cricketer, sir."

I gazed at him, dumb with astonishment.

"You've heard of my father, Sherlock Holmes?" asked my visitor.

I confessed that the name of the gentleman was not unfamiliar to me.

"And Mr. Raffles, my grandfather?" he persisted.

"If there ever was a story of that fascinating man that I have not read, Mr. Holmes," said I, "I beg you will let me have it."

"Well, then," said he with that quick, nervous manner which proved him a true son of Sherlock Holmes, "did it never occur to you as an extraordinary happening, as you read of my father's wonderful powers as a detective, and of Raffles' equally wonderful prowess as a—er—well, let us not mince words—as a thief, Mr. Jenkins, the two men operating in England at the same time, that no story ever appeared in which Sherlock Holmes's genius was pitted against the subtly planned misdeeds of Mr. Raffles? Is it not surprising that with two such men as they were, working out their destinies in almost identical grooves of daily action, they should never have crossed each other's paths as far as the public is the wiser, and in the very nature of the conflicting interests of their respective lines of action as foemen, the one pursuing, the other pursued, they should to the public's knowledge never have clashed?"

"Now that you speak of it," said I, "it was rather extraordinary that nothing of the sort happened. One would think that the sufferers from the depredations of Raffles would immediately have gone to Holmes for assistance in bringing the other to justice. Truly, as you intimate, it was strange that they never did."

"Pardon me, Jealous," put in my visitor. "I never intimated anything of the sort. What I intimated was that no story of any such conflict ever came to light. As a matter of fact, Sherlock Holmes was put upon a Raffles case in 1883, and while success attended upon every step of it, and my grandfather was run to earth by him as easily as was ever any other criminal in Holmes's grip, a little naked god called Cupid stepped in, saved Raffles from jail, and wrote the word failure across Holmes's docket of the case. *I, sir, am the only tangible result of Lord Dorrington's retainers to Sherlock Holmes.*"

"You speak enigmatically, after the occasional fashion of your illustrious father," said I. "The Dorrington case is unfamiliar to me,"

"Naturally so," said my *vis-à-vis*. "Because, save to my father, my grandfather, and myself, the details are unknown to anybody. Not even my mother knew of the incident, and as for Dr. Watson and Bunny, the scribes through whose industry the adventures of those two great men were respectively narrated to an absorbed world, they didn't even know there had ever been a Dorrington case, because Sherlock Holmes never told Watson and Raffles never told Bunny. But they both told me, and now that I am satisfied that there is a demand for your books, I am willing to tell it to you with the understanding that we share and share alike in the profits if perchance you think well enough of it to write it up."

"Go on!" I said. "I'll whack up with you square and honest."

"Which is more than either Watson or Bunny ever did with my father or my grandfather, else I should not be in the business which now occupies my time and attention," said Raffles Holmes with a cold snap to his eyes which I took as an admonition to hew strictly to the line of honor, or to subject myself to terrible consequences. "With that understanding, Jenkins, I'll tell you the story of the Dorrington Ruby Seal, in which some crime, a good deal of romance, and my ancestry are involved."

II
THE ADVENTURE OF THE DORRINGTON RUBY SEAL

"**L**ord Dorrington, as you may have heard," said Raffles Holmes, leaning back in my easychair and gazing reflectively up at the ceiling, "was chiefly famous in England as a sporting peer. His vast estates, in five counties, were always open to any sportsman of renown, or otherwise, as long as he was a true sportsman. So open, indeed, was the house that he kept that, whether he was there or not, little weekend parties of members of the sporting fraternity used to be got up at a moment's notice to run down to Dorrington Castle, Devonshire; to Dorrington Lodge on the Isle of Wight; to Dorrington Hall, near Dublin, or to any of his other country places for over Sunday.

"Sometimes there'd be a lot of turf people; sometimes a dozen or more devotees of the prize-ring; not infrequently a gathering of the best known cricketers of the time, among whom, of course, my grandfather, A. J. Raffles, was conspicuous. For the most part, the cricketers never partook of Dorrington's hospitality save when his lordship was present, for your cricket-player is a bit more punctilious in such matters than your turfmen or ring-side habitués. It so happened one year, however, that his lordship was absent from England for the better part of eight months, and, when the time came for the annual cricket gathering at his Devonshire place, he cabled his London representative to see to it that everything was carried on just as if he were present, and that everyone should be invited for the usual week's play and pleasure at Dorrington Castle. His instructions were carried out to the letter and, save for the fact that the genial host was absent, the house-party went through to perfection. My grandfather, as usual, was the life of the occasion, and all went merry as a marriage bell. Seven months later, Lord Dorrington returned, and, a week after that, the loss of the Dorrington jewels from the Devonshire strong-boxes was a matter of common knowledge. When, or by whom, they had been taken was an absolute mystery. As far as anybody could find out, they might have been taken the night before his return, or the night after his departure. The only fact in sight was that they were gone—Lady Dorrington's diamonds, a half dozen valuable jeweled rings belonging to his lordship, and, most irremediable of losses, the famous ruby seal which George IV had given to Dorrington's grandfather, Sir Arthur Deering, as a token of his personal esteem during the period of the Regency. This was a flawless ruby, valued at some six or seven thousand pounds sterling, in which had been cut the Deering arms surrounded by a garter upon which were engraved the words, 'Deering Ton,' which the family, upon Sir Arthur's elevation to the peerage in 1836, took as its title, or Dorrington. His lordship was almost prostrated by the loss. The diamonds and the rings, although valued at thirty thousand pounds, he could easily replace, but the personal associations of the seal were such that nothing, no amount of money, could duplicate the lost ruby."

"So that his first act," I broke in, breathlessly, "was to send for—"

"Sherlock Holmes, my father," said Raffles Holmes. "Yes, Mr. Jenkins, the first thing Lord Dorrington did was to telegraph to London for Sherlock Holmes, requesting him to come immediately to Dorrington Castle and assume charge of the case. Needless to say, Mr. Holmes dropped everything else and came. He inspected the gardens, measured the road from the railway station to the castle, questioned all the servants; was particularly insistent upon knowing where the parlor-maid was on the 13th of January; secured accurate information as to the personal habits of his lordship's dachshund Nicholas; subjected the chef to a cross-examination that covered every point of his life, from his remote ancestry to his receipt for baking apples; gathered up three suitcases of sweepings from his lordship's private apartment, and two boxes containing three each of every variety of cigars that Lord Dorrington had laid down in his cellar. As you are aware, Sherlock Holmes, in his prime, was a great master of detail. He then departed for London, taking with him an impression in wax of the missing seal, which Lord Dorrington happened to have preserved in his escritoire.

"On his return to London, Holmes inspected the seal carefully under a magnifying glass, and was instantly impressed with the fact that it was not unfamiliar to him. He had seen it somewhere before, but where? That was now the question uppermost in his mind. Prior to this, he had never had any communication with Lord Dorrington, so that, if it was in his correspondence that the seal had formerly come to him, most assuredly the person who had used it had come by it dishonestly. Fortunately, at that time, it was a habit of my father's never to destroy papers of any sort. Every letter that he ever received was classified and filed, envelope and all. The thing to do, then, was manifestly to run over the files and find the letter, if indeed it was in or on a letter that the seal had first come to his attention. It was a herculean job, but that never fazed Sherlock Holmes, and he went at it tooth and nail. Finally his effort was rewarded. Under 'Applications for Autograph' he found a daintily scented little missive from a young girl living at Goring-Streatley on the Thames, the daughter, she said, of a retired missionary—the Reverend James Tattersby—asking him if he would not kindly write his autograph upon the enclosed slip for her collection. It was the regular stock application that truly distinguished men receive in every mail. The only thing to distinguish it from other applications was the beauty of the seal on the fly of the envelope, which attracted his passing notice and was then filed away with the other letters of similar import.

"'Ho! ho!' quoth Holmes, as he compared the two impressions and discovered that they were identical. 'An innocent little maiden who collects autographs, and a retired missionary in possession of the Dorrington seal, eh? Well, that *is* interesting. I think I shall run down to Goring-Streatley over Sunday and meet Miss Marjorie Tattersby and her reverend father. I'd like to see to what style of people I have intrusted my autograph.'

"To decide was to act with Sherlock Holmes, and the following Saturday, hiring a canoe at Windsor, he made his way up the river until he came to the pretty little hamlet, snuggling in the Thames Valley, if such it may be called, where the young lady and her good father were dwelling. Fortune favored him in that his prey was still there—both much respected by the whole community; the father a fine looking, really splendid specimen of a man whose presence alone carried a conviction of integrity and lofty mind; the daughter — well, to see her was to love her, and the moment the eyes of Sherlock fell upon her face, that great heart of his, that had ever been adamant to beauty, a very Gibraltar against the wiles of the other sex, went down in the chaos of a first and overwhelming passion. So hard hit was he by Miss Tattersby's beauty that his chief thought now was to avert rather than to direct suspicion towards her. After all, she might have come into possession of the jewel honestly, though how the daughter of a retired missionary, considering its intrinsic value, could manage such a thing, was pretty hard to understand, and he fled back to London to think it over. Arrived there, he found an invitation to visit Dorrington Castle again *incog.* Lord Dorrington was to have a mixed weekend party over the following Sunday, and this, he thought, would give Holmes an opportunity to observe the characteristics of Dorrington's visitors and possibly gain some clue as to the light-fingered person from whose depredations his lordship had suffered. The idea commended itself to Holmes, and in the disguise of a young American clergyman, whom Dorrington had met in the States, the following Friday found him at Dorrington Castle.

"Well, to make a long story short," said Raffles Holmes, "the young clergyman was introduced to many of the leading sportsmen of the hour, and, for the most part, they passed muster, but one of them did not, and that was the well known cricketer A. J. Raffles, for the moment Raffles entered the room, jovially greeting everybody about him, and was presented to Lord Dorrington's new guest, Sherlock Holmes recognized in him no less a person than the Reverend James Tattersby, retired missionary of Goring-Streatley-on-Thames, and the father of the woman who had filled his soul with love and yearning of the truest sort. The problem was solved. Raffles was, to all intents and purposes, caught with the goods on. Holmes could have exposed him then and there had he chosen to do so, but every time it came to the point the lovely face of Marjorie Tattersby came between him and his purpose. How could he inflict the pain and shame which the exposure of her father's misconduct would certainly entail upon that fair woman, whose beauty and fresh innocence had taken so strong a hold upon his heart? No—that was out of the question. The thing to do, clearly, was to visit Miss Tattersby during her father's absence and, if possible, ascertain from her just how she had come into possession of the seal, before taking further steps in the matter. This he did. Making sure, to begin with, that Raffles was to remain at Dorrington Hall for the coming ten days, Holmes had himself telegraphed for and returned to London. There he wrote himself a letter of introduction to the Reverend James Tattersby, on the paper of the Anglo-American Missionary Society, a sheet of which he secured in the public writing-room of that institution, armed with which he returned to the beautiful little spot on the Thames where the Tattersbys abode. He spent the night at the inn, and, in conversation with the landlord and boatmen, learned much that was interesting concerning the Reverend James. Among other things, he discovered that this gentleman and his daughter had been respected residents of the place for three years; that Tattersby was rarely seen in the daytime about the place; that he was unusually fond of canoeing at night, which, he said, gave him the quiet and solitude necessary for that reflection which is so essential to the spiritual being of a minister of grace; that he frequently indulged in long absences, during which time it was supposed that he was engaged in the work of his calling. He appeared to be a man of some, but not of lavish, means. The most notable and suggestive thing, however, that Holmes ascertained in his conversation with the boatmen was that, at the time of the famous Cliveden robbery, when several thousand pounds' worth of plate had been taken from the great hall, that later fell into the possession of a well known American hotel-keeper, Tattersby, who happened to be on the river late that night, was, according to his own statement, the unconscious witness of the escape of the thieves on board a mysterious steam-launch, which the police were never able afterwards to locate. They had nearly upset his canoe with the wash of their rapidly moving craft as they sped past him after having stowed their loot safely on board. Tattersby had supposed them to be employees of the estate and never gave the matter another thought until three days later, when the news of the robbery was published to the world. He had immediately communicated the news of what he had seen to the police, and had done all that lay in his power to aid them in locating the robbers, but all to no purpose. From that day to this the mystery of the Cliveden plot had never been solved.

"The following day Holmes called at the Tattersby cottage, and was fortunate enough to find Miss Tattersby at home. His previous impression as to her marvelous beauty was more than confirmed, and each moment that he talked to her she revealed new graces of manner that completed the capture of his hitherto unsusceptible heart. Miss Tattersby regretted her father's absence. He had gone, she said, to attend a secret missionary conference at Pentwllycod in Wales and was not expected back for a week, all of which quite suited Sherlock Holmes. Convinced that, after years of waiting, his affinity had at last crossed his path, he was in no hurry for the return of that parent, who would put an instant quietus upon this affair of the heart. Manifestly the thing for him to do was to win the daughter's hand and then intercept the father, acquaint him with his aspirations, and compel acquiescence by the force of his knowledge of Raffles's misdeed. Hence, instead of taking his departure immediately, he remained at the Goring-Streatley Inn, taking care each day to encounter Miss Tattersby on one pretext or another, hoping that their acquaintance would ripen into friendship, and then into something warmer. Nor was the hope a vain one, for when the fair Marjorie learned that it was the visitor's intention to remain in the neighborhood until her father's return, she herself bade him to make use of the old gentleman's library, to regard himself always as a welcome daytime guest. She even suggested pleasant walks through the neighboring country and little canoe trips up and down the Thames which they might take together, to all of which Holmes promptly availed himself, with the result that, at the end of six days, both realized that they were designed for each other, and a passionate declaration followed which opened new vistas of happiness for both. Hence it was that, when the Reverend James Tattersby arrived at Goring-Streatley the following Monday night, unexpectedly, he was astounded to find sitting together in the moonlight, in the charming little English garden at the rear of his dwelling, two persons, one of whom was his daughter Marjorie and the other a young American curate to whom he had already been introduced as A. J. Raffles.

"'We have met before, I think,' said Raffles coldly, as his eye fell upon Holmes.

"'I—er—do not recall the fact,' replied Holmes, meeting the steely stare of the homecomer with one of his own flinty glances.

"'H'm!' said Raffles, nonplused at the other's failure to recognize him. Then he shivered slightly. 'Suppose we go indoors, it is a trifle chilly out here in the night air.'

"The whole thing, the greeting, the meeting, Holmes's demeanor and all, was so admirably handled that Marjorie Tattersby never guessed the truth, never even suspected the intense dramatic quality of the scene she had just gazed upon.

"'Yes, let us go indoors,' she acquiesced. 'Mr. Dutton has something to say to you, Papa.'

"'So I presumed,' said Raffles dryly. 'And something that were better said to me alone, I fancy, eh?' he added.

"'Quite so,' said Holmes calmly. And indoors they went. Marjorie immediately retired to the drawing room, and Holmes and Raffles went at once to Tattersby's study.

"'Well?' said Raffles impatiently when they were seated. 'I suppose you have come to get the Dorrington seal, Mr. Holmes.'

"'Ah—you know me, then, Mr. Raffles?' said Holmes with a pleasant smile.

"'Perfectly,' said Raffles. 'I knew you at Dorrington Hall the moment I set eyes on you and, if I hadn't, I should have known later, for the night after your departure Lord Dorrington took me into his confidence and revealed your identity to me.'

"'I am glad,' said Holmes. 'It saves me a great deal of unnecessary explanation. If you admit that you have the seal—'

"'But I don't,' said Raffles. 'I mentioned it a moment ago, because Dorrington told me that was what you were after. I haven't got it, Mr. Holmes.'

"'I know that.' observed Holmes, quietly. 'It is in the possession of Miss Tattersby, your daughter, Mr. Raffles.'

"'She showed it to you, eh?' demanded Raffles, paling.

"'No. She sealed a note to me with it, however,' Holmes replied.

"'A note to you?' cried Raffles.

"'Yes. One asking for my autograph. I have it in my possession,' said Holmes.

"'And how do you know that she is the person from whom that note really came?' Raffles asked.

"'Because I have seen the autograph which was sent in response to that request in your daughter's collection, Mr. Raffles,' said Holmes.

"'So that you conclude—?' Raffles put in hoarsely.

"'I do not conclude; I begin by surmising, sir, that the missing seal of Lord Dorrington was stolen by one of two persons— yourself or Miss Marjorie Tattersby,' said Holmes, calmly.

"'Sir!' roared Raffles, springing to his feet menacingly.

"'Sit down, please,' said Holmes. 'You did not let me finish. I was going to add, Dr. Tattersby, that a week's acquaintance with that lovely woman, a full knowledge of her peculiarly exalted character and guileless nature, makes the alternative of guilt that affects her integrity clearly preposterous, which, by a very simple process of elimination, fastens the guilt, beyond all peradventure, on your shoulders. At any rate, the presence of the seal in this house will involve you in difficult explanations. Why is it here? How did it come here? Why are you known as the Reverend James Tattersby, the missionary, at Goring-Streatley, and as Mr. A. J. Raffles, the cricketer and man of the world, at Dorrington Hall, to say nothing of the Cliveden plate—'

"'Damnation!' roared the Reverend James Tattersby again, springing to his feet and glancing instinctively at the long low bookshelves behind him.

"'To say nothing,' continued Holmes, calmly lighting a cigarette, 'of the Cliveden plate now lying concealed behind those dusty theological tomes of yours which you never allow to be touched by any other hand than your own.'

"'How did you know?' cried Raffles.

"'I didn't,' laughed Holmes. 'You have only this moment informed me of the fact!'

"There was a long pause, during which Raffles paced the floor like a caged tiger.

"'I'm a dangerous man to trifle with, Mr. Holmes,' he said finally. 'I can shoot you down in cold blood in a second.'

" 'Very likely,' said Holmes. 'But you won't. It would add to the difficulties in which the Reverend James Tattersby is already deeply immersed. Your troubles are sufficient, as matters stand, without your having to explain to the world why you have killed a defenseless guest in your own study in cold blood.'

" 'Well—what do you propose to do?' demanded Raffles, after another pause.

" 'Marry your daughter, Mr. Raffles, or Tattersby, whatever your permanent name is—I guess it's Tattersby in this case,' said Holmes. 'I love her and she loves me. Perhaps I should apologize for having wooed and won her without due notice to you, but you doubtless will forgive that. It's a little formality you sometimes overlook yourself when you happen to want something that belongs to somebody else.'

"What Raffles would have answered no one knows. He had no chance to reply, for at that moment Marjorie herself put her radiantly lovely little head in at the door with a 'May I come in?' and a moment later she was gathered in Holmes's arms, and the happy lovers received the Reverend James Tattersby's blessing. They were married a week later and, as far as the world is concerned, the mystery of the Dorrington seal and that of the Cliveden plate was never solved.

" 'It is compounding a felony, Raffles,' said Holmes, after the wedding, 'but for a wife like that, hanged if I wouldn't compound the ten commandments!'

"I hope," I ventured to put in at that point, "that the marriage ceremony was not performed by the Reverend James Tattersby."

"Not on your life!" retorted Raffles Holmes. "My father was too fond of my mother to permit of any flaw in his title. A year later I was born, and—well, here I am—son of one, grandson of the other, with hereditary traits from both strongly developed and ready for business. I want a literary partner—a man who will write me up as Bunny did Raffles, and Watson did Holmes, so that I may get a percentage on that part of the swag. I offer you the job, Jenkins. Those royalty statements show me that you are the man, and your books prove to me that you need a few fresh ideas. Come, what do you say? Will you do it?"

"My boy," said I, enthusiastically, "don't say another word. Will I? Well, just try me!"

And so it was that Raffles Holmes and I struck a bargain and became partners.